Also by June Faver

DARK HORSE COWBOYS
Do or Die Cowboy
Hot Target Cowboy

WHEN TO CALL A COWBOY

JUNE FAVER

sourcebooks
casablanca

Sourcebooks and the colophon are registered trademarks of
Sourcebooks, Inc.

Published by Sourcebooks Casablanca, an imprint of Sourcebooks.
P.O. Box 4410, Naperville, Illinois 60567-4410
(630) 961-3900
sourcebooks.com

Printed and bound in the United States of America.
OPM 10 9 8 7 6 5 4 3 2 1

Chapter 1

"YOU'RE BEAU GARRETT?"

Beau turned, eyeing the speaker, a man about his own age, mid-twenties. The man was not as tall as Beau, but beefy, wearing a T-shirt advertising a gym in Dallas.

"That's right." Beau put forth his hand, offering to shake with the stranger.

"You sonovabitch!" This pronouncement was followed by a rushing behemoth whose shoulder to Beau's gut took them both to the sidewalk.

Ah, shit! Beau's freshly starched western shirt was being ground into the dirt as his attacker prepared to take a swing. Beau dodged to one side, and the oncoming fist smacked into the concrete sidewalk.

A howl of pain and rage burst from his assailant.

Beau scrambled to his feet and swung a fist of his own, catching the man square in the nose. "Who the hell are you, asshole?" he demanded.

Blood streaming from the man's nose, but unfazed by the punch, he sprang to his feet. He swung his uninjured fist, grazing Beau's chin as he tried to dodge.

A kernel of anger burst in Beau's chest like an incendiary device being detonated. He set on the man, both fists delivering well-placed blows, mostly to the head and gut.

"Beau Garrett, you stop that right now."

The feminine voice sounded vaguely familiar, but

Beau managed to deliver one more punch that sent his foe to the sidewalk in a heap. Beau dropped his fists and turned to face the female who had spoken, only to receive a roundhouse blow to his cheekbone. He staggered backward, barely avoiding falling over the man on the ground. "Dixie?" he asked when his vision cleared enough to focus.

The irate redhead stood with both fists cocked. "What have you done?" she demanded. "Why did you attack my friend?" She glowered at Beau before going to hover over the man on the sidewalk. "Scott, are you okay? Let me help you."

"Dixie?" Beau repeated as though in a daze. His cheek and eye socket throbbed from her punch. "What are you doing here?"

She paused in her ministrations to the fallen man and glared up at him. "Well, in case you hadn't heard, my father died, and I'm here to make arrangements for his funeral."

"Oh, I'm sorry," Beau muttered. "I didn't know your dad was ill."

"He wasn't," she snapped. "Somebody shot him dead last night while he was closing up the store. Sheriff thinks it was a robbery. His bank deposit bag was missing."

"Sorry," Beau said again, feeling completely inadequate. "I—ah..."

Dixie helped the aforementioned Scott to his feet. Offering soothing comments, she led him toward a vehicle parked at the curb. "I'm going to take you to the local doctor. She'll fix you right up."

Beau watched as Dixie loaded the guy into the SUV and then took off in the direction of the doctor's office.

He huffed out a huge sigh, turning toward the store that had been his intended destination that morning. In his pocket was a check made out to Moore's Feed and Seed Store meant to pay the Garrett ranch tab for the previous month. Beau's father, Big Jim Garrett, had sat in his study the night before, writing checks to keep all the accounts current.

Sure enough, there was a hand-lettered sign in the feed store window that read CLOSED DUE TO DEATH IN THE FAMILY.

Beau swallowed hard. He found it difficult to accept that Mr. Moore had been killed. There had always been a Mr. Moore. When he was a boy, his dad had taken him into the feed store, and Vernon Moore had always been there. Later, when he was in grade school, he recalled being instantly enamored of the little girl with the bright-red curls. They had played together like puppies, Dixie being a complete tomboy and as likely as not, more ready to wrestle or climb a tree than sit down to a tea party with dolls.

"Dixie Moore," Beau intoned softly. His first crush. His first girlfriend. His first sexual partner. His shoulders sagged.

And then she was gone.

In the middle of their senior year, Dixie's mother had suddenly left town with Dixie. There had been no warning. No goodbyes. No way to keep in touch.

Losing Dixie had torn a hole in Beau's heart. He had never quite recovered and never found anyone to replace her. He'd gone to the prom alone and come home early.

Beau stared at the closed-up store. Someone would have to open the doors soon. All the ranchers in the area depended on Moore's Feed and Seed. It couldn't just cease to serve the community.

He climbed in his truck and drove back to the Garrett ranch. He was sure Big Jim would have something to say about the morning's events.

———————

Frowning, Big Jim Garrett stared at his youngest son. "Better get some ice on that. You're going to have a beaut of a shiner."

Beau slouched at the granite countertop in the Garrett kitchen. "I swear, he just called my name and then came at me."

Having raised three sons, Big Jim was used to mishaps that required ice. He kept several ice packs in the freezer for just such occasions. Selecting one, he tossed it on the wooden cutting board and pounded it with his fist to break up the chunks. "Here you go." He flung it on the countertop near his son's elbow.

Beau grunted and reached for the pack, placing it gingerly against his cheek, which was already swollen and turning purple.

"Nice job," Big Jim murmured. "And you said it was Dixie Moore who punched you?"

Beau nodded. "First, her boyfriend attacked me out of the blue, and then Dixie got off a shot. What is this? Beat on Beau Garrett day?"

Big Jim snorted. "Sounds like you got in a few punches of your own."

A wry grin spread across Beau's face. "That I did. We Garretts aren't exactly known for turning the other cheek."

Big Jim exploded with laughter. "That's for damn sure."

"What happened to you, Little Bro?" Tyler, Big Jim's middle son, entered the kitchen and slid onto the stool next to Beau. "That's quite a shiner you've got working there."

"Shut up," Beau responded.

"Remember Dixie Moore?" Big Jim asked. "She gave him that one."

"No way!" Ty grinned at Beau. "I remember her as a scrappy little hellion. What did you do to piss her off?"

"Not a damned thing." Beau tossed the ice pack down on the countertop and pounded it a few times with the side of his fist before gently applying it to his face again.

Tyler's expression sobered. "I heard her dad got killed last night. It's on the news."

Big Jim frowned. "That's what Beau was telling me. It seems little Miss Dixie is here to bury Vern."

Ty's brows drew together. "I wonder what she's going to do with the store."

"Well, for damned sure there has to be a feed store in Langston," Big Jim thundered. "Too many people around here depend on it."

Dixie had taken Scott to see the local doctor. Scott had sustained a broken nose and fractured two bones in his right hand when his fist impacted the pavement instead of Beau's face.

Now, Scott looked almost comic, with his right hand in a cast and the entire arm immobilized in a sling to remind him not to use it. He also had rolled-up gauze stuffed in his nasal cavities, and both eyes were turning black with bruising. In all, he looked like a petulant walrus with his two gauze tusks.

"Whatever were you thinking?" Dixie glanced over at Scott as he slouched in the passenger seat of her burgundy SUV. "I could have told you Beau would whip your ass."

"You know why," Scott said. Due to the gauze up his nose, he was mouth-breathing, and his voice was raspy and nasally.

Dixie figured Scott recognized Beau from the high school photos she had of him in her apartment. Somehow, she just couldn't put them away. And seeing him again was like stabbing her straight in the heart. He was even better looking as a man than he had been as a teen. His shoulders were broader, and his tall, lanky teen form had filled in with a solid bank of muscle.

She swallowed hard. It was the eyes that got her. *Those killer Garrett eyes*. Beau's hair was a little lighter than his two older brothers, but they all had those incredible blue eyes. Almost turquoise, ringed with black lashes all around.

When Scott and Beau had been fighting, she knew Scott was the underdog. Although he had greater muscle mass and was much heavier, he didn't stand a chance against Beau Garrett. And there was the fact that Scott had started the fight, so he had the element of surprise on his side. He would never think of himself as a loser… but in this match, he was far outclassed.

Beau Garrett could always whip his weight in wildcats and had done so, on occasion, while defending Dixie's honor.

She fought to control the smile threatening to break

out as she recalled how valiant Beau had been. Always her hero. *Well, almost always…*

And now she had her friend Scott trying to defend her honor against her former hero. *How sad is that?* She glanced over at her sullen protector and reached out to give him a pat on the arm.

"You're sweet, you know?"

"I'm a dumbass, apparently." Scott placed his good hand on top of hers. "But I love you, you know?"

"I know. Love you too. You're my best friend in the whole wide world."

He nodded. "I don't know what I would do without you—and Roger, of course."

Dixie smiled at the mention of Scott's lover and soon-to-be groom. "I'll have to thank him for letting you come with me. I don't think I could face this ordeal without you."

"I'm always here for you. It's terrible that your father was murdered." He shook his head. "This little town doesn't exactly look like a hotbed of crime."

She pressed her lips together, strengthening her resolve to tie up loose ends as fast as possible and try not to get caught up in whatever had happened to Vernon Moore. She couldn't imagine her mild-mannered father getting involved in anything that would get him killed. But then again, maybe she didn't know him at all anymore. She had been gone a long time. "Yeah," she intoned. "I'm sure the sheriff will deal with it."

He wagged his head from side to side, the tusks making a wide arc. "I don't understand," he said. "I can take anybody at the gym. I was on the boxing team in college. How come this punk cowboy can chew me up and spit me out?"

"Don't feel bad," she said. "He's no punk. That cowboy works hard every day. He's just one big muscle. And if memory serves, just mention a fight and all the Garretts would jump in." Shaking her head, she let out a chortle. "It wasn't the same kind of fight as in a gym with a referee. Those Garrett boys knew how to fight."

Scott made a guttural noise in the back of his throat. "One of them still does."

———

Beau saw the SUV around town, but Dixie always had her goon boyfriend with her. He ached to talk to her. To have a real conversation. He wanted to know why she and her mother had left town so abruptly and why she never contacted him. She knew he was in love with her. She knew he was serious about her. She knew…

Vernon Moore had always opened and closed his own store, but he had a full-time helper who had been pressed into service to keep the feed store in operation.

Beau pushed the door open and approached the counter. Pete, the clerk, looked tired and maybe a little dazed. Beau gave him the check he had been tasked to deliver from Big Jim. "How are things going?" he asked.

Pete shook his head. "Terrible. I can't believe old man Moore is gone. Somebody just shot him…right outside the door when he was locking up." Pete gave an exaggerated shudder. "Gives me the heebie-jeebies every night when I'm trying to close the store."

"I guess so," Beau agreed. "Isn't there another guy who works here?"

Pete grimaced. "Josh Miller, my cousin. He's been working part time since he was in high school. He's a big guy, and he could handle the heavy lifting when it got to be too much for Mr. Moore." He shook his head. "Vern kept him on because he felt sorry for Josh's mother."

"Yeah?"

"My aunt is a widow. Nice lady, but having a hard time getting by." He scratched his head thoughtfully. "Mostly, Josh works in the big shed out back. He receives shipments and rotates the stock so we can keep it fresh…does inventory. He loads the orders into customer trucks. That sort of thing." He shrugged. "You know Vern. Always a soft touch."

Beau nodded. Vern was known to allow some of the local ranchers to stretch their credit quite thin during a bad spell. "When is the funeral going to be held? I haven't heard anything about it."

Pete looked both ways as though about to spill a secret, but the only other customer was a lady pawing through the vegetable seed packets, and her two kids were squatted down petting the baby bunnies. "The medical examiner hasn't released the body yet. It was a murder, you know?"

Beau nodded, his patience wearing thin. "How about Vern's daughter, Dixie? Has she said what she plans to do with the place?" His casual question was tossed out in hopes Pete would tell him she planned to move back to Langston.

Pete shook his head, his expression dour. "Lil' Miz Dixie—she said she would put everything on the market. She can't wait to get back to Dallas." He shrugged.

"Who would have thought our little Dixie Moore would turn out to be a city girl?"

"Yeah," Beau said. "Who would have thought?" He huffed out a sigh and left the store, distinctly dissatisfied.

He stood for a moment, blinking in the sunlight after the dimness of the store. He couldn't imagine why Mr. Moore had been targeted, but he guessed someone had been desperate enough to rob an old man and then shoot him.

Beau climbed into his truck and started it up. The big diesel motor gave a little roar as he revved it. Slipping into gear, he backed out and pulled onto the main drag. Moore's Feed and Seed was located on the outskirts of town…the opposite direction from the Garrett ranch.

Beau drove slowly, taking in everything but keeping an eye out for the burgundy SUV. He spied his new sister-in-law's Jeep parked in front of the law office where she worked. His oldest brother Colton had married Misty just a few months ago, and the vehicle was a present he bought for her. Beau could have killed some time by pulling in and chatting with her, but he figured she had work to do and he would just be in the way.

At the next intersection, he glanced down the street and located Dixie's automobile in front of the church. He sucked in a breath and blew it out, puffing his cheeks as he did so.

Might as well give it a try. Surely she won't punch me in church.

He pulled in beside her car and turned off the motor. What if her boyfriend was with her? Beau squared his shoulders. *So what? That guy would be an idiot to go after me again.* He climbed out and pocketed the keys.

Although his footsteps appeared sure and confident, Beau's gut was doing flip-flops. He had no idea why he was anxious about seeing Dixie again. Taking a deep breath as he sprinted up the steps, he paused with his hand on the brass door pull to consider what he might say to the girl who had left him and never looked back. He swung the door open and stepped into the cool darkness. It took a moment for his eyes to adjust. Walking deeper into the interior, he made his way to the back hall, which led to the church office and various rooms used for Sunday school classes, Boy Scout and Girl Scout meetings, and other gatherings.

There was a certain lemony smell to the church. It was always clean, immaculately so. Everything was polished and ready for the next group or class or sermon to commence. As he strode toward the church offices, he was glad the hallway was carpeted. At least his arrival wouldn't be announced. Nearing the open doorway, he peeked inside, but the church secretary was not at her desk. He heard voices coming from the pastor's office. He recognized the sonorous voice belonging to the minister and Dixie's lighter feminine tone.

Beau leaned against the wall outside the doorway, not able to hear the words spoken, but he gathered Dixie was making arrangements for Vern's funeral. In a few minutes, he could tell the voices seemed to be concluding their business and the pastor was walking her to the door. Beau hoped the irate Scott wasn't in attendance.

"Thank you so much," Dixie said. "I'm sure the service will be lovely."

"I hope to see you at Sunday services soon, young lady."

"I'm afraid we won't be staying in town. I'll return to Dallas after the reading of the will."

The pastor murmured some comforting words, and Dixie stepped through the door. The big smile on her lips evaporated as soon as her eyes locked on Beau. "You! What are you doing here?"

He shrugged, all the while prepared to duck if she swung a fist. "This is my church. I show up here every Sunday with my whole family."

Dixie's green eyes narrowed, and she let out a derisive snort. "Not all of your family."

Puzzled, he spread his hands. "Yes, unless somebody's sick, we all show up."

Her mouth curved up in a sneering farce of a smile. "Well, isn't that just like you Garretts. You get to pick and choose who you call 'family.'" She gave him a glare that would have killed him dead, had it been a weapon, before she sailed past him down the hallway.

Feeling as though he had been struck again, Beau watched her depart. "Wait! What are you talking about?" He hurried to catch up with her.

She ignored him. Head held high, she strode through the church, placing both hands on the exit door, but Beau grabbed the big brass handle and held it fast.

"I mean it, Dixie. What are you talking about?"

He watched her profile as a series of emotions played out across her face. "You know," she said in a whisper.

"No, I don't know. Please talk to me."

Heaving a sigh, she finally met his gaze. "We have nothing left to say to each other, Beau. Nothing at all." With that she shoved him aside and pushed through the door.

Beau trailed after her, watching as she opened her car with the remote and swung up into the driver's seat. In an instant, she had backed out and driven off in the direction of the Moore ranch.

He could follow her if he wanted, but he couldn't bring himself to do so since it was pretty clear he was persona non grata to one Miss Dixie Moore.

Hearing a noise behind him, he turned to see the pastor exiting the church. "Oh, hello, Beauregard. I didn't know you were here. Did you need to see me about something?"

"Um, no—yes, sir. When is Vernon Moore's funeral going to be held?"

"This coming Tuesday at ten in the morning. The viewing will be the day before from two to six p.m. I hope the Garrett family will come to pay their respects."

Beau nodded curtly. "You can count on it, sir."

━━∿∿━━

Dixie drove toward her childhood home, tears flowing down her cheeks. "How could he? How—how could he?" She hiccupped. "Damn you, Beau Garrett. How dare you act the innocent?"

Heaving a sigh, she pawed through her handbag with one hand, searching for a tissue. She mopped at her face and gave her nose a hearty blow. "Enough of that. I will not allow Beau Garrett to cause me to shed another single tear." Straightening her shoulders, she clasped the steering wheel with both hands.

She had grown up on the Moore family ranch located about ten miles east of town. Her father raised Charolais and Black Angus beef cattle and grew some of the feed

for his herd. He had never considered himself a farmer
but rather a store owner and a gentleman rancher.

And someone killed him. An involuntary shiver
snaked down her spine. How could someone have murdered her father? She tried to moisten her suddenly dry
lips. Now she would never have a chance to confront
him…to ask him why…to make things right. She had
always thought there would come a time when they
would see each other again.

Dixie slowed the vehicle and turned in at the farm-
to-market road leading to the ranch house. Seeing the
house brought the ache of tears back to her throat. She
swallowed hard, remembering how happy this view had
made her as a child. Riding the bus after school, she
always felt a little tug of joy at the first sight of her home.
Her mother would be inside waiting for her with a hug.
There would be a snack spread out on the kitchen table
to fortify Dixie for homework. And her mom always
asked her about her day, whom she had played with,
and what her teacher said. Those early mother–daughter
after-school chats had bonded them, making her mom
the person Dixie could pour her heart out to. Whenever
she had needed her mom, she was always there for her.

But now, her mom remained in the city, unwilling to
attend the funeral of the man she had been married to
since she'd been a teenager.

When her mother had first taken her to Dallas, Dixie
had thought it would be a temporary arrangement, but
her mother had purchased a condo and settled in.

At first, Dixie kept expecting to hear from Beau, or
at least from her dad, but apparently he had no use for
her either.

Her mother had filed for divorce a few months later, she said because her husband had disowned Dixie. Being abandoned by her father had left a huge void in Dixie's life. Where was the man who had treated her like a princess when she was young, who had attended her basketball games and track events, who had applauded when the calf she'd raised won a ribbon at the county fair?

Dixie choked back tears as she pulled into the drive leading to the house. Her father had planted pecan trees along the driveway when Dixie was a child. Now they had grown tall and were covered with clusters of green pecans in shells. Soon they would be ready for harvest, but Dixie was certain she would be back in Dallas by that time. After all, she had her business, and as the sole owner, she had to be present to make sure it was running right.

She pulled up close to the house and turned off the motor. *Who am I kidding? I can run everything online.* Her craft store was more of a hobby than an actual business, but she did turn a profit and had regular customers. Promoting it and filling orders via computer took up very little time but provided a healthy payday.

She got out and slammed the door with a vengeance. Truth was she couldn't wait to get back home to Dallas where everything she held dear was waiting for her.

Chapter 2

THE ENTIRE GARRETT CLAN TURNED OUT FOR THE VIEWING. Three pickup trucks with the Garrett Ranch logo emblazoned on their sides pulled up in front of the funeral home. Beau drove his dad, Big Jim, while his brothers Tyler and Colton drove up with their families tucked inside. Misty insisted she wasn't up for the viewing, so she stayed outside with the kids while the adults trooped inside to pay their respects.

Beau was nervous. He wanted a chance to talk to Dixie again but didn't relish creating any kind of a scene or being rebuffed in public.

There was quite a crowd. Vernon Moore had been a good man, and he was well known all around the area, so there was a large turnout.

Beau trailed behind his family, hoping they would break the ice.

Vernon Moore's casket was open in the front of one of the rooms designated for viewings. His lovely redheaded daughter sat by herself in the front row, her back straight as an arrow, and she stared directly ahead.

Eula Mae Salter, retired elementary school teacher, slipped into the chair beside Dixie. Dixie's face broke into a smile when she recognized one of her former teachers. Miss Salter embraced her, and Dixie appeared to be shedding a tear. Beau stayed out of sight as all of his family members queued up to offer condolences. Several clusters of locals stood around the room, speaking in low voices. Three ranchers in the corner near where Beau loitered expressed concerns that the heir might close the feed store.

Beau returned his attention to where Dixie Moore was seated.

Tyler was introducing his wife, Leah, to Dixie. They chatted for a while, and Dixie seemed to be thawing a bit. Leah was incredibly warm and gracious. If anyone could break down Dixie's walls, it was she.

Beau heaved a sigh. It was now or never. He stepped in front of Dixie and extended his hand. "Hey, Dixie. I'm really sorry you lost your dad."

She had reached for his hand before she realized who he was and tried to withdraw it immediately, but he leaned down to kiss it softly.

"Beau," she breathed. "I—uh—"

"I just wanted you to know that I'm here for you if you need me." Beau gave her hand a squeeze but released it.

Dixie's eyes flashed fire. "Yeah, like you've always been there for me?"

Beau dropped onto one knee, bringing him down to her eye level. "Dixie, you're the one who left me. I had no way to contact you. What are you talking about?"

Dixie glanced around anxiously. "Have a little respect. I'll thank you to keep your voice down."

"Sure, but can we talk?" Beau gazed at her, addressing the pain in her eyes.

Her lips tightened. "I really don't have anything to say to you."

"Well, Dixie, I have a couple of things to say to you," he responded. "Please give me a few minutes. We have a lot of history between us."

Dixie's eyes narrowed. "Yes, we certainly do, but history is not going to repeat itself. Just leave me alone, and don't make a scene." She glanced around again.

He grimaced. "Where's your boyfriend? Why isn't he here with you?"

"If it's any of your business, Scott had to go back to Dallas. His job—"

Beau stood up. "I really am sorry about your father, Dixie. He was a fine man."

"So you say," Dixie bit out.

Beau gazed down at her. Now she seemed to be angry with her father as well as with Beau. "I do say, Dixie. And I want you to find some time to talk to me in private. You owe me that much."

Her face reddened, and she sucked in a sharp breath.

He held up both hands in an "I give up" gesture and stepped away from her. *That didn't go well.*

Big Jim was engaged in a low-pitched conversation with the three ranchers gathered in the back corner.

Beau walked to join his brothers and their wives. "Will one of you take Dad home? I need a chance to talk to Dixie by herself, and I'm willing to wait her out."

Colton placed a big paw on Beau's shoulder. "Yeah, I noticed she looked pretty frosty when you were talking to her just now. What's all that about?"

"Beats the hell out of me," Beau said. "I'm pretty certain that if I have a chance to talk to her all alone, I can figure out what she's so all-fired mad about."

Tyler nodded to where Dixie sat. "She sure does seem to have a bug up her butt about something. Are you sure you want to find out what it is?"

Colt nodded. "Yeah, you might want to back off."

Beau cast a glance to where she sat, ramrod straight. "No, I can't let it go. Whatever I did to offend her, I want to make it right. I mean, we used to be…" His voice trailed off.

Ty and Colt exchanged a knowing glance.

"You do what you think needs doing," Colt said, giving him a last thump on his shoulder. "Don't worry about Big Jim. We'll take Dad home."

Beau slipped out and drove around until he saw the crowd had thinned at the funeral home. Dixie's burgundy SUV was still parked in front, so he tucked his silver extra-cab pickup under the shade of a large elm in the park across the street. About twenty minutes later, he saw Dixie emerge from the funeral home. Her shoulders sagged as though the weight of the world was upon them. The funeral home director walked a few feet behind her and appeared to be speaking to her. She paused and shook his hand before descending the steps and walking to her car. Her head was down, and she pressed the remote to unlock the vehicle.

Beau's jaw clenched. He wished he could lift some of that weight off her shoulders. Dixie was obviously affected by her father's death, even though she seemed to have a huge chunk of anger festering in her gut… anger toward both Vern and Beau, even if he hadn't a clue what he had done to earn her hostility.

Dixie sat for a few moments before pulling down the visor to stare at herself in the mirror. She wiped her eyes and blew her nose.

Good. He was glad to see for sure that she was still human. A few tears shed for her dad were proof positive of that.

She started the SUV and pulled out, heading for the Moore ranch.

He followed at a respectful distance, slowing as she turned off the highway. On the way he found himself deep in the past, recalling all the times he had driven this same route. Turning onto the farm-to-market road, he trailed far enough back to remain invisible. When he got to the Moore ranch, he drew to a stop beside her vehicle.

Dixie lifted her gaze as she stepped from the SUV. He heard her expel a disgusted breath as he approached. "Can't you just leave me alone?" Even with her eyes reddened, she was beautiful.

Beau shook his head. "I've never been able to leave you alone. You know that."

Her mouth twitched. "That's over and done with." She moved as though to go into the house, but Beau cut her off.

He reached for her, wrapping his fingers around her forearm. "Please give me a few minutes. I deserve that much at least."

Glancing toward the house, she heaved another sigh. "You deserve a kick in the ass. If my dad hadn't been killed, I wouldn't have come back here, and you would never have bothered to get in touch with me. Why should I waste another breath on you?"

"Dix, I dogged your father for weeks trying to find out where you were, but he kept telling me he didn't know. He said you and your mom just disappeared."

"Don't insult me by lying. I know better." She jerked her arm free.

Puzzled, Beau took a step back. "Dixie, why are you

so mad at me? I've never done anything to hurt you... nothing that I know of."

She crossed her arms over her chest. "Look, I need to get inside. I have...things to take care of in there."

Beau glanced at the door, but Dixie strode to it and turned, barring the entrance with her very presence. "Please, Dixie. We have a history. I'm just trying to tell you that I'm here for you. Whatever you need, please let me know."

"If you value our so-called history, just leave me the hell alone." She turned and opened the door just enough to slip inside.

The door closed behind her, and Beau heard double locks tumble into place. He stood for a moment, glaring at the barrier before shaking his head. He let out a mild expletive and turned on his heel to walk back to his truck. Just for fun, he slammed the door. It wasn't nearly as satisfying as he'd thought it would be.

The fact that the girl he'd loved since grade school just called him a liar and told him to stay away was like pouring vinegar on a fresh cut. He couldn't believe it still hurt so much.

Beau had just been a kid when she left. Of course he'd been heartbroken. But he was a man now. Surely he could man up and walk away if that's what she wanted.

He started the truck, revving the motor a couple times, but he still felt impotent.

What had happened to the great love of his life? Why had Dixie left him so suddenly? Why had she completely abandoned him? Why had her father insisted that he didn't know where she was?

Beau slipped the truck into gear and pulled slowly

away. He headed home, puzzling over the questions battering his brain.

———⁓———

Dixie peered out from behind the drapes to witness Beau's departure. She had mixed feelings. On one hand, she was relieved that he had gone, but on the other hand, she was dismayed to discover she felt a loss. Why, after all this time, should she feel anything for Beau Garrett? After all, he was the one who had abandoned her.

She watched the dust settle and then closed the drapes. Turning, she gazed around the quiet living room. Nothing had really changed since she'd left. The piano, where she had practiced after her music lessons, was still in place against the far wall. She swallowed something that felt like a tangle of barbed wire at the back of her throat. It appeared that her father had not removed the sheet music she had last used. That surprised her.

It had surprised her as well that he had not changed a thing in her room. It was as if he had kept it as a shrine to his daughter. That is, as a shrine to the little girl he had been proud of...not the girl she had become. Not the girl he had betrayed by turning his back on her when she needed him most. *Daddy, how could you stop loving me?*

Dixie pressed her lips together, determined not to waste any more tears over something that had happened in her past. She had a future waiting for her back in Dallas.

I just have to tie up loose ends here and get back to my life. She turned resolutely, wiping away tears with the back of her hand. She made it to the kitchen without breaking down entirely. Slumping onto a chair in the cheerful dining area, she gave vent to all the pent-up emotions that had bombarded her since she had once again collided with Beau Garrett…her lover, her betrayer, her tormentor. *Why can't he just leave me alone?*

Her mother's ringtone sounded, and Dixie pawed through the pocket of her jacket. "Mom? Is everything okay?"

"Sure, my dear. We're fine. But I can tell everything's not okay on your end. You've been crying."

Dixie sniffled. "A little."

Her mother made a scornful sound. "Don't waste your tears on your father. He kicked us both out. Hurry up and get everything done so you can come home. We miss you."

"I'm trying." She swallowed hard. "It's probably just being here in this house. I have so many memories of my life before—before everything happened."

"You mean before your father turned his back on us…before he threw us to the wolves."

It pained Dixie to hear the rancor in her mother's voice. "I know, Mom."

"All you have to do is get through the funeral and the reading of the will. Then put everything on the market and get back here."

Dixie nodded. Her mom made it sound so easy. "It's just that…I saw Beau Garrett today. He's—"

"Oh, no! Not that wretched boy. I hope he didn't bother you."

The venom in her mother's voice caused her to cringe. She had heard this many times in the past. "No,

Mom. It was just that all the Garretts came to the visitation. It was…it was difficult to get through."

"Well, I'm sure it was. Those people have no business coming anywhere near you." She snorted. "Evil. They're all evil—and…and heartless."

She didn't feel compelled to relate to her mother that Beau had attempted to talk to her numerous times since she had arrived. She couldn't face that diatribe. "Not a problem. Just a couple more days, and I'm out of here."

Dixie said goodbye and tucked the phone back in her pocket.

Sitting in the kitchen with its bright yellow daisy-print curtains overwhelmed her with nostalgia. She clasped her hands together, determined to muster up something good from her childhood. Generally, her dad left for work before she got to the breakfast table, but on Sunday they always enjoyed a big family breakfast before leaving for church. She recalled her father as being jovial and kindhearted.

He often took her fishing on Sunday afternoons. Just the two of them in a small motorboat out on the river. Time to talk and dream out loud about the future. Her dad had assumed Dixie would take over the store someday and run the ranch when he was unable to do so. Dixie had thought this would be her future. Now it was only her painful past.

Beau drove around for a while, ending up parked by a stand of mesquite trees, staring, without seeing, at his dad's champion herd of Charolais. The big beef cattle grazed, oblivious to Beau's turmoil.

Sadly, he came to the conclusion that he was still in love with Dixie Moore. He also came to the conclusion that, for some reason he couldn't fathom, she hated the very sight of him. Six years had passed, and he still didn't have a clue as to why she had disappeared just before graduation and why she was being so frosty now.

He huffed out a frustrated sigh and smacked the heel of his hand against his steering wheel. *Why won't she talk to me? Did our relationship mean nothing to her?*

Reluctantly, he shoved the key into the ignition and gave it a turn, feeling a moment of validation as the powerful diesel engine roared to life. But it only lasted for a moment.

He drove back to the Garrett ranch house, feeling deflated with no idea of how to reach Dixie when she was completely closed off to him.

Perhaps he could kidnap her. Tie her up and force her to talk to him...*how?* He might enjoy being close to her again, but he couldn't force her to talk to him...couldn't make her tell him why she was so angry with him.

Beau stepped down from his truck and slammed the door for emphasis. He stomped inside and tossed his Stetson on the bentwood coat rack just to the right of the front door.

In the kitchen, he took a beer from the refrigerator door and popped the lid off his longneck, accidentally knocking over one of the stools pulled up at the counter.

"What's all that racket?" Big Jim strode into the kitchen, his face like a thunderstorm. He stood glowering at his youngest son. "What's wrong?"

Beau sighed and righted the stool. "Nothing really." He slouched onto the stool.

Big Jim's eyes narrowed. "Something. Might as well tell me. You know I'll find out eventually."

"It's Dixie Moore. She's making me crazy, Dad." He took a long swallow of his beer.

A half smile softened Big Jim's craggy features. "Ah, Son. You always were hung up on that little gal." He got another beer and slid onto the stool at the end of the counter.

"It's more than that. I mean, I accept that she dumped me, and I accept that she's moved on...but she's madder'n a cat in a rainstorm, and I have no idea why. She won't talk to me. She keeps telling me to stay away from her."

"Well, maybe you'd best do just that. Leave her the hell alone." Big Jim shook his head. "You're not the only one stymied by those Moore women. Poor old Vern was completely baffled when his wife up and left with their daughter. He swore he hadn't the slightest idea why they vamoosed."

Beau's chest tightened. Too well he remembered his own anguish when Dixie disappeared just before the end of their senior year. He recalled feeling confused, going over everything that had passed between them, searching for anything that might have caused her to leave him. He swallowed hard, averting his gaze. "Yeah, me too. I kept hounding Mr. Moore. I thought he was holding out on me when he said he had no idea."

"Vern felt bad for you. He knew how much you cared for that little gal."

"I still do, apparently. I thought she loved me too, but now she treats me like some dirt she tracked in and can't wait to get rid of." He sipped his beer, washing down the taste of tears at the back of his throat. "She used to be so sweet. I really thought we had something."

"Son, I was there when you were moping around. You wore your pain like a blanket. Wrapped it around you and dragged it everywhere. Gotta say I wasn't happy to see her back here again."

"It doesn't look like she's going to be here any longer than she has to. She's itching to get back to Dallas."

Big Jim made a derogatory sound in the back of his throat before raising his longneck in a salute. "Good riddance. Maybe your life can get back to normal."

Beau clinked the base of his bottle against his dad's. "I can't even remember normal."

The funeral was a solemn affair. The whole town turned out to see Vern Moore off and pay their respects. The person they paid their respects to sat glum and ill at ease, counting the minutes until it was over. She was just glad Scott was there with her. Without him by her side, she would have to face the entire Garrett clan, Beau in particular.

Dixie clung to Scott's hand, the one that wasn't in a cast, and occasionally rested her head against his strong shoulder. His face was still bruised from his encounter with Beau, but he was looking somewhat better.

She didn't cry. She was actually a little angry, having thought she would someday have a chance to confront her father and ask him why he had betrayed her. Why had he thrown her out when she needed him most? Even abandoning his wife of eighteen years. How could a man do that?

It was a good thing her mom had had some money from her trust fund. Otherwise they would have starved. Her mother had never worked outside the home, and Dixie had been just a girl—a seventeen-year-old girl with a problem.

Dixie heaved a sigh, tracing the seam in Scott's cuff with one finger. She knew she was lucky to have such a good, solid friend by her side. At least all the onlookers would think she had a man in her life and that she had gotten over Beau Garrett.

How ironic that Scott is acting as my *beard for a change*.

When the pastor intoned his final prayer and the mourners stood, Dixie and Scott stood to follow the casket to the hearse. They got into the black car provided by the funeral home and were driven to the cemetery by a very solemn driver in a black suit.

One more ordeal and this charade will be over.

"Hang on, sweetheart. We're almost done here." Scott stroked her hair with his big hand.

"I'm okay."

"You're breaking my heart." He shook his head. "You just look so sad."

Dixie swallowed bile at the back of her throat. "I am sad."

He kissed her temple. "I didn't realize you had any feelings for your dad."

A tear trickled from the corner of her eye, dribbled down the side of her nose, and fell on her breast. "I have feelings. So many feelings."

The car turned in at the cemetery and pulled close to where Vernon Moore would be buried. The hearse had stopped just ahead, and the long line of mourners jockeyed for parking along the narrow roads.

Dixie wiped her tears, making a vow not to show any emotions to the citizens of Langston. Especially not in front of the Garretts. The driver came around to open her door, and she stepped out, surprised that the sun was shining and a slight breeze lifted her hair. She blinked and sucked in a few lungfuls of the fresh country air. Yeah, there was probably something better about living in Langston as opposed to Dallas. There were clear blue skies, and the air didn't smell of car exhaust and manufacturing waste products. A few big puffy cumulus clouds dotted the sky.

She could make it through this day. All that would be left would be the reading of the will. After that she would list everything with a real estate agent who specialized in ranch country and wait for it to sell. Maybe someone in the area would buy the store. *That would be good*. Yeah, she hoped for a local buyer.

"Let's get this over with." Scott spoke close to her ear. Cupping her elbow, he urged her toward the little rise where folding chairs had been set up and a canopy erected to keep the sun off the family…of one.

Dixie nodded, allowing him to escort her to the open pit where her father would lie for all eternity. The pallbearers had placed the coffin atop the wide woven straps that would lower the casket.

Oh, Daddy. Why didn't you stand by me?

"Look at her." Colton Garrett shook his head. "Cold as ice."

"Maybe she's just...controlling her emotions." Misty, Colt's wife, gazed up at him.

"Our little Dixie has been like an iceberg since she rolled back into town." Big Jim took a wide stance and shoved his hands deep in his pockets. "Vern deserves better than this."

Beau felt the weight of his family's distaste. Some part of him wanted to defend her, but he couldn't find the words. His heart was breaking all over again, but not for the woman who sat dispassionately beside her father's grave. He was mourning anew for the girl he had been in love with. The girl he would always love. Not the cold, standoffish woman who stood wrapped in her lover's arms near the casket.

A strand of her long red hair blew across her cheek. Just for a second, he ached to smooth it down...just for a second.

The girl he loved was gone forever, and in her place was this cold, emotionless stranger. He'd better get over it and accept that he couldn't recreate the past—that it didn't matter what Dixie was so mad about or that she wouldn't talk to him. He echoed his father's stance. Boots planted wide apart and his hands in his pockets, gazing at the woman who used to be his girl.

Chapter 3

Scott went back to the city, but two days after the funeral, Dixie drove herself into Langston to meet with Breckenridge T. Ryan, the only lawyer in town and her deceased father's attorney. She parked on the street in front of his storefront office. This was the last task before she could go home to Dallas. She realized she'd been holding her breath and released it slowly.

Just get out of the car and get this over with. I'll never have to come back to this town again. I'll never have to see any of these people again. She heaved a sigh. *I'll never have to see Beau Garrett's face again.*

Dixie climbed out of the car and strode purposefully into Breck Ryan's office. A small metal cowbell clanked against the glass. A lovely young woman with long dark hair sat behind a desk in the big open space. Dixie remembered that she was married to one of the Garrett brothers. The oldest one, Colton.

Dixie managed a fake smile as she approached.

"Oh, hello, Dixie. We were expecting you." She came out from behind the desk and embraced Dixie awkwardly, giving her pats on the shoulder. "So sorry about your father. He was such a nice man."

"Um, thank you, uh—"

"It's Misty."

"You're married to Colton Garrett." Dixie felt herself stiffening.

"Yes." She gave a gracious smile. "I just wanted you

to know we're all here for you. Anything you need, just let any of us know."

Dixie nodded furiously. "Yes, thanks. I'll do that."

"Well, Breck is all ready for you, so let me show you right in." Leah led her to a closed door with the name BRECKENRIDGE T. RYAN emblazoned in gold letters. She knocked and opened the door.

Stepping over the threshold, Dixie froze in her tracks. All of the air seemed to be sucked out of her lungs. Sitting across the desk from Breck Ryan was Big Jim Garrett, looking as uncomfortable as she felt.

"Am I early?" she asked.

"No, you're right on time. Take a seat." Breck gestured to the other chair. "I believe you know Mr. Garrett."

Dixie swallowed hard. "Um, yes." She sat down, moving the chair slightly away from where Big Jim sat. "I can wait until Mr. Garrett finishes his business."

Breck spread his hands. "Mr. Garrett was invited to join us this morning because he was mentioned in your father's will."

Dixie's stomach was roiling. She couldn't imagine what her dad would leave to Big Jim Garrett in his will, but she nodded, keeping her gaze averted. She supposed they had been friends.

Breck unsealed the document, spread it open, and began reading it.

All she heard were a bunch of words she didn't fully understand, most of which followed a *whereas*.

"I, Vernon R. Moore, state that I still love my daughter, Dixie Lee Moore, although I have not seen her in years. I am still hurt by the way she and her mother, my former wife, abandoned me and never looked back.

However, I leave all my worldly property and possessions to my only daughter, with the stipulation that she live on the ranch in the home we once shared for a period of not less than one year and that she take part in the management of the store and the ranch during that time.

"I will rely on my good friend, James Garrett, to oversee this arrangement and assist her with anything she needs to settle in. If Dixie Lee refuses to abide by my wishes, then her right to my property shall be null and void and James Garrett will become the sole heir to my estate."

Dixie's mouth fell open. "Wha—" She struggled to comprehend. "What did you say?"

Breck folded the documents and tapped them on top of his desk. "Basically, your father's will gives you his entire estate, but in order to inherit, you have to return to Langston, live in your childhood home, and run the ranch and feed store." His gaze chilled her. "Is that plain enough for you?"

Big Jim cleared his throat. "I assure you, Dixie, I knew nothing of this arrangement."

"Oh…" She stood, turning from one man to the other. "Oh." Gathering her purse and keys, she almost ran from the office, past Misty's desk, and out onto the sidewalk. She got into her car as quickly as humanly possible and drove out of town. She made it back to the ranch house in record time, only to sit in her car and stare straight ahead.

The lawyer's words kept echoing in her head. What did her father mean that they had abandoned him? She and her mother hadn't abandoned him. He had kicked them out and locked the door behind them.

She was still gripping the steering wheel. Slowly, she managed to uncurl her stiff fingers and climb out of the car. It only took her about fifteen minutes to gather a few things and get on the road back to Dallas.

———

"She just walked out?" Beau was flabbergasted. "How could she just walk out?"

Big Jim shrugged. "Well, that's what she did. Breck and I just sat there like a couple of idiots, staring at each other." He sat down heavily on one of the chairs on the deck behind the house, gazing up at the brilliant sky as the sun made its way west.

For his part, Beau paced back and forth. "I can't believe she would walk away from the ranch…the store…" He swallowed hard. "Her home."

"I swear to you, that's just what happened."

Beau halted in his path. "It sounds like old Vern's will was his way of getting her back here."

"But it backfired. The will stipulates she has to live in the house and run the ranch as well as the feed store for one year, or—" He paused.

Beau heaved an impatient sigh. "Or she gives up all rights to the property and you inherit everything. That about right?"

"That's about right."

"Well, hell!" Beau had been hoping for a miracle in which Dixie would decide to stay in Langston. He had hoped her change of heart would have something to do with him. He had hoped she would realize she was still in love with him. *Yeah, right.* Well, a man could dream, couldn't he?

"You got to remember one thing. Vern had no idea he was going to be murdered, so he probably thought his daughter would be a lot older and maybe have some business skills…" He heaved a defeated sigh. "Can you fetch me a beer out of the fridge, Son?"

"Sure, Dad." Beau returned to the large kitchen where his mother had lovingly prepared meals for her family. He opened the fridge and pulled out two longnecks, flipping the caps into the trash can.

He pushed out the back door and slapped one of the bottles into Big Jim's waiting hand. Beau clinked his bottle against his father's before hoisting it to his lips. The cold liquid rolled down his throat, cooling the fire burning in his chest. *How can she leave me…again?*

"I guess that little lady was just not interested in living in a small town. Miss Dixie isn't the same girl who left Langston. She's gotten all citified on us."

Beau let that sink in and shook his head sadly. "Well, I guess there's only one thing left to do. I'm going to go to Dallas."

———

"Why, that contemptible, underhanded jerk!" Mamie Moore's voice was shrill. She gazed up at Dixie, her eyes and mouth wide open. "How could he do that to you?"

Dixie shrugged. "He kicked us out before. Why would you think he would treat us any better when he was dead?"

"Well…well…" Mamie's hands fluttered in the air. "Don't worry about it. I still have some money left, and you have a nice little business going. We'll be fine."

"That's what I was thinking, Mom." Dixie pressed

her lips together, forming a thin line. "Daddy didn't love me at all…but…" She recalled the strange language of the will. Why did he think she had abandoned him? After all, her mother had tried over and over again to change his mind. She had pleaded with him to find forgiveness in his heart, but he had remained cold and distant.

"We're going to be fine." Mamie nodded vigorously. "We have the condo, and it's all paid off. I've got my savings. We don't need that much. It just isn't worth it for you to give up a year of your life to go back to that horrid place where everyone treated you so badly. It's not worth it at all."

Dixie considered the vast amount of grassland, the thousands of head of beef cattle, the lovely rambling house, and the successful feed store. She blew out a deep breath before wrapping her arms around her mother. "I'm sure we'll be fine."

—∞—

The next day, Beau called on Misty, his ultra-smart sister-in-law, and asked her to try to find Dixie Lee Moore in Dallas, Texas. He walked into the offices of Breckenridge T. Ryan, Esquire, and explained to her what he needed.

"I'll see what I can do," she said, entering the information into her computer. "Let me see what I can find online."

The door swung open, and Breck Ryan strode inside. "Good morning, Misty. Beau. Do you need to see me?"

Beau shook his head. "I'm just borrowing a little of your office manager's time."

Misty laughed. "I'm just a secretary. Give me a break."

Breck folded his arms across his chest. "No, I think you're more than that. I couldn't do half of what I do without you keeping me straight."

"I do the best I can." To Beau she said, "Let me work on this, Beau. I'll call you if I can find something."

"Come on into my office," Breck invited. "You and I can catch up while Misty is looking for whatever it is she's looking for." He swung the glass-paned door open and gestured for Beau to enter.

The lawyer tossed his Stetson on a hat rack and took a seat behind his wide mahogany desk. Beau sat opposite, trying to relax.

"Tell me what I can do for you." He eyed Beau critically. "What's on your mind?"

"It's Dixie Moore. I need to find her."

Breck leaned forward. "Mind if I ask why? I know you were sweet on her in high school, but she's been gone a few years." He spread his hands. "Trust me, the woman who came in here yesterday was not the same sweet kid."

Lifting his shoulders, Beau shook his head. "I—I don't know. I just have to find her. I have so many questions. I can't let her go without some answers."

Breck raised one dark brow. "I hear ya." He opened a desk drawer and removed a folder. He pried open the clasp, spilling the contents on the desktop. "I think I have what you need right here." He pawed through the papers and found what he was looking for. He tossed a card across the desk.

Beau seized upon it. It was the business card of a detective agency in Dallas. He flipped it over. A squeezing sensation in his chest triggered an intake of breath.

The name Dixie Moore was hand-printed along with an address and a telephone number. "How did you get this?"

"I had to locate her when Vern was killed. She was the heir. She'll inherit everything—that is, if she comes back to Langston."

"So you paid a private detective to find her?"

"That I did. If you want to talk to little Miss Dixie, there's your chance."

Beau stared at the words on the card. The letters seemed to dance before his eyes. This was Dixie's world...where she lived. He could just drive to Dallas and knock on her door. Simple as that. Maybe he could get some answers. Maybe she would kick him out, but at least he would have tried.

He stood and extended his hand, giving Breck's a hearty shake. "Thanks. Thanks a lot."

To Misty, he murmured, "Cancel the search...just never mind," as he strode out the door.

***

"Sweetie, your mother's crazy." Scott lifted her chin. "She's not that old, but she's very bitter. She's asking you to give up your birthright." He had come over soon after Dixie had called to tell him she was back. He still wore a cast on his right forearm since his hand was not fully healed.

Tears stung Dixie's eyes. "I—I don't know, Scott." She glanced toward the stairs leading up to her mother's bedroom.

"Years from now, you'll kick yourself if you let this opportunity go. You owe it to yourself. You owe it to—"

"I know," she said, sniffling. "I'd just hate to go back

to Langston. Everyone there treated me like—like..." She cast about for an analogy but came up blank.

A tear trailed down her cheek, and Scott wiped it away with his thumb. "Don't cry, sweet girl. You know I'm here for you. I'll drive to Langston every weekend, if you need me. Roger won't mind. He knows you're like a sister to me. We'll always be like family."

"I know, but—"

He interrupted her with a finger to her lips. "It's only a year. It will pass in a flash. You'll see."

She sucked in a deep breath and eased it out. "You think so?"

He flashed a grin. "I know so. You can run your business from your home in Langston, and I'm sure you can deal with the feed store. I mean, how hard can that be?" He spread his hands. "Farmers come in and buy feed...right?"

A throbbing in her temple signaled the beginning of a headache. *How hard can it be?* Did he have any idea how hard it was to run a ranch? How hard it was to run a business? Scott worked at a day spa and gym, flattering middle-aged women and showing them how to use exercise equipment.

She nodded. "I'm sure you're right. I'll think about it."

"You can sell everything in a year. All that property has to be worth a bundle. Don't blow it away."

"A year." She thought about spending the next twelve months in Langston. Twelve months in a small town where she would run into all the Garretts. Where she would run into Beau everywhere.

"It will go by in a flash," Scott assured her. "We can get you through this, and then, when you sell it all off, you can go anywhere you want. You can do anything you want."

"I'll think about it," she reiterated.

Big Jim stood, his hands fisted on his hips, glaring at his youngest son. "Are you sure about this?"

"Yeah, Dad. I'm sure. I can't get on with my life until I get some answers from Dixie. If I have to chase her down to her home turf to find out why she left me so suddenly, then that's what I'm going to do." He opened his closet and took out several nicely starched western shirts and Wranglers on hangers and laid them across his bed. "I just need to do this."

Big Jim looked doubtful. "You don't need to. You want to."

"Yes, I do." He stuffed his toiletries into a dopp kit and rolled some underwear into a duffel bag. He abandoned his packing efforts and turned to his dad. "Look, I know you don't understand, but this is just something I have to do. I can't leave things unresolved between us."

Big Jim huffed out an impatient snort. "You and Dixie Moore? I thought she made it clear she didn't want anything to do with you, or Langston, when she went running out of town after the will was read. Running away for the second time, I might add."

"Yeah, well..." He couldn't think of anything to rebut his father's assessment. At that moment, his cell phone sounded.

His father rolled his eyes and walked away.

Beau answered the phone, noting that the call came from the office of Breckenridge Ryan. "Hello?"

"Beau? It's Misty. I have news for you."

He raked his fingers through his thick dark hair. "Let 'er rip."

"Well…Dixie Moore is coming back to Langston. She called Breck a little while ago to tell him she intended to return to Langston and live up to the terms of her father's will."

Beau sat down on the edge of his bed. "She's coming back?"

"That's what she said."

"Okay, thanks." He hung up and sat staring into space. *She's coming back. I have a year to win her over.*

Beau gave her a week. He thought that should be enough time for her to get settled in…and for her to get used to the fact that she would have to deal with him for a year.

He gripped the steering wheel with both hands as he drove to the Moore ranch. He gave himself a pep talk about keeping his cool and not losing it if she shut him out—again.

When he turned his silver double-dually truck in at her ranch, he slowed, rolling to a stop in front of the house. He killed the motor and sat, gazing at the rambling one-story ranch house. Dixie's SUV was in place, so he figured she was inside. He hoped her boyfriend was not. It wasn't that he was afraid of the muscle-bound oaf, but he didn't want to do anything to upset Dixie. It was too important to him to be able to communicate with her.

Man up, Beau.

He opened the door and stepped down out of the

truck, hoping he could break through the wall Dixie had built up against him. Sucking in a chest full of air, he then blew it all out. He strode across the porch and rang the doorbell. *Nothing.* No sounds from within.

He knocked this time, but again, the house remained silent. He figured she had peeked out and decided not to open the door to him.

Just as he turned to go, he heard her laughter…and her voice. She was talking to someone and coming closer.

Beau stood frozen on the porch, watching as Dixie rounded the corner, hand in hand with a young red-haired girl. A strangling sensation wrapped his throat. Undeniably, this was Dixie's clone. *She has a child—a daughter.*

He struggled to draw a breath. "Dixie," he gasped out.

Dixie's gaze lit on him, and she stopped in place. "B—Beau," her voice rasped.

The child turned her attention to him as well. She was Dixie's spitting image, except for her eyes. Garrett eyes. Bright, turquoise-blue eyes ringed with a fringe of black lashes stared back at him.

Beau felt as though he had been sucker-punched. He dropped to one knee, unable to speak. Obviously this was his daughter. The question was why had Dixie hidden the child from him?

—ᴧᴧᴧ—

Dixie had known this moment was coming. She had rehearsed her lines a hundred times in her head. She had intended to be cool and aloof, letting him know her boundaries in no uncertain terms—but now she stood staring at Beau, unable to react.

Her throat constricted as she saw tears gather in Beau's eyes. Seeing this big man drop to one knee had jarred her, but now that tears had formed in his eyes, the eyes identical to her daughter's, she couldn't function. She could barely breathe.

"Mommy?"

"It's okay, baby." Resolutely, Dixie continued, stepping up onto her porch. "Beau Garrett. Meet my daughter, Ava. She's five years old."

Still on one knee, he stared at Ava and then raised his gaze to Dixie's. "My daughter." It wasn't a question.

"Yes." She felt her lips tighten. "The daughter you denied. Now, she's just my daughter."

A strange, animal-like sound curled up out of Beau's throat. He stood, his face changing as he rose. "Just what the hell are you talking about?"

Dixie raised her brows, giving him a stern look. "I'll thank you to watch your language." She ruffled her daughter's curls. "Ava, why don't you go on in the house and find your teddy bear. I'm sure he needs some company. I'll be with you in a minute."

Beau's gaze followed Ava as she climbed the steps and entered the house. When he turned back to face Dixie, his face was the picture of rage. His color was heightened, and a muscle in his jaw worked.

"I can't believe you never told me about Ava. I was sick with worry when you disappeared." He shook his head and stomped to the end of the porch. "I can't believe you did that to your father." Pivoting, he strode back to her. "What kind of monster are you, Dixie Moore?"

Anger spiraled through Dixie's chest. She could hardly breathe. "How dare you pretend you didn't know about Ava! My mother went to your home and begged your father to acknowledge my pregnancy." Her voice came out as a raspy whisper, since she didn't want to alarm Ava. If she were to scream at Beau, as every molecule of her being wanted, she might fly at him with her fists. *How dare he pretend? Is he mocking me?*

Beau regarded her through slitted eyes. "I assure you my father would never do that. If he knew you were pregnant with his grandchild, he would have gone straight to the preacher to arrange our wedding. My dad's not like that."

"Ha! Shows what you know. Your dad is a big, egotistical bully. My mother said he laughed and called me a slut."

"He would never do that," Beau reiterated, leaning so close she itched to slap his face.

"Are you calling my mother a liar?" She was aware her voice had become shrill.

He straightened his shoulders. "It appears so."

Chapter 4

BEAU DROVE HOME. IT MIGHT BE TRUE THAT HE EXCEEDED the speed limit, but encountering an officer of the law was the last thing on his mind. He took the turn way too fast, squealing his tires. The truck rocked as he drove through the horseshoe-shaped arch gating the entrance to the Garrett spread. His truck bumped over the cattle guard, jarring his teeth together. A cloud of dust rose behind his vehicle as he tore down the private road to the Garrett ranch house.

Stomping on the brakes, he swerved to park next to Big Jim's truck. He jammed the gears into park and jumped out, stomping into the house. "Dad! Dad, where are you?"

"What's all the racket?" Big Jim came out of his study, frowning.

Beau raked his fingers through his hair. "I've got to know, Dad. Promise you won't lie to me."

"What the hell?" Big Jim's brows came together as he fisted his hands on his hips. "Have I ever lied to you?"

"Not that I know of, but I'm just saying, you have to be straight with me. This is too important."

"Come on in the kitchen. You look pretty hot under the collar. I'm going to have a glass of sweet tea, and I'm gonna pour one for you." Big Jim headed to the back of the house.

Beau released a frustrated sigh before following his father to the kitchen. Slumping onto a stool, he leaned both elbows against the counter. He watched Big Jim's movements as he selected two tall glasses, filled them with ice from the refrigerator door, and topped them off with tea from a pitcher in the refrigerator.

"Now, what is all this about?" Big Jim took a sip before sliding onto another stool.

"Dad, did Dixie's mother ever come to talk with you?"

"Not that I recall." He took another hit of tea. "I barely remember her. Seems she was always scowling." Big Jim cocked his head to one side. "You wanted to talk about Mrs. Moore?"

"Maybe I should have started off congratulating you."

"For what?"

"For one thing, you're a grandfather."

"You mean Leah's little daughter, Gracie? I love her like she was my own blood. You know that."

"No, I was thinking about the daughter Dixie Moore gave birth to when she left high school before graduation." He raised his glass in a salute before taking a sip. "My daughter."

Big Jim set his tea down hard and leaned forward. "What did you say?" His bushy brows rose toward his thick shock of silver hair.

"You heard me. Dixie Moore has a beautiful little daughter, and she's mine."

"Well, I'll be damned." A slow smile spread across Big Jim's craggy face. "A daughter, you say?" Big Jim let out a whoop and smacked his open palm down on the countertop.

"Dad, it's not a laughing matter. Dixie insisted her mother came to this house and told you about the pregnancy. That's what she's been so all-fired pissed off about."

"Never happened," Big Jim growled, suddenly serious. "We would have gone straight to the preacher to get you two married."

"That's what I figured." Beau slumped against the counter. "Damn! I can't believe I have a daughter." He leaned his forehead against his hands. "She's just beautiful."

"I can't wait to meet her."

Beau let out a snort. "Good luck with that. Dixie and I had a fight. She's convinced her mother came here to tell us Dixie was pregnant and that you called her a slut and turned her away."

"That's a bald-faced lie!" Big Jim exploded.

"That's what I told her." Beau raked his fingers through his hair again. "That's when she went inside and locked the door."

"What is it you want to do?"

Beau's chest grew tight. "I can't imagine having a child and not being able to be with her, but Dixie is so hostile, I don't know how we can work that out. I mean, she hates me."

"Well, Son…" Big Jim hesitated. "I'm pretty sure you have some rights. If it's okay with you, I'll give Breckenridge Ryan a call."

Beau shook his head. "No, Dad. I'm hoping we can work past this. She's just operating on some bad information. I don't know where she got the idea her mother talked to you."

"That Mamie Moore always had a burr under her saddle. I seem to recall your mama saying she was real difficult to work with. She seemed to think that because she was from the city, she was way better than the local women. Couldn't be bothered to do any church work or even socialize with others."

"The only times I ever saw Mrs. Moore were when I picked Dixie up at her house. Mr. Moore was always glad to see me, but I got the idea that Dixie's mother disapproved of me for some reason."

Big Jim let out a hearty bellow. "Well, she was right. You did knock up her daughter."

"Yeah, there's that." Beau shrugged. "But even when we were kids, she didn't seem to want me to play with Dixie. I guess she never liked me."

"Don't worry about it. I'll make sure you get a chance to be a father to that little girl."

Beau held up both hands. "Settle down, Dad. I don't want to run roughshod over Dixie. I'm hoping we can work things out, and…and I have my daughter to think of."

Big Jim made a scoffing noise deep in his throat. "I do believe you're still sweet on little Miss Dixie."

———

Dixie wouldn't cry.

She didn't want to upset Ava. So she plastered on a big grin and stifled the anger choking the breath out of her. *How dare he call me a liar?* After all the misery Beau and his stuffed-shirt father had caused her and her mother, how could he insult her as well? Dixie was boiling inside.

"Mommy?" Ava gazed up at here with concern. "Are you okay?"

"Sure I am, honey. I was just trying to figure out what to fix for our dinner."

"Macaroni," Ava crowed.

"Let's see what we've got. Want to help me?" At Ava's eager nod, Dixie gathered her in a hug and carried her to the old-fashioned kitchen.

She settled Ava at the table and rummaged through the pantry. *Yes, there's a box of macaroni and cheese. What else?*

She pushed things around, locating a can of peas and another can of fruit cocktail. What a sad excuse for a meal. "Okay, tomorrow we have to go into town and shop for food."

Ava clapped her hands together.

"We'll go early before—before it gets crowded." *With Garretts.*

Dixie prepared the simple meal, and afterward she and Ava curled up on the comfortable overstuffed sofa in the den. After all the stress, she could feel the tension slowly drain from her body. Ava nestled against her, happily settling in for an evening of television. They watched *Modern Family*, but after the first ten minutes, Ava's eyes grew heavy, and her head dropped against Dixie's shoulder.

How nice that her daughter could feel so comfortable even though Dixie was a basket case. She huffed out a sigh. Maybe it was because Ava felt secure with her mother even though the surroundings were new for her. She buried her face in her daughter's hair, inhaling the sweet fragrance and planting a kiss at the same time.

Dixie gazed around the room. Time seemed to have stood still in this house. Her father had not changed a thing. The house was in need of a thorough cleaning and had a sort of musty odor. Maybe she would clean everything and open all the windows. She supposed her dad spent more time out on the ranch with his horses and cattle or at the feed store in town. Obviously he hadn't paid much attention to the old family home. Or maybe it had just missed a woman's touch.

Slowly she came to the realization that this house now belonged to her...or it would at the end of the year, along with everything else in her father's estate. She felt the immediate weight of owning all that property, like a heavy mantle settling around her shoulders. She took several deep breaths. *Not a problem.* In twelve months, she would have this place spruced up and on the market.

All she had to do was hang in here for the next twelve months, and she could sell off all the property...and return to Dallas.

Her life in Dallas was so simple. She shared a condominium with her daughter and her mother. She had an online store that brought her an adequate income and gave her a creative outlet. She got to spend time with Ava, and then there was Scott, her best friend who loved her like a sister. He was always there for her, ready to accompany her anywhere. He was the perfect date. He was quite handsome and was built like a Mack truck, but...he was in love with Roger.

She was a little irritated with Scott for urging her to return to Langston to claim her inheritance...Ava's inheritance too. She knew he was right. There was too much at stake, and most of all, she couldn't allow that bastard Big Jim Garrett to profit from her father's death, even if it was going to be a miserable year. Even if her father had turned his back on her when he learned she was pregnant…even then, she needed to preserve his estate for her daughter. That was something she had to do, for Ava—for herself.

Mostly, she was furious with Beau. Her anger was based in the pain he had inflicted when he first denied fathering a child with her. And that pain had festered into a smoldering rage.

—⁓—

Early the next morning, Dixie logged into her online business and took care of the new orders, processing credit and debit cards and forwarding orders to the manufacturers. This was the ritual she used to begin most days.

Dixie checked the balance in her business account and gave a little hum of satisfaction. At least some things rolled along nice and steady no matter what else was going on in her life.

She closed her laptop, pausing for a moment with her hands clasped on its smooth surface.

The image of her father's smiling face flashed into her brain, the smiling, kind man he used to be…before he decided he had no use for a pregnant daughter or for the wife who sided with her.

Her eyes misted up, but she blinked away any traitorous tears that might attempt to ruin this day. What was done was done. The father she had adored had not supported her. She had to let it go.

Dixie swallowed hard, recalling that her father had been murdered. Some lowlife thief had killed him over the day's receipts. And now she would never have an opportunity to face him, to ask him why he had treated her so unkindly.

"Mommy," Ava called. "I'm done."

Dixie plastered on a smile. "That's my good girl." She slipped her laptop into a carrying case and put it away. Lots of sensitive information there.

She cleared away Ava's breakfast dishes and gave her a quick washup. "You ready to go to town?"

Ava bobbed her head, grinning in response. She had no idea what this town had to offer, but she was eager to take it on.

Dixie secured Ava in her car seat and set out for Langston. Ava was singing to the radio. Dixie, on the other hand, was tight-jawed. She dreaded going in to Langston. She dreaded the possibility of seeing any of the Garretts. For that matter, she dreaded seeing anyone she had known previously. There would be questions, questions she did not care to answer.

Not going to let the bastards get me down.

She had to get into some kind of regular routine. Shopping for food would be a normal part of her life, so she needed to toughen up and be able to survive here in Langston…just for a year.

Turning in at the parking lot in front of the relatively small grocery store, she found a parking place and turned off the motor. "Here we are, honey."

She pried Ava out of her safety seat and headed inside. Just as she heaved her daughter into the grocery cart, her cell phone rang. She answered before checking the caller ID.

"Miss Moore? It's Breckenridge Ryan."

Her stomach did a tumble and roll. Another person she wanted to avoid. "Um, yes?"

"Could you come to my office today? We need to discuss your father's business obligations."

"Does it have to be today?"

Silence. She could imagine his fierce frown.

"You have employees who need to be paid." His tone was terse. "And we need to get you on the signature card at the bank."

"I see." She considered her options. "Look, I'm at the grocery store. I can be there in about thirty minutes." She said goodbye and disconnected.

Ava stared at her with wide eyes. What was she thinking?

Dixie made a quick circle of the store and found a small cooler, which she filled with milk and other cold or frozen items. She congratulated herself on taking care of her business so quickly as she queued up at the checkout stand.

"Why, who is this pretty little thing?"

Dixie whirled around. An elderly woman stood behind her in line, her cart empty save for two six-packs of Boost and a package of adult diapers. The woman's face crinkled into a grin. "Aren't you the Moore girl? And this little one is your spitting image."

Nodding mechanically, Dixie kept a grip on the cart and her debit card.

"Shame about your dad. Vern was such a good man. Never missed a Sunday at church."

Dixie swallowed hard, recalling that it was her father who took her to church every week while her mother stayed in bed. Did that make him a good man?

If so, how could he turn his back on her when she needed him most?

"I hope to see you in church this Sunday. I think this little one will be in my daughter's Sunday school class. Is she four or five?"

"Five," Dixie croaked out. "She's going on six." She began placing grocery items on the conveyor belt.

The old woman reached out a hand to stroke Ava's hair. "Lovely hair, and those eyes. You don't see eyes like that every day."

"No...no, you don't." She banished the image from her brain of another with those eyes.

Dixie placed her cold items back in the cooler and stowed the groceries in the back of the SUV and Ava in her car seat. With no pleasure, she headed for Breckenridge T. Ryan's law office.

Misty Garrett, Breck's secretary, greeted her with a smile. "Hello, Ms. Moore. It's so good to see you again."

Dixie stiffened. "Um—it's good to see you as well."

Misty's gaze was fastened on Ava, confusion registering on her face.

"There you are," Breck bellowed from inside his office. The door stood open, and he motioned for her to enter. "Sit right down."

Dixie lifted Ava in her arms and carried her into the office, closing the door behind her. "I have groceries in the car. What do you want?" She remained standing, aware of her open hostility, but considering the attorney's contempt at the reading of the will, she didn't care what he thought of her.

He stared at Ava. "Didn't know you had a daughter."

"Well, now you know." Her voice was terse. She adjusted Ava on her hip.

"Now I know." He opened a folder on his desk. "You need to pay the men who are working at the feed store."

"Okay, how do I do that?"

A muscle in Breck's jaw twitched. "First, you need to sign these checks." He fanned out two checks and placed a pen onto the desk beside them. Dixie released her pent-up breath and placed Ava in one of the chairs across from Breck before seating herself in the other. She reached for the pen.

The payees' names were Peter Miller and Joshua Miller. "Same last name?"

"Cousins," Breck bit out. "Pete has been employed by your dad for many years, but when the work in the warehouse got to be too much for him, Vern hired Josh part time to do the heavy lifting."

Dixie signed her name to both checks and pushed them toward Breck.

"Now, you need to take this card to the bank across the square. Take your ID as well."

"What is this?"

"A signature card. I've contacted the bank to make arrangements for you to be able to sign on the business account as well as Vern's private accounts."

Dixie's shoulders sagged. "Oh." This step weighed heavily on her. It felt so permanent. "Do I have to?"

Breck made a scornful sound. "Of course. The checks are worthless without a valid signature. Be responsible for once."

"For once?" Dixie jumped to her feet, leaning across the desk. "What do you know about my life?"

Breck gazed at her, steely-eyed. "I know you and your mother abandoned Vern Moore and never looked back. He was devastated."

She felt as though he had punched her in the gut. "No! No, that's not what happened. My...my father threw me out...for...for—" She glanced at Ava, sitting wide-eyed in the chair.

Breck drew in a breath and let it out. "I see." He shook his head. "This doesn't agree with the story your father told me."

"You don't know. You weren't there," she shot back.

Breck gazed at her impassively. "And you weren't here."

Dixie gathered her daughter and stomped out of the office, startling Misty as she closed the door so hard the glass panel rattled. Her hands were shaking by the time she got to the bank. She had to sit in the car for a few minutes, gripping the wheel. How did this lawyer have the nerve to accuse her of abandoning her father? It was the other way around.

Now she was wondering what kind of story her father had told people when his wife and daughter left. Had he concocted some sort of fable to cover his own actions?

"Mommy?" Ava's voice from the backseat jerked her out of her reverie.

"Sorry, honey. Mommy was just thinking." She removed Ava from her car seat and entered the bank. They were shown to the office of one of the bankers, where she signed the card and presented her identification.

"Miss Moore, we were so sorry to learn of your

father's death. He was a pillar of the community." The banker presented a pitying expression.

"Thank you," she said.

"We hope you will continue to carry on in your father's footsteps." The banker leaned toward her, a hopeful expression on his face.

"It appears my daughter and I will be residents for a year. After that, I don't know."

This was obviously not the response he was looking for. He gazed at her dolefully, pursing his lips and tenting his fingers on his desk.

She stood and reached for Ava's hand, but the little girl grinned and dashed out the office door. "Ava, stop!" Dixie hurried after her.

She stopped short, almost stumbling when she saw the two tall men who had just entered the bank lobby. Both men wearing Stetsons and Wranglers. Both men broad-shouldered. Both men the bane of her existence.

Straightening her spine, she regarded both Beau and Big Jim Garrett. Her heart leaped into her throat, cutting off her ability to take in air.

Grinning, Big Jim dropped to one knee and held out his arms as Ava ran straight at him. He lifted her, standing as he raised her high above his head. "Whoa! Who is this little runaway filly?" He appeared to be delighted to be holding Ava.

Dixie cleared her throat. "That is my daughter, Ava. Put her down."

Big Jim tickled Ava on her tummy. "Aw, we're just getting acquainted here."

Beau, for his part, looked stricken. He reached out to stroke her hair.

Big Jim passed Ava to Beau, whose face was a smorgasbord of emotion. His brow furrowed, but he was grinning.

Dixie realized he was close to tears and felt a stab of sympathy but quickly squelched it. No way she was going to feel sorry for Beau Garrett. Pressing her lips together, she strode across the polished granite floor. "Put my daughter down."

"Aw, Dixie. Can't we just get acquainted with each other?"

"Not now. We need to leave."

Beau gave Ava a kiss on the cheek and set her on her feet. "Dixie, you need to accept that I'm her father. I want to be her father."

"You had your chance, but you turned your back on me." She took Ava's hand. "Now, I'm turning my back on you." She left, aware that every eye in the bank followed her as she led her daughter out the door.

~~~

Beau swallowed what felt like a roll of razor wire at the back of his throat. He tasted unshed tears. He hadn't known how quickly he would grow to love the little girl with the big blue eyes. He hadn't known how it would hurt to have her ripped out of his arms.

"Tough break, Son." Big Jim clapped him on the shoulder. "That is one mighty sweet little girl."

Beau couldn't find the words to describe how he felt about this child, this little girl who stared at him with eyes the same color as his…the same shape as his…

"It's okay, Son. We'll work out something." He turned and strode to the office of the bank president.

Beau leaned against the granite-topped table with slots hosting forms for deposits, withdrawals, and various other transactions. The polished stone felt cool and smooth.

He tried to sort out his feelings. Years ago, Dixie had ripped the heart right out of his chest when she took off without looking back. Now, he knew she'd left because she was pregnant, but why hadn't she had the decency to tell him? He was in love with her. They were young, but they could have made it work. He would have married her—if only he had known.

But why was Dixie spouting all that anger? She acted as though he had done something wrong. It was as though she had suffered directly because of his actions. As though he had purposefully inflicted some intense pain upon her. She was angry and bitter.

"I'm done here. Let's go." Big Jim appeared by his side.

Beau huffed out a sigh and followed Big Jim out of the bank. He climbed into his father's truck and closed the door much harder than necessary.

Big Jim gave him a sideways glance before pulling out. He drove the few blocks to Moore's Feed and Seed.

"I'll take the order in," Beau offered, his hand on the door handle.

"I'll go with you." Big Jim swung out of the truck, heading for the entrance. He stepped up onto the wooden deck and glanced back to see if Beau was coming.

"Sure, Dad." Beau followed, blinking when he stepped into the unlit store from the bright sunlight.

"Hey, Pete." Big Jim greeted the man behind the counter. "How's it going?"

Pete gave a wide grin. "Pretty good day so far. Breck Ryan just dropped off our paychecks. Josh and me ain't got paid for the past couple weeks." He took a folded paper out of his breast pocket and flashed it before returning it to its place. "It's good to have a little money in my pocket."

Big Jim tossed a folded paper on the counter. "Order me some more of that high-grade supplement for calves. We got a bumper crop comin' up. Have you met your new boss yet?"

Pete shrugged. "I saw her at the funeral, but other than that, I ain't seen her since she was a feisty little teenager."

Josh Miller raised a garage-type door in the back wall, pushing a dolly loaded with bags of mulch. He nodded at Beau and his father but continued on to a corner where bags of potting soil, compost, and mulch were piled. He jerked his head to indicate the large man following in his wake. "Got some coffee, Pete? Troy here needs caffeine bad."

"Sure, help yourself." Pete gestured to the coffee-maker behind the counter.

Troy glanced at the Garretts and then edged closer to Pete to fill his thermos with coffee. He screwed the top on and strolled toward the back in the direction of the loading dock.

Big Jim raised an eyebrow, but Pete just shook his head. "Truckers making deliveries. They think this is Dunkin' Donuts."

Big Jim heaved out a sigh. "I figured you should know about Dixie, should she decide to get herself in here." His mouth tightened. "Vern wanted his daughter to take over the management of his ranch and his business." Big Jim shook his head. "You two need to be aware that she should be coming in here and she has the right to, you know…inspect the books."

Pete shrugged. "She can do that. We got nothin' ta hide."

"I want you to show her the business," Big Jim said. "I mean, teach her how to run it. It's what Vern wanted."

Pete nodded. "I hear ya, Big Jim, but I'm not sure I know everything about the business. Vern was a good boss, but he took care of all the business stuff hisself. He always closed up the store all by hisself. I would lock up the outside doors and go home."

Big Jim expelled a deep sigh and leaned his forearms against the counter. "Anything different about the night Vern was killed?"

Pete's eyes opened wide. "Why, no…not that I can recall." He stroked his chin thoughtfully. "Me an' Josh finished our jobs, you know…closin' down stuff."

Big Jim nodded.

"An' then I said g'night to Vern, and we left." His shoulders slumped. "Then the next mornin' when I come to work, the doors were all locked up and there was yeller plastic ribbons all around."

"Crime scene tape?" Beau offered.

"Yeah. That stuff." Pete's face morphed into one of deep depression.

Big Jim clapped him on the shoulder. "I know it's hard, but just hang in there, and I'll bet Vern's daughter will take a load off."

Beau had a hard time imagining Dixie working here, but he kept his mouth shut. He watched Josh heave the bags on top of others of the same variety. Josh was a few years older, but Beau remembered him as sort of a screwup. This was probably the best job he would ever land.

His father waved him over, and they left together.

"How about it, Beau? Do you want me to go to Breck Ryan to see if you have some legal status in your daughter's life?"

Beau shook his head. "I want to give Dixie a chance to simmer down first. I hope we can work out whatever has got her so all-fired furious with me."

"Sure, we can give it a little time." Big Jim heaved himself into his truck.

Beau climbed in, and they headed back to the ranch. "I don't know why she's so messed up. She's got it into her head that I somehow betrayed her...and that you turned her mother away when she went to talk to you."

"Never happened." Big Jim smacked the heel of his hand against the steering wheel. "Believe me, I'm just as much in the dark as you are."

Beau was oblivious to the countryside whizzing by. He didn't see the fields or the cattle or even the few and far between vehicles on the highway. The image dancing before his eyes was of a beautiful red-haired woman with hurt in her eyes.

―⁓―

Dixie drove back to the Moore ranch as fast as the speed limit allowed. She stowed the groceries and settled her daughter with a bowl of ice cream in front of the television before stepping far enough away to give her mother a call in Dallas.

"Yes, my darling. Is everything all right? Are you coming home?"

Her mother's voice infused Dixie with a sense of calm. "We—we're okay."

"Because if you're rethinking your terrible decision to return to that miserable little town out in the middle of nowhere—"

"Mom, please…we're fine." Dixie sank onto a cushy chair and pulled her feet up under her. "I just have to ask you something."

"Well, you know you can ask me anything. How's my favorite granddaughter?"

Dixie chuckled. "Your only granddaughter is doing well. Please, I have to know something."

There was silence on the other end of the line.

"Mom, something isn't right here. Beau and his father are acting like they didn't know a thing about me being pregnant."

Her mother made a scoffing sound. "Of course they're acting the innocents. Those Garretts are ashamed of the way they treated us."

Dixie's brow furrowed. "They sure aren't acting like they're ashamed of anything."

"Well, of course not. Big Jim Garrett has always had a giant ego and a lot of gall. His sons have inherited his bad genes. Just ignore those villains, and don't let them anywhere near our precious Ava."

"Too late for that."

She disconnected after listening to more of her mother's recriminations against the whole Garrett clan. Her mother seemed to hate all of them as well as the entire town of Langston.

Dixie leaned back in the chair, staring up at the ceiling. There were cobwebs on the ceiling fan. *Need to clean that.*

Her mother's words reverberated in her head. Langston wasn't really such a bad town. She did have some good memories. Lots of them, in fact, before... before...

Dixie closed her eyes, reviewing images of her childhood. Her dad kept late hours at the store, but Sundays belonged to him. First he would make her breakfast and then take her to church. Then there were many adventures, from taking his little boat out on the lake for an afternoon of fishing to riding horses together or just taking a walk to enjoy the leaves turning colors in the fall. No, she couldn't think about him. Too many sad memories later in their relationship.

Her thoughts drifted to Beau. They had been playmates in grade school. This natural affinity flowed into being high school sweethearts, and those feelings had led to sexual experimentation. She couldn't regret the outcome, but she wished she hadn't had to pay such a high price.

She had been in love with him. So deeply in love she could feel it in every molecule of her being. She'd thought he loved her too. She'd thought they would be married someday. They talked about going to college and whether they should get married before or after they graduated.

Silly girl. Naive girl. Stupid girl.

But she still couldn't regret their coupling when Ava had been the result.

A wave of sorrow washed over her. Better to think about her father. Better to get it all out and put it behind her. Better to move on.

The room was closing in on her. This was where she

had climbed onto her father's lap with a storybook. He seemed to have endless patience, not even rolling his eyes when she kept presenting her favorites.

She jerked upright. It was this very chair in which her father had read to her, sometimes the same stories over and over again.

In spite of her resolve, tears spangled her lashes and drooled silently down her cheeks. She let them fall, unchecked.

She jumped when her phone sounded with Scott's ringtone. She picked up the call and greeted him.

"Hey, sweet thang. I miss you." His voice wrapped around her like a comforting blanket. One that she needed at that precise moment.

She rubbed her tears away with the heel of her hand. "You must be clairvoyant. I really needed to hear your voice."

"I'll come see you Friday evening. We can have the whole weekend to hang out. If you need me to do anything, I would be happy to bring my toolbox. I'm pretty handy, you know. How does that sound?"

"Sounds great. I thought you had to work this weekend."

"I did, but I managed to trade with a couple of guys. I gotta see my girls."

She grinned. It was great that he and Roger loved Ava as much as they loved her. Perhaps Ava was a surrogate daughter the two men needed. Having these men around gave Ava some male influence in her life. *Good to have friends*.

Chapter 5

BIG JIM SLIPPED INTO HIS OFFICE AND CLOSED THE DOOR.
No point in disturbing the family, especially Beau. Big
Jim knew he was acting against Beau's wishes, but he
was pretty sure he was acting in his youngest son's
best interest.

He made the call he had been putting off.

"Breck? Sorry to call you at home. It's James Garrett.
I just needed a little advice."

"Sure," Breck said. "Whatever you need, Big Jim.
You know you can always count on me."

"Now, I want you to consider yourself on the clock. I
aim to pay you for this session."

"Forget it. Just tell me what's up."

"Well..." Big Jim made sure his office door was
closed tight. "I wanted to talk to you about Dixie Moore.
You know she is the mother of my granddaughter, Ava?"

He could hear the smile in Breck's voice. "Yeah,
I believe I heard something about that. In fact, Dixie
brought her to my office the other day. Lovely little girl.
Congratulations, Big Jim."

"She's a mighty precious little girl, but that mother of
hers is a bit flighty." He heaved a sigh. "I don't quite
know how to say this, but...I don't trust her. You know
she ran off to Dallas and Beau didn't have any idea why?"

"Seems I heard something about that too."

"I just want to make sure we don't lose Ava again."
Big Jim cleared his suddenly husky throat. "I've taken

her right to my heart, and I know Beau is so happy to be her papa. Is there anything we can do to ensure her mama don't just take off again?"

"Of course there is," Breck said. "But are you sure you want to set off that little box of dynamite?"

Big Jim made a noise somewhere between a groan and a growl. "Y'think it would cause trouble?"

"No, Big Jim. I think it would cause the apocalypse." There was a long pause. "I think you should just stay cool, enjoy getting to know your granddaughter, and be nice to Dixie. If she tries to disappear again, it's not like she will just evaporate. She's got a base in Dallas. We'll sue for parental rights on Beauregard's behalf. Don't worry about it."

Big Jim leaned back in his chair. "You're sure?"

"I'm sure. Don't make waves. Family rifts are hard to mend. Play nice, my friend."

Big Jim disconnected, feeling somewhat relieved but still not trusting.

—⁓—

The next morning, Dixie's phone sounded. She thought about not answering it when she saw the caller ID. Heaving a sigh, she answered. "Hello, Mr. Ryan. What do you want this time?"

There was a pause on the other end. "Miss Moore. You need to go to the feed store today. Pete Miller is going to show you the books. He's expecting you this afternoon."

"I don't need to see the books," she said. "I'm not questioning his accounting."

Breck snorted. "Well, Pete is no accountant. He's just been doing his best since your father died. Under the terms of your father's will, you are to take over the day-to-day management of his businesses. His businesses are now your businesses."

She sat down hard. This was news that she couldn't handle on her feet. "His businesses?"

"The feed and seed store is a thriving business," Breck said. "Every ranch in the area depends on it. The store is a part of this community, and we need it to continue to thrive. As the new owner, you need to gut up and take over the reins."

"I don't know how to be a store owner."

Another snort. "I thought you had some kind of store in Dallas."

"I have an online store. A boutique really."

"Same thing."

"It is most definitely not the same. My customers place orders online. I do not have store hours or have to stock shelves or wait on customers."

Breck let out a loud and disbelieving yelp. "How the hell do you run a store and sell things without having products in stock?"

Dixie felt her face flush. "I'm in e-tail. My stores are up in the cloud."

"Cloud?"

"I'm just the middle man. I advertise and show the products, and when someone orders, the actual seller ships it out. I make a profit off the order, but I don't have any investment in stock or warehouse space. I just run their Visa or Mastercard, pay the seller, and put my profit in my bank account. It's not that hard to understand."

"Good to know that you have some sort of business acumen."

Dixie shrugged, annoyed that this obnoxious lawyer was questioning her. "It's not a big deal. I wanted to have income and stay at home with my daughter. I'm just a small-time entrepreneur."

"Well, you better put on your boots and step up, girlie. Pete is expecting you. Your father's businesses do require hands-on management."

"What else?" she asked. "What other businesses did my dad have?" She heard a sharp intake of breath and then a slow and noisy release.

"The ranch. Your father left you the ranch. There are cattle grazing out there. There are horses. There are thousands of acres under tillage." His voice revealed his irritation.

"Oh."

"I'll bet you didn't even know that the Garretts have been making sure your animals are taken care of while you...mourn your father."

Was that sarcasm?

Dixie was glad she had chosen to sit down. "What do you mean?"

"I mean, young lady," he said, his voice taking on a strident tone, "every single day, the Garretts—your neighbors—they go over to make sure your horses have food and water. The cattle are grazing, but they still require some oversight. The ranch is a business, and you will learn to manage it." He disconnected.

Dixie sighed. "My life just keeps getting better and better."

Grappling with the idea that the Garretts had been taking care of her livestock, she came to a decision.

———

Beau was sitting in his father's office, logging in some receipts for tax records, when the doorbell chimed. He wasn't aware of any appointments his dad may have made. People rarely dropped by without calling first.

He got up and peered out the window, surprised to see Dixie's SUV pulled up close to the house. He lost no time in getting to the door and throwing it open.

"Dixie?"

She looked beautiful. Her skin was translucent. He had to fight with himself to keep from pulling her to him and kissing every inch of her. But he stood like some kind of idiot, just staring at her.

The breeze lifted a strand of hair, blowing it across her cheek.

By reflex, he reached out to smooth it away from her face. His fingers trailed along her cheek, caressing her jawline. He swallowed and dropped his hand.

"Beau, I—" She faltered.

He cleared his suddenly husky throat. "What can I do for you, Dixie?"

Heaving a sigh, she gestured to the SUV. "I brought your daughter for a visit."

Beau looked at the car, seeing the bright-red hair in the backseat. He turned back to Dixie. "You brought her?"

"I know we have our differences, but I won't put Ava in the middle of it." With one backward glance at him, she strode to the vehicle to remove Ava from her car seat and lead her to where Beau stood. "Ava, this is Beau."

He held out his hands, and Ava reached for him. He

thought his chest might burst wide open. "Hey, Ava. How are you?" His voice broke as the child leaned toward him and he gathered her in his arms.

She stared at him, her eyes wide.

"Oh, man. She's so beautiful. She looks so much like you." He tore his gaze from his daughter to the woman he had created her with, albeit unknowingly. "Come inside?" He asked Dixie.

She nodded, stepping up onto the porch.

He gestured for her to enter and carried Ava inside. "Let's go to the kitchen. Ava, would you like something to drink? I'm pretty sure we have some juice." He gave himself a mental head slap. Could he think of anything dumber to say? He set her on her feet, and she scurried to Dixie's side.

Ava gazed at him, alert and perhaps wary.

"Juice would be nice." Dixie seated Ava at the table and took the chair beside her.

Beau removed a bottle of apple juice from the refrigerator and placed it on the table. He was aware that Dixie watched him as warily as Ava. He took two glasses out of a cabinet and returned to the table. His hand shook when he poured the amber liquid into the glasses.

Dixie scooted one of the glasses toward Ava. "Be careful, honey."

Ava took the glass in both hands and lifted it to her lips.

Beau tried to soak up every molecule of the child. He longed to touch the red curls cascading around her cherubic face. He longed to become her father in every sense of the word.

He managed to swallow, although his throat was constricted. "Thank you."

Dixie nodded. "It was time." She took a deep breath and blew it out.

"I don't want you to think I've changed my mind about returning to Dallas after this year is over. I won't abandon my mom. I mean, she's always stood by me."

Beau felt as if he'd been punched in the gut. The air had been sucked from his lungs. "Back to Dallas?" he gasped. "I—I had hoped you might want to get settled in here."

"Well, I'm sorry to disappoint you, but I have to keep moving forward. I can't go back." She shrugged. "I have a life there. Friends and different interests."

He swallowed hard. His stomach tightened like a fist. It wasn't fair. He'd just met his daughter. Surely he should have a chance to get to know her—surely he should get a chance to win Dixie back. After all, they had a child between them. That should count for something. "I see."

Dixie's cheeks reddened. She gazed at her hands and then swept the curls back from Ava's forehead.

"Well, I hope you figure out that you have a lot of friends here. Me, for instance." Beau's stomach clenched. "I—I want you to be happy."

"Thanks." Her voice dropped to a lower level. She turned to Ava and placed her phone in front of her. "You can play your game, honey."

Ava grinned and began poking the screen, accompanied by a rush of music that brought a circus to mind, but she seemed to be totally engrossed.

"Can I ask you a question?" Beau tried to keep his voice low.

"Sure."

He glanced at Ava. "Could you please give us a chance?"

Her lips tightened, and she shot him a look of pure venom. "What right do you have to ask me that question?"

He reached out a hand and lightly stroked it over Ava's hair.

Ava looked up at him and grinned. An amazing, dimpled grin that ground its way into his soul.

"I guess it's because I've always been in love with you and I don't see how you could stop loving me. I don't see how you could have left me and not told me about Ava." He spoke carefully, not raising his voice or giving any hint about how he was raging inside. Nothing that a child might pick up on. *Nice and easy*.

Dixie stood up suddenly. "How dare you ask me that question?"

"I dare because I have nothing to lose. I died inside when you left me. Surely you knew how much I loved you...I still do."

He looks so hurt. How can he look so hurt?

Dixie stared at Beau. He looked incredibly earnest. If she didn't know better, she would buy into his innocent act.

She exhaled slowly, trying to control her temper. She couldn't lose control in front of her daughter. *This was a bad idea*.

"I know you used to love me," he said. "I just don't know when you quit."

"I think we're done here." She turned to Ava. "Drink up, honey. We need to go."

Ava looked disappointed but handed over the phone

and finished her juice. She grinned at Beau before she set the glass on the table.

Beau held out his hands, and Ava reached up for him, a sweet smile on her face. He lifted her in his arms. "Ava, you sure are a pretty girl. Can I give you a hug?"

She nodded and threw her arms around his neck.

Dixie watched this interaction with growing apprehension. *Oh, no. She really likes him.*

Beau put his hand on the back of Ava's head and kissed her cheek.

Are those tears in his eyes? "I can take her now." She reached for her daughter, but Ava had a stranglehold on Beau's neck.

"I'll take her to your car." His voice was low and controlled.

Dixie regarded him coolly. "All right." She fished her keys out of her purse and turned to leave. At the front door, Beau reached around and opened it for her. *Always a gentleman…at least for show.*

She fumbled for the car key and clicked the remote. She was surprised when Beau opened the back door and placed Ava in her car seat. She was grinning at him, her eyes alight.

"You be a good girl, okay?" His voice sounded sincere, like he really cared.

Ava nodded furiously. "I will," she crowed.

With obvious reluctance, he closed the door and then turned to Dixie expectantly.

"Okay, then." She took a step back. "I'll see you around."

Something flickered in his eyes. "Damned right you will." He stepped forward, pulling her into his arms. His intense gaze held her in place as he lowered his mouth to hers.

A whimper escaped her throat as their lips touched. She had forgotten how his kisses made her feel. She seemed to be melting into him through no will of her own. His tongue plundered her mouth. Long-dormant feelings roiled through her body.

He threaded his fingers through her hair, holding her in place. His kiss deepened, stirring an ache low in her belly.

Mindlessly, her arms circled his neck as her pulse throbbed in her ears. She pulled away, gasping for air. "No," she wailed. "I can't do this. Let me go."

He held her for a moment, the blue eyes stripping away her barriers, and then dropped his arms and stepped away.

Dixie climbed into her SUV and tried to close the door behind her, but Beau stepped in close.

"I love you, Dixie, and I love that little girl. You can't just disappear on me again. It's not right."

She huffed out an impatient breath. "You have some way of showing it." Reaching for the door handle, she was relieved when he moved out of the way. She slammed the door, hit the door lock, and turned the key in the ignition.

Glancing back, she saw that Ava was grinning and blowing kisses to Beau.

This was a mistake. This was a terrible mistake. She pulled away from the house and made for the highway, all the while aware that Beau had awakened the feelings she thought she had buried. With one kiss, one very long and passionate kiss, he had taken her back to that place where she had been so very much in love with him.

He stood on the porch, watching the burgundy SUV as it drove out of sight. A cloud of dust trailed behind. A profound sense of loss surged through him.

When Big Jim and Colton returned to the ranch, they stomped into the house, laughing and obviously enjoying themselves. It was Colt who noticed Beau's silence.

"What's up, Little Brother? You look like a storm cloud." Colt tossed his Stetson on the hat rack beside the door.

Beau remained tight-lipped, unwilling to share his pain.

Big Jim raised a brow. "What happened? What's got your panties in a wad?" He slung an arm around Beau's shoulder and swept him along as he made his way to the kitchen.

Beau shook his head. "I don't want to talk about it."

Big Jim and Colton glanced at each other. "Dixie Moore," they said in unison. Big Jim took three long-necks out of the fridge and set them on the granite countertop.

Colton reached for a bottle and leaned back against the kitchen counter. "C'mon. Bro. Get it off your chest. What did she do this time?"

Beau heaved a sigh. "She came over."

Big Jim's fierce brows rose. He made a scornful sound at the back of his throat. "Well, she didn't burn the place down. That's a good thing." He took a seat on one of the stools and flipped the cap off his beer.

"What did she want?" Colton regarded him with curiosity.

"Dixie came to see me." Unexpected tears sprang to his eyes. He gave them a swipe with the back of his hand and then pinched the bridge of his nose to quell the tears. "She brought my daughter."

Big Jim came off the stool. "Your daughter? She brought the girl here?"

Colton turned to Beau. "Dad told me your big news. Congratulations, Little Brother."

Beau nodded. "Ava is beautiful. She looks like Dixie did when she was a little girl, except—"

"Except what?" Colton had frozen in place, one of his big paws gripping the beer bottle.

"Except Ava has blue eyes."

Big Jim sat back down on the stool, grinning. "And that's a good thing, Son. Good news, indeed." He and Colton clinked their bottles together. "Prettiest little girl I've ever laid eyes on." He took a long swallow of beer.

"Congratulations, Bro." Colton lifted his bottle. "Nothin' better than kids."

"So, when do I get to spend some time with my granddaughter? I mean, officially?"

"I have no idea. Dixie told me she was planning to go back to Dallas after the year is up. She says she can't abandon her mother...but she could abandon me easily enough."

"Bad idea." Big Jim let out an exasperated huff. "What are you going to do about it?"

Beau shrugged and left the kitchen. He grabbed his hat from the rack and stepped outside. He wasn't sure what he could do about the situation, but he couldn't just sit around brooding. He thought better on his feet, so his feet took him to his truck. He swung into the cab and started the motor. Not sure where he was headed, he drove toward the highway. The sun was just setting in the western sky, sending long fingers of salmon and purple reaching across the horizon.

He drove into Langston and made a circle of the town square. The businesses had mostly closed up, with only restaurants and bars showing signs of life. He thought about stopping in somewhere, but he wasn't hungry and not in the mood to socialize.

He made another circle and then headed back out of town. Once on the highway, he figured out where he wanted to go.

Dixie showered and pulled on a long tee-type nightgown. She looked in on Ava, who slept soundly, one arm flung over her head, the other embracing a plush toy.

A rush of warmth flooded her chest. *I love you so much*. Still grinning, she had just silently closed the door when she heard the sound of tires on the gravel drive.

The fact that she and her daughter were alone on this vast ranch hit home. A tingle of fear spiraled around her spine. Who could be coming to call so late at night? She sucked in a deep breath and let it out slowly. Not the time to panic. Her dad had kept a rack of weapons in his study. Hopefully, the array of rifles and shotguns were still loaded. Unfortunately, her ever-responsible dad did not have any loaded weapons in his home office, and she had no idea where he'd kept the ammunition.

Well, whatever. Maybe the appearance of being armed would be enough. She gathered her courage and grabbed a rifle. Without turning on any lights, she crept toward the front of the house. *Best to face the intruder head-on.*

Peeking out the front window, she recognized Beau's truck as it came to a stop and the headlights were turned off. The vehicle stood like a silver behemoth, shining in the bright moonlight.

She froze, unable to think. A sense of numbness settled over her, followed by a flood of emotion. She had felt so empowered when she took Ava to see him, but now she was paralyzed.

She didn't think she could face him again. She wasn't prepared. Above all, she had to keep Beau from discovering how his kiss had affected her. "I'm over him." The sound of her own voice startled her. "Yes, I'm over you, Beau Garrett." she whispered.

Warily, she watched him open the driver's-side door and climb out. He took a stance, feet apart, hands fisted on hips, seemingly staring at the house.

A shiver ran through her, and this time it wasn't fear. Just seeing the broad set of his shoulders and the well-filled Wranglers caused a roiling in her nether regions. She huffed out a breath. "Oh, for heaven's sake." She propped the rifle against the wall and let the curtain fall into place.

Dixie flipped the light switch and threw open the front door. "Beau, what are you doing here?" She leaned against the doorjamb and crossed her arms over her chest.

Beau lifted his chin. A smile flicked across his mouth. *Oh, that mouth.* Dixie swallowed again.

He walked toward her, taking long, athletic strides, quickening her heartbeat with every step nearer. "Dixie…" His voice rolled out, deep and intimate. "I needed to see you."

"N—needed to see me?" She heard the catch in her own voice and straightened her spine.

"Yeah." He strode through the doorway, managing to gather her in an embrace, lift her off her bare feet, and kick the door closed with one booted heel.

Just like that.

Her heart was trying to beat its way out of her chest. Staring up into his eyes, she understood the meaning of *weak in the knees*.

He gazed at her mouth as though it was the last cookie on the plate, yet he held back, prolonging her misery.

"Oh, for goodness' sake. Just kiss me!"

The smile went wall to wall. "Yes, ma'am." He lowered his head, brushing her lips with his gently at first and then attacking her mouth hungrily.

She couldn't think...couldn't breathe. It was as though Beau was infused into every molecule of her being. Wrenching her mouth away, she tried to assemble her thoughts. "Wait! What—what was it you wanted?"

He let out a snort. "You...I want you." He found her lips again and kissed her all the way across the room, where he lowered her onto the sofa. "Ava...where is she?" His voice was ragged with desire.

"Asleep—in her bed." Her breath came in gasps. "Oooh."

He was touching her in places she hadn't been touched in a while. His hand slipped under her nightshirt, gliding from her thigh and up to her hip. "You stopped wearing panties?"

"I was on my way to bed."

"Good idea." He scooped her up and headed down the hall toward the bedrooms.

"Stop! Where are you going?" she hissed.

"Your room."

"No, Ava is sleeping there."

He paused in the hallway. "Where then?"

She clung to his shoulders, her heart throbbing in her ears. "The guest room. Take me there." She pointed to the room at the end of the hall.

He quickly covered the distance and leaned down for Dixie to twist open the doorknob.

The door swung open slowly, noiselessly. It felt unused, empty for eons. Beau carried her inside and closed the door behind them. Placing her on the bed, he landed beside her, his weight causing the bed to bounce.

With no preamble, he pulled her to him and took possession of her mouth, sucking her lower lip into his mouth and working it with his tongue.

She emitted a low moan, just as his kiss deepened. His hands skimmed her body, the thin cotton knit nightshirt doing little to hide her nipples' eager response to his touch. She pushed him back, sitting up. "Listen here, cowboy...one of us is definitely wearing too many clothes." She concentrated on unbuttoning his shirt, aware that he was staring at her like a puma ready to pounce.

He stripped his western belt out of the loops of his Wranglers, unzipped them, and pulled his shirt tail out. *How helpful*.

Dixie pushed his shirt off his shoulders, her fingertips grazing his warm, muscled skin.

He shrugged out of the shirt and then stripped the nightshirt off over her head. His gaze skimmed over her body, causing her to shiver.

A wave of shyness washed over her. The last time he'd seen her naked she had been seventeen. Now she'd had a child and weighed a bit more.

He stroked his hand over her body, cupping a breast and circling her nipple with his thumb. "How can one woman be so beautiful?"

A flush of ridiculous pleasure washed through her, while a blush painted her cheeks. "That's nice of you to say."

"Aw, Dixie. You've never been stuck on yourself, but someday you gotta look in the mirror. You are a complete hottie."

She made the mistake of looking into his eyes, and felt herself being pulled in—hypnotized by his magnetism. Having no will of her own, she reached for him, slipping her arms around his neck and pulling him toward her.

Their lips met in a kiss that set fire to the kindling that had been ignored for so long. An aching passion swirled low in her belly.

He pulled away and quickly started removing his remaining clothes.

Damn! He's even hotter naked. She noted the well-developed muscles in his shoulders and arms. *Not an ounce of fat*. His abs were beyond six-pack. Maybe a twelve-pack. As he worked to remove his boots and divest himself of the rest of his clothing, he was unknowingly giving her a show.

Once free, he turned to her, encircling her in his arms.

"Wait! Wait, dammit!" she said.

A wry grin lifted one side of his mouth. "What am I waiting for?"

She laughed, noting he was obviously more than ready to jump on her. "Do you have some protection? I don't think we're in a position to make another baby."

His grin went full throttle. "I'm willing. I'll make all the babies you want and love every single one of 'em."

She couldn't help but laugh. "Beau, seriously—"

"Right here, baby. I gotcha covered." He reached for his Wranglers and pulled out a handful of colorfully packaged condoms.

"How many times are you planning to—" She stopped short.

"I want to make sure you're satisfied." He winked and swept her into his arms.

She fell back onto the bed, taking Beau with her. His warm flesh seeming to melt against her. She arched her back, rubbing her nipples against the light dusting of hair on his chest.

He sucked in a breath and lowered himself on top of her. He kissed her neck. He kissed her shoulder. He kissed her breasts, suckling each nipple in turn. He started to move lower, but she sank her fingers into his thick hair, holding him in place. "Hold on, cowboy. I've had enough of the appetizer. If you're intent on satisfying me, I'm ready for the main course." She wrapped her legs around him to make her point.

"Yes, ma'am," he murmured. Finding her warm and wet, he quickly applied a condom and eased into her.

"Oh, Beau!" She had almost forgotten how it felt to be joined to this man—this man she had loved most of her life.

He began to stroke inside her, slowly at first and then picking up rhythm. Dixie raised her hips to meet his thrusts. She felt the gathering tension low in her belly. Her breath was labored as she struggled to keep up with her very athletic partner.

Beau knew her body. He knew where and how to touch her, and he was doing a damned fine job of it.

She matched his thrusts as the choreography of their dance raced to a climax. Gripping him with both her arms and legs, she writhed against him, bringing exquisite pressure to her core. *Yes!* A tsunami of an orgasm grabbed her and rode her like a demon, turning her inside out and making her groan softly to keep from screaming.

When she could catch her breath, she opened her eyes to find Beau grinning at her.

"Ready to go again?"

"Beast!"

"Hey, I'm the man who loves you. I'm the man who just rocked your world." He kissed her damp temple. "And I'm willing to do it again," he whispered close to her ear.

Chapter 6

THE NEXT MORNING, DIXIE OPENED HER EYES CAUTIOUSLY. She was cradled in Beau's arms, her head cushioned on his big, cushy bicep. She tried to feel regret over her actions of the previous evening but couldn't. She had been aching to be in Beau's arms since she had first laid eyes on him again. Yes, she hated him, but she loved him as well.

Now what? Now, I get up. It would not do for Ava to wake up and discover a naked man in the guest room… or her mother snuggled in his arms.

Dixie gazed at Beau's face. He looked so relaxed. A smile curved his lips. He appeared to be happier than she had seen him since her return. She sighed and tried to slip out of his arms, but they tightened around her.

"Whoa! Where do you think you're going?"

"I need to get up."

"Do you? It's not fair for you to take advantage of me and then just toss me aside."

She snorted. "Oh, is that the way it happened?"

He nuzzled her neck. "I just came over to talk, and you jumped on me. I had no choice other than to try to satisfy your voracious sexual appetite."

She laughed in spite of her resolve, resting her head against his shoulder. "Yeah, you stick with that story, cowboy."

Beau rolled her onto her back and kissed her. Kissed her so well she forgot about climbing out of bed. Forgot about everything except the lips kissing her and the hands caressing her.

"Mommy?"

They jerked apart, turning to stare at the wide-eyed little girl standing in the doorway.

Dixie cleared her throat and gathered the sheets around her. "Yes, darling. Mommy will be up to make your breakfast in a minute. I'm sure you're hungry."

Beau pulled the sheets to cover himself. "Good morning, Ava."

She grinned at him, drawing closer to the bed.

"Ava, honey…could you go on and get your clothes on? I'll have your breakfast made by the time you get done."

Beau winked at her. "I'll race you. Bet I get dressed before you do."

Ava let out a shriek of laughter and tore out of the room.

Beau threw back the covers and pulled on the Wranglers he had tossed beside the bed. "Go get dressed. I'll handle this." He fastened his belt but left off his shirt and boots. Barefoot, he headed for the kitchen.

Dixie closed the door behind him and gathered her clothes. In no time she had her nightshirt on, but it wasn't enough. She paced around the guest room. Ava was in her bedroom, with all the clothing she had packed for the two of them. And here she was in her nightshirt with no panties.

She heard the sound of Ava's footsteps zooming down the hall. At first Dixie thought her daughter was headed for the guest room, but she passed it by and ran to the kitchen.

Dixie expelled a sigh of relief. Thankful for the

reprieve, she slipped from the room and tiptoed to her own bedroom. Once inside, she pulled off the nightshirt and scrambled for clothes. She mounted a chaotic search to locate her underwear and found a not-too-wrinkled shirt. Finally, she slipped into her jeans and sandals. Yeah, this would work. Her hair was a mess, so she ran a brush through it and found a scrunchie to twist it up. Glimpsing herself in the mirror, she drew to a stop. Her skin glowed. Her eyes were alert. She looked happy.

Really happy.

She hadn't felt this way in a long time. Pressing her lips together, she closed her eyes. *Don't let me down, Beau. Not again.*

—⁓—

Beau had found a skillet and was laying strips of bacon in it when a little red-haired bundle of energy came zipping into the kitchen. "Well, look who's here."

"You beat me," she said.

"I wanted to hurry and fix your breakfast." He gestured to the table. "Why don't you sit down and talk to me while I work?"

She nodded and followed his direction. Once she had arranged herself, she sat grinning at him.

"Tell me what you like to do, Ava."

"I like to color and cut and glue." She giggled. "And glitter. I like to glitter."

"I see." *Boy, do I have a lot to learn about little girls.* "What else? Do you have any pets? A dog or a cat?"

She shook her head, setting the fiery curls into motion. "Nuh-uh. Gramma won't let us have any." For a second her lower lip jutted out, and then she sighed. "Do you gots a dog?"

"Yes, we have several dogs at the ranch…and cats too."

"I wish I had a dog and a cat." Ava rested her cheeks on her fists. Again the slightly pouty look.

"And we have horses. Lots of horses and cattle—you know, cows."

"Cows?" Ava's big blue eyes followed him around the kitchen.

"What are you doing?"

Beau turned to find Dixie, fully dressed, standing in the doorway. "Um, making breakfast." He pointed to Ava with the spatula. "Our daughter is hungry."

Dixie's brows lifted ever so slightly, but she didn't say anything.

"You're running a little light on groceries. No eggs. But there is old-fashioned oatmeal in the cupboard, so I've got some on the stove. And we have bacon and toast. Hope that will satisfy your…appetite." He winked at her.

She shook her head but smiled. "That will do." She went to the cupboard and took out glasses. "We have orange juice and milk."

"I gave Ava the last of the milk, so we'll put that on our shopping list."

"Mmm," she murmured.

He figured she was feeling a little pressured. Maybe he should back off. But this was everything he had ever wanted right in this room. He couldn't let these two slip through his fingers.

Dixie poured the juice into two glasses and set them on the table. When she turned around, she looked wary.

He concentrated on arranging the bacon and toast on a platter and scooping the oatmeal into bowls.

When he placed the food on the table, he saw that Dixie had brought brown sugar and butter. Her voice was soft and husky when she spoke. "Thanks for doing this, Beau."

He leaned down to brush a kiss against her temple. "My pleasure." He took a seat and reached for the brown sugar, adding a couple of spoonfuls to his oatmeal.

"I want some," Ava said, pushing her bowl toward him.

"Uh, didn't you forget something, young lady?" Dixie asked.

Ava heaved a sigh. "May I please have some?"

"Sure," he said but glanced at Dixie to make sure it was okay. *Yeah, I can get the hang of this parenting thing.* "What do you ladies have planned for today?"

"I have to go check out the feed store. I know nothing about running it, but I guess the clerk can tell me what's going on."

"Pete. His name is Pete," Beau said. "He's been working with your dad for a long time, so I'm sure he can teach you the ropes in no time at all. And there's a part-time guy who works there too. His name is Josh. He's younger, and he handles some of the heavy lifting."

She shrugged. "If you say so."

"Would you like me to go with you?"

"No…yes…I don't know." A muscle near her eye twitched. "I wish I didn't have to go, but my dad's will…you know?" She reached for a slice of bacon and bit into it fiercely.

"I know." He stroked her arm. "Everything's going

to be all right, Dixie. Once you get to know your way around, it will be easy."

She heaved a sigh. "I sure do hope so. This is going to be a long year."

Beau felt as if the wind had been knocked out of him. *A year?* It sank in on him that she was dead set on getting back to Dallas. *No matter what.* So he had a year to change her mind.

~~~

Dixie was in a daze. Somehow, with no particular plan in place, she had wound up with Beau Garrett back in her life. She still couldn't imagine how he had remained ignorant of the fact that he had fathered a child, but the truth was he seemed to be thrilled with the situation.

He couldn't take his eyes off Ava, although he did appear to be treading carefully. Now they were playing like June and Ward Cleaver at home—only this wasn't really her home.

She finished the oatmeal and reached for another slice of bacon. Silently chewing, she observed the interaction between Ava and Beau. She knew her daughter really hadn't comprehended that this tall, handsome man was her father. Ava didn't even know what a father was supposed to be.

Dixie heaved a deep sigh. Whatever was happening between them was a direct result of Beau's barging in on her last night. When she had opened the door, it was as though her hormones had exploded. He wore his "take no prisoners" expression, and that alone set her soul on fire. Her protests were forgotten, as she gave in to the flame that had been burning low in her belly since she had first laid eyes on him again.

No regrets. Sex had always been good, but this was phenomenal. Now she was faced with the aftermath. The man who woke up beside her had now fixed breakfast for her and her daughter. He seemed to have taken his place as a part of the family, and she wasn't sure how she felt about it.

"If you ladies want to get ready, I'll load the dishwasher, and we can go to town."

Dixie nodded, motioning for Ava to finish. "We might as well get this over."

She pawed through her meager wardrobe and chose a jacket, thinking it made her look more professional. As she pulled it on and made sure Ava was dressed appropriately, she came to the conclusion that she was glad Beau was going with her. Glad he would be beside her when she assumed the role of owner at the feed store. Just glad…

She gave her hair a final fluff. Maybe she had taken a little extra care with her makeup, and maybe she wore her most flattering skinny jeans. Maybe she wanted Beau to react…although his reaction was pretty strong last night when she wore a shapeless sleep tee and her clean, shiny face. A giggle escaped her throat, disregarding her efforts to stifle it.

Somehow, in spite of the events of the past few years, she was thrilled that Beau was still in love with her.

Dixie wanted to take her SUV into town, but instead Beau loaded Ava's safety seat into the backseat of his truck, and in no time they were on their way to Langston. The familiar countryside whizzed by in a blur. Beau made light conversation, mostly with Ava.

Dixie was aware she wore a smile, and she felt lighter inside than she had in some time. Maybe things would work out between them. No, that wasn't what she wanted. Her plan was to get through this year and get the hell back to Dallas. She was a city girl now.

She wanted her daughter to have the privileges of growing up in a city with art galleries and theaters. Well, at least that was what her mother wanted for Ava, and somehow Dixie had found herself going along with it.

Beau drove through Langston to the opposite edge of town where Moore's Feed and Seed was located. He pulled to a stop right in front and climbed out. Before she could get out, he had opened the door and offered his hand.

"Thanks." She stepped down way too close. Gazing up into his incredible blue eyes, she could almost feel the heat radiating off his body, or maybe it was hers.

He grinned and tipped her chin up, brushing a quick kiss over her lips before opening the back door to retrieve his daughter.

Dixie turned away, hiding a smile. *Good kiss*. Then her gaze connected to the two men staring at her from the open doorway of the feed store. A rush of heat rose from her chest to paint her cheeks. *Not a good first impression on the men who are supposed to be my employees*.

Beau lifted Ava out of the truck and kept her in his arms as he strode into the store. "Hey Pete…Josh. I brought Ms. Moore in so you could show her the ropes."

Josh, the younger man, openly stared at Dixie,

checking her out from head to toe and letting his eyes linger on her figure.

The older man, Pete, gave her a lopsided grin. "Howdy, Miz Moore. Sorry 'bout your daddy."

"Thanks." Dixie swallowed hard. She remembered all the time she had spent in this building as a child. Pete had been here then, but not the other guy.

"Dixie needs to learn the business, Pete. Why don't you show her the layout, and then we can get into the way you run this place?"

Josh gave a little wave. "I'll just be getting back to work."

Dixie nodded and turned back to Pete.

"Um, sure." Pete motioned to her and gave her a quick tour of the building, starting with the smaller sacks of grain and seed, garden implements, flower and vegetable seeds, and a selection of fruit and shade trees lined up outside the front door. "Come November, we'll bring in some pine and fir trees to sell to folks around here for Christmas trees."

"I remember the Christmas trees," she said. A rush of nostalgia crowded her chest. She recalled her father letting her pick out the best tree to take home. She also recalled that her mother had found fault with every one of them.

"And in this other room we have a selection of chickens, baby chicks, and supplies." He led the way, pointing out different breeds and commenting on their characteristics as though she should know about them. "These are Wyandotte, and these are Orpingtons," he said proudly. "We carry different exotic breeds from time to time."

"Um, they're very nice." The smell was not pleasant. "Who cleans up after them?"

Pete beamed proudly. "Me an' Josh do it all around here."

"Mommy," Ava shrieked. "Look at the bunnies."

When Dixie found her, Ava was on her knees in front of a cage of various breeds of baby rabbits, a gleeful expression on her face. "Oh, Mommy, can I have a bunny? Please?"

"Of course not. You know Gran won't allow any pets. I know she won't stand for any animals in the condo." She glanced around to find Beau frowning at her. He stood with his feet apart and his arms crossed over his chest. A muscle by his mouth twitched.

Oh, brother. She realized the mention of her home in Dallas had been like a slap in the face to Beau. Well, it was out there. He had to realize she would be going home eventually.

Ava looked stricken, her lower lip trembling. "Gramma's so mean. She never lets me have anything I want."

"Honey, I—"

"Can't I just have one bunny? Gramma won't know." Ava's voice turned whiny.

"We'll see. Right now I have to find out about this business. Just play with the bunnies while I work."

Ava was clearly put out, but she did as directed and patted the small animals through openings in the cage.

"Is this all?" Dixie asked.

"Well, there's the shed," Pete offered. "I better get Josh to show you around back there. He's the one who's in charge out back."

"What's back there?"

Pete shoved his hands in his pockets and scuffed his

toe on the cement floor. "Um, we just call it 'the shed.' It's where we store the big things. Mostly different kinds of seed for the ranchers to plant. We have to make sure it's fresh and available each season."

Dixie nodded, pretending to make sense of what he was saying.

Encouraged, he brightened up. "And we have big bags of feed for different kinds of animals. Hay, of course."

"Of course."

Pete used an overhead speaker to call for Josh to come "up front" while Dixie turned to Ava, who was squatting next to the rabbit cage with Beau close beside her.

Beau met her gaze. "Don't worry. I'll stay here with Ava while Josh is showing you around."

She felt a rush of gratitude. The sight of his dark head so close to their daughter's fiery-bright one made her breath catch.

Josh came into the building through a wide sliding metal door. He looked big and brawny, as though used to lifting heavy things. He touched his forehead with two fingers in a kind of salute. "Miz Dixie." His sweat-stained shirt was open down the front, showing off his muscled torso and six-pack. The sleeves had been torn off so his biceps were on display as well. His expression hinted at humor as he visually cruised her body.

She struggled to maintain eye contact, faltering under Josh's admiring, somewhat insolent stare. "Josh."

Pete frowned at him. "Josh, straighten up and button your shirt. I want you to give Miz Dixie a tour of the shed."

He appeared to be surprised. "There's nothin' to see back there. Just feed and seed, like the sign says." He gestured to the name of the store, painted in large letters on the back wall.

Pete planted his fists on his hips. "Just take her on a tour of her property, you numbskull. This is her place, and she wants to look around."

Josh made a low growl but motioned for her to follow him. He stomped out the same door through which he had entered and down a set of steps to reach the driveway. His boots crunched through the gravel to a larger building out back. "There's the loading dock," he said.

"Why is it so high?" She hurried to keep up with him as he took the concrete steps two at a time.

He let out a rude snort. "It's the same height as the beds of the big semis that make the deliveries." He held up a hand to halt her progress. "You better stop right here. You can see everything without anything falling on you or getting your pretty little self dirty." He eyed her again, this time focusing on her cleavage.

She stepped far enough away to avoid smelling his sweaty stench. "So, what am I looking at?" She was staring at colorful bags stacked high. There was a second floor with what looked like a conveyor belt.

Josh raised a beefy paw, waving it toward the inside wall. "That there's cattle feed. All different kinds, and there's feed for other kinds of animals too." He turned to the other wall, gesturing in that direction as well. "An' all that is seed. We got cotton. We got corn. We got grain sorghum, and we got winter rye. We got about any seed the ranchers around here might want to plant."

"Mmm." She made a noncommittal noise, as he seemed to require some kind of response. "What's up there?" She gazed at the second story.

"Mostly hay. I got a conveyor belt to get the bales down so the ranchers can just pull up outside and I can load 'em right up." He seemed quite proud of the fact.

She swallowed hard, her gag reflex working over-time. "Great job, Josh. Thanks for the tour." She turned toward the exit and got out as quickly as she could, holding her breath until she had cleared the building. It didn't smell much better outside, as the air was musty. She headed down the steps and across the gravel parking lot. When she had returned to the feed store, she looked around for Beau and Ava. She found them each holding a baby rabbit, their heads close together.

Ava spotted her and squealed. "Mommy! Look at my bunnies."

Beau glanced up at her, a sheepish grin on his face. "I couldn't resist."

"What? I told you we couldn't get a bunny."

"But Mommy...Beau said he would take care of them for me." She held one up for inspection. "This is Bertram, and that one is Anastasia. Beau helped me name them. They're so soft and cuddly. I love them."

Dixie drew in a breath and let it out slowly. No point in blowing her top in front of her employee.

Beau shrugged. "She was crying. I couldn't take it. Don't worry about taking the rabbits to Dallas. I'll take good care of them when you go to visit your mother." He gave her a pointed look. "I know we both want to make our daughter happy. Does this work for you?"

She swallowed hard, resisting the urge to smack him one. "Why, yes, Beau. That works for us, and you'll have a nice herd of rabbits to add to the Garrett ranch stock." She allowed a smug smile.

He gave a hoot of laughter. "Fair enough." He gave Ava's curls a tweak. "I'll build a nice hutch for Bertram and Anastasia in the backyard."

She stood up and threw her arms around Beau's neck. He looked startled at first but then folded his big arms around her, and Dixie thought he was blinking back tears.

At least he cares for our daughter…and me. He cares for me.

"Let's get ready to go home. Is there a box or something to take the rabbits in?"

"Why, yes'm. We stock these pet carriers so customers can take their new pets home safely." Pete stopped and scratched his head. "Of course. Since you're the owner, you can take any one you want."

She nodded. "I want."

Beau lifted Ava onto the countertop so she could supervise the loading of bunnies into their crate. A bag of premium rabbit food was hefted onto the counter with directions for providing the best care for Ava's new pets.

Dixie told Pete that she had absorbed as much as she was capable of for one day and would return the next day to examine the books.

He appeared to be relieved. "That's good. I'm not sure I understand the books myself." He swiped his hand over his sparse hair. "Your daddy, he had his own way o' doin' things."

Beau loaded them in his truck again and this time made a stop at the local grocery. "We need to restock the pantry."

They left the truck windows open for the rabbits and went inside, holding hands with Ava.

Dixie acknowledged that this felt good. She didn't

want to think about how comfortable the entire situation had become. *Or why…*

Dixie dropped Ava's hand and selected a grocery cart, rolling it out into the aisle. She was suddenly aware of other customers staring at them. She felt her cheeks burning but kept her gaze averted.

"We need milk," Beau said, seemingly oblivious to the stares. "And we better get a couple of cartons of eggs."

She sucked in a breath, nodding. "I—I should have made a list."

"We can wing it. Let's just go up and down the aisles and pick up what we want to eat."

Dixie felt a constriction around her chest. Beau obviously was planning on eating a lot more meals at the Moore ranch. "Yeah."

They went down each aisle, and between Beau and Ava, the cart was soon filled with food.

"Do you like rutabagas?" Beau asked Ava with a straight face.

She giggled and insisted that she didn't.

"But have you ever met a rutabaga?"

She shook her head vehemently.

"No rutabagas," Dixie insisted. "Now, listen here, Beau Garrett. We have more food than we can eat in a month."

Beau looked over the haul. "This wouldn't last more than three days in the Garrett kitchen."

Dixie rolled her eyes and pushed the cart to line up at the single checkout counter.

An elderly woman in line turned, a smile spreading across her face. "Why, hello, Beau." She looked at the young girl in his arms. "And who is this lovely young lady?"

Without missing a beat, he responded. "Good to see you, Mrs. Conway. This is my daughter, Ava."

The lady oohed and aahed over Ava and then turned to Dixie. "And this is your…?"

"My friend, Dixie." He slipped an arm around her shoulders.

The woman peered at her. "I remember you. Dixie Moore."

A flush of heat roiled up from her chest. "Um—"

"Mrs. Conway was our third-grade teacher, Dixie. You remember her."

"Um—yes. Of course. Good to see you again, Mrs. Conway."

When the cart full of groceries had been scanned, Beau swiped a card before Dixie could get hers out of her purse.

By the time they were able to get out of the grocery store, they had been intercepted by several other people, and Beau dealt with them the same way: proudly introducing Ava as his daughter and reacquainting Dixie with her neighbors.

She was still in a state of shock, having intended to remain a hermit until such time as she could return to Dallas. Of course, she would have had to shop for food, but without Beau Garrett as an escort, she might have been unnoticed.

Dixie was unusually silent on the drive back to the Moore ranch.

Beau noticed that she pressed her lips together several times and stared out the window at the passing countryside.

Ava, however, kept up a lively conversation, mainly about her new pets. "I love my bunnies. Bertram has more brown on him, and Anastasia has more white. Do you think they love each other?"

"I'm pretty sure they're good friends," he said, glancing in the rearview mirror at her blissful expression.

He stole a quick peek at Dixie again, but she was deep in thought. He hoped she wasn't planning on telling him to stay away. They had been dancing around the subject of her intention to return to Dallas. Beau couldn't imagine that she would ever leave him...not after last night, but she had been apart from him for years and had undoubtedly had relationships in the intcrim.

His chest tightened, but he reasoned that a woman as beautiful as Dixie would not be likely to sit on the shelf for long. He didn't like to think that any other man had ever held her, let alone made love to her, but she had a big burly boyfriend in Dallas, and surely they had an active sex life.

Beau slowed down to turn onto the road leading to the Moore ranch. *I can't let that happen. No matter what, I can't let Dixie go back to Dallas...not with my daughter.*

When he pulled up in front of the Moore ranch house, he put the truck in park and turned off the motor.

Ava had fallen asleep, slouched against the bunny crate.

"Home sweet home," he said softly as he released his seat belt.

Dixie heaved a huge sigh. "Beau, I—"

He steeled himself, prepared to handle whatever she had to say.

"Beau, I just want to thank you for taking care of the

stock. Mr. Ryan told me that you and your family had been coming over to feed the horses and cattle. I could never do this by myself." She stopped, drew in a deep breath, and let it out slowly. "I mean—it's hard for me to say thank you when I'm so confused."

He reached for her hand and kissed her palm. "Dixie, you know I love you. I would do anything for you... and for Ava." He gestured to the contents of the truck interior. "This is everything I've ever wanted."

She blinked and looked away. "I want to believe you, Beau, but I—"

"Shh...don't worry about it. I'm here with you now, and what we have is amazing."

"But what about everything that's happened? It's not like we can go back and just erase everything that came between us. There's a lot of hurt there."

Beau leaned closer to her, sliding his arm around her shoulders. "No, we can't go back, but we can go forward. Dixie, this is our life, and we need to stick together for the sake of our child if nothing else. Ava deserves a family."

"This is just happening too fast." She closed her eyes and pressed her fingertips against her temples.

"We have all the time in the world." He kissed her cheek. "Just hang in with me. We can work things out, I promise."

She nodded. "I'll try." She turned to face him. "I just wanted you to know how much I appreciate everything you're doing for me...and I want to thank your father and brothers too."

"Speaking of which, would you feel comfortable if my family could spend a little time with Ava?"

"Oh." Her brow furrowed.

"My dad is so thrilled to be a grandfather. It would mean a lot to me if you would allow him to get to know her."

"He hates me."

"No, baby. He doesn't hate you. He's my dad. When he and my brothers realized how much it hurt me when you left…well, maybe they were just a little protective."

Her expression registered pain and confusion. "Let's get Ava inside."

"Sure." He knew enough to back away. He had pushed, and now she was shutting down. "I'll carry her inside and come back for the groceries and rabbits."

Dixie nodded and went ahead to open the door.

Beau released Ava from her seat belt and gathered her in his arms. He slipped through the door Dixie held open and gently laid the sleeping child on the sofa. He felt a tug at his heart as he watched her roll onto her side, her curls falling over her brow and her lashes dark against her pink cheeks. He was still in awe that he could have contributed to the genetic makeup of such a beautiful creature. Now all he had to do was make sure he could remain in her life.

"A little help here," Dixie called from the entryway.

Giving one last glance at Ava, he rushed to take the rabbit cage from Dixie and set it down in the hallway. "I'll carry in the groceries."

"I'm not helpless, Beau. You know that I've carried groceries into the house for years without your help." She gazed up at him mischievously. The dimples flickered in her cheeks.

He smiled, hoping her good nature had been restored.

"Well, now you don't ever have to carry groceries by yourself."

"Well, I guess you can help me." The dimples flashed again as she whirled around, heading for the front door.

Beau followed, grabbing her in his arms and turning around once they had cleared the house. "Dixie, honey…I'm just so happy to be back with you. It's like my life has had a hole in it and you just healed me. You know how much I love you, don't you?"

She struggled to get out of his arms. "Honestly, Beau. I'm trying to just take it day by day. I don't know if we're back together…but we're—"

"I'll take it day by day."

Chapter 7

THE NEXT MORNING, BEAU GRABBED DIXIE AND DELIVERED a soul-searing kiss before she climbed into her car and headed back to Moore's Feed and Seed. She hoped that, without Beau and Ava as distractions, she might be able to concentrate on understanding the books as explained by Pete.

Beau told her he planned to spend the day entertaining Ava and building a rabbit hutch.

Damn! That man knows how to make my toes curl. She shook her head, but a huff of laughter escaped her throat.

After a remarkably cozy dinner the previous evening, Beau and Dixie had kissed their daughter good night and put her to bed. Then an uncomfortable few moments while they considered their situation, but that didn't last long. One tentative kiss led to another, more confident this time. A trail of clothing littered the hallway as they stumbled over each other on their way to the guest bedroom.

Dixie giggled. Oh, yeah. Last night, Beau demonstrated many possible ways to pleasure a woman...well, he was on his way when she gave up and demanded satisfaction. "Now!" she'd whispered.

She reached the intersection with the highway and turned toward Langston. In time, she arrived in front of Moore's Feed and Seed. Heaving a sigh, she climbed out, straightening her shoulders before entering the store.

Pete rushed forward to greet her, appearing a little anxious. "Miss Moore, I...uh...I'm—" He broke off awkwardly and then cleared his throat. "I mean, welcome to the store—your store."

"Thanks. I'm not a bookkeeper, Pete, so you're going to have to explain things to me." She gave him a smile to reassure him. "I mean, really break it down for me."

He nodded several times, his head bobbing up and down rhythmically, but remained staring at her without moving.

She flashed him a grin meant to encourage. "Okay, let's get this party started."

Pete bobbed a few more times and led her to a small office in the back of the building. He punched a button on the phone and asked Josh to come to the front office.

In a few minutes, Josh presented himself. He looked reasonably well kept, but his shirt was once again unbuttoned and the sleeves torn off, showing off an impressive array of muscles.

Pete gestured for him to button up his shirt, and he complied, huffing out a groan and rolling his eyes.

Totally immature. Dixie supposed Josh was competent in his usual duties, but he was definitely a smart ass. She frowned as he openly ogled her.

"Josh, you need to stay up front and let me know when customers come in. I'll be here with Miss Moore for a while."

Josh smirked and gave her a wink. "Sure thing, cuz." He turned and strolled to the front of the store.

"Well, he certainly has an attitude," Dixie said.

"Aw, he's a good kid," Pete protested. "He's just had a hard life."

Dixie snorted. "He's not a kid. He's older than I am, and he needs to get it together if he's going to work here."

Pete blinked a couple of times. "I guess I can tell him to straighten up."

"Show me the books, please. I'm ready to learn how my dad's business has been doing."

Beau had wanted to take Ava to the Garrett ranch but hadn't wanted to risk ticking Dixie off since their relationship, at this point, was so tentative.

So he did the next best thing. He invited Big Jim to the Moore ranch. Of course, being Big Jim, he arrived with a big bang.

Beau heard his father's powerful truck roar up the drive and come to a stop with a couple of toots of the horn. By the time Beau and Ava got to the front door, Big Jim was out of the truck.

"Whooee! I'm ready to build a hutch for those bunnies." He strode up to the house and squatted down to grin at Ava. "And how are you today, little lady?"

She leaned against Beau and ducked her head.

"Take it down a notch, Dad." Beau stroked his hand over her mop of curls. "Let's get acquainted."

"Sure, Son. I didn't mean to come on too strong." Looking a bit disappointed, he stood up. "So, I brought some lumber and tools."

Beau gave Big Jim a pat on the shoulder. "Thanks a lot, Dad." To his daughter, he grinned. "Ava, I want you to meet my daddy. You can call him—" He turned back to Big Jim.

"Grampa!" Big Jim's grin went wall to wall.

"Um, yeah. Ava, this is your grandfather...Grampa."

Ava stared up at her grampa, her eyes wide.

Big Jim squatted again. "Nice to meet you, Ava. Would you like to help me build a home for your bunnies?"

"Yes, Grampa." Her curls bounced as she nodded enthusiastically. "My mommy says my bunnies need to have their own home." She leaned a little closer and lowered her voice. "She doesn't think they should live inside this house."

Big Jim nodded, his expression serious. "I understand. My dear departed wife felt the same way about my horses." He then invited her to help unload the back of his truck.

Beau watched his father become an oversized playmate to a five-year-old. He opened the door as Big Jim and Ava carried lumber and other supplies through the house to the fenced backyard. Beau's chest felt tight. He wished he could have been there when Ava was born. He wished he could have heard her first word and seen her take her first step. Now, he was determined that he and his family would always be a part of her life. After all, Ava Moore was a Garrett.

—⁓—

When Dixie pulled into the driveway, she sucked in a breath. There were two big silver double-dually extra-cab pickup trucks in front of the house.

She sat for a few moments, immobilized by fear, her heart beating out a little pitty-pat. "Wait a minute. This is my house. I'm not afraid to go in there." She pulled the key out of the ignition. "I don't care how many Garretts are in there."

She climbed out and slammed the door, doubly irritated when she found the front door ajar. She stormed inside, prepared to face down the whole pack of Garretts, but found the house eerily silent. Room by room, she searched for Beau and, more important, her daughter, but the house appeared to be empty. A tingling sensation coiled around her spine. *Okay, this is weird.*

Suddenly the sound of laughter erupted from the backyard. She wondered if the damned Garretts were having a party on her back porch.

Dixie opened the sliding door and stepped out onto the screened-in back porch. "Oh!"

Beau and his father had built some kind of structure with a pen around it. They were laughing with Ava, who seemed to be carrying on a lively conversation. The expression on her daughter's face allayed all of Dixie's fears.

Beau saw her, and a wide grin spread across his face. "Dixie! Come on out and see your brand-new rabbit hutch."

Ava whirled around. "Mommy! I made a bunny house. Beau and Grampa helped me." She ran to Dixie's arms as soon as she stepped off the porch. "See!"

"Grampa?" But Ava was dragging her by the hand to admire the hutch.

"What do you think?" Beau asked. "Do you think Bertram and Anastasia can be happy in their new home?"

"Um, yes. I'm sure they will be. It's—"

"Isn't it pretty, Mommy?" Ava gazed up at her expectantly.

Beau and Big Jim were gazing at her too. They all looked extremely proud.

"Well, yes," she said. "It's a palace fit for a prince and princess."

Ava clapped her hands and danced around, her gleeful expression causing Dixie's throat to constrict. Beau and his father had made her daughter happy. She choked back the taste of tears. "Thank you so much, Beau... Big Jim."

"No need for thanks, Dixie. You'll find there's nothin' I wouldn't do for my granddaughter—your little girl. Or for you." Big Jim held out his hand, and she reached for it without thinking. His grasp was warm and callused. "Aw, c'mon, Dixie. We can do better than that." He leaned closer and clasped her in a warm embrace.

Dixie stiffened and then took a deep breath and released it. She wrapped her arms around Big Jim's torso, returning the embrace.

When he released her, she saw Beau and Ava grinning at them.

"We have an important decision to make," Beau said. "We have to choose the perfect color for the bunny palace. Any thoughts?"

Dixie smiled. "Color?"

"Yeah, I was thinking purple, but Ava wants blue. And Dad was thinking bright pink."

Big Jim let out a loud guffaw.

"Uh, I'm not sure... How about something earth-toned? You know, brown...or beige?"

Ava made a face, and Beau turned his thumb down.

She shook her head and laughed. "Okay, then. Blue it is."

The look on Beau's face caused a flutter in her chest.

It was as though she had crossed over some bridge into another dimension.

"I think we've done enough work for one day," he said. "How about if I fire up the grill and throw on some steaks? Anybody else hungry?"

"Oh, yeah," Big Jim said. "Let's get that fire goin'."

"Steaks? I don't believe I have any steaks on hand." Dixie tried to recall what was in the refrigerator and freezer. *Certainly not steaks*.

"Gotcha covered, babe. Dad sprung for dinner."

Big Jim shrugged. "I thought we should break bread as a family." He arched a brow and gazed at Dixie. "That's okay, I hope."

The word *family* hit her like a punch in the gut. "Mmm, yes. It's fine." *Am I being assimilated as a Garrett?*

Beau left the fire-building to Big Jim and Ava and followed Dixie into the house.

She kept her eyes averted and her lips pressed together. *Oh, brother. I'm in it now. Too soon...way too soon...*

She opened the refrigerator and stared inside at the bags of food Big Jim had hastily stowed. "Oh, my!"

"I'm sorry, Dixie. My dad was...um...overenthusiastic."

She reached for one of the bags and set it on the countertop. "Veggies. Looks like Big Jim was hungry for a salad...and corn on the cob...and potatoes." She laid out all of the vegetables.

Beau could not penetrate the defensive wall she had erected. "Hell, Dixie. If you're mad at me, it's okay to just come right out and say it. I can't take this distance between us. It's like you've locked down."

She glanced up, green eyes revealing not anger but anguish. "I—I'm just having a little trouble with all this…this—"

He took her in his arms, cradling her head against his shoulder. "Baby, I'm sorry if I went too far. I was happy to spend a day with Ava. And my dad…he's thrilled to be a grandpa."

"You don't understand. I haven't ever been a part of so much…family. It's somewhat overwhelming." She lifted her face to gaze at him. "You have your dad and two brothers…and your brothers are married with kids." Her lower lip trembled. "I guess I've always been a loner."

"Loner? Are you kidding me? You were always Little Miss Everything in school. You went out for all the activities from debate to school plays. You were a joiner."

She pulled away and shrugged. "I guess, but all those organizations were things I could leave behind. They weren't a forever thing…but family is…"

He pulled her closer, placing a kiss against her temple. "Yeah. Family is forever." He held her until he felt her rigidness ease away.

She gazed up at him. "I may not have much in the way of family, but I have friends."

"Yeah, I met your dear friend Scott." Beau shook his head. "He's a complete bozo."

She heaved a sigh and ducked her head. "Scott is not a bozo. He's my best friend."

"Dixie, I'm your best friend."

"I mean, he's my friend. Not my boyfriend."

"Friends with benefits?"

She grinned at that. "No benefits at all."

He felt as if a huge weight had been lifted from his shoulders. "So, you're not…involved with your friend?"

"No. When Scott made a run at you, he was trying to get you to stay away from me."

Beau let out a yelp and lifted her off her feet. He spun around several times before setting her down. "He did a helluva good job of that. Face it, Dixie. We were meant to be together."

Ava ran in to the kitchen and stopped, hands on hips. "Grampa says for you two to get a move on. Those steaks can't bring themselves." She mimicked Big Jim's deep voice.

"Yes, ma'am," Beau said, trying not to laugh at her stern expression. "You go tell Grampa we're on our way."

She grinned and raced back out the way she had come.

"Guess we better get on it." He removed the steaks from the butcher's paper and arranged them on a platter. "Ready?"

"You go ahead. I'll make the salad." She looked a little sad.

"I wish you could be happy that we're all together now."

"I want to be happy, but I have so many questions." She shook her head. "Things just don't add up."

"We'll figure it out. Just don't give up on us."

———※———

When Beau had gone outside, Dixie set about preparing the vegetables. She rinsed the potatoes and set them in the microwave to nuke but didn't turn it on. Then she washed salad ingredients and let them drain in a colander.

She went into the living room and sank onto the sofa, her phone in hand. She selected a name and pushed the button.

"Hello, sweet cheeks. How is life in the boondocks? Is it dreary? You must miss the company of intelligent life-forms."

She had to laugh. *Good old Roger*. "As a matter of fact, I was hoping you might be able to bring your great big brain and come for a visit. I warn you up-front, I plan to use you."

He let out a snort. "I refuse to shovel cow dung or pick cotton."

"It's not cotton season, and the cow dung just sort of sits there and fertilizes the pasture."

"In that case, count me in. What do you need?"

Dixie raked her fingers through her tousled hair. "It's the books at my father's store—my store now. I can't understand a thing. It may be me, or it may be the very sweet guy who is trying to explain them to me. He has just been doing counts and recording numbers since my dad was killed." She heaved out a sigh. "Maybe you can cut through the red tape and help me set up something simple that I can keep up with. I'm also expected to run the ranch."

"Ah, say no more. Roger to the rescue."

"You are the very best, Roger. Having a brilliant and talented CPA at my side is all the help I need."

"I think the Golden Boy planned to drive out to the wilderness tomorrow anyway, so we can come out there together. He's standing right here looking hopeful."

"Of course," she said. "Um, you might want to warn him that Beau and I are sort of back together again."

She heard Scott shout in the background, followed by several colorful curses.

"Whoa! How did that happen?" Roger asked.

"I'm not sure, but I think it's a good thing. I mean, he is Ava's father, and there seems to have been some kind of misunderstanding. I haven't figured it out yet, but things are pretty good between us."

Roger rang off, promising to drive to Langston with Scott the following day, which would be Friday. Now she would have two houseguests.

Dixie pocketed her phone, feeling immensely better. Just having her two pals around would restore some sense of normalcy. Maybe her life wouldn't be so Garrett-centered.

———

After dinner, when they had all enjoyed steak, baked potatoes, and a nice salad, Dixie was surprised when the two Garrett men began clearing the table.

"What are you guys doing?"

Beau frowned. "What do you mean? We're just cleaning up."

"Yes, but..." She stopped herself, realizing that her mother had always taken complete charge of everything having to do with meals—the cooking, the serving, and the cleanup. She had almost said it was "woman's work." Mamie Moore's claim. "I appreciate your help, gentlemen."

Big Jim nodded in her direction. "We Garretts always pitch in."

She couldn't imagine her own dad doing the same. Not that he wouldn't if asked. But Mamie guarded her kitchen fiercely. Maybe she felt empowered in the kitchen. Maybe the vast ranch and business in town were too much for her. Maybe she had staked a claim on that one room and refused to cede any of her power.

Sadly, she had not shared any of her knowledge with her only daughter. Now, Dixie was away from Mamie's gastronomic talents and responsible for providing meals for her young, growing offspring. *Maybe I should get a cookbook.*

She helped carry the leftovers to the kitchen and found containers to store the extra salad. She watched Beau and Big Jim as they went about their task of scraping and rinsing the dishes before stacking them in one side of the sink.

Big Jim said good night, spending extra time with Ava. Then he left, a wide grin on his face. The sound of his big diesel motor roaring to life heralded his departure.

"Beau, you can stay here tonight, but you'll have to leave tomorrow morning. I have guests coming early tomorrow."

He held her by the shoulders, staring deep into her eyes. "What do you mean? Who's coming?"

She exhaled. "I asked my friend Roger from Dallas to come help me."

"Help you? Dixie, you've got me. You've got the entire Garrett clan on your side. Just tell me what you want us to do."

"Um, how sweet. I appreciate your enthusiasm, but I need a specialist. I want you to go home tomorrow morning or tonight if you prefer. I need to entertain my guests over the weekend. Roger is a CPA, and he's going to help me figure out how to unsnarl the books at the feed store. My dad had a more complicated system than I know how to deal with. There are things that are taxed and other things that aren't. My head was swimming." She heaved a sigh. "Sadly, I'm pretty sure that Pete has just been jumbling things together, and I have no idea how to separate things."

"Oh." Beau appeared to be a little miffed, but he nodded. "I see. Well, just let me know what I can do to help."

She leaned up to give him a kiss on the cheek. "Thanks, Beau. I appreciate you."

He made a growling sound in the back of his throat. "Yeah, well, I'm going to appreciate you mightily just as soon as we put our daughter to bed."

Chapter 8

SATURDAY MORNING, DIXIE LAY NESTLED IN BEAU'S ARMS. She opened her eyes cautiously, not really certain she wanted this little slice of nirvana to end.

Knowing how organized and punctual Roger was, she figured that he had roused Scott out of bed at the crack of dawn, loaded him with coffee, and the two were zooming their way toward Langston.

Beau looked so peaceful. A rush of emotion filled her chest. She supposed it was an equal mix of lust and love.

She sucked in a breath. *Okay, I love him…but can I trust him?* Her mother's words kept echoing in her head. Words that made her mistrust all things Garrett.

She was pretty sure there had been a major misunderstanding. Knowing her mother, who could be hot-headed at times, she figured that there had been some kind of confrontation between Mamie and Big Jim, which she may have embellished, but what puzzled her most was Big Jim's very convincing delight in becoming a grandfather. She couldn't understand how he could refuse to acknowledge the kinship when she was a pregnant teen and do such a turnabout six years later.

"What are you thinking about, Miss Dixie?" Beau kissed her temple and snuggled her closer. "You look a little sad, but I'm willing to pitch in and exert myself to make you happy." He rolled her over on her back and began kissing his way down her body.

"No! Wait! Stop!"

He raised his head, clearly puzzled. "What?"

"I have to get up. You have to leave." She struggled to recover her composure.

"Right now? You must be kidding."

"No, really. I have to get up and get ready. I need to get the mess at the store straightened out, and I need help to do that. I'm supposed to actually take over running the store. How can I do that if I'm swimming in the financials?" She struggled to untangle herself from Beau's ardent attentions and the tangled sheets. "Please get up and leave."

He propped himself up on one elbow, gazing at her appreciatively. "If you're going to be that way about it, how about if I take Ava home with me? I would love to entertain her today while you're working."

She knew Roger and Scott would be anxious to see Ava but decided to acquiesce. "Okay. That will be great. Let me help her get dressed." She threw on a robe and made shooing motions at him. "Get a move on, cowboy."

"Yes, ma'am," he drawled.

She raced down the hall to wake Ava and get her dressed.

In a reasonably short period of time, Ava was up and dressed and delighted to be spending the day with Beau.

Dixie stood on the porch waving goodbye, having gained Beau's promise to feed their daughter a hearty breakfast at the Garrett ranch. She heaved a sigh before returning to the house for a quick shower.

———

A short time later, a shiny black Audi pulled up to the house, disgorging two males.

Dixie heard one toot of the horn and rushed to

greet them. "Hey, guys. I'm so glad you're here." She embraced both men and then gestured to the house. "Please bring your stuff inside."

Scott carried his duffel bag, along with Roger's more elegant leather bag, and a garment bag with Roger's freshly starched shirts laid over the cast on his wrist and forearm.

She directed them to the guest room she had hurriedly freshened up. Clean sheets and air freshener had worked their magic.

"Where's my girl?" Scott asked.

"Yes, where's that little heartbreaker? I've missed her so much." Roger peered at Dixie over his glasses frames.

Dixie moistened her lips, nervous under his scrutiny. "Well, Ava is spending the day with her father and grandfather at the Garrett ranch."

"Crap!" Scott shouted. "Don't tell me you let that jackass cowboy get to you?"

Roger's brows seemed to have climbed up to his hairline. "Do tell?"

"There seems to have been some misunderstanding. I haven't sorted it out yet, but Beau had no idea I was pregnant, and his father may have been in the dark as well. I'm not sure what happened. You know my mom. She gets hysterical about any little thing."

Roger rolled his eyes. "Yes, we know. Drama queen to the max."

Scott appeared to be livid. "I can't believe you just let him come over and—" He smacked himself on the forehead with his open palm. "Wait! Just what is your relationship with Cowboy Bob? Please tell me you didn't let him—?"

Dixie shrugged. "I'm afraid so. Trust me. I know he loves me, and he's crazy about Ava."

"Who wouldn't be?" Roger regarded her steadily. "But if you're truly happy, and you seem to be, then we're happy for you."

Scott made a scoffing noise and folded his arms across his chest.

Dixie heaved a sigh. "Thank you, gentlemen. Have you eaten?"

"We grabbed a bite on the drive here. I wanted to take a look at those books as quickly as possible. Come on. Time's a-wasting."

"Thanks a lot."

Dixie climbed in the Audi with Scott in the backseat, still pouting. They chatted on the way into Langston, arriving at the feed store just as Pete was sweeping the front entry. He looked surprised when she emerged from the sleek black car and even more so when the two men climbed out.

"G'mornin', Miz Dixie." Pete's brow furrowed. "I was just tidying up out here." He glanced up and down the street. "Ready for some customers."

Dixie wondered why he might be nervous but greeted him with a cheery smile. "Good morning to you too, Pete. These are my friends, Scott and Roger. Roger is a certified public accountant, and he's going to try to help me understand the bookkeeping system my dad used." She shrugged, trying to look like a brainless female and not a suspicious business owner. "I'm hoping he can set up a simpler system that will be easier for both of us to use." She brandished a bright smile.

"Oh, well. That's good. I don't understand it at all.

I've just been counting the daily receipts and writin' 'em down." He ducked his head. "Y'know…since your daddy…um—"

"Was murdered. Since he was murdered in cold blood." She heard the anger in her own voice and released a deep breath.

Roger put his hand under her elbow as though she needed help ascending the steps, but with Roger doing it, the gesture was sweet and not crippling. "Let's get to it, shall we?" he said.

She nodded and led the way to the small office.

"You two knock yourselves out," Scott said. "I'm going to look around."

"Just avoid the baby bunnies," Dixie warned. "Ava fell in love with two of them, and now, thanks to Beau and his father, we have a rabbit hutch in the backyard."

Scott flapped his hand at her. "Don't worry about that." He chuckled. "No room for rabbits at our place."

Dixie and Roger spent the next few hours sequestered in the small room. It held a desk and a chair and an old-fashioned ledger in which Vern had kept careful records up until the time of his death.

Finally, Roger closed the books and gathered all the paperwork together. "I'm done," he announced. "I'm going to take this back to your place and reconcile everything. Then I'm going to install a simple electronic book-keeping program that you'll be able to access online."

"That would be wonderful, Roger. I can't tell you how much I appreciate your help."

"My pleasure, darling." He rubbed his eyes wearily. "Right now I have a headache and I'm starving. Is there a decent place to eat in this quaint town?"

"Yes. We have three quite nice restaurants. One Mexican, a steak house, and a diner that has mostly home-style meals. Take your pick."

He rubbed his temples. "Anything. Just get me out of this little cave. I probably need some fresh air." He followed her into the store. "Could you please round up Scott and bring him out front? I'm going to wait in the car."

"Sure. Be right there." She walked Roger to the front and watched him descend to the street level before returning to search for Scott. She checked the entire store, but he was nowhere to be found. "Pete, do you know where my friend Scott went?"

Pete looked up from his task and nodded. "Yes'm, Miz Dixie. Big fellah with lots of muscles? He went out back an hour or so ago. I ain't seen him since."

Dixie nodded and exited by the back door leading to the cavernous shed and loading dock. "Scott?" No response, so she called again. "Hello? Anybody here?"

An eerie silence greeted her. She couldn't imagine where he had gone.

"C'mon out, Scott. We're hungry, and Roger has a headache." She was vacillating between anxiety and anger. Was he playing some kind of game? Or had he connected with that grungy Josh guy? Maybe he was holed up in a corner somewhere, bored out of his mind, waiting for the business tasks to be over. She was pretty sure he wouldn't be having scintillating conversations with Josh.

Cautiously, she climbed the stairs to the loading dock and peeked into the yawning maw of the so-called shed. *Total silence.*

A coil of fear spiraled around her spine. Her heart was trying to beat its way out of her rib cage. "Scott?"

Dixie sucked in a deep breath, inhaling the intermingled odors of grains, fertilizer, and an incredible amount of dust. She crossed the concrete floor as silently as she could, peering both ways as she went. No sign of Scott or, for that matter, Josh. She huffed out a sigh and planted her fists on her hips as she surveyed the space. There didn't appear to be anyone on the second floor either. Just bales of hay and lots of bags of grain stacked up to the ceiling. *What the heck am I paying Josh for, anyway?*

"Okay, guys. I'm getting pissed off. Where the hell are you?" Her voice sounded small in the immense warehouse area. She noticed a door in the far wall and made her way toward it, picking her way around various products in bags and boxes. Jerking the door open wide, she found a narrow walkway outside lining the back wall. It was a couple of feet down to the ground level, and she spied an old-model Chevy sedan parked at the far end.

She glanced in the other direction and almost lost her balance. There on the ground below her lay a crumpled body and a lot of blood.

Scott...

She wanted to scream, but it clotted in her throat, constricting her ability to breathe. Frozen in place, she struggled to remain upright as the horizon seemed to tilt. She closed her eyes, stepping back from the doorway, and took several deep breaths. When she regained her equilibrium, she spun around, retracing her steps back through the shed, down from the loading dock, and across to the store.

Lips clamped together, she reached for the old

wall-mounted phone behind the checkout counter. Remarkably, it had a rotary dial. Stunned, she stared at it, trying to remember what her fingers were supposed to do.

Nine-one-one got her to a cheery-sounding woman. "Sheriff's office. How can I help you?"

"Please—come to the feed store—the shed behind the store." She swallowed hard. "There's a dead person back there."

Pete stopped sweeping. "What?"

Dixie gave her name, and before she had hung up, she heard the sound of sirens screaming through town and winding down behind the store. She raced back outside and down the stairs to meet the somewhat-corpulent sheriff struggling to emerge from behind the wheel. Two deputies peeled from the second vehicle.

"I'm Sheriff Rollins. What's this about dead people?" the red-faced man huffed out.

Dixie gestured to the shed. "My friend... He's— behind this building. Back there..."

The sheriff and deputies ran around the shed with Dixie bringing up the rear and Pete a distant follower.

She drew up short, keeping her distance from the bloody and crumpled form.

"This man's still alive, Sheriff," one of the deputies shouted.

The sheriff called his office, asking for an ambulance and Dr. Ryan, the local doctor.

Dixie covered her mouth with both hands, afraid to look...afraid not to...

"Gosh! What a mess." Pete stood beside her, shaking his head. "What coulda happened?" He squinted, frowning. "Is that Josh a-layin' there?"

She stifled a shudder, managing to whisper a single syllable. "No."

A car came around the back corner of the building and screeched to a stop near where they stood.

Dixie recognized the blonde woman who leaped out carrying a small bag. Dr. Ryan knelt beside Scott. "Help me roll him over," she ordered the deputy. When Scott was flopped onto his back, his cast was covered with bright-red blood. Placing her stethoscope on his chest, the doctor sighed and turned to the sheriff. "How far out is that ambulance? We need it now." She rolled up the instrument and stuffed it in the bag before concentrating her efforts on Scott, inspecting his wound and using gauze pads to stanch the blood.

The sheriff squatted down on one knee nearby. "So, what's going on here, Dr. Ryan? How'd he get so cut up?"

She shook her head. "There is a gunshot wound in his chest. Right now, he's bleeding out if we don't get him to the hospital quickly."

"Gunshot?" The sheriff turned his fierce gaze on Dixie. "Did you hear gunshots, young lady?"

She shook her head. "I didn't hear a thing. We were in the little office working on the books."

Pete shifted from foot to foot, his hands gripped tight together. "I—I don't think so. I was cleaning the cages. You know…the chicks and baby rabbits?" He looked at Dixie hopefully. "I wonder where Josh got to. Maybe he heard something."

Sheriff Rollins stood up, hands on hips. "Well, where the hell is Josh? He must have heard the sirens."

"I don't exactly know. It's not his break time, and his

car is still here." Pete pointed to the old car at the far end of the building.

"Hellooo?" Roger had entered the shed and appeared in the doorway above. "Oh, my precious," he gasped before his eyes rolled up in his head and he took a header off the platform and onto the walkway below.

Now, two men were laid out on the ground, with an anxious doctor hovering over the two of them. Roger, a gash open on his forehead, lay bleeding beside Scott.

In a few minutes, another siren approached, finally ending when an ambulance pulled up behind the doctor's vehicle. Two attendants emerged with their own bags. All three healthcare professionals worked over Dixie's two friends until they were loaded into the ambulance and driven away.

The doctor started to get into her car, but Dixie stopped her.

"Please tell me about my friends. Are they going to be all right?"

The doctor shrugged. "I need to go. The man in the suit may have a concussion, and the other has lost a lot of blood." She got in the car and peeled out after the ambulance.

Dixie stood shaking as she watched the doctor's car disappear.

<center>~~~</center>

Beau was determined to give Ava a great day on the Garrett ranch. He had called ahead to be sure everyone would be expecting the little princess and be on their best behavior.

When they arrived, his sister-in-law Leah had

prepared a sumptuous breakfast, including her incredible light and fluffy biscuits.

Ava seemed to be delighted with everything, especially the fact that there were other children living at the ranch. Leah's daughter Gracie was eight, and Misty's little brother Mark was twelve. After eating, the kids took her out to show her the baby animals.

Beau, Leah, and Big Jim stood together watching the children interacting.

"I just can't believe you didn't know about this lovely little girl, Beau," Leah said. "How did you lose touch with Dixie?"

Beau shook his head. "Beats the hell out of me. One day we were together. Just two happy high school seniors, planning to go to college and then get married. That was the plan." His chest swelled with an ocean of pain. *How the hell did I lose her?*

Leah tilted her head. "So, what happened?"

He blew out a frustrated sigh. "Damned if I know. She just disappeared. Her crazy mother took off with her somewhere. It was completely nuts. They left her father and didn't look back. I never could figure out what happened…or why it happened."

Leah's brow furrowed. "I don't understand. You mean Dixie's mother just abandoned her husband and left town with her pregnant daughter? That sounds deranged."

"Tell me about it."

"That's not the half of it," Big Jim supplied. "Her mother filled her head with all kinds of nonsense about us."

Leah shook her head. "Well, I'm glad you're back together. I hope everything works out between you two."

Big Jim adjusted the brim of his Stetson, tilting it just a bit to the right. "You for damned sure better marry that girl, Son. I can't lose that little ray of sunshine." His gaze followed the bright-red crop of curls as Ava romped around with the other children.

"Doing my best, Dad."

After lunch, Beau saddled up one of the horses and took Ava for a ride around the ranch, showing her just a part of the vast property. He drew up beside a stream that ran through the property and lifted his daughter down.

"I like this horse, Beau. He's pretty." She turned to look up at him.

"It's a girl horse." He led the horse down to drink from the creek. "Listen, sweetheart. Did your mommy tell you that I'm your father?"

Ava nodded her head seriously.

It felt as though his heart swelled double its normal size. He swallowed hard. "Do you think you could call me Daddy instead of Beau?"

She stared at him, wide-eyed. "You mean like a mommy and a daddy?" she whispered.

"Just like that." He leaned down to hear her.

She threw both her arms around his neck, whimpering softly.

He stood up straight, cradling her in his arms. "Oh, honey. I didn't mean to make you cry. Please don't cry. You don't have to call me Daddy or anything if you don't want to."

She was crying full-out now, seemingly inconsolable. "Noooo," she wailed. "I want you to be my daddy. I never had a daddy before." She buried her face against his neck.

"Honey, I am your daddy. There's no way I'm ever going to let you go. We're family."

She pulled away slightly to gaze into his eyes, her cheeks wet with tears. "We are?"

"Yes. You're my little girl. You will always be my daughter. That means we're family."

"But Gramma says she's my family…just Gramma an' Mommy an' me."

A muscle in Beau's jaw tightened as he contemplated Mamie Moore. "Well, sweetheart, we'll have to let her know that all the Garretts are your family too. We all love you." He kissed her damp cheek. "Especially me."

By the time they got back to the ranch, it was late in the afternoon.

Big Jim stood on the porch, waiting impatiently. "See here, Son. You can't hog all the time with my grand-daughter. I got two storybooks down from the attic that used to be your favorites." He reached up for Ava, a wide grin in place.

Beau helped her from the saddle and then rode the horse to the stable, confident his daughter was in good hands.

His oldest brother, Colton, was in the stable before him, tending the stock. "How's it going, Little Brother?"

"Great. Ava just agreed to call me Daddy. I feel like my insides are flying." He dismounted and set about removing the mare's saddle and blanket.

"She's a sweet little girl," Colton agreed. "But the best thing is the way she's got our old man wrapped around her little finger. I swear he's mellowed a lot since you brought them together."

Beau chuckled. "Yeah. Who would have thought it?"

"So, what's going to happen if Miss Dixie decides to take off for Dallas after the year? You know it would break Dad's heart."

"Mine too. I guess I'm going to do everything I can to keep them here. Whatever it takes."

Colton's expression told him that he didn't for a minute trust that Dixie would stay.

Beau didn't bother arguing because Colton always thought he was right and Beau didn't feel like wasting his breath.

Beau rubbed down the mare and gave her a quick once-over with curry brushes. "Good girl," he said, patting her neck. He led her to her stall and gave her fresh water and grain.

The two brothers walked back to the house together.

The minute they entered, Leah called out to Beau that his phone had been making funny noises.

He patted his pockets, realizing he'd left his cell behind when he'd taken Ava for a ride. He checked it and saw several messages from Dixie. He didn't bother to read them but immediately called her. "Dixie? Are you all right?"

"Oh, Beau! I was so worried. Why didn't you answer?"

"Sorry. I took Ava for a ride around the property and down to the creek. I stripped off my shirt and changed to a tee before we left, and my phone was in my shirt pocket. Everything is fine. My dad is reading to her now."

She released a sigh that sounded like frustration.

"Is there something else going on?"

"There is. I'm at the hospital in Amarillo. There was a—a problem at the store."

"What happened? Are you okay?"

"Yes. I'm fine, but my friend Scott is in the hospital. So is Roger."

"What? How did they wind up in the hospital?"

"Oh, Beau. It was horrible. Roger was helping me in the office, and when we got ready to leave, I couldn't find Scott." She whimpered. "I went looking for him, and he was lying out back behind the shed, all bloody. Someone shot him."

Beau's gut tightened. He couldn't stand the muscle man, but still…

"I called the sheriff, and he got Dr. Ryan to come out. She said Scott was alive but had lost a lot of blood." She stopped to take a breath. "And then Roger came out and saw Scott, and he fainted. I swear he pitched off onto the walkway headfirst and gave himself a concussion. So now both my friends are here. I just don't know what to do. Roger is supposed to be okay. He got a few stitches, but they're keeping him for observation. Poor Scott is in critical condition." Her voice ended in a wail.

"Hold on, Dixie. I can drive to the hospital to be with you."

"Nooo. I'm okay. Just take good care of Ava for me. I don't want her upset. She's crazy about these men. Scott is like her big playmate, and Roger spoils her something awful."

At the mention of Scott's name, Beau's chest tightened. *Playmate, right.* He vividly recalled their encounter. "Okay, just calm down. Don't worry about Ava. I'll take good care of her."

"Please tell her I love her, but she's going to have a sleepover at your house."

"Are you sure you don't want me there with you? I

mean, everyone's here for Ava. I don't think she would miss me."

"No, stay with Ava. Just knowing she's safe with you will give me one less thing to worry about."

Beau reluctantly agreed, frowning long after she disconnected.

"What's the matter, Bro?" Colton asked.

"There's been another shooting at the feed store. That big, moosey guy who's a friend of Dixie's…apparently someone shot him, but he's not dead." Beau shook his head. "She said her other friend fell and bashed his head open… so now both her friends are in the hospital in Amarillo."

"At the feed store? That place is jinxed. Something's going on. I wouldn't want my wife to work in a place like that. Maybe you can convince your girlfriend to hire a manager for the store."

Beau made a scoffing sound. "This is Dixie we're talking about."

Colton shook his head and smacked Beau on the shoulder. "You're a better man than I am, Bro."

Beau's hackles rose, hearing Colton's opinion of Dixie, but then Colton had never experienced her sweet and loving side. He sucked in a deep breath and let it out all at once, glowering at his oldest brother.

"Sorry, Beau. I know you're touchy about the subject of Dixie."

"Because you don't know what you're talking about." Beau's chest was so tight it felt as though a steel band was binding him. "When we were in second grade, you were in middle school. I don't recall you paying much attention to any of the kids I went to school with. What do you actually know about Dixie?"

Colton's mouth tightened. "I know she hurt you...hurt you so bad I didn't think you would ever get over it."

"Well, I am over it, and you need to get over it too. Dixie's Dallas friends have been injured, and she needs my support." Beau stomped away before things escalated.

He found his dad and brought him up to speed on the events at the feed store.

Big Jim's face reflected his concern. "Another shooting at the feed store?"

"That's what Dixie said. She's at the hospital with her Dallas friends right now."

"Well, there you go. Wonder what the city fellas stirred up."

"Dunno, but I want you to take care of Ava. Dixie was worried about her."

Big Jim made a scoffing noise. "Of course I will. You know I will guard that little angel with my life."

"I know. I just want to go into Langston and find out what happened firsthand."

"Take your brother with you. See what kind of trouble the two of you can get into."

Beau kissed Ava on the forehead and told her to be good for her grandpa. By the time he walked out the door, Colton was already in his truck with the motor running.

He motioned for Beau to get in. "Thought I ought to drive, since you might get upset at what we find."

"Will you stop treating me like your little brother?" Beau climbed in and slammed the door closed.

"Take it easy, Little Bro. I'm just here to help." He put the truck in gear and headed toward town.

Beau took a deep breath and blew it out. "I know. I just want to find out what's going on at the feed store. If it's dangerous for Dixie to be there, I'm going to be on her like her own shadow, and she's not going to like it."

Colton shook his head. "Lucky you."

"Knock it off, Colt. You know how I feel about Dixie."

"Sorry, Bro. I just hope she doesn't take off on you again...especially not now that you know about Ava."

Beau's chest tightened as his brother spoke aloud his own worst fear.

When they arrived in Langston, they found the feed store was still a beehive of activity. There were two sheriff's department vehicles blocking the drive to the back of the property. Pete Miller was sitting outside the front of the store. He'd pulled a metal folding chair outside and sat staring vacantly and looking particularly dejected.

Colton parked, and the brothers walked up to where he sat.

"Hey, Pete. How are you holding up?" Beau asked.

He looked up, a dazed expression on his face. "I—I don't know what happened." He sucked in a wheezy breath. "I mean, how could that guy have gotten shot and I didn't hear a thing? I was working right inside the front here."

Beau shook his head. "I don't know, man. That's a tough one."

"An' my cousin, Josh. He's nowhere to be found."

"Where are the deputies?" Colton asked.

"Out back. They've been going over everything with a fine-tooth comb. I mean everything." He met Beau's gaze uncertainly. "They told me to stay up here away from the crime scene."

"We'll check it out," Beau said, giving him an

awkward clap on the shoulder. With Colton close on his heels, he beat a path through the store and out to the loading dock. He heard voices coming from behind the warehouse and went behind the building.

There a deputy held up his hand to stop them. "Hold it right there, Beau. You too, Colt."

"Hey, Leon. I just want to know what's going on. My—my fiancée owns the feed store. She's at the hospital with the guys who got hurt."

The deputy nodded. "I heard you and Dixie were back together. Hope it works out this time."

"Me too." Beau took a wide stance, his hands at his waist. "C'mon, Leon. Help me out here."

"I can't let you contaminate the scene. The forensic team is here from the city. They're going over everything now."

"I understand, but can you just tell me what happened?"

The deputy looked around and lowered his voice. "There was a shooting. One man got shot in the chest, and supposedly, nobody heard a thing." He looked a little irritated, fisting his hands at his waist and then dropping his right to caress his holster.

"That's what my fiancée said. It's weird that nobody heard the gun go off."

"The story is that two folks were shut up in that office in the front building and the clerk was in a room where they have ducks quacking and chickens clucking. He didn't hear a thing either."

He peered past the deputy, noting an area of ground stained dark with what was most certainly blood. In addition to the two deputies guarding the scene, there were two other individuals wearing plastic gloves who seemed to be collecting samples. An old vehicle stood at the far end of the building with all the doors open, while another tech leaned into the cavernous trunk.

Colt shook his head. "This place is jinxed for sure."

Beau hated to admit his brother was right. Now he had to worry about how to keep Dixie away from this place. He couldn't let his headstrong girlfriend endanger herself...no matter what Vern Moore's will demanded. Maybe she could hire a manager for the store. He could just imagine how that was going to go over.

Chapter 9

AFTER RETURNING TO THE RANCH, BEAU CHECKED IN ON AVA and then drove in his own truck to Amarillo. He pulled up in the hospital parking lot and called Dixie as soon as he strode through the doors.

Her voice was just above a whisper. "Beau, is everything all right with Ava?"

"She may be a little spoiled when you see her. But she's safe at home with the entire Garrett clan eating out of the palm of her hand." He heard her heave a relieved sounding sigh. "I'm here in the hospital lobby now. Where exactly are you?"

"Oh, I'm coming down. Wait there." In a few minutes, she emerged from the elevator and raced to his open arms.

"It's going to be okay, baby, I promise. I won't let anything happen to you or Ava."

Her shoulders were shaking as she wept against his chest. "I just can't believe this happened. It's all my fault."

"That can't be right. You didn't cause this." He rhythmically patted her back.

"I—I did. If I hadn't asked Roger to come help me with the books, both of my friends would still be safe at home in Dallas. Don't you see? It's all my fault." She raised her tear-stained face to gaze up at him.

"I don't think so. What happened was terrible, but you didn't cause it." In the face of her grief, he felt totally ineffectual. "I'm really sorry, baby. Why don't you let me take you back to the ranch? You look...tired."

"No, I don't think I should leave them. I mean, they have no one else." She grabbed his hand. "Come up and meet Roger. He's just the dearest man in the world...and he's so worried about Scott."

"Are they related? Brothers or something?" He gazed into her agonized face.

Amazingly, she smiled, laughter shaking her shoulders. "N—No, they are a couple."

Beau frowned. "A couple? You mean like...a couple?" She nodded.

"You mean boys who like boys?"

"I mean, Roger and Scott are a couple. They've been my very best friends for years." She leaned her forehead against his chest. "I can't bear it that Scott might die."

Beau stroked her hair. "Yeah, that would be terrible. Why don't you let me take you home for tonight and I can bring you back bright and early tomorrow morning?"

"Is...is Ava missing me?"

He chuckled, brushing a strand of hair away from her face. "I know you'd like me to tell you that our daughter is just pining away for her mama, but that wouldn't be the truth." He brushed a kiss across her lips. "Truth is right this minute, my daddy is reading to his newly discovered granddaughter. Leah has a big meal on the stove, and then Leah is going to lend her one of Gracie's nightgowns and bed her down with her own daughter."

Dixie's lips trembled. "Is she...happy?"

"Sure is. She's been playing with Gracie and Mark and all the animals. She's going to sleep like a newborn baby tonight."

"Good. I'm glad she's having a good time. Something positive to come out of this horrible day." She half turned and then whirled back to face him. "Just come upstairs with me. I want you to meet Roger. He's such a good guy."

"Sure thing." Beau seized upon the opportunity to step into the world she had kept hidden from him for so long.

Dixie grabbed his hand and pulled him to the bank of elevators. Once inside, she selected a floor, and the elevator rose a couple of levels. When the doors opened, she led him down the hallway and past the nurses' station. "Roger is stable. They're just keeping him overnight for observation since he suffered a concussion when he fell." She stopped in the middle of the hall, lowering her voice. "Scott is in the ICU downstairs. He's in critical condition, and they say he might not survive the night. I just don't know if Roger could live through losing Scott."

"What can I do to help?" Beau asked.

"Just don't mention anything about Scott. I'm trying to keep Roger's spirits up."

He followed her into the darkened room, his gaze falling on a man lying in bed, a bandage across his forehead. The overhead light was off, so the small fluorescent lamp on the bedside table gave the room an eerie quality.

"Dixie? Is that you?" The man on the bed reached out.

"Yes, I'm back. Roger, this is my friend, Beau Garrett. He's—"

The man lay back on the pillows. "The baby daddy." He pronounced it as though it was a bad thing.

Beau's spine stiffened. "That's right. I'm Ava's daddy."

Dixie poked Beau in the ribs. "Roger Parsons has

been my friend for years. He's a certified public accountant. He was helping me—"

"When someone hurt Scott." Roger sat up, his face riddled with pain. "Did you find out anything else about his condition?"

She shook her head. "No change."

Roger dropped his face in both hands, weeping openly. "Oh, Dixie. What am I going to do if I lose him? He's my whole life."

"Don't go there," Dixie said. "Let's keep positive thoughts. He's going to pull through."

Roger's shoulders shook, and Dixie handed him a tissue. "There, there. Don't even think that. Scott is tough as nails. He's going to be fine."

He patted her hand. "Thank you, dear girl. You're a ray of sunshine."

"I wanted Beau to meet you now that we're back together. He's been getting to know Ava. His whole family has been wonderful."

Roger blew out a caustic snort. "Where were they when you needed them? This fellow was markedly absent." He gestured to Beau as though he were of no consequence.

Beau considered the condition of the man hurling insults at him and bit back his response. He folded his arms across his chest, regarding him stonily.

Dixie heaved a sigh. "There seems to have been some kind of miscommunication. Beau and his family knew nothing of my pregnancy." She glanced up at Beau, placing her hand against his chest. "I don't know what happened yet, but I know that Beau would have been thrilled had he known."

Roger made a scoffing noise in the back of his throat.

"Seriously, Beau's father has been so excited since he got to meet Ava. He's taking care of her now."

"Mr. Parsons, I was deeply in love with Dixie then, and I still am. I was crushed when she just disappeared. You don't have to believe me, but I can't stand by and hear you making these accusations without speaking up. My dad would have marched me right to church to marry this girl. He's all about family."

Roger eyed him, appearing to be unconvinced.

Dixie cleared her throat. "I just wanted you to meet Beau. Scott met him before—"

"Yes, I remember when this young ruffian thrashed poor Scott. Broke his nose."

Beau started to speak, but Dixie put a restraining hand on his arm. "Come on now. You know that Scott started it. He attacked Beau without warning, and Beau just fought back. He didn't even know I was back in town then."

"So you say." Roger's mouth was pursed as though he had just sucked a lemon.

"I'll be running along now," Beau said. "Dixie, I think you should come home and get some rest. You've been going since early this morning."

"No, I want to stay here until they release Roger. I feel so bad about what happened."

He drew her toward the door. "I don't think my presence is doing anything but ticking your friend off. Let me know if you need anything." He dropped a kiss on her cheek and followed it by brushing his fingertips along her jawline.

Her eyes teared up, but she shrugged. "You just take good care of Ava."

He aimed a curt nod toward the bed and ducked out, feeling torn about leaving. He drove back to the ranch, still rankling over Roger's dismissive tone. *The baby daddy? Really?*

His mood evaporated when he entered the ranch house and was tackled by his daughter.

"Daddy," she squealed. "Wait till you see what I made."

Being called Daddy was the salve his wounded feelings needed. "What did you make? Mud pies? I seem to recall that your mother had a great recipe."

"No way." She wrinkled up her nose. "Come on, Daddy." She dragged him to the kitchen where Leah stood behind the counter, a big grin on her face.

"Yeah, Daddy. See what your lovely daughter created." She made a sweeping gesture toward a tray of cupcakes.

"I made this one specially for you." Ava searched the array of treats and selected one. She whirled around, dimples in play, brandishing a gaudily decorated cupcake.

"Oh, man! That is one beautiful cupcake."

Ava rocked back and forth rhythmically. "You like it?"

"Nooooo." He gave her a look of mock horror. "I love it. This is the prettiest thing I've ever seen…next to you, of course." He ruffled her curls, and she collapsed in a fit of giggles.

The cupcake had at least an inch of yellow frosting on top with a hefty load of multicolored sprinkles.

Leah pointed to the top. "You'll notice that Ava embellished it with a big blue *D* for *Daddy*. Isn't that special?"

"Indeed it is," Beau agreed.

"Eat it, Daddy," Ava urged.

"Um, can I save it for dessert? I want to look at it for a while." He carefully set it back on the platter. "But I have to take a picture of this so I can preserve this beautiful masterpiece." He whipped out his phone and took a quick snap.

Ava seemed delighted, giggling and jumping around.

"Big Jim was just waiting for you to get back here. He's got the fire going and the steaks marinating." Leah pointed to the deck in back of the house. "Maybe you ought to go tell him you're here."

"Good idea." He winked at Ava and strode out through the French doors and onto the deck. "Hey, Dad," he called.

Big Jim was sitting in a deck chair, nursing a beer. "'Bout damned time. Did you bring Dixie?"

Beau felt his lips tighten. "Nope. That stubborn little heifer is going to spend the night at the hospital with her Dallas boyfriends."

Big Jim sat upright. "Did you say 'boyfriends'?"

Beau huffed out a sigh. "Yeah, but don't worry. They're a gay couple." He stood with his thumbs threaded through his belt loops contemplating his own words.

Big Jim made a scoffing noise deep in his throat. "Well, don't that just beat all?"

"Dixie says they adore Ava and have been very good to her too."

Big Jim rolled his eyes. "You don't say? So these boys are both in the hospital?" He pulled himself to his feet and set his beer on a side table.

"Apparently, the one who came with Dixie when she first came back—"

"You mean that big jackass who attacked you out of the blue? That guy is gay?"

"Yep. His boyfriend is a kind of nerdy guy. Dixie said he's an accountant. He came to help her unscramble the feed store books."

"Lordy! What next?" He reached for a pair of tongs and lifted the lid of the barbecue grill. "I hope you're hungry."

"I could eat."

Big Jim grunted and uncovered a bowl of steaks that had been marinated and lovingly patted with his own special spice rub. He carefully placed each slab of meat on the grill rack and closed the lid. He eyed Beau before reaching for his beer. "So these city boys…what happened to 'em?"

"Colt and I went to the feed store, and it seems the muscle guy got shot, but nobody heard a thing. So, that guy's in pretty bad shape. The nerdy guy saw his boyfriend all bloody and took a nosedive onto a concrete walkway. Fainted dead away. His head was bandaged. They're just keeping an eye on him, but for some reason, Dixie felt like she needed to hold his hand all night."

Big Jim made a few clucking sounds with his tongue and opened the grill. "Well, ya gotta give the girl points for loyalty. That's all I gotta say about it." With that he used the tongs to rearrange the steaks on the grill and closed the lid. "How about getting me another beer out of the cooler?"

Beau selected a longneck for his father and one for himself. He flipped the caps off both and slapped one in Big Jim's outstretched hand.

After dinner, Leah gave Ava a bath and dressed her in one of Gracie's outgrown nightgowns. When Ava was ready for bed, she held her arms up to Beau, and he felt his heart melt in his chest. *So this is what being a father is all about.*

He picked her up, and she squeezed his neck with both arms.

"Will you tuck me in?"

Beau carried her to Gracie's room and tucked her in. "Good night, princess."

"Where's my mommy?" Ava's blue eyes demanded an answer.

He swallowed, searching for a way to soften the truth. "Uh, your mommy went to the hospital to keep a friend company. He—he got hurt."

"Who got hurt?"

"A man named Roger…he had an accident."

She sat up straight. "Uncle Roger? He's hurt?"

"Um, just a little. He fell down and bumped his head." At Ava's quick intake of breath, he patted her shoulder. "He's fine. The doctor is sending him home tomorrow."

Her lips trembled, and she looked like she was going to cry.

"Don't worry. Your mommy told me to take really good care of you tonight. She's going to be here tomorrow, so go to sleep, and tomorrow will be here before you know it." He smiled encouragingly.

"Will you stay with me while I go to sleep?"

Beau kissed her on the forehead and ended up rubbing her back until she was fast asleep. *Yeah, I can get the hang of this daddy thing.*

———

Roger slept soundly. A nurse had delivered his meds earlier, and now he lay on his back, snoring lightly, his mouth slightly agape.

Dixie stood and tiptoed out of the room. She wanted to call Beau but knew it was too late. Her back was hurting from sitting for so many hours. She made her way to the cafeteria but found it mostly shut down. There were coffee, tea, milk, and various soft drinks. Her food choices were limited to dry cereals, wrapped sandwiches, chips, and a few tired-looking salads. She settled for a ham-and-cheese sandwich and a bottle of chocolate milk.

The woman sitting on a stool beside the cash register barely looked up from her paperback novel to take Dixie's money.

She was the only person in the cafeteria, and she didn't feel like eating in the empty void. Tucking her sandwich and drink in her purse, she walked down the silent hallway to the elevator.

She stepped out on the second floor and followed signs to the area designated *Intensive Care Unit*. There was a little more activity here. At the nurses' station, one woman in scrubs was industriously scribbling in a chart, while another chatted on the phone. Neither paid any attention to her.

Dixie slowly made her way down the hall, noting the patient names inscribed by the doors. She swallowed hard when she found Scott's name. Her throat seemed to have closed up, and she couldn't draw a breath. *Scott…*

"Miss?" The aide who had been on the phone appeared by her side.

Dixie straightened her spine, pulling herself together. "My friend...how is he doing?"

The aide's lips tightened. "Are you family?"

"Well, no...but he's one of my best friends."

"You'll have to talk to the charge nurse, but we can't give any information out if you're not his family."

Dixie nodded, her stomach roiling. "I—I just want to see him." She stepped into the room, her gaze fastened on the inert figure on the bed. "He—he looks awful."

"I'll get the charge nurse." The aide pushed the call button, never taking her eyes off Dixie.

Scott's skin was ghastly pale. His usually robust color had faded away. He was sporting a breathing tube as well as an IV and a heart monitor.

"Is he—is he going to die?" Dixie choked out the words.

"Ma'am?" The charge nurse appeared at her side.

"Scott? Is he going to die?"

The charge nurse gave out a snort. "Not if we can help it. Are you a relative?"

"I'm a close friend. His..." She swallowed again. "His fiancé was injured too and can't be with him, so I'm just checking for his fiancé."

The nurse's face reflected compassion. "Yes, dear. Well, perhaps you can talk to his doctor when he makes rounds tomorrow morning." She made clucking noises with her tongue and then suddenly brightened. "But he's young and was in remarkably good shape before the incident, so you tell his fiancée she's a lucky girl and to just keep praying for his recovery."

Dixie stepped closer, reaching out a finger to stroke his arm. The one that wasn't hooked up to the IV. She leaned close to his ear and spoke just above a whisper. "Scott, can you hear me? I'm telling you that you've got to live. There are so many people who love you. There's me and Ava and Roger. We all need you to pull through." She placed a kiss on his cool cheek. "We're counting on you."

"Get some rest, miss. You can check on him tomorrow."

Dixie returned to Roger's room without waking him. She ate her somewhat-dry sandwich, washing it down with the chocolate milk. The image of Scott's pallid face was etched on her brain.

―――◦◦◦―――

The next morning, Dixie jerked awake when a cheery nurse's aide brought Roger's breakfast tray.

"Good morning," she chirped, setting the tray on the overbed table before helping Roger to sit up and plumping his pillows. She took the cover off his plate and asked him if he needed anything else.

Roger eyed her nervously and shook his head. When the young woman had gone, he gestured to the tray. "Do you want any of this? I don't think I can eat a bite until I find out how Scott is."

"You need to eat, Roger." Dixie stifled a yawn. "I checked on him a few hours ago, and he was hanging in there."

Roger gave her a weak smile.

"Here, let me fix your cereal. Hot oatmeal. Do you want the butter and sugar in it?"

He nodded, reminding Dixie of a petulant child.

"And you have a poached egg and some ham. That looks wonderful."

He took the eating utensils from her. "I know what you're doing. Just go find some breakfast for yourself, and I'll do the best I can with this…this…" He waved his fork.

"I'll grab something and be back in a flash." As soon as she cleared the room, her bright smile faded. She took the elevator to the ground floor and tromped to the cafeteria. The good news was that the aroma of freshly prepared food assailed her senses as soon as she pushed in the door. She ordered a couple of eggs over easy, toast, and coffee to go and paid with her debit card. Clutching the bag, she returned to the elevator and found herself pushing the button for the ICU floor. The doors opened silently. She stepped out and made her way back to Scott's room, heaving a sigh of relief when she saw that his bed was still occupied. She had feared, most of all, returning to find the bed empty.

Dixie glanced back over her shoulder, but nobody seemed to be paying any attention to her. She slipped into the room and crossed to where Scott lay. He was still hooked up to an excess of wires and tubes. He had a breathing tube, and an IV, and leads were attached to his chest. Lights blinked, and something else pinged rhythmically. A machine displayed Scott's heart rate and blood pressure.

Good boy. Just keep blinking.

She pulled the chair close and sat near Scott's side. "Good morning, sunshine," she said. "I brought my breakfast." She held up the bag as though he could see it. "I would share, but you have to open your eyes first."

Scott's chest was mostly covered with a large amount

of bandage, but at the top, amid the proper amount of carefully manicured chest hair, she saw a couple of sutures closing an ugly dark-red line.

A roiling of her gut squelched any desire for food, but she remembered her purpose and plastered on a smile as though he could see her through his closed eyelids.

She opened the bag, took out the Styrofoam carton, and popped it open. "Yummy. I wish you could see how pretty my breakfast looks. Really fresh." Her voice caught.

"What are you doing here?"

Startled, Dixie turned to see the blonde doctor leaning against the doorjamb, her arms crossed over her chest.

Dr. Ryan from Langston. "Um, I just wanted to spend some time with my friend, Scott."

The doctor crossed the room and began to examine the inert patient. "Your friend, huh?"

Dixie straightened her shoulders, feeling a little defensive. "Yes, Scott and I are friends."

The woman took Scott's chart and opened it.

"You may not remember me, but I brought Scott to you when he made the mistake of picking a fight with my—my boyfriend, Beau Garrett." Dixie said.

"Ah, yes. I remember. You're Vernon Moore's daughter. I'm Camryn Ryan." She chuckled. "Or as some people around here think of me, I'm that young lawyer Breckenridge Ryan's wife."

Dixie had to smile at that reference to the small town mentality. "Yes, I'm Dixie Moore."

"Your friend Scott is my patient." She scribbled in the chart and flipped a page to read intently. "I understand his home is in Dallas?"

"He came to help me. His—my other friend Roger is a CPA. I have an online business, so my bookkeeping system is not all that complicated. I needed some help trying to figure out my dad's bookkeeping system, and Roger is brilliant."

"Good to have friends," Dr. Ryan said absently. "Especially brilliant friends."

"Roger Parsons fell and hurt his head when he saw Scott lying there covered with blood."

Dr. Ryan glanced her way. "Another patient of mine. I expect to release Mr. Parsons this afternoon. I'll be making rounds on his floor later."

Dixie sucked in a breath and pressed her lips together, steeling herself to ask the question she feared most. "Can you tell me about Scott? Is he—is he going to be okay?"

"Your friend Scott is not out of the woods. I don't want to give you false hope."

Dixie nodded, trying to stave off the threat of tears. "I'll hope anyway."

Chapter 10

"What's wrong, Son?" Big Jim settled into a chair alongside Beau on their backyard deck.

For his part, Beau's face was drawn into a frown. "Nothing, Dad."

Big Jim snorted while simultaneously giving Beau a smack on the back of his head. "Don't lie to your daddy, boy. Your face looks like you ate something that's thinking about coming back up. I repeat, what's wrong?"

Beau released a lungful of air. He had been watching his five-year-old daughter play with his eight-year-old niece. "Just thinking."

Big Jim gestured to where the girls romped around under the trees. "That sight alone should bring a big grin to your face."

"Aw, it does. I've never been happier in my life. It's just that…" He raked his fingers through his hair. "Somebody murdered Ava's grandfather, and I don't think that Sheriff Rollins is taking it seriously."

"Of course he is. How come you think he isn't?" Big Jim leaned forward, resting his elbow on his knee.

"In light of the fact that Dixie's friend got shot in broad daylight at the same store where Vern Moore was shot, you would think he would put two and two together."

"I'm sure he's working on it."

"Don't think so. I called the sheriff's office this afternoon. Your friend Sheriff Rollins doesn't see any connection between the two crimes. They've written off Vern Moore's murder as a botched robbery, and they are suspicious of the guy from Dallas just because he's a stranger from the city—even though he has a bullet hole in his chest."

"Damnation!" Big Jim exploded. "Ed Rollins may not be the brightest bulb in the drawer, but he's a good man. He'll figure it out eventually. It's not your problem, Beau."

"Yes, it is. Anything that affects Dixie is my problem, and she's in this up to her neck."

Big Jim's bushy eyebrows rose high on his forehead. "You wouldn't know she gave a darn about her father's death. That little lady was cold as ice when she rolled into town for Vern's funeral. You wouldn't even know they were related from all the tears she shed."

Defending Dixie against his opinionated father's condemnation was not a fight he could win. Beau pulled himself out of the chair without glancing back at Big Jim. "You don't know Dixie," he murmured as he strode across the yard to join the girls in their game of chase.

"All of this belongs to the Garretts?" Roger waved his hand to include the grazing land on both sides of the private road leading up to the Garrett household.

Dixie made a scoffing noise in her throat. "This and much, much more. Big Jim owns thousands of acres of prime farmland. He has quite a herd of cattle, and he raises horses, most notably a line of beautiful black Arabian horses."

"Blah blah blah," Roger intoned. "Sounds terribly boring to me."

Dixie patted him on the arm and slowed to pull up in front of the ranch house. "You just don't appreciate the hard work it takes to put that steak on your plate. It's really a wonderful life."

Roger turned to gape at her. "Your mother should hear you talking this way. She would wash your mouth out with soap."

Dixie's mouth tightened. She wasn't sure why her mother had lied to her, but she was too angry to confront her or to share her feelings, even with a friend. "Well, let me say that I had a pretty good childhood, and…and my dad had a lot to do with that." She released her seat belt and swung out of the car before Roger could respond. She noted his surprised expression as she crossed in front of the car.

Beau threw open the front door before Dixie had made it to the porch.

"There's my girl." He met her halfway with a bear hug that lifted her off her feet. "Missed you." The kiss he planted on her may have melted the polish off her toenails.

"Whoa, cowboy," she breathed, crushed against his hard torso.

"Our daughter missed you too." He set her on her feet, and then his gaze settled on the man sitting in the car. "Is that the guy who was in the hospital? He looks sorta irked."

"That's just Roger. He has mastered the art of being irked." She turned to give Roger a finger wave. "Mostly, he's a great fan of my mother's…mostly because she fawns over him and cooks goodies for Scott and him."

Beau lifted a hand to wave at the man in the car too but received no response.

"Where is Ava?"

"Ava is out back. Let's go surprise her." Beau led her into the house and through to the backyard.

Big Jim stood up when he saw her. "Hello, Dixie. It's sure been a pleasure having Ava with us." He cleared his throat. "Gonna miss that little sweetheart around here."

Dixie forced a smile. "I'm sure she's enjoyed herself. Thanks for taking care of her."

"No thanks needed. I hope both of you can think of this as your second home."

Her stomach twisted in anger or confusion, she couldn't tell which. This just didn't agree with her mother's version of things. "I appreciate it, Big Jim." She turned to Beau, who appeared to be enjoying the exchange. "Where's Ava?"

He gestured to the backyard where Ava was running with two older children, a girl and a boy. The sound of her daughter's laughter was like a curative to her troubled mind. For a moment, all three adults stood on the covered back deck, grinning in unison at the carefree sight.

Ava spotted Dixie and squealed, "Mommy!" She ran straight across the length of the yard and into Dixie's open arms. "Mommy, I missed you."

"I missed you too, my precious girl." Dixie buried her face in Ava's hair, noting a different scent. "Who washed your hair?"

"Aunt Leah. She let me wear Gracie's clothes. They're too little for Gracie now." She turned to wave at the two children who stood silently regarding her from the far end of the yard. "But they fit me just right." She smoothed the fabric of her shirt.

"Um, very pretty," Dixie said. "I'll wash the clothes you borrowed, and we can return them."

Ava's brow puckered. "No, Mommy. Gracie's mom gave them to me." She jammed her hands in the pockets of her jeans.

"Well, that was very nice. I hope you said thank you." Dixie wasn't sure how she felt about her child wearing secondhand clothing, but it was an emergency, and the shirt looked very pretty on Ava.

The sound of a horn beeping interrupted her thoughts.

"Oh, I forgot about Roger. He's waiting for us in the car. We better go now."

"Let me say goodbye to my little princess." Big Jim squatted down to give Ava a hug and kiss on the cheek. "You come back and see me real soon. I love you."

She responded by hugging his neck. "I will, Grampa. I love you too."

Dixie could not have been more surprised. Big Jim Garrett declaring his love for her daughter, who apparently loved him right back. Dixie had to stop herself from giving away her inner turmoil. She spread a smile across her face and started to retrace her steps. "Let's go, Ava."

They were stopped by Leah and Misty, who had to give hugs and say goodbye.

"She's such a dear," Misty said. "Please bring her back soon. My little brother Mark took it upon himself to be her personal watchdog. He wanted to be sure she knew her way around the ranch."

Dixie thanked them both and ushered Ava out the

front with Beau trailing behind. She turned to stop him. "Thanks for taking such good care of her."

Beau regarded her a little sadly, his blue eyes tearing a hole in her heart. "You don't have to thank me for taking care of my own daughter, I loved every second of it."

She leaned her forehead against his chest. "I know…I mean, thanks for being there for us—for me."

He kissed the top of her head before leaning down to gather Ava in his arms. "C'mon, baby. Let's get you in your car seat." He carried her out to the car and opened the back door.

"Hi, Uncle Roger," she called out. "You have a booboo on your head."

Beau fastened her in the seat and gave her a kiss on the forehead. "Be a good girl, Ava. I love you."

Ava clasped his neck. "I love you too, Daddy."

He closed the door and reached for Dixie. "You be careful. I don't want you going back to the feed store until the sheriff catches the shooter." He stroked the side of her face. "I love you, you know?"

"I know." She tried to resist his magnetic attraction. "I gotta get to the house. I'll probably be going back to the hospital with Roger to check on Scott. He hasn't regained consciousness."

"I can pick Ava up tomorrow morning if you want."

"I'll call you." She thought to give him a quick kiss, but Beau had other ideas. His kiss would have been enough to make her clothes fall off if they had been alone. As it was, she drew back, breathing hard. "See you tomorrow."

She climbed in the car and started it up without

glancing at Roger. Beau stood in front of the vehicle as she backed out, gazing at her with a tender expression.

"So that's how it is, huh?" Roger asked.

Dixie turned around and headed back to the highway. "That's the way it is."

Beau watched Dixie's car until it disappeared. He had a bad feeling about her "friend" Roger staying with her. The man obviously despised all things Garrett, and Beau wasn't secure enough in his newly revived relationship with Dixie that he trusted it to last.

Apparently Dixie's mother had filled her head with falsehoods about the Garrett family and about her own father. He hoped she finally saw the truth of the situation, but then again, her emotions had been put through the wringer already. He wasn't sure she could take much more.

One thing he was sure of. He wanted to slap the smirk off Roger's face.

Beau kicked a pebble with the toe of his boot. It went skittering across the drive, landing in a grassy area where his mother had planted forsythia bushes, now covered with bright-yellow blossoms. He turned and stomped onto the front porch, surprised to find Big Jim leaning against the doorway.

The expression on his face was not pretty.

Beau heaved a sigh, anticipating a tirade from his dad.

"Well, if that don't beat all. What's Miss Dixie doing now?"

"She's going to be babysitting her friends, at least until the one in the hospital is stable, or…or—"

"Dead," Big Jim pronounced solemnly.

"Yeah."

"Not good for Ava to be around all that—"

"Yeah."

"I mean, Dixie should have left Ava here with us... where she's safe." Big Jim's mouth was drawn down at the corners.

"Yeah." Beau didn't want to venture more, but he did. "I offered to pick Ava up in the morning, and Dixie said she would call me."

Miraculously, Big Jim's whole countenance morphed from despair to hope. "Yeah?"

Beau grinned at his father. "Yeah, Dad."

———

Roger was silent on the drive to the Moore ranch.

For this, Dixie was extremely grateful. She felt certain that she would get an earful when they were alone, but for now, Ava was holding court.

Dixie's daughter sat in her car seat and prattled on at length. She explained that her daddy had taken her on a horse ride and shown her lots of pretty places. And she talked about her "aunties" Leah and Misty, who cooked good things and helped her with her bath, and she talked about "Grampa," the wonderful man who showed her the baby calves and let her feed the chickens. "An' Grampa read me a story at night and kissed me right here." She placed her index finger in the middle of her forehead.

"Right there, huh?" Dixie glanced in the rearview mirror.

Ava nodded furiously. "Yes, Grampa loves me."

Roger made a sound and did an elaborate eye roll but managed to hold his tongue.

"Daddy loves me too. He said I was the little princess of the Garrett family."

Dixie's heart was being squeezed by an invisible vise. She struggled to draw a full breath. "Well, you're a very lovable young lady." She turned off the highway and onto the road to the Moore ranch. Mature trees reached limbs across to each other, as though the narrow road had torn them apart. When she pulled into the driveway leading to the house, she drew to a stop, dreading to find out what her houseguest had to say about her love life.

Without looking at Roger, she got out and busied herself releasing Ava from her seat. Once Ava was on her feet, she raced around the car and up to the front door like a bundle of wild red-haired energy.

Roger climbed out slowly, turning to gaze at Dixie over the roof of the car. "You're allowing this family of hicks to turn your girl into the princess of cows and chickens." His face reddened. "You cannot permit the Garretts to contaminate her with their rural mentality. I mean, she is going to attend the extremely exclusive Fairfield Academy in the fall. You have no idea how many strings I had to pull to ensure her admission to the kindergarten class. If she doesn't get in now, she'll be reduced to"—he shuddered—"public schools."

Dixie steadied herself against the car when she felt she was in danger of falling flat on her face. "What? How come I didn't know about this?"

Roger spread his arms wide. "It was supposed to be a surprise. Mamie said you would be thrilled." He appeared to be genuinely put out.

"You and my mother cooked this up between the two of you without consulting me at all?" She was aware that her voice had taken on a strident tone. "I would advise you to step off the attitude right now. I am truly furious." She tucked her small handbag under her arm and strode up to the front door, a somewhat-tight smile plastered on her face. "I'm coming, Ava." She jangled the keys.

"Hurry, Mommy. I need to potty." Ava jumped from foot to foot. "And I hafta feed Bertram and Anastasia."

Dixie hurried to open the door, and her daughter raced inside. Dixie turned to find Roger leaning against the car with his arms crossed over his chest. "Please come inside, Roger. You just got out of the hospital, and you should be taking it easy."

Another eye roll, but he pushed away from the vehicle and stomped up to the house like a petulant child.

She gestured to the open door and, when he passed, followed him inside. *It's going to be a long night.*

The next morning, Dixie called Beau. "I—I hope I'm not calling too early."

Beau smiled, her voice warming his insides. "Never too early for you. This is a working ranch, you know? Dad taught us to roll out early, no matter what."

He heard her heave a deep sigh.

"What can I do for you this morning?"

Another sigh. "I have to take Roger back to the hospital, so…if you could come get Ava, that would be very helpful."

"You know I will. Jumping in the truck right now."

He stuck his wallet in his back pocket and grabbed his keys. "I'll be over there as soon as I possibly can."

"And Beau, I wonder if you might be able to go by the feed store. I haven't talked to Pete since the—the shooting. If you could just check in with him and make sure he's doing okay. I—I'm doing such a shitty job of managing the store." She made a sniffling sound. "And my life."

"I'll be right there. Just remember that I'm always on your side." He had left the house and was in the process of climbing up into his truck when he heard a tiny whimper.

"I'm glad somebody is." She disconnected.

By the time Beau pulled into the driveway at the Moore ranch, he was torn between concern for Dixie, who seemed to be miserable, and anticipation of spending another day with his daughter.

He climbed the porch and had just lifted his hand to knock when the door flew open.

"Daddy! I'm a-post to go home with you."

Beau lifted her over his head and then snuggled her in his arms. "Okay, I'm game. What else do you want to do?" He eased into the house to see if he could get more direction from Dixie. "Where's your mommy?"

Ava's face fell. "Mommy and Uncle Roger are fighting."

Beau tucked Ava under his arm in a football carry and went into the kitchen, where Dixie and Roger were silently drinking coffee. "Good morning," he said and leaned to kiss Dixie's cheek. "Anything in particular you want me to do at the feed store?"

She gazed at him sorrowfully. "Just give Pete some support. I feel so bad that I'm not there for him."

Roger made a scoffing noise in his throat. "Well, you certainly don't have to neglect your employee on my behalf. I'm sure you care more about him than you do about my poor, poor Scott."

Dixie turned slowly, crossing her arms over her chest. "Seriously, Roger?"

Beau controlled the urge to smack the man slinging barbs at Dixie. "Um, maybe you and Ava can grab an extra outfit and something to sleep in? That way we'll be prepared for anything at Casa Garrett." He set Ava on her feet.

"Good idea." Dixie took Ava's hand and left the room.

Beau folded his own arms across his much wider chest and stared at Roger.

"What are you looking at, cow hand?"

"I'm looking at a man who needs a change of attitude, because I'm fed up with your mouth. It was no big deal when you were bashing me, but I draw the line on you sniping at Dixie."

Roger's eyebrows rose high on his forehead. "I beg your pardon?"

"I'm just letting you know that you better climb down off that high horse and stop being a jerk to Dixie. She's been through a lot, and she is bending way over backward to help you out."

Roger's face reddened. "Why, I've never been spoken to in this manner. Now you listen—"

"No, you better listen to me. You need to stop treating Dixie like dirt." He uncrossed his arms and took a step toward the irate man. "Because if you keep it up, you will be picking your teeth up off the floor. I won't allow her to be abused."

"Here we are." Dixie swept into the kitchen with Ava, who had a small backpack. "We picked out a nice outfit for play and a dress for church in case you happen to have Ava on Sunday."

"I got my toothbrush too," she crowed.

"We're all set then," Beau said. "I need to get Ava's car seat out of your car, and we'll be on our way." When Dixie grabbed her keys and led the way out the front, Beau turned to give Roger an intense stare. He pointed to his own eyes with two fingers and then pointed those same two fingers at Roger. The *I'm watching you* sign caused Roger to draw back frowning.

Beau followed Dixie and Ava outside. He removed the car seat, installed it in the backseat of his truck cab, and then settled Ava inside.

"I haven't had a chance to make breakfast." Dixie gnawed her lower lip, and then gave a half-hearted shrug. "I hope that Ava can have some cereal or something at your place."

"Not a problem." He drew her into his embrace and gave her a kiss. "Anything in particular you want me to do at the feed store?"

She shook her head. "I have no idea what needs to be done. I am so out of my element here."

He stroked his fingertips across her jawline. "You haven't had a chance to really settle in. You're right in your element here…with me." He lifted her chin and kissed her again. She seemed to relax a little, her body losing some of its tension.

"Thanks for everything, Beau. Take good care of our daughter."

"I will. You don't let that Roger guy bully you. He's

an ass." She started to object, but he stopped her with a kiss before climbing into his truck.

When he arrived at the Garrett ranch, he brought Ava into the house and found most of his family gathered in the large kitchen. Everyone gave Ava a hearty greeting.

Big Jim waved Ava over and started filling her plate. "You come right on over here, young lady. I've been saving you a special place right here." He patted the chair beside him.

Ava's face lit up, and she scampered over to give Big Jim a hug and climb onto the chair.

"C'mon, Son. Sit down and eat this fine food my lovely daughters-in-law prepared for us."

Misty laughed. "All I did was arrange the bacon on the baking sheets and pop them in the oven."

Leah smiled. "That was a great help." Leah leaned closer to her husband, who gave her a kiss on her temple.

"If my singing career goes belly-up, we can always open a restaurant. Leah can cook, and I'll wash dishes." Ty winked at Leah, who gave him a murderous look.

"Now that sounds like a heckuva deal." Big Jim toasted her with his coffee cup.

"You gotta grab a couple of these biscuits, Bro." Colton gestured to a basket filled with light, flaky biscuits.

Beau had intended to drop Ava off and go straight to the feed store, but the aroma of bacon and fresh-baked biscuits got to him. "Don't mind if I do." He filled a plate and took a seat beside Colton.

"What are your plans today, Little Bro?" Colton's voice was low-pitched.

Beau doubted anyone else at the noisy table overheard. "Dixie asked me to go by the feed store and give Pete a hand." He spoke just above a whisper.

Colton gave a slight nod. "Good. I'm sure old Pete must be overwhelmed. I'll go with you. Maybe we can lend him some muscle."

Beau considered for a moment, making a show of chewing his food. "Yeah, Bro. That will be great. I hope Pete can tell me if there's been any progress on the case. Old Vern was murdered right outside the store, and nobody's doing much about it—at least not anything they're sharing with Dixie."

Big Jim cleared his throat. "I believe I'll be tagging along with you two. I'm pretty sure these ladies will be able to entertain Ava for a while."

Beau and Colton exchanged a glance. "Um, sure, Dad," Beau said. "The more the merrier."

After breakfast, Big Jim herded his oldest and youngest sons to his own big silver truck. Colton was quick to slide into the backseat, leaving the front passenger seat for Beau. Beau sent him a look that fully expressed his lack of gratitude.

By the time they arrived in Langston, Beau was up to speed on Big Jim's opinion of just about everything.

Fortunately, he hadn't had to add anything to the monologue because Colton supplied the requisite "Really?" and "You don't say." Beau reasoned that Colton was the better-trained son because he had been around longer.

Big Jim pulled up in front of Moore's Feed and Seed and cut the engine. "Well, boys, let's go give old Pete a hand."

All three Garrett men piled out of the truck and ascended the steps to the store, their boots sounding like a thundering herd stomping across the wooden platform. Once inside, they found Pete sitting on a stool behind the cash register. He was slumped against the wall and appeared to be dozing, but he jerked awake when the trio's bootfalls interrupted his state.

"Hey, there, Pete," Big Jim called out.

Pete blinked several times and straightened his shoulders. "Good to see you, Mr. Garrett. How can I help you?"

Big Jim clasped Pete's hand warmly. "Aw, we come to help you, Pete."

Beau interrupted, earning a frown from his father. "Actually, Pete…Dixie asked me to stop by and see if you need anything. She is still hanging with those two fellows who were injured."

Pete swallowed visibly. "I see. Well, that would be good. You know, my cousin Josh ain't never come back. He musta got real scared when that big guy got shot."

Beau fisted his hands at his waist and took a wide stance. "You mean you haven't seen Josh since the shooting?"

"That's for sure." Pete nodded. "Josh was in the shed earlier that morning, but when we found that guy a-bleeding out back, Josh was nowhere to be found." He jerked his head toward the rear of the building. "His car is still there. I know he wouldn't just run away and leave his car behind." Pete rubbed his eyes with both hands. "And he's got money due come payday."

The back door opened, and two big, burly men came stomping inside. They headed for the little counter where Pete kept the coffee urn filled. One of the men gave Pete a nod and then looked over the Garrett men before filling his thermos. The other man filled his thermos and popped the stopper in the top. "Yer outta java, Pete. I cleaned you out."

"Okay," Pete called after the retreating forms.

"You must make a mean cup of coffee, Pete," Colton said.

Pete shrugged. "Vern always had me make coffee for the customers, but then the truckers found out it was here, and they started loading up." He scratched his head thoughtfully. "I'm pretty sure Josh told 'em."

"Does Josh have a gun?" Beau asked.

Pete shrugged. "Well, sure. Everyone around here has a gun. Don't you?"

"Well, sure," Colton said.

Big Jim made a scoffing sound. "Of course. We've all got guns—shotguns and rifles."

"Scott was shot with a 9 mm. The doc recovered bullet fragments from his chest," Beau pronounced. "So they're looking for someone with a handgun—a Glock, maybe."

"How the hell do you know this?" Big Jim's voice boomed out.

"I asked the deputies who were standing guard." Beau shrugged. "It seemed like the most direct way to get a straight answer."

Big Jim frowned. "I hope the sheriff knows his deputies are giving out information."

"Your friend Sheriff Rollins probably doesn't know as much as his deputies." Beau was aware that challenging his father, especially in public, was not a good idea. He sucked in a breath and tempered his tone. "I'm just worried about Dixie. This is her business, and there have been two violent acts committed right here by person or persons unknown. I don't want her to be in danger, so, yes, I'm interested in finding out what happened."

There was a moment when Beau's intense blue eyes and Big Jim's equally intense blue eyes were locked.

Colton slapped Beau on the shoulder. "Well, I don't blame you, Bro. I wouldn't want Leah anywhere around here until the crimes are solved...right, Dad?"

A muscle near Big Jim's mouth twitched. "I suppose that's reasonable. I'll see what my 'friend' the sheriff will share with me."

"Thanks, Dad." Beau turned back to Pete. "Now, what can we do for you today?"

Pete appeared to be frozen in place, apparently not used to the spirited exchange between father and son. "Um, well, I suppose the best thing would be to check on the shed. I can't really lift those big bags of feed that are out back. There are a couple of orders that need to be filled. Maybe if you fellows could line up the bags on the loading dock, I could manage to get them into the back of the customers' trucks."

"Sure, we can do that. Just show us what to do. Maybe if you called those folks to tell them they can pick up their orders, we might be able to load them for you." Big Jim started for the back without waiting for the others, but they quickly fell into step. They traversed through the store, past the small animal enclosures and racks of flower and vegetable seeds, then outside and across the yard to the shed.

When all four men had climbed the stairs to the loading dock, Pete pointed out the large sacks of seed he needed moved to the edge of the dock.

"We'll get you lined out, Pete," Big Jim bellowed. "What's up there?" He pointed to the loft at the far end of the building.

"We store some of the product up there. Things that aren't usually ordered, but Vern had a couple of customers he ordered special for…and the big rolled bales of hay. There's a conveyor belt up there to move them down to ground level."

"That's handy," Big Jim said. "We'll take care of everything."

Pete seemed grateful to be escaping the Garretts' company, retreating to the safety of the store.

"Okay, let's get these bags shifted to the dock." Beau and Colt grabbed the first of the bags, and they sidestepped out onto the loading dock.

"Hope it doesn't rain," Colt said, casting a glance at the clear blue sky.

"Not a chance," Beau said. "But we can find a tarp around here somewhere."

They returned to the shed and hauled the next bag out onto the loading dock while Big Jim wandered around the shed, poking into things. The two brothers stacked the bags into two areas, separating them into the two different orders. Just as they went inside to get the last of the bags, they heard Big Jim yell from above.

"What the hell? What are you doing there?" This was followed by the sound of a scuffle.

Beau and Colton lost no time in racing up the narrow metal staircase. When they reached the loft, they found Big Jim holding a small dark-haired woman by her shoulders.

She struggled to free herself, kicking at him and trying to bite his arms.

"Whoa! What you got there, Dad?" Beau grasped her from the back, earning himself a head butt to the chin and her bare feet kicking against his legs.

Big Jim glowered at the young woman. "Just hold on there, girl. What are you doing up here?"

"Hey, there's more of 'em!" Colton shouted from behind the large bales. "Stop!"

Beau was amazed when his brother emerged from the hay holding two more young women by the arms.

Big Jim called the sheriff, and within minutes the sound of sirens could be heard but wound down to a wail outside the shed. Moments later, the sheriff and two deputies ran inside, calling out for Big Jim.

Big Jim leaned over the edge of the loft. "Up here, Sheriff. We got three suspicious characters who sure don't belong here."

The young woman in Beau's arms went limp, tears streaming down her face. She began speaking to the other girls in Spanish. The younger girls broke into tears, wailing at the top of their lungs.

The sheriff came puffing and panting up the staircase, his face red and with beads of sweat gathered on his forehead. "Whatcha got there, Big Jim?" He stood bent over with his hands on his thighs, trying to catch his breath.

"We were trying to give Pete a hand with the loading dock when we found this bunch up here." Big Jim pointed to a space behind the large hay bales. "They seem to have made a little hidey-hole back there."

The three young women had collapsed down to the dusty, straw-covered wooden floor. They sniffled and wailed softly, seemingly resigned to their fate.

Sheriff Rollins, having recovered somewhat, mopped

his brow before stuffing the sweaty handkerchief back in his pocket. "Do any of you girls speak English?"

This was met with silence and surly looks from the first young woman, who sent scathing glares all around before tossing her hair and sitting up straighter.

"Okay, if that's how you gonna be…" The sheriff turned to his deputies and made a motion for them to move in. "Well, let's show these girls the amenities of our finest jail cell."

The girl Beau had helped subdue was trying to appear cool, but he could tell she was frightened. She was probably sixteen or seventeen. The other two were even younger. "Look, Sheriff, these girls are just kids."

The deputies busied themselves applying handcuffs to all three young women, which set off a new round of high-pitched wails. They were hustled to their feet, and then the deputies led them down the stairway.

The older girl was last to go. She threw one final baleful glare at Big Jim, and then her gaze lit on Beau. Her image remained seared in his brain long after they had left the loft.

Chapter 11

Big Jim parked his truck and led the way into Tio's Mexican Restaurant. Two of his sons followed behind. They were grim and silent.

Big Jim removed his Stetson and hung it on a peg beside the entry. Beau and Colton followed his example.

"Good to see you, Mr. Garrett." Milita Rios, the owner's daughter, greeted them with a smile. "You want a table or a booth?"

"A table would be best, Milita. We need a little shoulder room." Big Jim trailed behind her to a round table and took a seat facing the entry. Beau and Colton took a chair on either side.

Milita laid a menu in front of each man and departed, only to return a few moments later with three glasses of ice water. She noted the untouched menus and raised an eyebrow. "I take it you gentlemen know what you want."

Big Jim raked his fingers through his thick silver hair. "Sure do. Bring us three of the Monterrey Platters and some sweet tea."

Beau wasn't sure he had an appetite for that much food, but he hadn't the appetite to argue about it either. He passed his unopened menu to Milita, who collected them all and retreated to the kitchen. She returned quickly with a bowl of salsa and a tray of warm corn tortilla chips.

Other diners wandered in and were seated. In a short time, Milita brought their tea. She set the tall glasses down on paper coasters and then leaned back and crossed her arms over her chest. "It's probably none of my business, but I've never, ever known three Garretts to be sitting around a table with glum faces and not talking to each other." She gave each of them a searching look. "So, who's going to tell me what's going on? You know I'll find out eventually."

"Sit down," Big Jim said, his voice gruff. When Milita slid into the chair across from him, he shook his head. "I'm not one to gossip, but you might be able to help."

She leaned forward, gazing at him earnestly. "Of course, Mr. Garrett. I'll help if I can."

"You know the troubles at the feed store?"

She nodded. "I've heard about Mr. Moore getting killed and then some other guy who got shot there — and now Josh Miller is missing." She glanced around. "People are saying he probably got killed too."

A muscle near Big Jim's mouth twitched, but he was silent.

Beau took a deep breath and jumped in. "We were at the store this morning, trying to help Pete, and we found three girls in the loft—three very young Hispanic girls who appear to speak no English."

"In the shed behind the store?" Milita clasped her hands on the table. "You do know I speak fluent Spanish?"

Big Jim nodded. "That's what I was thinking. Maybe you can help the sheriff out by having a chat with those young ladies."

She looked around the restaurant. "Well, sure. After the lunch crowd is served, I can go over to the sheriff's office. You can let him know." She pushed back from the table and stood, smoothing her skirt. "Right now, I have customers to wait on." She gave them a wink and went to work the room.

"Good idea, Dad," Beau said. "And I thought you brought us here because it's your favorite restaurant."

Big Jim gave out a snort. "I can always eat Mexican food, but I did happen to think maybe Milita could help those girls." A wry smile spread across his face. "Every once in a while the old man has a good idea."

Milita came out of the kitchen balancing three platters and set them on the table. "Enjoy, gentlemen."

"This was definitely a good idea," Colton said as he picked up his fork.

Beau followed suit. Suddenly his appetite had returned.

———

At the hospital, Dixie and Roger learned that Scott had improved but was still not out of the woods. He had not regained consciousness.

Dr. Cami Ryan tried to convince them to go home. "Seriously, there is no point in you two hovering. This man needs to heal. His body has sustained a lot of trauma, but he's a remarkably strong and fit person. I have hopes that he will bounce back, but do not disturb him." She turned to Dixie. "I heard you have a little girl. You should be with her."

Dixie nodded. "I'm sure you're right, but my friend Roger needs me too."

Roger straightened his shoulders. "No, she's right. Go be with Ava. Don't allow her to become more countrified. I'll stay here with Scott."

"But I—"

He patted her hand. "No, you're a mother first. I'll call you if there's a change."

Dixie finally agreed to leave but promised to bring Roger's car back that evening.

Roger's lips tightened. "Don't let that cowboy drive my Audi." He handed over the keys.

Dixie huffed out a sigh. "Roger, you've got to get over this grudge you have against Beau. Look at me. I'm happy…really happy."

Roger gazed at her sadly. "I believe you are. I just can't get over all the things Mamie told me about the Garretts and about your Beauregard in particular." He shook his head, sadly. "You know I love you dearly and I'll try to give him the benefit of the doubt."

"That's all I ask." She smiled and gave him a kiss on the cheek. "Don't be such an old fusspot, Roger. I promise you'll like my cowboy if you give him half a chance. He's the real deal."

Roger made a noise in his throat that sounded more like a growl than agreement. "I'll call when there's a change."

After their meal, the restaurant crowd had thinned out. Big Jim had called the sheriff to let him know that Milita would be coming by to help him communicate with the three girls.

"Beau, why don't you accompany Miss Rios to the sheriff's office? Colton and I can hang out here for a while to pass out menus and ice water."

Colton expelled a hearty laugh. "Seriously, Dad?"

"Seriously, Colt. We can handle this place for a while. Beau, you hustle up Milita and let me know what the sheriff has to say." He unclipped his keys from his belt loop and passed them to Beau. "Take care of the young lady."

Beau retrieved his hat and escorted Milita to his father's truck.

She settled into the passenger seat, chuckling. "I never thought I would see the day when Big Jim Garrett would wait tables at my father's restaurant."

Beau started up the truck and slipped it into gear. "Aw, my dad is pretty versatile. He knows all about hard work, and he made sure we know it too." It was two long blocks to the sheriff's office, and he parked right in front.

When he and Milita entered the building, a deputy pointed them to the back.

"Come on in here," the sheriff called. "I kept the three girls separated. It seemed like the older one was trying to shut the other two up. Y'know? Like she was bullying them."

"How can I help you, Sheriff Rollins?" Milita gazed at him steadily.

"If you could find out what these girls were doing at the Moore shed, that would be a great thing." He lifted the sheriff's department cap from his head and scratched the top of his thinning hair. "They might be runnin' away from somethin' bad." He asked one of the deputies to bring in the two younger girls. When the deputy ushered them into the large office, they appeared to be terrified, clinging to each other and wide-eyed.

Beau tried to blend into the background, squeezing into a corner.

Milita's expression morphed from concern to a

pleasant smile. "*Buenas tardes, muchachas. Mi nombre es Milita Rios. Estoy aquí para ayudarles. ¿Están en problemas?*"

The girls glanced at each other and then reached for Milita. They began babbling at the same time.

Milita's brows drew together. "*¿Dónde están sus padres?*"

After a long, chaotic conversation, Milita gathered the girls in an embrace. "Sheriff, these two girls are sisters. This is Sofia. She's fourteen, and her sister Ana is only thirteen. They're from Matamoros, just across the border from Brownsville. They've been kidnapped by Valentina, the older girl."

The one named Sofia clasped Milita's hand and began speaking, her voice drenched with emotion. "*Ella nos engañó. Ella ofreció a llevarnos a casa, pero estábamos drogado.*"

"She says that Valentina offered them a ride home, but they were drugged. These poor girls have no idea where they are."

Beau leaned forward. "How did they get from Mexico all the way up here to north Texas? That's a long way to travel without knowing where you're going."

The girls drew back, clinging to each other.

He stepped back, holding his hands up in a surrender gesture. "Tell them I'm not a bad guy."

Milita conversed at length with the two girls, who vehemently shook their heads and gestured. When Milita leaned back in her chair, her expression was sad but composed. "These young girls were kidnapped by this Valentina and her boyfriend, who has a big truck. The girls were transported in the back of the truck and woke up inside, bound with duct tape. Then the three girls were unloaded here several days ago. They're confused since they were drugged and in the back of the truck. Then they were taken up to the loft and heard what sounded like gunshots. Valentina told them they better stay quiet or they would be killed. So they have been huddled together. She told them that another truck would come to pick them up." She shook her head, her lips pressed tightly together. "Can you imagine what these horrible people had planned for these young girls?"

Beau had a pretty good idea of the fate that awaited them had they not been rescued. "Just glad we found them, but can you ask them about the gunshots again? See if they remember any other details."

Milita asked more questions. For the most part, the girls responded but shook their heads. She turned back to Beau. "They said when they heard two shots they stayed very quiet behind the bales of hay. They heard sirens and were afraid they would be discovered. Valentina told them stories of how badly the ICE agents treated young girls."

Beau fisted his hands at his waist. "She did, huh? Sheriff, don't you think it's about time you questioned this Valentina?"

"Um, yeah. Say, Beau, is your papa coming over?"

"Big Jim specifically sent me over to represent him. He and my oldest brother are at the feed store right now." Beau figured stretching the truth a bit would motivate the sheriff to follow through.

The sheriff stood up and tucked his shirt in under his substantial gut. "The other girl is still in holding." He signaled to the deputy to go get her.

Milita held up both hands. "Wait, Sheriff. I don't think these girls need to be exposed to that young woman. They're really afraid of her."

The sheriff scratched his chin. "Well, I suppose we don't have to question her in this room. We can step into another office right across the hall."

Milita spoke to the girls in Spanish, and they moved closer together, fear on their faces. When Milita rose to follow the sheriff, the older girl reached out to grab her hand. Milita leaned down to pat her shoulder and say something in a soothing voice.

Beau noted the girl looked more confident. She released Milita, who crossed to the door and slipped out. Beau followed her to the other office.

In a few minutes, the deputy brought a very sullen Valentina in, and the sheriff motioned for her to be seated. She tossed her hair before dropping into the chair but kept her gaze averted.

The sheriff sat heavily behind the desk. "Now, listen here, young lady—"

She rolled her eyes and turned in the other direction. "*No entiendo*," she murmured.

"Well, fortunately for you, we have someone right here who speaks fluent Spanish." Beau gestured to Milita, whose expression could best be described as scathing.

Valentina huffed out a dramatic sigh and crossed her arms tightly over her chest. "Okay, I speak some English."

"Tell us how you happened to be hiding in the loft."

"I—I was kidnapped. Some men grabbed me and those others. They said they would kill me if I didn't stay quiet."

Beau's lips tightened. "Sounds like you speak English just fine."

"Them other girls tell a different story," the sheriff said. "They told us it was you who arranged their kidnapping and that you and your boyfriend brought them up here."

She made a scoffing sound. "They're lying. I would never do that. I am a very nice girl."

Beau fisted his hands at his waist. He wanted to punch something. Anything. "That remains to be seen. When are you expecting to hand the girls off to their buyer?"

"I have no idea what you're talking about. I'm a victim here."

"You just keep telling yourself that," the sheriff said.

"What is the name of your boyfriend with the truck?" Beau's voice sounded harsh to his own ears.

Valentina placed one hand on her breast. "I—I have no boyfriend."

"I'm a-gonna have the deputy take you back to your cell." The sheriff stood up abruptly. "I suggest you make yourself comfortable, 'cause you're a-gonna be in a cell for a long, long time."

Valentina's face reflected pure venom with just a flash of terror. The deputy took her by the arm and escorted her back to the holding cell.

"So, what now?" Milita asked. "What's going to happen to Sofia and Ana? They're just innocent babies."

The sheriff sat back down. "First, we'll try to locate their parents and verify their story. In the meantime, I'll just call social services outta Amarillo to come and git 'em."

That seemed reasonable to Beau, but Milita was troubled.

"Oh, that sounds so cold," she said. "They're already scared to death."

The sheriff flapped his hand at her in a dismissive gesture. "Aw, those social ladies are real pros. They'll know how to take care of them girls…until their parents can get together with 'em."

"That sounds good, doesn't it?" Beau asked. He wanted to get back to the feed store and share what he had learned.

"I'll stay here with Sofia and Ana until something is settled for them." Milita turned to return to the other office. "Tell my father I'll be there in time for the dinner crowd."

"Um, yes. Sure." Beau made his escape and drove back to the restaurant. He noted that the restaurant was empty except for Big Jim and Colton, who had settled at a table with Mr. Rios and were enjoying coffee and pie with him. Beau pulled up a chair, and Mr. Rios brought him a slab of blueberry pie and poured coffee into a cup before returning to his chair.

Beau explained that Milita got involved with the two young victims and had promised to return to work by the time the dinner crowd began arriving.

Mr. Rios shook his head and grinned. "Ay, that girl. She has a soft heart. She loves children, puppies… anything that needs a home." He pushed back from the table. "I guess I better call in another waitress."

On the drive back from the hospital, Dixie called the Garrett ranch only to find that her daughter was not missing her at all.

In fact, Ava said, "Oh, Mommy. I'm having such a good time with Gracie. We're playing dress-up. Can't I stay a little longer?"

Dixie had asked to speak to Leah, who told her the girls were about to have lunch. She invited Dixie to dinner and assured her the entire Garrett clan would love to see her.

So, instead of driving to pick up her daughter, Dixie was home alone.

She unlocked the front door to the Moore ranch house. It swung open slowly, yawning into a great abyss of blackness. Somehow she was reluctant to enter. It was deadly silent.

A tingle of fear spiraled around her spine. She huffed out a sigh and straightened her shoulders before striding inside.

Kicking out of her shoes, she shed clothes as she made her way to the bedroom...her childhood bedroom.

She chose a pair of shorts and a tee to wear with her sandals. Then she sat on the bed. The bed she had last slept in as a teen.

"Okay, I have to stay here for a year. I better start kicking the ghosts out." She began by taking down the poster and the bulletin board covered with all kinds of memorabilia from high school. She gazed at the things she had thought important enough to save and steeled herself as a wave of nostalgia swept over her.

Dixie swallowed hard. "Just get this room cleared out." She took down the curtains, running a finger over the dusty mini-blinds. When she dumped out her dresser drawers, she realized her father had kept everything exactly the same as she had left it. In a short time, the room was stripped bare of any personal items except for the bed coverings. The next step would be to take Ava to the hardware store to pick out just the perfect color to paint her new room.

It dawned on her that she would have to face another chore. Clearing out the master bedroom. Her father's room.

That door was at the end of the hall, and it was closed. She hadn't opened it since her return to Langston. Couldn't open it. Until now.

She stood in the hallway, biting her lower lip. *Just go in*. Yet she stood frozen, unable to enter.

Dixie turned, accepting that she was a coward. She got a few feet down the hall before she let out a howl of anger. "No! It's just a room." She whirled around, marched to the intimidating door, and threw it open. So much for bravado. She took a moment to gather the courage to step inside.

The room was dark and smelled like her father's Old Spice aftershave. She pressed her lips together and flipped on the light. The overhead lamp had tear-shaped faceted crystals that sent spangles of light onto the ceiling and walls.

Apparently Vern Moore had not been so determined to keep the memory of his beloved wife, Mamie, intact. He had changed the bedspread and drapes. The walls were still an off-white, and the only other remnant of Mamie was a wallpaper border she had glued to the wall close to the ceiling. It had been popular at the time, but staring at it now gave Dixie a case of the creeps, as though being here somehow violated her father's privacy.

"Oh, Daddy," she whispered. "What really happened? Did you disown me?"

Her question lingered in the stale air and remained unanswered. She heaved out a sigh. "I can do this. It's not going to be any easier tomorrow."

She pulled the dark-green bedspread off along with the rest of the bedding and left it in the hallway. Next she took down the matching drapes, adding them to the pile. The room already appeared brighter and even more so when she raised the mini-blinds. She unlatched the windows and raised them to let in some fresh air.

Dixie turned around in a full circle, gazing at the major alteration resulting from her simple changes. *I can do this…I really can.* Suddenly, she felt much better. Less of an intruder…more as if she had a right to be there.

"Okay, Daddy. I'm going to clear out the rest of your stuff and figure out how to make this room fit for the new lady of the house." She took a wastebasket and sat down at the dresser her mother had used to apply her makeup and style her hair. It appeared that her father had removed all traces of his former wife. Dixie opened the drawers, but most were empty. A single bobby pin slid across the bottom of one drawer to assure her that she had not imagined that it had once been crammed with the beauty tools of one Mamie Moore. Capturing the errant bobby pin, Dixie held it for a moment and then dropped it in the wastebasket. She opened the smaller drawer, and her stomach did a tumble and roll when she saw it was stuffed with envelopes. Unopened envelopes that had been mailed and returned.

Dixie couldn't draw a breath. Her chest felt as though

a tight band was constricting her airway. The address on the letters was the condominium she shared with her mother in Dallas.

Her hand shook when she reached out to tentatively touch the envelopes. They were arranged in neat bundles, each bound together with a wide rubber band.

At first she couldn't identify the pounding sound, but then she realized it was her own heartbeat, pulsing in her ears. She swallowed hard, steeling herself to examine the envelopes.

She lifted the first packet out of the drawer, cringing as though she had been punched in the gut when she saw the addressee—*Miss Dixie Moore*. These letters had been sent to her...by her father.

There! In her mother's own handwriting...the words *Return to Sender. Wrong address.*

Swallowing hard against the taste of bile rising in the back of her throat, she slipped the rubber band from the first packet. She shuffled through the unopened envelopes, noting that they were fairly recent and the date stamps indicated a weekly letter from her father.

Two opposing emotions battled inside her. Fury that her mother had lied to her. Rage that she had dealt such painful blows not only to her daughter but also to her husband, destroying the once-close father–daughter relationship.

And for her father she felt the ache of regret. Shame for believing that he could abandon her, that he would stop loving her.

"I'm so sorry, Daddy," she rasped out as twin rivulets of tears streaked her cheeks.

Dixie Moore was not the kind of woman to dissolve

into tears at the drop of a hat, but now, she wept and
wept, bawling at the top of her lungs. She found a roll
of toilet paper in the bathroom and ripped it from its
wrapping. She stomped around the house, alternately
crying, blowing her nose, and dropping crushed tissue
in strategically placed wastebaskets.

When the rage had subsided to a murderous simmer,
Dixie dashed cold water on her face and gazed at herself
in the bathroom mirror. Her eyes were puffy and her
skin mottled, but she had regained her composure.

She still had to go to the Garrett ranch for dinner and
to retrieve her daughter. She didn't want any trace of
tears to upset Ava, and God forbid if Beau observed that
she had been crying.

Instead she focused on her mother. She replayed
every single lie she had been told subsequent to discovering that she was pregnant. Mamie Moore had cut
off everyone with whom Dixie had had a relationship,
except for her very supportive mother.

She took out her phone several times, ready to roast
her mother verbally, but each time, she put it away. *Not
going to let her off the hook that easily*. No, she owed
her mother a face-to-face confrontation, although the
way she was feeling at the moment, it might be their last.

Her cell sounded, but the ringtone wasn't her mother's. She sighed and accepted the call. "Hello?"

"Miz Dixie? This here's Sheriff Rollins. I hope I
didn't catch you at a bad time."

Concerned, Dixie assured him that it was not a bad
time. She couldn't imagine why the sheriff was calling
her. Maybe he had news about her father's death. Maybe
he had arrested the killer.

"Ma'am, I regret to inform you that your place of business has once again been the location of another crime."

Dixie's stomach clenched with fear. *Not Beau.* "What—what happened now?"

"This afternoon, three young women were found hiding up in the loft out back o' your store. They say they been kidnapped."

"What? I don't understand."

There was a chortle on the other end of the line. "Well, Miz Dixie, that makes two of us. It seems your store has been involved with human trafficking for some time. You wouldn't know anything about that, would you?"

Dixie groped for words. Kidnapping? Slavery? "Um, Sheriff Rollins, I have no idea what's been going on. I just inherited the property, so I can't say what's transpired in the past, but I can assure you that I knew nothing about anything illegal…and I think if you knew my father, you know he would never condone anything that was against the law."

He cleared his throat noisily. "Yes'm, Miz Dixie."

―〜〜―

When they arrived back at the ranch, the Garrett men separated, each with a different purpose in mind. Big Jim headed to the stables, while Colton made a quick phone call to touch base with Misty, who was still at work in town.

Leah was in the kitchen preparing dinner, with the three children gathered around the table.

Ava looked up when Beau entered the room.

"Daddy!" She pushed away from the table and ran to greet him. The sight of her face always gave him a stab of joy. How could he have missed her birth…the first years of her life?

He shook off all negative feelings as he stooped down to scoop Ava into his arms. He lifted her up and gave her a tickle on the tummy. "How's my girl?"

"I'm having fun. Mommy is coming to dinner, and she's going to take me home." She looked confused for a moment. "To the other place."

Beau carried her out onto the patio and closed the sliding-glass door behind them. He settled into a deck chair with Ava on his lap. "It sounds like you don't know where your home is anymore."

Ava stared at him, her eyes wide. "My gramma says my mommy and me live with her."

"I see." Beau worked his jaw to keep from grinding his teeth together. "Well, I think you have two more homes. You have a home where your mommy is staying now. She owns that house and all the land that goes with it. It belongs to you as well."

Ava nodded her head wisely, as though she understood.

"But since I'm your daddy and this is my home, it's also your home."

She flashed a quick grin. "And Grampa. This is where my grampa lives…and…and my Auntie Leah and Auntie Misty." She gnawed her lower lip. "And Uncle Colton and Uncle Tyler. Oh, and Mark and Gracie?"

"That's right. And we're all your family, so you have a home with us wherever we are."

That response seemed to satisfy her, and she dropped her head back against his shoulder.

He heard the door slide open and then close again. "Well, this looks cozy."

Ava lifted her head, and her face lit up. "Mommy!" She scrambled out of Beau's arms and ran to greet Dixie.

Beau stood, smiling to see both his redheads locked in a hug. "Hi, baby."

Dixie straightened, laughing. "Which one of us was that directed to?"

She looked happy. Maybe too happy. Her eyes were bright, and her smile was wide, but something was a little off.

Beau couldn't put his finger on it, but there was something simmering right under the surface. She was upset about something. He hoped it wasn't anything he'd done.

He approached warily. "You're both my babies." He wrapped his arms around Dixie and gave her a kiss on the cheek. "You look...beautiful."

There was the tight little smile again. "Thanks. You must have missed me."

"That's for sure. I think Ava has had a good time playing with her cousins."

Dixie's brows drew together. "Cousins?"

"Sure. Tyler is my brother, and his wife's daughter must be Ava's cousin."

Dixie nodded uncertainly.

"And Colton is also my brother. His wife's little brother must be a second cousin too."

She was laughing now. "That's stretching it a bit, don't you think?"

He kissed her nose. "Maybe, but more family is always better...at least that's what I believe."

The door slid open again, and Big Jim gestured for them to come inside. "Break it up, you two. Leah is putting dinner on the table. Let's eat." He held out his hand to Ava, who scampered inside.

Beau drew Dixie into his arms and planted a kiss on her lips. She seemed to relax a bit as he gazed into her eyes. "I love you, y'know?"

This elicited a genuine smile. "I know." She released a deep sigh. "I love you right back...you know?"

"Yeah, I know." He gave her another squeeze before gesturing to the open doorway.

The long table was set, and some of his family were already in place. His middle brother, Ty, waved them over.

"Dad is serving our meal right up." Ty seemed to be in particularly high spirits.

Beau seated Dixie beside Ty and took the chair next to her. "What's up, Bro? You look like you're about to bust. Going on another big tour?"

Ty's grin went wall to wall. "Nope. I'm going to be recording some new songs, but no tour until next year."

Big Jim brought a platter of fried chicken to the table. "Make way, kids. Leah's been slaving over a hot stove, so let's get this dinner on the table."

Tyler jumped up eagerly. "Let me help." He went to the breakfast bar separating the kitchen preparation area from the dining area. Leah had placed several dishes there, and Tyler began carrying things to the table.

Colton came into the room with Ava, Gracie, and Mark. "All hands have been washed," he announced. The children took their places at the table. Misty caught up with Colton, and they walked arm in arm to take their seats. Soon, the entire Garrett clan had gathered around the table.

Beau's chest tightened as he gazed around at the family he loved. This was the way it was supposed to be. All he had to do was make sure Dixie and Ava remained a part of this tribe.

"Who wants to say grace?" Big Jim asked.

The three children immediately raised their hands.

"I think it's Mark's turn," Big Jim pronounced, which caused Mark to grin and sit up a little taller. He reached to hold hands with those on either side of him, which caused a chain reaction of hand-holding. He said a simple blessing: "And please bless my family. Amen." This was followed by a chorus of amens.

Beau glanced at Dixie, who seemed to have been overcome with some kind of strong emotion. He squeezed her hand and brushed a kiss on it before he released her. "Okay, baby?" he whispered, and she nodded.

Tyler pushed his chair back and stood. He tapped his spoon against his glass of iced tea. "If I can have everyone's attention for one minute. I know you're anxious to partake in this great meal my beautiful wife has prepared, but we have some exciting news for you."

There was a hush as everyone turned to stare at him.

"I wanted to share with you that the love of my life, my beloved wife, and I are expecting a baby around Christmastime." He leaned down to give Leah a kiss as those sitting around the table broke out in cheers and applause.

"I'm going to be a big sister," Gracie announced proudly.

"And you're going to do a fine job of it, I'm sure."
Big Jim beamed at her.

Beau reflected that his father's happiness seemed to
be centered around his children and grandchildren. *It's
all about family*.

"Who wants a leg?" Big Jim roared. Both Gracie and
Ava raised a hand.

Chapter 12

DIXIE DROVE HOME WITH AVA SECURED IN HER SAFETY SEAT right behind her. She glanced in the rearview mirror and saw that her daughter was drowsy, her beautiful blue eyes heavy-lidded.

The rearview mirror also revealed a pair of headlights following behind.

She couldn't suppress her smile.

Beau.

He was following along behind and would spend the night. That alone brought a smile to her lips.

Dixie was a little anxious to see how Ava felt about the newly stripped bedroom, but she thought the opportunity to choose her own paint colors might please her little darling, and it would be fun to share this experience. She hoped Ava's color choice would not be dark purple or neon green.

Dixie had folded all the bedding and draperies from the two rooms and would donate them to some local charity. She figured she would stage her seduction of Beauregard Garrett in the guest room, which was decorated with heavy burgundy drapes and bed coverings. It hadn't been updated since the eighties. But at least it had clean bedding in place and smelled nice, thanks to a little recent attention. She wasn't sure she could sleep in her father's room yet. Not until she had stripped the memories from it. But she could claim the guest room as her temporary nesting place, at least until the redecorating process was complete.

By the time she pulled to a stop in front of the Moore ranch house, Ava was fast asleep. She turned off the motor and killed the lights. In a few seconds, Beau was parked beside her. With a finger to her lips, she signaled Beau to be quiet.

With as much stealth as possible, Beau climbed out of his truck and came to release Ava from her safety seat. "Come on, sweetheart. Easy does it." He arranged her in his arms and followed Dixie up to the house and through to the bedroom now designated as Ava's.

He glanced around at the bare walls and bed made up with sheets and a summer-weight blanket. He shot Dixie a questioning glance, but she pulled back the bedding so he could slide Ava into bed.

Dixie gently removed Ava's outer clothing and snuggled her under the sheet and blanket.

Beau gestured to the bare walls and windows. "What's going on?" he whispered.

She drew him out into the hallway. "I thought I would make some changes."

He looked puzzled. "Changes? What kind of changes?" His intense blue eyes seemed to bore right into her soul.

"Nothing too serious," she said. "Just a coat of fresh paint and maybe new bedding to match."

"Sounds like a good idea. What brought this on?"

Dixie reached up to unbutton the top buttons of his western shirt. "I just thought I should settle in. After all, I am going to be here for a while."

A smile played around his mouth. "Yes, you are."

"A year, at least." She finished the buttons and flipped open the buckle on his belt.

"At least," he agreed, stripping the belt from the loops.

She took a few steps toward the guest room. "And I thought Ava needed her own room. Maybe you can go with us to pick out paint colors."

Beau reached around her to open the door to the guest room and made a gesture for her to enter. "After you." His expression started a tingling sensation spiraling around her chest. She stepped into the dark room and turned around to face him.

He was gazing at her fondly. "That sounds like a great idea. I'd be happy to help pick out colors for Ava's room." He shrugged out of his shirt and arranged it over a chair. "I'm so glad you've resigned yourself to your fate. You belong here…with me."

Her breath caught in her throat. She gazed up into his eyes. "I do?"

He lifted her chin. "Yes, you do. You and Ava belong with me." His kiss was tender yet stirred her to the tips of her toes.

Dixie sucked in a breath and blew it out. "Well, we better get those clothes off so you can show me that I belong with you."

"Happy to oblige."

Dixie started to shed her own clothes, but only got as far as removing her denims. She realized that she had left her best lingerie back in Dallas. Maybe she could drive to Amarillo for a little retail therapy because she really would like to knock Beau out with something luscious.

When she started to unbutton her shirt, strong arms

wrapped around her and pulled her back to lean against his chest. Beau took over her task. His fingers worked the tiny buttons, opening them all the way down. Then he placed his palm flat on her stomach. "I cannot believe you grew our daughter right here and I didn't even know about it."

"Yeah, well, those were really sad times for me. Not turning me on."

Slipping her shirt from her shoulders, he kissed the side of her neck. "Sorry I wasn't there for both of you."

Dixie turned to face him. "Me too." She leaned her cheek against his chest. "I don't want to talk about sad things. I've had enough sad feelings for one day."

"Then I'll just tell you how much I love you. I loved you then, and I love you now. I'm going to love you when you're a wrinkly little old lady."

This made her laugh, really laugh with her head thrown back. "What makes you think I'm going to be a wrinkly old lady? I will use sunscreen."

"Mmm." He made an appreciative noise. "I'll rub it on for you."

She was laughing when he nudged her toward the bed. "How generous of you."

"Yeah, that's me. Generous to a fault." He gave her another nudge. "Now I'm going to help you with the rest of those clothes." He released the clasp on her bra and cupped her breasts in his slightly callused hands. "I thought these were pretty when you were a teen, but now these are a work of art."

"You don't have to say that."

He gathered her in his arms and pulled her against his chest. "I'm just stating the truth. I think I'm a boob man."

She was laughing again. She liked that he made her laugh…that he made their lovemaking fun. "Did you know that I love you?" She had spoken the words in a rush, and now she was staring into Beau's remarkable blue eyes…eyes that reflected so much love he didn't even have to say the words. She grabbed his face with both hands and kissed him. He lifted her against him, and she wrapped her legs around his torso. If he only knew how hot he was, how the desire to jump on him was always hovering at the edge of her consciousness.

His hands cupped her bottom, holding her even closer. He took two steps to the bed and climbed onto it, rolling on one shoulder to lie on his back with Dixie on top of him. He reached up to brush one of her errant curls away from her face. "You love me? I sure do hope you do because I'm crazy in love with you."

She gazed down at him. *Such a beautiful man.* "Good," she whispered. "I've got you where I want you. So pucker up and kiss me while I'm hot."

He reached up, taking her face in both hands. "Yes ma'am." He drew her close, kissing her lips tenderly and then more vigorously. His hand grazed down the side of her body, setting a tingling in its wake, from her breast down her ribs to her hip and grabbing a handful of her buttock.

Her body seemed to ignite anyplace he touched, no matter how casually.

He rolled her onto her back and began to trail kisses from her shoulder to her breasts. His lips and tongue teased, suckled, and caressed her breasts, causing her to catch her breath and arch toward him, eager for more pleasure as he was dealing it out. She was on fire.

Flames spread from her taut nipples, from his mouth suckling and teasing her, burning a path to her core.

His was kissing her stomach, causing an explosion of feathers to whirl around in her stomach.

"Such a cute little belly button," he whispered before exploring it with his tongue. He traced a path lower, grazing his way to her mound.

She gasped when he found his target. Spiraling waves of passion lapped at her in time to the rhythm of his sensual massage. The pressure increased, driving her closer and closer to the edge of the abyss.

"You're torturing me," she groaned. "I—I can't…"

He laughed and kissed the inside of her thigh. "I'm loving you."

"Come here!" she commanded. Her strong thighs encircled his hips, drawing him to her. Her short nails skimmed his skin.

Beau hesitated a moment, then reached for a condom in the pocket of his Wranglers. As he entered her, he gazed into her eyes.

Dixie let out a soft moan as their bodies connected and again with every stroke that reached deep inside her. She held him tightly, lifting her hips into his thrusts. When the first waves of her orgasm washed over her, she went rigid. "Oh, Beau," she cried out.

He grinned, continuing to thrust into her. "I love you, Dixie," he whispered.

She whispered his name and grabbed him around his waist, matching his thrusts. As her passion built again, she was aware of Beau holding her tenderly. When she climaxed again, Beau gripped her, exploding inside her.

She kissed his neck, tasting the salt of his sweat,

feeling his pulse beat against her lips as he pulsed inside her.

In the morning, Beau awoke with Dixie in his arms. This was the way he wanted to start every day. He knew his dad probably had lined out a bunch of tasks for him on the Garrett ranch, but he planned to spend as much time as he could with Dixie and with Ava.

Getting to know the amazing little creature he had cocreated had him entranced. He had gone from free-as-the-breeze bachelor to daddy with the first meeting.

He stared down at Dixie's beautiful face, so similar to Ava's. Her hair was the same fiery red, and her fair skin had the same high color in her cheeks and lips. He was glad he had been able to contribute Ava's eye color. *Yeah, those eyes stamp her as a Garrett. Can't deny those.*

After a rousing night of lovemaking, his tempestuous darling was at peace, her auburn lashes resting on her cheeks. She was even lovelier as a woman than she had been as a girl.

"Are you staring at me?" she asked without bothering to open her eyes.

"As a matter of fact, I am." He brushed a strand of curls off her face.

She giggled, opening her eyes wide. "Why?"

"'Cause I love you. 'Cause I can't seem to get enough of you."

She let out a most unladylike snort. "Seems to me like you got a healthy dose of me last night. In fact, I'm not sure I can walk straight yet."

"Not a problem. I'll carry you anywhere you want to go."

That elicited another giggle. "You will? I would have had a second helping of those buttery mashed potatoes and cream gravy last night if I had known."

He kissed her cheek gently. "It's fine with me. I'll love you if you gain a ton. You'll always be beautiful to me."

She punched him on the arm. "Oh, Beau. You always say the right thing."

"I hope I always do the right thing."

She gazed up at him, suddenly vulnerable. "What is the right thing?"

Here goes. "With all my heart, I believe the right thing is for you to agree to marry me. I promise to love you for as long as I live. I'll take care of you and Ava and protect you always."

She seemed to be frozen in his arms. A beautiful nude statue. She didn't even blink.

He felt as though his chest was compressed in a vise. Time stopped as he waited for her to respond in some way. Would she laugh and blow him off? Maybe she would recover and be angry. He held his breath.

"Oh, Beau. That is the most wonderful thing anyone has ever said to me."

"Actually, there was a question in there. In case you missed it, here it is again." He gave her a more thorough kiss. "Will you, Dixie Moore, please marry me, Beauregard Garrett, and make me the happiest man on the planet? Will you spend your life with me and raise our daughter with me? Will you meld into the Garrett family that also loves you and Ava? Will you join the chaos that is a part of being a Garrett as long as we both shall live?"

Her chin quivered, but she caught her lower lip between her teeth and then grinned. "Actually, I think that sounds like a great idea. Dixie Lee Moore Garrett. Dixie Garrett." She giggled. "Mrs. Beauregard Garrett."

He fixed her with a skeptical glare. "Is that a yes?"

"Yes, it is a definite yes. I will marry you." Tears spangled her lashes.

"Aw, baby. Please don't cry. There's been enough tears between us. I just want to do everything in my power to make you happy."

She sucked in a ragged breath. "I am happy. I'm very happy." She wrapped her arms around his neck, and he rolled onto his back, carrying her with him.

"It's about time. Just think, we could have gotten married years ago and been old married folks by now. We might have another little one running around." He drew back to glimpse her face, but she looked strained. "Dixie? What's wrong?"

"Oh, Beau. I'm so mad and hurt and…and angry." She brushed tears away with the back of her hand. "Mostly, I'm sorry I hurt you, and I'm sorry I hurt my father."

He stroked her shoulder with his fingertips. "But we're both here now. We survived all the misery, and we can be together forever."

Shaking her head, she made a sound like a newborn kitten. "But my father is dead. Someone murdered him, and I'll never have a chance to make it up to him."

Beau recalled how devastated Vern had been after Dixie's departure, but he neglected to share that memory. Instead, he continued to stroke her shoulder and murmur soothing words. "I'm sure your dad knows how you feel. He was always so proud of you." This set off a new round of tears.

"I—I'm so mad at my mother I could just strangle her." A huge tremor shook her body. "She—she lied. She lied to me all these years."

Beau had suspected as much but thought he should keep his mouth shut. *Not a good time for I told you so.* "Dixie, I hate to see you so upset. Maybe you can think about our beautiful daughter and the life we have ahead of us. Don't look back. It's too painful right now."

She nodded. "You're right. I have to think about Ava. She's going to start school next fall. She's so ready for kindergarten." A sudden smile ripped through the tears. "She is really excited about it. We need to go shopping for school clothing, and…and I want to paint her room."

He smiled in return, encouraged by a flash of good humor. "That sounds awesome. I hope I'm included in both projects."

"Well, I was going to ask you to help me paint, but are you up for all that girly shopping?"

He laughed, deep in his chest, shaking her atop him and eliciting a laugh in return. "Of course. I'm thrilled to be Ava's daddy. I want to know how to shop for little girls. I want to see her try on girly stuff."

"You're on." She laid her cheek down on his chest, appearing to be far more relaxed. "I guess we better get up. Ava will be coming to find us. She's addicted to breakfast."

He gave one of her buttocks a playful swat. "We better feed our girl."

She started to move off him but then settled in place. She took his face in both her hands. "Thank you, Beau.

I found letters my father tried to send me but my mother returned. I've been so angry with her…and so hurt for my father." She leaned down to kiss him tenderly. "But you helped me to feel more centered. I'm still angry, but at least I can focus on something besides choking my mother till she turns purple."

"What are you going to do?"

"I'm going to take care of Ava and make love with you as often as possible." She rolled over and swung her legs off the side of the bed. "I'm going to figure out how to manage the feed store and run this ranch, and along the way, I plan to find out who murdered my father and shot my friend Scott."

Beau sat up and reached for her, but she was on the move, locating underwear and a robe and shrugging into them. "Wait a minute. That sounds dangerous. I do not want you to do anything unsafe. Just be patient and let the sheriff deal with it."

She turned to him, tying the belt to her robe. "Obviously, you have forgotten who you are dealing with. Patience is not one of my virtues." She winked before leaning down to pick up his hastily removed Wranglers. "You better get your britches on, cowboy. It's show time." She tossed them on the bed.

Beau climbed to his feet and searched for his underwear. He was glad she seemed to have recovered some of her good spirits, but knowing her as he did, he was afraid her impetuous nature might put her in danger.

Dixie sashayed out the door, casting an amused glance back at him before closing it behind her.

Beau heaved a deep sigh. He pulled on his Wranglers and zipped them up. At last, he located his socks and boots, donning them as quickly as he could. All the while he tried to figure out how he could manage to placate Big Jim while staying glued to Dixie and Ava. He had to protect his females.

—⁓—

Their breakfast together was pleasant enough. Dixie made bacon and eggs, while Beau and Ava made the toast. Conversation was light, mainly concerned with Dixie's announcement about painting the bedrooms and an excited discussion about color preferences.

"Pink?" Dixie gazed at Ava. "That's your favorite color?"

Ava nodded furiously. "Yes, Mommy. I want to paint my room pink…with purple too."

As Dixie started to object, Beau interrupted. "I think that's a great choice. I like red and yellow best myself. We can go check out paint colors this afternoon."

Dixie wrinkled her brow. "First, we have to take the Audi to Roger. He needs to have transportation, and I need to check on Scott. I'm such a bad friend."

"Okay, Ava and I can follow in my truck. Then we can pick out some paint."

Her brow cleared. "Okay. That works. Now let's eat up so we can get on the road."

—⁓—

Beau trailed a safe distance behind the dark-blue Audi in his pickup truck. Ava was secured in her child safety device on the passenger side of the backseat. She continued an animated conversation with no sign of wearying, commenting on everything they passed.

"Oh, that cow has very big horns." She pointed to a herd grazing close to the barbed-wire fence as they drove along the highway.

"That cow is a Texas Longhorn bull. He belongs to Harold Maxwell."

"Is he a boy cow?"

Beau grinned at her in the mirror. "Yes, Ava. A cow is a girl, and a bull or a steer is a boy."

Ava seemed to consider that for a moment. "What's the difference between a bull and a steer?"

Beau swallowed hard, not sure he wanted to have that conversation with his daughter at that particular moment. "Um, they're both boys." He pointed out the window. "Look! There are some more cows. The black ones are called Black Angus, and the ones with the light color are called Charolais."

She then bombarded him with questions about the different cattle breeds. He explained that they came from different countries. *Yes, a much safer topic of conversation…and a good one for a rancher's daughter.*

Eventually, they arrived in Amarillo, and Beau pulled into the parking area at the hospital. By the time he found a parking spot and wrangled Ava out of her car seat, Dixie was waiting for them at the entrance. She appeared to be slightly anxious. Her arms were crossed over her chest, and her jaw was tight.

Beau held Ava's hand, but he also reached out to Dixie, hoping to comfort her.

Dixie surprised him by sliding out of her tension like shedding a coat. A smile lit up her face as she laced her fingers in his. "How was the trip?"

"Great," Beau said.

"Daddy told me all about cows and bulls and steers," Ava piped up.

Dixie's footsteps faltered. "What?"

"Not that discussion," Beau said. "Just commenting on the livestock we passed."

The hospital entrance doors opened silently, and they stepped inside.

"Do you want us to wait here in the lobby?" Beau asked.

Dixie drew in a deep breath and heaved it out. "I'm not going to hide you from Roger and Scott. They're a part of my life, and you and Ava are a part of my life. I need to have something gel, so you just come right along with me and face the wrath of a slightly bitter, middle-aged gay man…one who has been brainwashed by my mother." She huffed out a sigh. "I don't blame Roger. My mom is very convincing. She kept me under her spell for years."

Beau shrugged. "Sure, but why does he dislike me? I've never done anything to him."

"My mother. She painted you and the entire Garrett clan as heartless beasts who turned your back on me when I was a teen. Roger drank all the Kool-Aid."

"So did you."

"I did, but I'm over it. Now I need to set Roger straight."

Beau smiled. "Isn't he gay?"

Dixie rolled her eyes. "All right, smart ass. I want Roger to know the truth."

Beau slowed. "You don't have to force me on him. I can just be on the sidelines. He's probably concerned about his Scott."

"No!" Her voice took on a sharp tone. "I'm tired of having things hidden. From now on, I'm living my life right out here in the open. People can love me or just run away."

They stopped in front of the elevators, and Ava ran forward to push the button.

Beau pulled Dixie closer and grazed her temple with a kiss. "I'm one of the people who loves you."

The elevator door whished open, and they stepped inside. Dixie selected a floor, and they rode in silence until the door opened again and they stepped out. Beau felt reluctant to make any waves. He thought Dixie had made up her mind, so he lifted Ava into his arms and followed her to the nurses' station. She asked for Scott's room number, and the charge nurse said that Ava could not visit.

Beau felt greatly relieved when the nurse pointed out a waiting area. "Ava and I will just wait for you over there."

Her face wore a one-sided smile that might be considered a smirk. "You're not off the hook, Mister. I'll be back." The latter was said in her best Arnold Schwarzenegger impression.

Beau took Ava to the waiting area and settled into a green plastic upholstered chair with her on his lap.

There was an elderly couple sitting together. They looked tired and stared vacantly at the television. For her part, Ava was staring at the couple.

Beau sorted through the reading material and found a very old issue of *Highlights for Children*. "Let's look at this one, okay?"

Beau found a short story and began reading it to Ava in a low voice. That's how Dixie found them. He looked up when he heard footsteps on the polished floor. Unfortunately, a scowling Roger trailed behind her. He appeared to have downed a bottle of vinegar judging by his expression.

"Ava, your Uncle Roger wanted to say hello." Dixie looked a bit strained but bore a determined smile.

Beau let the magazine slide to the floor and stood with Ava in his arms. "Roger," he said, nodding at the beetle-browed man.

Roger hesitated then nodded as well. "Beauregard." He held out his arms for Ava, who leaned toward him.

Reluctantly, Beau released her, but Ava seemed to genuinely like the man.

With the child in his arms, Roger's demeanor changed, and he actually looked friendly. He strolled toward one of the windows, engaging Ava in conversation.

Dixie closed the distance between them, and Beau slid his arm around her shoulders. He was gratified that she leaned into him and wrapped her arm around his waist.

When Roger turned, his face registered a moment of shock before recovering its cool facade. He crossed the room and stopped in front of them. "I better be getting back." He kissed Ava on her cheek and set her on her feet. "Goodbye, darling. I hope to see you soon." He turned to leave, but Dixie called him back.

"Hang on a minute, Roger. I wanted you to be the first to know that Beau proposed and I accepted. If my mother hadn't lied her head off, it would have happened long ago. But we're together again, and we won't be parted."

Roger took a few steps back toward them but stopped uncertainly.

"I just wanted you to know because you and Scott

have been my dear friends and I love you both. I hope we will continue to be close." She gazed at him steadily, demanding something from him.

Roger drew himself up to his full height. "Well, Scott and I love you too, and Ava is a part of our family. Of course we will always be close." He stood for a moment, looking quite uncomfortable.

Then Dixie moved away from Beau and threw her arms around Roger in an enthusiastic embrace. When they separated, Roger held his hand out to Beau, who clasped it in return. "Congratulations. You're getting the best woman on the planet...and the best girl." His eyes were moist, and he swallowed hard.

Beau shook Roger's hand and gave him a hearty slap on the shoulder. "Don't I know it? Dixie has always been the best, and now I have Ava too. I'm a very lucky man."

Roger went back to his vigil, and Dixie looked up at Beau. "I guess we can go now."

Beau sensed she had leaped over some kind of hurdle, at least in her own mind, because she appeared to be much more relaxed. "Are we going to pick out some paint now?"

"You bet."

Chapter 13

DIXIE FELT CONTENT. SHE WAS STRAPPED INTO THE PASSENGER seat of Beau's truck with Ava behind her. A country song was playing softly on the radio. Beau's mouth was curled up at the corners. She hoped he was feeling content too.

Ava kept up a constant commentary on whatever they passed. She was gripping a wad of paint samples, some of which were actually colors Dixie could agree to. She was hoping for one of the soft pastels and hoping to misplace the neon-orange paint chip.

"I'm going by your very own feed store," Beau announced. "We need food for the bunnies. Bertram and Anastasia are hearty eaters."

"Sure. If I were a good and responsible employer, I would be there every day…like my dad was." Dixie suppressed a shiver as she realized how her father had ended up.

"You've had a lot going on," Beau said.

She liked that he was always defending her, or was he making excuses for her? Either way, it was kind of sweet and very annoying at the same time. "Well, it's good that we're going to the feed store. I'm sure Pete will appreciate us even showing up."

Beau winked at her. "He will." He drove through the town of Langston to the site of Moore's Feed and Seed on the far edge of town. When they arrived, they found Pete sitting behind the cash register looking particularly morose.

She tried to appear cheery, which she knew came across as totally fake. "How are you doing, Pete? Is everything going well around here?" She grinned fatuously.

Pete raised his brows. "I—I don't know. I guess everything's going okay, except for...you know...the girls in the shed. That was not your everyday occurrence." His mouth tightened. "An' then that guy got shot out back..."

Beau leaned over the counter to shake Pete's hand. "It's been a bad time, all right. You just hang in there, Pete."

Dixie edged closer to the counter. "Why don't you and Ava go and pick out the tastiest bunny food while Pete and I talk business?"

Beau gave her a smart-aleck salute, and he and Ava headed for the back room to shop for the rabbits. Dixie sincerely hoped they didn't fall in love with any more cute animals.

She leaned on the counter and gave her employee her full attention. "So, how are you really doing, Pete?"

"I—I guess I'm okay. I don't seem to be able to keep up with everything without Josh. I haven't felt comfortable to even go out to the shed since...you know?" He spoke in a low voice, and he looked frightened.

"How about if you show me where it all happened? Do you think you could do that?"

Pete's mouth twitched. "Well, I guess I could do that. Don't you want to get Beau to come back there with us?"

"I think we'll be all right. It's broad daylight."

"Yes'm, Miz Dixie. Right this way." He took a key off a hook behind him.

Dixie followed behind Pete out to the back, down

a flight of stairs, and back up onto the loading dock. Pete fumbled with the lock and then pulled up a wide overhead door that rattled and shook on its climb up to the high ceiling. There was an ominous silence to the void within.

She saw row after row of bagged feed for animals and various seed for planting. The bags were huge, and she couldn't imagine how one person could lift one, but she supposed that a man as strong as Beau wouldn't have a problem. There was a forklift in the corner to the back, and the high windows allowed the late-afternoon sunlight to brighten the space.

She raised her eyes to the overhead loft. "Is that where the girls were hiding?"

Pete glanced around nervously. He nodded. "They was up there, all right."

"I want to see it. Is that the way up?" She pointed to a metal staircase affixed to the far wall.

Pete's voice reflected terror. "That there's the only way to get up to the loft."

Although Pete's tension was causing her stomach to turn flip-flops, she nodded at him pleasantly. "Okay, I'm going to have a look around." She headed for the stairs, aware that Pete was not following her. She made it halfway up the stairs before glancing back at him, but his panic was apparent. *Okay, I'm on my own.*

When she reached the loft, she felt a little less anxiety. The upper level was filled with large bales of hay and huge bags of feed. There was another garage door–type opening toward the loading dock and a conveyor belt that could be directed to whatever waited below. But the opening was sealed up tight.

She found the place the girls must have been hiding. They could not have been seen if they were seated behind the big rolls of hay lined up in the front row. Smaller rectangular bales were stacked against the far wall, and that was where they had hunkered down. Some of the bales had been rearranged out of their orderly stacks to provide cover, she supposed. Dixie saw something stuffed down on the floor with loose hay pulled over it. When she reached for it, she realized it was a small clutch purse. It was scuffed and of cheap quality, but there was something inside.

Reluctantly, she unzipped the top and saw there was a lipstick and mascara, a small amount of cash, and a cell phone complete with charger. *Well, well, well…this should be interesting*.

She poked around a bit more and then descended the stairs with the purse under her arm.

Pete wasn't exactly pacing. It was more as if he was shifting from foot to foot. *Definitely nervous*. When he spotted Dixie, he froze and his brow cleared, perhaps a little too forcibly.

"Uh, Miz Dixie. Are you ready to get outta here now?" He edged toward the gaping exit to the loading dock.

Dixie strolled toward him, unwilling to let him off the hook. "I think you can level with me, Pete. You know something. What's really going on?"

Pete swallowed hard, his Adam's apple bobbing up and down in his ropey throat. "Well, y'see…" He wrung his hands together. "I mean…"

She put her hand on his shoulder. "It's okay, Pete. I haven't been here much, but I really do want to help."

To her dismay, he broke into tears and collapsed against her shoulder. She was forced to pat his back and say soothing things to the shaken man.

"I'm so afraid," he moaned.

"What are you afraid of?" she asked, although she knew good and darned well he had plenty of reason to be fearful.

He drew back, gazing at her, wide-eyed. "It's everything. Everything that's been happening around here." He swallowed again. "First, that terrible thing that happened to your daddy."

Dixie was careful not to show the pain that statement dealt her. She nodded, accepting that the murder of her father was indeed a terrible thing.

"An'—an' then that poor young feller got shot." Pete's body was racked with a tremor. "An' Josh...he just vamoosed."

"Vamoosed? You mean he disappeared?" Dixie heaved a sigh. "And now you're afraid he was also murdered?"

Pete's eyes opened even wider. He glanced around both ways over his shoulders and then lowered his voice. "No, Miz Dixie. I was thinkin' that he musta been kilt, but then Josh showed up at my place last night. He's scared to death. He saw who shot your friend."

"What?" Dixie's grip on his shoulder suddenly tightened. "Your cousin told you he knows who shot Scott? You have to tell the sheriff. Let's call him right now." She took a few steps toward the loading dock, but Pete pulled away.

"No! I swore to Josh that I wouldn't tell no one. He's on the run, and he don't want to get kilt too."

He ducked his chin. "An' now I've gone and run my mouth off to you."

Dixie whirled around to face him. "You can't withhold information like that. It's too important. If Josh was the only witness, he has to come forward." She folded her arms across her chest and tilted her head to one side, a position that always conveyed to her daughter that she meant business.

Pete backed up, raising his hands in supplication. "Now, Miz Dixie, I can't do that. Josh is my kin, and you can't expect me to turn on my own kin."

They stared at each other for what seemed like an eon.

Finally, she fisted her hands on her hips and tried another approach. "Do you think Josh would talk to me?"

Pete pursed his lips. "I dunno. I can ask him if he shows back up. I give 'im some money, so I don't think he's a-comin' right back."

"Fair enough," she said. "If he comes back, please tell him I can give him money if he'll talk to me. I need to know what happened to my friend." *And my father*.

Beau had taken it upon himself to make sure all the caged animals were fed and their cages cleaned. It appeared that Pete was falling behind now that he was by himself.

Ava was keeping a half dozen baby ducks entertained while Beau arranged fresh paper in the bottom of their crate. He had washed and refilled their water and food containers.

When he glanced up, Dixie was staring at him. She looked upset but seemed to be holding it together. "Hi, baby. Did you get done with…whatever it was you wanted to do?"

"I—I guess." She glanced back at Pete, who had settled himself behind the cash register again. "Are you about done here?"

"I thought I would make sure the critters had food and water and a clean place to live. I don't think Pete has had time to do it all."

A smile broke through. "That's sweet, Beau. You were always the responsible one."

He gave out a hearty laugh. "Have you met my father?"

"Oh, yeah."

"Look at the duckies, Mommy," Ava said. "They like me. Can't we take them home?"

Dixie shot Beau a grimace that clearly said *No, we do not take ducks home*.

Beau responded by gently picking up two of the ducklings and placing them back in their clean quarters. "I think these ducks are already taken. Pete is just keeping them for someone."

Ava looked disappointed but graciously surrendered the ducklings. "I really like this one." She handed over the last one but gave it a kiss on the head first.

Beau secured the enclosure and got to his feet. "Let me wash up, and we can get on the road. I'm anxious to know which paint color you choose for your room."

Ava's face lit up. "Green. I like the green."

Beau cleaned up and came to meet Dixie and Ava at the front of the store. He noted that Pete appeared to be more depressed than he had been previously. He wondered if Dixie had anything to do with that.

When they got in the truck, she said, "I need to stop

by the sheriff's office before we go home. I—I found this little purse up in the loft where those young women were hiding. There's a phone in it."

Beau's jaw tightened. "Why were you looking around up there?"

"I told you. I'm going to find out who murdered my father. I'm sure there are clues in this phone."

Beau started the truck and drove to the sheriff's office. "You stay here with Ava. I'll run this in to the sheriff." He swung out of the cab with the purse before Dixie could react.

He strode through the doors and looked around. "Where is the sheriff?"

A deputy sat behind a desk, typing on a keyboard. He didn't look up. "In his office."

"Tell him I'm here…Beau Garrett."

The deputy glanced up without any particular interest. He picked up the phone and, after a brief conversation, told Beau to go on back.

He found the sheriff behind his desk with his booted feet up on his desk. "C'mon in, Beau. Take a load off." He gestured to the chairs across from his desk.

Beau seated himself and tossed the purse on the cluttered desk. "I've got Dixie and our daughter waiting out in the truck, Sheriff, but we thought you should take a look at this."

The sheriff took his feet down and leaned forward. "What's this?"

"Dixie was poking around up in the loft where those girls were hunkered down, and she found this. Must have belonged to one of them. There's a cheap cell phone in there. It might have some info you can use."

The sheriff slipped the cell out of the clutch. "How does this one work?"

Beau took it from him and turned it on. He scrolled over to the contacts but only found one. "This guy. He must be the one who left them there. Maybe he shot the guy."

The sheriff made a note of the number.

"Why don't we see if there are any texts?" Beau scrolled down the list. "Here's a whole script of their conversations. Some of the words are in Spanish, but you might be able to catch up with him through these."

The sheriff jumped to his feet. "Whooee. You betcha! Hey, Gene. Come on in here."

In a short time, the man who had been at the desk came shuffling into the office. "Whatcha' got, Chief?"

"Beau here brought a phone from the place those girls were found. I wan'chu ta write down all the chats that are on here an' git the phone numbers. I want it all." He handed the cell to the deputy, who shuffled off again.

Beau rose as if to leave. "Speaking of the girls, how are the two younger ones? Are they still locked up?"

"Nah. Some social worker out of Amarillo came an' took 'em off. Said she would try to git 'em back to their parents." He sorted around in his desk drawer and came up with a business card. "Lorene Dyer, LSW, whatever that means."

"Let me jot down her number. I'm sure my dad would want to make sure they're okay."

The sheriff flipped the card across the desk at him. "Take it."

Beau took his leave and returned to the truck.

Dixie leaned forward to put her finger to her lips. "What happened?" she whispered.

He glanced back at Ava, who appeared to be dropping off to sleep. "The sheriff is going to follow up on the texts in the phone."

She leaned back, appearing disappointed.

He started the truck and shifted into gear. "There was only one contact. That's probably the guy."

"Ooh, that's great. How can we find him?"

"We don't. The authorities will handle it." He gave her a stern look he hoped would squelch her enthusiasm.

———

Beau took Dixie and Ava to the Moore ranch, leaving them to determine which colors to paint the bedrooms. He returned to the Garrett ranch only to receive his father's merciless teasing.

Big Jim gaped at him, open-mouthed. "Look who it is, Colt. That's one of your little brothers…can't recall which one."

"Very funny, Dad. I just needed to do some things with Dixie and Ava." He removed his Stetson and tossed it on the rack near the front door.

"I figured," Big Jim said. "How is my little granddaughter doing? You should bring her over here more."

"Well, I needed to be over there. The good news is that we got paint samples today. I'm going to be helping paint Ava's room. It was Dixie's room when she was a girl."

Big Jim and Colton exchanged a glance.

"That sounds promising," Colt said.

"It sure does sound like little Miss Dixie is planning

on sticking around for a while." Big Jim slapped Beau on the shoulder.

"That's my plan." Beau frowned. "But you know how stubborn she has always been. Now she's decided that she's going to solve her father's murder."

Big Jim made a scoffing sound. "Well, that's just crazy. Tell her to let the sheriff do his job."

"I tried, Dad, but today we went to the feed store, and she got Pete to take her up to the loft where those girls were being held." He shook his head. "She poked around up there and found a purse…a little one with a cell phone in it. I took it to the sheriff, and there was just one contact. Some man. He must be the one who brought those girls, and there were a lot of texts between him and the older girl, Valentina."

Big Jim looked surprised, his blue eyes opening wide. "That sounds promising. Surely even our old duffer of a sheriff can follow up on a solid clue like that."

"You'd think." Beau shook his head, not trusting that their sheriff would follow through. "I just want this to all be over so we can get on with our lives."

Big Jim put his arm around Beau's shoulder and walked toward the stables. "Do you think Dixie is going to stay? Are you going to be able to hog-tie that little filly?"

Beau stopped beside a corral and leaned against the wood rail. "Something happened, Dad. Dixie said she found some letters her father wrote to her in Dallas and her mother refused. She's been reading his letters, and it's clear that her mom lied to her about her father disowning her." He raked his fingers through his thick hair. "She's furious with her mother and feeling guilty for believing that her dad would throw her out. I think that's part of her drive to find Vern's killer."

Big Jim leaned both forearms on the railing. "I don't blame her for being mad, but she's just a girl—a young woman and a mother. She owes it to Ava, and to you, to stay alive."

"I—uh, I asked her to marry me, and she said yes."

Big Jim's whole countenance morphed from concern to joy. "Well, how about that? That's the best news I've heard in a long time." His grin widened. "I'll have all three of my sons married and settled…with children."

"I hope I can get her down the aisle. You know Dixie."

Big Jim's bushy eyebrows waggled up and down. "Indeed I do. Crazy as a fruit fly half the time."

Beau had to smile at that. "Yeah, but I love her. She's the one."

Big Jim smacked the heel of his hand against the railing. "She always has been."

Dixie spread the paint chips out on the bed in the room that was now Ava's. "What do you think?" Somehow, she had managed to misplace the neon-orange and lime-green paint samples.

"I like the purple," Ava said. Unfortunately she pointed to the darkest value on the spectrum.

"Hmm… Well, maybe we can lighten it up a little. How about this one?" She moved Ava's finger to the lightest lilac at the other end of the strip of paper.

Ava's brow furrowed, and her lower lip jutted out.

"Or how about this nice pale pink? That's pretty too."

"I want the purple."

"How about we let Daddy help us decide? He's the one who is going to be helping me with the painting."

Ava considered this for a moment and then nodded her head once. Probably certain that she could twist him around her little finger.

Dixie brought Ava to the kitchen and set about figuring what to prepare for dinner. Suddenly, the house felt very empty. After her discovery at the feed store, she was more than a little anxious. There had been something strange going on at the store for some time. Something that had gotten her father killed and her friend shot.

She tried to shake off the uneasy feeling and concentrate on foraging for food for her daughter. All the doors were locked up tight, and she had one of her dad's handguns nearby but safely out of Ava's reach.

The window coverings had been closed up as soon as they got home, so the house was even gloomier.

She kept glancing over her shoulder anyway. Finally she decided to make mac and cheese from a box, with wieners and canned peas on the side.

Dixie grimaced as she dished the food onto two plates and set one in front of her daughter. Ava seemed to think this meal was acceptable and reached for one of the wieners, grasping it in one hand while taking a big bite.

"Glad you like it," Dixie said as she poured milk into Ava's glass. "Here you go." She turned to replace the milk in the refrigerator, and her breath caught in her throat. *There! No, it's gone*.

She turned on the outside light, spilling light onto the backyard. *Nothing*.

She stood for a minute staring out the kitchen window, where she was certain she had seen a face peering at her. Her heart throbbed rhythmically in her ears, loud as thunder. She thought perhaps it was shaking her body, so she gripped the edge of the countertop for support.

Okay, I'm imagining things. Get a grip.

Most of all, she didn't want to frighten her daughter. She needn't have worried because Ava was happily munching her wiener. "Don't forget to eat your macaroni."

"I'm eating," Ava sang out.

Dixie jumped when she heard a loud knocking on the front door. "Stay right there," she ordered Ava as she surreptitiously retrieved the handgun and covered it with a dish towel.

Dixie crept to the front door and jumped again when the knocking began again.

"C'mon, Dixie. Open up."

Relief washed through her as she recognized Beau's voice. She tucked the dish towel–wrapped handgun under her armpit and managed to get both locks unlatched and the door opened.

Beau's grin faded when he saw her face. "Baby, what's wrong?" He strode through the door and reached for her, but she backed away, reaching for the weapon under her arm.

"Wait! Let me put this away." She showed him the gun and went to replace it among her father's arms collection. When she returned, Beau had closed and locked the front door and met her as she came down the hallway.

"Armed and dangerous? What's got you scared?"

She swallowed hard. "Oh, Beau. I'm afraid, and I don't like being afraid."

He opened his arms and folded her in an embrace.

"I—I thought I saw someone looking in the window… but when I turned on the light outside, there was no one there."

"Want me to check around outside?"

She shook her head. "No. I've been pretty antsy since we got back from the feed store. I just let things get to me."

He placed a kiss on top of her head, drawing her closer.

She tucked in tight, clinging to him in return. He felt so strong, so invincible. Surely nothing bad could happen when she was in Beau's arms. Surely he would protect her and their daughter. "Are—are you going to stay tonight?"

He drew back to gaze into her eyes. "I'm going to stay. I'm kind of addicted to you."

"Good. I guess I got spooked going into the loft and finding the purse. It made it all so real." A shiver coiled around her spine. "I really need you tonight."

He let out a low-pitched chuckle. "That sounds good."

"Mmm—have you eaten? I have a really pitiful excuse for an evening meal. Ava seems to like it."

"Sounds great." He followed her into the kitchen, where he was greeted by a delighted, wiener-waggling Ava.

"Daddy, I want purple."

Beau kissed her on the forehead and took a seat beside her. "Purple is a nice color."

Dixie spooned macaroni and cheese onto a plate and added peas and wieners. When she placed the plate before him, he grinned.

"I can't believe it. My mother used to serve me a

meal just like this when I was Ava's age." He scooped up a bite and put it in his mouth, chewing blissfully. "Good times."

Chapter 14

DIXIE AWOKE WITH A START. SHE WAS ALONE AND NAKED in the guest room bed. She distinctly recalled falling asleep mashed up against a very powerful chest, wrapped in extremely muscular arms. The fear that had been strangling her since her visit to the loft had evaporated. She'd slept without dreaming, comfortable in the knowledge that Beau would protect her and Ava.

An aching void of abandonment yawned in her chest. No, Beau hadn't abandoned her. She had abandoned him…and her father. She had been gullible enough to believe her mother's lies and had hurt two people she loved very much…people who loved her.

Dixie curled into the fetal position, wrapping her arms around the pillow that had cradled Beau's head. She inhaled the scent of him, somehow drawing power from his essence.

Straightening her limbs, she rolled onto her back and stretched out in all directions, trying to take up as much of the queen-size bed as possible.

The sun was up, so she might as well be too. *A new day. Wonder how I can screw this one up?*

Dixie put her feet on the ancient area rug, its pattern of flowers dull and worn. The clothes she had worn the previous day were strewn around the room, landing wherever Beau had tossed them.

A wry smile settled on her face as she recalled their

previous night's lovemaking. *Yes, the man does know how to haul the mail.*

She slipped into the clothes she had worn before, realizing her bag and the rest of her wardrobe was still in the room that was now officially Ava's...the room that might soon be purple.

When she had dressed and finger-combed her hair, she ventured out into the hallway. A delicious aroma beckoned her to the kitchen. There she found her man slaving over a hot stove. Well, it was more that she found her hot man-slave working in front of the old gas range.

"Mornin'," he called out pleasantly. "You were sleeping so pretty, I didn't want to disturb you."

She closed the distance between them and was rewarded with a kiss that tasted like bacon. "Mmm... been sampling the wares?"

"Perks of the job," he said. "Now, if you'll go awaken our baby girl, I'll scramble up some eggs."

"Deal!" She went to Ava's room and silently opened the door.

Ava was curled on one side, her arm thrown around her toy giraffe. Her innocent expression caused a warm sensation in Dixie's heart. She tiptoed across the floor to sit on the edge of the bed. Ava's big blue eyes opened, and she stretched.

"Good morning, precious. Daddy's making your breakfast, so I'll help you get dressed."

Ava was slow to start in the morning, but she willingly slid out from under the covers and stood blinking sleepily.

Dixie gathered some clothing and held Ava's hand

to lead her into the bathroom for a hand and face wash, a quick brushing of teeth, and a finger sweep through the mop of red curls. "Now you're ready. I hope you're hungry because Daddy's been working so hard."

When they made their appearance in the kitchen, Beau had plated up their breakfasts and was pouring juice into glasses. "There are my beautiful females. Come sit down and gear up for the day."

He pulled out a chair for each of them and sat himself down with a wide grin on his face.

Dixie sipped her juice. "Do you always get up so early?"

"Indeed I do. The day starts pretty early on a working ranch. We have chores to do."

That announcement hit Dixie like a cold slap. The last thing she wanted to do was ranch chores, the tasks she had frequently experienced with her dad. But, she reasoned, there were things that needed doing. Maybe she could figure out how to hire them done.

Ava picked up a slice of bacon with her fingers and munched it gleefully. "I'll help you, Daddy!" she crowed.

"Atta girl! I knew I could count on you." He gave her a high five then swung his attention to Dixie.

She huffed out a sigh. "Oh, all right. I'll help. I presume this includes mucking out horse stalls."

He was grinning now. "Of course. You'll have a great time."

"Mmmpf," she muttered. "My favorite task."

Big Jim Garrett's fierce brows were drawn together as he gazed around the breakfast table. His oldest and middle sons were gathered with their respective families, but where was the youngest? He felt a muscle near his mouth twitch.

He had no doubt where his errant son was holed up. Beau had always been crazy nuts about that little red-headed girl, and now he had two of them to be demented over. Big Jim huffed out a snort. *Can't blame him. That little Ava is a heartbreaker*.

He cleared his brow, seeing that several of his family members were staring at him with an obvious question about his temperament. He forced a brief smile and reached for his mug of coffee.

"Um, what's on your list for us today, Dad?" Colton pressed the question, but the entire adult assemblage seemed to hold their breath.

Big Jim took another sip of coffee and then carefully set his cup down. "Nothing in particular. Just the regular chores. I thought you boys might ride with me over to check on that herd of Charolais in the east place."

"Sure, Dad." Ty nodded but exchanged a glance with Colt. "We can get right on our chores and then ride out. I think we could use a little time in the saddle."

Big Jim slathered more butter on his biscuit and then dipped it in egg yolk before stuffing it in his mouth. "You know, Leah, your biscuits are the best I've ever tasted. We should get you entered in the county fair. You could knock the socks off that county extension agent."

Leah laughed, and Misty covered her mouth with both hands.

"What are you girls giggling about?"

"Well, these biscuits were made by the very capable Misty Garrett."

Misty's face had turned bright red, but Colt hooked

an arm around her neck and planted a kiss on her temple. "Good job, honey."

Misty recovered a bit. "Leah has been teaching me. I want to be able to feed my little family when we build our own place."

"We'll be fine," Colt said.

"Speaking of which, how is your dream house coming along, Tyler?"

Ty wiped his mouth on his napkin and half turned to face his dad. "The construction is pretty much complete. Just a few cosmetic things. Leah just picked out her kitchen countertops and cabinets last week."

"You got appliances and furniture?" Big Jim asked.

Ty shrugged. "Well, no, but—"

"I want you two to go into Amarillo this weekend and pick out your appliances and some furniture on me. Consider it a late wedding present."

Ty and Leah looked at each other in surprise.

"But, Big Jim, you gave us a plenty big wedding present when we got married." Leah was wide-eyed.

"Well, you can consider this an early baby present. Now don't argue with me about this. My mind is made up." Big Jim mopped up his plate with the rest of his biscuit.

The family continued with their normal activities. Misty got ready for work and loaded Mark and Gracie into her vehicle to drop them off at school in town. When she and the children were gone, Ty and Colt quickly cleared the table and loaded the dishwasher. Leah protested that she could do it, but Ty gave Leah a kiss and told her to rest.

"You're treating me like I'm sick," she protested. "I'm just having a baby."

"You're having my baby, and that gives me the right to baby you." Ty shooed her off to watch television in the den, while he prepared to join his father and brother, who waited near the front door. They both had their hats on and were halfway out the door.

Ty reached for his hat, and once outside, he carefully locked the front door with his key.

Big Jim saw this and frowned. "What's going on, Son?"

Ty frowned right back. "With all the crazy stuff happening in town, I don't want to leave her alone with the door unlocked." A muscle in his jaw twitched. "Just too much evil in the world today."

Indeed there had been chores. The stables smelled just as inviting as she recalled from her girlhood. But Beau had pitched in and done most of the heavy lifting, shoveling manure out of the stalls and leaving her to spread fresh hay on the stable floors.

Ava seemed to be entranced as she observed her parents' efforts from her perch atop the railing of one of the stalls.

"I want to get down, Mommy," she called. "I want to pet the horsies."

"You can take a ride with me as soon as we get the horse stalls cleaned up." Beau winked at her. "We have to clean their house for them."

"Why?" Ava persisted.

Dixie caught Beau's eye. "Because they can't do it for themselves. Like your bunnies. They can't clean their own house, so Daddy has to shovel it out."

Beau shook his head. "Thanks."

"That's the reason parents don't always say yes." She smiled pleasantly.

He huffed out a sigh. "Message received." He turned to give her the full effect of his blue laser eyes. "I'm pretty sure Anastasia is P-R-E-G-N-A-N-T." He spelled it out in a whisper, which amused Dixie.

"It's okay," she said in a loud whisper. "She can't spell that word."

His brows drew together. "Can she spell M-U-R-D-E-R?"

Dixie drew up straight. "No. Of course not."

"Well, we need to talk about what happened to your dad…and your friend." He glanced at Ava, but she seemed to be ignoring them, singing in a low voice and brushing two curry brushes across each other, making a rhythmic accompaniment.

Dixie pressed her lips together, dreading what he had to say.

He stepped closer, his voice low. "I happen to love you, in spite of that thick concrete skull of yours."

"And I love you, in spite of your overbearing alpha-male caveman brain."

He nodded. "Agreed. But I do not want you to even think you can go nosing around these—these crimes. It's too dangerous, and I forbid you to go into the feed store again."

Dixie made a scoffing noise in the back of her throat and fisted her hands on her hips. "I beg your pardon. I do not think you are in a position to forbid me to do anything, Beau Garrett. I do not need your permission to do anything."

He took a breath and seemed to be choosing his

words before speaking. He leaned closer and spoke in a low tone. "Maybe not, but if you love me and you love Ava, you won't put yourself in harm's way." He stroked the back of his hand over her cheek. "I can't lose you twice."

Dixie couldn't look away.

Beau held her pinned in place with the power of his intense gaze. To be fair, his expression was kind and his words loving...but he was drawing a line.

"I—I want to find out who murdered my father," she whispered. "I have to know."

Silence.

"How would you feel if someone killed Big Jim? I know you wouldn't be sitting on the fence." Dixie held his gaze, though she could feel her color rising.

"I'm not going to play games about 'what ifs.' Big Jim is not the issue." A muscle near his mouth twitched. "The real issue is that you hurt your father by believing that he would turn his back on you. He was devastated. We both were. I was just a kid, but I knew he was hurting as much as I was."

Dixie felt a stab of pain, as though he had struck her. Tears sprang to her eyes and rolled down her cheeks, unchecked. "How could you be so cruel?"

"Baby, I'm not trying to hurt you, but I just don't believe you're thinking right about this thing with your dad." He pulled her against him. "You've got to step back and let the sheriff do his thing. You don't have to find your father's killer to atone for hurting him."

Dixie buried her face against Beau's T-shirt, damp with his sweat but it smelled like love and protection to her. She knew he was right. How could he see everything so clearly? How could he know how guilty she felt for having believed her mother's lies?

He stroked her hair and kissed the top of her head.

"Beau?" Her voice sounded wimpy, even to her own ears. She cleared her throat. "Thank you…for loving me, no matter how hard my head may be."

He rocked her back and forth in his arms. "Don't worry about anything, Dixie. We'll find out who's responsible for the trouble at the feed store. I just want you to stay away until this is resolved."

"But my daddy's will says I have to take over the management of the store and the ranch in order to inherit. If I don't, Big Jim gets everything."

Beau made a scoffing noise deep in his throat. "You don't actually think my dad wants your ranch or the store, do you?"

She reflected for a moment. "I don't know. He might want the land."

Beau rolled his eyes. "He does not want your land. My dad wants only the best for you. You're Ava's mom, and he adores his grandchild."

Yes, she reasoned. That was true. She knew that Big Jim was wrapped around Ava's little finger. Maybe Beau was right. She pushed away from him. "No, I have to go work at the store. It's in the will. Breckenridge Ryan says I have to take part in the management. I have to learn."

"How about if I'm your proxy? I know poor old Pete is just overwhelmed there all by himself, and you're not able to help with the actual heavy lifting."

She let out a petulant little snort. "And just what am I supposed to do?"

"You can count the money." He grinned. "I know you like that."

"Are we done in here?" Ava asked.

"Um, yeah." Beau stepped away from Dixie. "Just going to take this out to the compost pile." He wheeled the wheelbarrow of horse dung out of the stables.

"Mommy," Ava asked. "Why do we have a compost pile?"

Dixie regarded her small doppelganger with a serious expression. "Beats the heck outta me."

Chapter 15

BEAU WASHED UP AT THE FAUCET BESIDE THE BARN, AND when he returned to the stable, he found that Dixie had already selected the mare she would ride and had saddled her.

He was a little disappointed that he hadn't been able to take care of his woman but also proud of her independence. Ava was watching her mother and he reasoned that this independent spirit was imprinting on her little psyche.

Good role model.

"You ready?" Beau gave her a sideways glance as he selected a roan gelding for his ride. He slipped the reins onto the horse's head and arranged the bit in his mouth.

"We decided to get a head start. The day is getting away from us. Ava wants to take a ride."

He let out a playful snort. "And you didn't saddle a horse for me?"

"Sorry. You'll have to saddle your own horse, cowboy. You've got more muscles than I do." She gave him a wink. "But I'll bet cleaning out the stables gave you a workout."

He cocked his head to one side. "Nah, I'm tough. I do a lot more work than this everyday." He held out his arms to her.

She slid into his embrace, offering up her soft lips for his kisses. "You're right. I'm sorry. I didn't think." She pushed away a bit. "I've just been alone for so long, I've forgotten what it means to be a part of something bigger than just me—and Ava, of course." She waved a hand to where Ava sat, making her own kind of music.

"Of course." He spread a colorful blanket across the gelding's back. "But now you have me to deal with. I'm in love with both of you, and I want us to take care of each other."

She let out a giggle. "Seriously? You don't appear to need anyone to take care of you."

Silence.

He couldn't speak. It wasn't as though he could explain his need. He couldn't put it into words. His pain over having her disappear from his life and the fear that she could do so again. He tried to appear confident, but Dixie Lee Moore was his Achilles' heel. His vulnerability.

He lifted a saddle off the rack and slid it onto the gelding's back. "Let's take our daughter for a ride, shall we?" His voice was distinctly husky, and he turned away to cinch the saddle under the horse's belly. When he turned back to face Dixie, she was gazing at him with a questioning expression.

Beau heaved himself up into the saddle and then leaned down to lift Ava onto the saddle in front of him. He turned to Dixie and gave her a wink. "Are you coming, Miss Independence?"

Beau thought Dixie enjoyed their ride. He kept Ava on his horse, thus allowing Dixie to ride with more abandon. Seeing her so happy gave him great pleasure.

Ava seemed to be quite blissful as well, sitting in

front of him with a tenuous grip on his wrist. She commented on everything they encountered and appeared to be confident in the saddle...at least in her daddy's saddle.

After a pleasant ride around the property, Beau was able to convince Dixie to stay home while he checked on things at the feed store. "I won't be long unless Pete needs a hand with something. You know he can't lift anything heavy."

She nodded. "I appreciate it, Beau. I'm really not up for sad Pete today."

He gave her a kiss. "Just chill, and I'll be back in a while." He turned to leave, grabbing his Stetson as he headed for the door.

"Come home soon," she called after him.

Home? Beau climbed in his truck and drove away, wondering where his home would be. He'd always thought he would spend his life on the Garrett ranch, but perhaps Dixie had other ideas.

When he arrived at the feed store, he found Pete in the same place he'd left him. He was sitting on a stool behind the cash register, looking haunted and glum.

Beau thought Pete must have dropped some weight because his skin seemed to be hanging on his face and his pallor was ashier than it had been. "Hey, Pete. What's going on today?"

Pete seemed to focus and shook his head. "Not much. I got a couple of orders for pickup, but I ain't got no idea where Josh had stuff stored out there." He heaved a deep sigh. "I guess I'm a little scared to go out there, truth be told."

Beau frowned and fisted his hands on his hips.

"Can't say that I blame you. Maybe we can figure it out together."

Pete nodded, seemingly relieved. "That'll be good, Mr. Beau. I can use a little help for sure." He shook his head and squeezed his eyes shut. "I'm so worried about Josh, I don't know what to do. He's my little cousin, y'know?"

Beau visualized the beefy Josh, who towered over Pete but was the "little" cousin. "I know. Maybe he's all right."

Pete nodded vigorously. "He was, the last time I saw him, but he sure is hurtin' for cash. I'm supposed to ask Miz Dixie for his last pay."

Beau tried to keep his expression neutral, though he felt like grabbing Pete and shaking some sense into him. "You've been in touch with Josh?"

Pete began blinking rapidly. He looked from side to side, though the two men were alone in the store. "Um, well…yes. He come by my place. He's scared to death." He swallowed hard, his Adam's apple bobbing up and down. "I'm scared too." He looked as though he might break down in tears at any moment.

Beau placed his hand on Pete's shoulder. "It's okay, Pete. I understand. I'm here to help." The look of gratitude he received in return made Beau realize how totally terrified Pete must be. "I'm sorry we've kind of ignored you, Pete. I've been keeping my eye on Dixie and—and our daughter. I have to keep them safe too."

Pete nodded, his forehead beaded with sweat. "That's what you gotta do."

"But Pete…I'm going to either be here to help you or hire someone to work along with you. I don't want you to be here by yourself."

"Oh, Mr. Garrett. That's a load off my mind." He mopped his brow with his sleeve. "Lordy! I been so scared, but I didn't want to let Lil' Miz Dixie down."

"No problem. Let's get those orders ready to go. You show me where the items are and how many. I'll get them out on the loading dock for easy pickup."

Pete gave a tremulous smile and a thumbs-up. Together they worked on filling the orders and arranging the items on the loading dock in two areas. Pete then called the customers to let them know they could come pick up their orders.

"I don't know about you, Pete, but I could eat a buffalo, hooves and all." Beau put his shirt back on over his tee. "I'm going to get us some food from the diner. Are you going to be okay here by yourself for a little while?"

Although Pete was clearly not okay, he nodded in agreement. "Good man. You hold down the fort, and I'll be right back." Beau ducked out and drove his truck straight to the sheriff's office. He called in an order to be picked up at the diner before loping inside and asking to see the sheriff.

"He's gone home for lunch," one of his deputies said. "Can I help you?" He gazed at Beau questioningly.

"Um, maybe. I just need to leave a message for the sheriff. I'm Beau Garrett, and my—uh—my fiancée is Dixie Moore."

The deputy nodded. "I know who you are. You're Colton's little brother."

Beau bit his tongue, knowing he would wear this dubious title his entire life. "Yeah, that's me...the little brother." This was somewhat ironic since Beau towered over the deputy.

The deputy must have realized the humor of the situation. He gave a wry smile and shook his head. "I'm Fletcher Shelton. I went to school with Colt." He extended his hand and gave Beau's a hearty shake. "Call me Fletch. Is there anything I can do for you, or do you want to wait for the sheriff to come back?" He shrugged. "The sheriff has been known to take some long lunch hours."

Beau considered this. He needed to grab lunch and return to the feed store before Pete imploded.

Fletch gestured to a chair across from his desk. "Take a load off. I didn't say this, but the sheriff has also been known to take a nap after lunch—for a couple of hours."

Beau sat down heavily. "It's about the troubles at the feed store. I need to report a new development."

The deputy took out a legal pad and noted the date and time. "Go ahead. I'm working on the feed store shootings."

"Are you looking for Josh Miller?"

"Oh, hell yeah. We don't know if he's layin' dead somewhere, rotting away." He smacked his hand on the desk in front of him. "Trust me. We are very actively searching for one Josh Miller."

At Fletch's nod, Beau made the decision to tell what he had been told. "Pete, the man who works at the feed store, is Josh's cousin. He told me that Josh has come to him for money. He says that Josh is terrified of whoever shot the guy behind the shed, and he's hiding out." Beau paused and pressed his lips together. Something just didn't make sense about this story. "I figured that if you could question Josh, you could find

out what he saw. You know, get a description of whoever did the shooting?"

Fletch was making rapid notes. "I'll go right over and
question Pete."

Beau threw up his hands in a cautionary gesture. "No.
That's not going to work. Pete told me this in confidence. He's so scared he can hardly function. I thought
you might be able to watch his place and when Josh
contacts him, you could grab him, not Pete."

Fletch frowned, his brows almost meeting in the
center of his face.

"Pete is about to have a stroke as it is. I can't let you
spook him." Beau arranged his features to appear as fear-
some as Fletch. "If you bring Pete in, you'll never get Josh."

"I guess you're right. But how do you think we can
get Josh if he's hiding out?"

"I can give Pete some cash to give to Josh, so that
might draw him out."

Fletch smacked his open palm on the desk again.
"Great idea. We'll have to watch Pete to see when Josh
makes contact."

"I'll hit the ATM and grab some cash. Pete is waiting
for me to pick up lunch, so I better be on my way." Beau
stood and reached out for another handshake.

Fletch stood and grasped Beau's hand firmly. "Say,
are you working at the feed store now?"

"I'm just helping out. I really don't want Dixie to be
there. She's determined to find out who killed her father,
and it's pretty obvious the two crimes are connected.
I told Pete I would try to hire someone to take Josh's
place. You know, so Pete won't be so scared and to take
over the shed."

Fletch squinted and tilted his head to one side. "Interesting."

When Beau arrived back at the feed store, Pete was standing near the front door, as though anxious for his return.

"I was a-thinkin' that maybe you got lost."

"No, man. I got us some of those pulled pork sandwiches from Tiny's Diner. And Crystal said you really liked their potato salad, so I got some of that too." Beau set the bag on the counter and began dividing up the food. "Woo-hoo! A big pickle on the side."

Pete's distress seemed to evaporate when he saw the food. "That does look mighty tasty." He sat down on the stool behind the counter and reached for a napkin.

Beau unwrapped his sandwich but remained on his feet. "By the way, I did stop and get some cash for Josh. Poor guy. He must be really worried."

A wave of relief washed across Pete's face. "That's awful nice, Mr. Garrett. I know Josh will appreciate it." He took the lid off his container of potato salad and eyed the contents appreciatively. "Best potato salad around."

"I agree." He chewed a few bites of the meaty sandwich and then reached for a napkin. "By the way, will you be able to get in touch with Josh to let him know you have some cash for him?"

"I—I got his cell phone number right here...somewhere." Pete patted his shirt pocket absently but then spooned some potato salad into his mouth with an expression that reflected pure bliss.

"Um—maybe you ought to save that phone number to your cell, Pete. It would be terrible if you lost it."

Pete swallowed his bite and paused, the spoon halfway to his mouth. "I don't have me one of them cellular phones. I'm either at home or here at the store, so I just use the landlines if I need to make a call... Heck! I don't actually call very many people."

Beau let that sink in and finished his meal. He was just discarding the remnants when the little bell over the front door clanked against the glass and Deputy Fletcher Shelton strolled in. He had shed his uniform and wore cowboy boots, Wranglers, a western belt, and a white T-shirt.

"I heard you might be looking to hire some help? I'm strong and willing to learn." Fletch flexed his muscles while wearing a wide grin.

"That's right," Beau said. "I think you might do just fine."

Pete stroked his chin. "Say, don't I know you? You look mighty familiar."

Without missing a beat, Fletch stepped closer. "I'm Herb and Ellen Shelton's oldest son, Fletcher. I've lived here all my life."

Pete grinned back, nodding his head. "Local boy."

Beau gestured toward the back of the store. "Let me show you the shed out back. That's mostly where we need help."

When he had escorted Fletch to the shed's loading dock, he slid open the door and closed it behind them. "What's going on?"

Fletch looked particularly pleased with himself. "I called the sheriff, and he said I could go undercover... so here I am. I figured if I was here I might be able to keep an eye on things and maybe contact Josh." He looked particularly proud of himself. "It's my first time undercover."

Beau related that Pete would be contacting Josh by phone from either the store or his home phone, and Fletch assured him that he had things under control. The two walked back inside, and Beau left Fletch with Pete for training.

Beau exited the store, feeling both relieved and anxious. He hoped that Fletch would be able to take Josh in peacefully. Josh was kind of an ass, and if he was running scared, he might be more so. The muscle-bound oaf had dropped out of high school, but Beau thought he had to know something about the criminal acts that had been carried out at the feed store. Definitely, Josh was a part of the human trafficking that involved the three young girls discovered hiding in the loft. But what did he know about the death of Vern Moore and the shooting of Dixie's friend Scott?

Big Jim was surprised when the sheriff called him. He retrieved his phone from his shirt pocket, listening to the man on the other end. He heard an overview of the feed store situation. Somehow, he doubted that the sheriff had come up with this idea all on his own, and he planned to cross-examine his youngest son to find out the real story.

"How about the two young girls?" Big Jim asked. "Did they get home to their parents okay?"

There was a silence that drew out way too long on the other end of the line.

"Well, not exactly…"

Big Jim got a sick feeling in his stomach. "What the hell does that mean?"

"Um—well…them two little girls went to Amarillo with that social worker lady. She was able to get in touch with their parents, but they can't afford to pay for the bus tickets to get the girls back to wherever they live in Mexico."

Big Jim felt his jaw tighten. "Well, where in the hell are those two girls staying?"

The sheriff cleared his throat. "I believe the social worker has them staying in some kind of juvenile center."

Big Jim exploded. "With a bunch of delinquents? How can that be right?"

The sheriff dithered a bit. "I believe there are some children who have been removed from their homes for some reason…runaways…petty theft…drugs."

"Gimme the name and number of that social worker lady. I'm gonna give her a piece of my mind."

The sheriff gave him the information, but his voice sounded anxious. "Now, be careful, Big Jim. We don't want to make any waves."

"Waves!" Big Jim's voice took on a belligerent attitude all its own. "Now see here, Sheriff. I plan to go full-fledged tsunami on her ass." He disconnected abruptly.

"Big Jim, are you all right?" It was his daughter-in-law Leah. "I could hear you all the way in the dining room."

Big Jim expelled a deep breath. Gentle Leah was the last person he wanted to unload on. "Oh, just got a call from our glorious sheriff. He told me that those sweet little girls who got kidnapped are now staying with a bunch of damned juvenile delinquents in Amarillo because their parents can't afford to transport 'em."

He blew out another lungful of air as he tried to get his temper under control.

Leah's big blue eyes opened wide. "Transport them? Makes them sound like cattle."

Big Jim stood with his fists planted on his hips. "Don't it though? This social worker lady contacted the parents, but they couldn't afford bus fare for the girls to go back to Mexico."

Leah covered her mouth with her hand. "Oh, no! After all they've been through, and the best they can do is put them on a bus? Those girls are so young to be traveling by themselves." She looked at him imploringly. "How can we get them home? I'll help if I can."

Big Jim stood staring at her. "How can one little person have such a big heart?"

Leah giggled. "I'll have you know that I'm a tall woman."

"Not when you hang around with the Garrett men. You're a downright miniature." He stroked his chin. "But I'll call this social lady and see how we can get the girls home."

She threw her arms around his waist. "Oh, thank you so much. I'll be happy to help. Let me know what she says."

Big Jim went into the kitchen and slid onto one of the stools at the dining bar. He figured he should be sitting down for this. "Is there something to write on around here?"

Leah sat beside him, pen in hand and a small notepad. "Put it on speaker, and I'll take notes."

Perfect. Big Jim punched in the number the sheriff had given him. "Miss Lorene Dyer, LSW?" He paused for her to respond. "This is James Garrett. I'm calling about the two young girls from Mexico. The ones who were kidnapped and rescued in Langston."

The woman explained to him that she was not able to give any information about the children she was supervising.

"I understand that," he said. "I just wanted to see if my family could help them get home."

The woman's frosty demeanor evaporated. "Well, that would be wonderful. The girls don't speak English, so their stay at Harvest House is very difficult." She cleared her throat as though showing any emotion was not allowed. "Would you like to contribute to their bus tickets down to the border?"

Big Jim stifled the urge to yell at the woman. "No, we would not. We would like to take the girls to meet their parents at the border. Can you arrange that as quickly as possible?"

She sputtered and stammered. "Why, no. That will not be possible. We can't just release these very young girls to a complete stranger. They have been traumatized. They were kidnapped with the intent to sell them into some kind of slavery. Maybe sex trafficking. I cannot turn them over to you."

Big Jim drew in a deep breath, filling his lungs. But before he could formulate a response, Leah had scooted the phone closer to her.

"Miss Dyer? This is Leah Garrett. I'm sure the girls are frightened, but it would be cruel to send them all the way down to Mexico on a bus. Anything could happen to them on that long ride. We want to protect them. You can call our sheriff to ask about the Garrett family." She smiled at Big Jim. "We're good people."

—ᴍᴍ—

Beau called Dixie to tell her he was on his way but that he was going to check in at the Garrett ranch.

"Of course you are," she sang out. "I swear, that Garrett umbilical cord doesn't stretch very far."

He laughed, a single syllable. "It's in the Garrett DNA. We check on each other. I've neglected all my usual duties, so just going to touch base with Dad and then I'll be at your service, baby."

"Ooh, that sounds good. I'm making dinner." A deep chuckle erupted from her throat. "And you know that's always an adventure."

"I'll take my chances. See you later." Beau returned the cell to his pocket and drove to the Garrett ranch. He turned in at the horseshoe-shaped arch, his tires bumping over the cattle guard.

When he entered the ranch house, some kind of an uproar was coming from the rear of the house. He tossed his hat on one of the pegs by the front door and went back to the kitchen. "What's going on?" he asked. He noticed his next older brother's face was red and Leah's brow was furrowed.

"Well, look who showed up," Big Jim said. His face seemed to be more purple than red.

Beau looked from man to man, not venturing a comment.

Tyler made a growling noise in the back of his throat. "Would you tell my father that I forbid him to take my pregnant wife to Mexico?"

Beau took a step back, raising his hands in supplication. "Don't drag me into this war."

Big Jim shot a fierce glare at Tyler. "Not a war. Leah and I are just trying to do something nice for those poor little Mexican girls who got kidnapped."

"Just calm down, everybody," Leah said. "It's not that big a deal. Big Jim and I were talking to the social worker who took charge of those two young ladies." She rolled her eyes up to the ceiling. "Honestly, we were just trying to get them back to their parents in Mexico."

"Mexico!" Tyler exploded. "I'm not having my pregnant wife traipsing off to Mexico with my father, no matter how noble the cause."

"Well, I can't take those two little girls down there by myself," Big Jim said. "I mean—they're little girls."

Beau crossed his arms over his chest. "Why don't you just go with them, Ty? You traipse all over the country when you're touring with your band. Why not just take a little trip with Leah and Dad—and those two girls?"

The silence was so heavy the air itself seemed to have gained weight.

"That's a good idea," Leah said. "But who would keep Gracie?"

"I'm pretty sure she can come stay with us at the Moore ranch. She can play with Ava, and if Dixie's cooking doesn't kill us all, everything will be okay."

Leah exchanged glances with her husband and father-in-law. "That doesn't sound bad at all."

In the end they agreed to make the trip together and that Beau would pick Gracie up after school and take her to the Moore ranch to spend the night when they were to pick up Sofia and Ana in Amarillo.

Beau smacked one fist into the other open palm. "Bam! It's all settled. Any other world-shattering problems you need me to solve for you?" He looked from one to the other. "Well, then...I guess I'll be going to eat Dixie's wonderful cooking and hope Ava and I survive."

"Hold on a minute there," Big Jim's voice boomed out. "What's the status of your involvement with this ranch? Should I still count on you to perform your usual duties, or are you permanently on some kind of leave of absence?"

"Aw, Dad," Ty said. "Beau's just trying to get his relationship going again with Dixie. There's a child involved."

"I know that," Big Jim snapped. "But this is a working ranch. I need to know if I can count on my youngest son to show up and lend a hand now and then."

"Dad," Beau said. "You know you can always count on me." He raked his fingers through his thick hair. "I'm trying to make sure both Dixie and Ava stay in my life. And Dixie needs help with her ranch and the store. I know you like having that little girl around." He gave Big Jim a questioning look.

"You know it." Big Jim huffed out a snort. "You just do whatever you have to do to make sure Dixie doesn't go running off to Dallas again."

"I'm trying, but if she goes to Dallas, I'll be following her there."

⁓

"Well, could you be any later?" Dixie threw her head back so she could look down her nose at the very tall man.

"Yeah. I'm pretty sure I could. Do you want me to leave and come back again later?"

"I put Ava to bed, and she was upset that you weren't here to kiss her good night." She turned back to the stove. "I'll heat some food for you. It was delicious when I first cooked it."

"Ummm—looks—interesting," he said. "What was it?"

She raised her head slowly, giving off a cool vibe. "I can put this away, and you can make your own PB and J. Your choice."

"No, I want some of that." He pointed at the pot on the range. "I just wanted to know what to call it."

"George," she said. "It's called George."

Beau laughed, shaking his head. "C'mon. Give me a hint."

"It's chicken."

"Mmm…good to know. Dish me up some of that… uh, chicken stuff."

"You are cruisin' for a bruisin', Beauregard Garrett." She glopped some of the contents of the pot onto a plate and stuck it in the microwave. When it was heated, she placed it on the table in front of Beau. "Sweet tea?"

"Sure. Hey, this smells great." He picked up a spoon and scooped some into his mouth. "It tastes great. Are those mushrooms?"

Dixie rolled her eyes. "My favorite fungus. Just eat and don't piss me off any more than I am."

"Aw, don't be mad at me. I've been busy all day."

She leaned back against the countertop, folding her arms across her chest. "I noticed. Did your daddy have you dancing to his tune?"

He looked up at her, the blue eyes intense as a double dose of laser beams. "No, Dixie. I went to the feed store to help Pete. He mentioned that he'd told you about his cousin Josh paying him a visit. But you didn't happen to mention it to me. What's up with that?"

"Oh." She gnawed her lower lip. "Well, I didn't know it was important."

He made a snorting sound. "As if."

"Okay, I didn't want to upset you."

"Keep going. I'm sure you're going to hit the truth eventually." He scooped another bite of the chicken into his mouth. "George is really good."

Dixie felt her color rise. At that moment, she regretted the tendency to blush, a side effect of her red hair. "I was hoping to meet with Josh in case he could tell me something about the person who shot Scott…and maybe my father."

Beau gave her a knowing look, waving his spoon at her. "I figured it was something like that." He shook his head, looking very disapproving. "I'm disappointed to say the least. I thought you understood that I'm trying to keep you and Ava safe."

Dixie clenched her hands together, interlacing her fingers. She tried to keep her voice level. "I know that. I'm just trying to do my part."

"Your part is to take good care of Ava and stay the hell away from the feed store. I went to the sheriff's office to alert them that Josh was roaming around the area and that he was in contact with his cousin."

"You did what?" She gripped her hands together tighter.

"I brought the sheriff's office in on this. Leave it to the professionals."

Dixie swallowed hard. She was outraged, but strangely, she could see his point of view. She was offended that he'd ordered her to stay away from her own store and that he thought it was her place to be safe at home, caring for Ava. She realized her fingers had turned white with the grip she had on them and relaxed them slightly. "I see. Well, I guess I have no choice but to stay home and take care of Ava."

He grinned and raised his glass of iced tea in a salute. "That's my girl."

Simmer…slow simmer. She tilted her head to one side and gazed at him sweetly. "Don't you worry that I could smother you in your sleep?"

He let out a derisive snort. "Not likely. When I get done with you, you'll be way too tired."

Chapter 16

BEAU TOOK A STEAMY SHOWER AFTER HE FINISHED EATING, but Dixie made it even steamier when she stepped in with him.

He stared at her, wondering how one woman could be so beautiful.

Her fiery-red curls were piled on top of her head and held with a couple of clips. The warm water brought a pinkish glow to her skin. Her eyes were shining, and her lips were slightly open...an invitation to a kiss.

"Hey, did you want to scrub my back?" He handed her the soap and his washcloth.

"Sure, I can do that," she said. "Or I can scrub your front." She lathered the soap with both hands and rubbed suds over her breasts and stomach.

Pure lust roiled through his entire being. "Dixie," he breathed. He leaned down to kiss her lips and lifted her against him.

Her warm, soapy breasts melded against his chest, imprinting on him like a hot branding iron. She writhed against him, sending currents of heat to his already-attentive erection.

Dixie wrapped her arms around his neck, lifting herself higher against him.

"You're killing me here," he murmured.

She issued a smug grunt to go along with her smile. Her long, soapy legs wrapped around his torso with torturous deliberation.

He pressed her against the wall, kissing her and letting his hands explore her body. Gazing into her eyes, he stroked her thigh and pressed his hardness between her legs.

She sighed, just the tiniest whimper of pleasure, bringing a grin to Beau's mouth.

"I don't have a condom handy."

"I don't care," she said. "Give me all you got, cowboy."

He chuckled close to her ear. "You can't take all I got."

Her thighs tightened as she rotated her hips, rubbing his already-engorged shaft.

He swallowed hard. She was demanding he make love to her. What if they created another child? He considered this for half a second before easing inside her. He held her against the shower wall and thrust into her, increasing his rhythm and intensity.

She grazed his shoulder with her teeth and uttered little mews of ecstasy, grinding herself against him, satisfying herself as she drove him over the edge. She came to orgasm, shuddering as she gripped him with all four of her limbs.

Beau's climax came hard and heavy. They clung to each other, gasping for breath. The warm water streamed over his shoulders and down his backside, grounding him to his surroundings.

Her breath rasped in his ear. "That was—"

"Yeah, it was."

—⁓—

Damn! He's gone again. Dixie lay in the tangle of sheets, naked and languorous in the aftermath of the previous night's great sex. She heaved out a deep sigh, smoothed the sheets on both sides of her, and pulled the covers up to her chin, figuring that if she had been awake earlier, she might have participated in yet another incredible sexual marathon event.

In truth, she was glad Beau didn't awaken her at the god-awful early morning hour that he routinely awoke, but she would have liked to wake up to a repeat performance of his very enthusiastic lovemaking from the night before. A performance that etched a permanent impression on her psyche. She couldn't repress the giggle that bubbled out.

Although Beau made certain she had no unfilled needs and was thoroughly sated during their nightly encounters, somehow she always woke up with an aching need for more. *Get back here, boy! You got work to do.*

Dixie was pretty certain she would have no trouble getting his immediate attention, but he would have to be there with her, his muscular and athletic form available as her playground.

She huffed and turned on her side. The sun was barely up. Now a long day of basically alone time yawned before her, since she had been forbidden to go to the store. She threw back the covers and groped around for her robe. She tucked her cell phone in the pocket should Beau find time in his busy schedule to give her a call.

Padding barefoot to the kitchen, she found that Beau had made coffee, so she could forgive him for his early departure. Indeed, he was thinking about some of her basic needs. Pouring a cup, she went around opening drapes and blinds to let the burgeoning sunlight enter her domain.

Grabbing her laptop, she opened the back door, stepped out onto the covered porch, and inhaled deeply. *Nothing like that good old fresh country air*. She reflected that, were they still in Dallas, the air would carry traffic sounds and the aroma of emissions from said traffic and various manufacturing enterprises. *No, living at the ranch is definitely a healthier choice*.

Dixie sank onto one of the chairs and took another sip of coffee before opening her laptop and logging into her business site. She took care of the orders received the previous day and forwarded them to the various wholesalers and then leaned back to gaze out at the beautiful countryside. There were a few shade trees, a couple of pecans, and an oak. But most of her "backyard" was lush green grass that hadn't been mowed in a while with a scattering of bluebonnets and some tiny yellow daisy-like flowers. The grasses sparkled with dew in the early-morning light. Altogether a pleasing picture.

Her reverie was broken by her mother's ringtone. She raised her head and set the coffee cup on a small table. *Might as well get the battle on now*. She sighed and answered the call. "Hello, Mother."

"Oh, thank God! Dixie, where have you been? I've been so worried about you. Are you all right? Did that dreadful Garrett boy do something to you?"

"As a matter of fact, he did," Dixie said. "I know the truth now. I know how you lied to me, and I never, ever want to speak to you again. Please don't call me."

Abruptly, she disconnected and shoved the cell back in the pocket of her robe. "That's one thing off my list. Divorce lying mother." She drew a line in the air as though drawing a line through an item on her imaginary list.

Big Jim, along with Colton and Tyler, had just finished cleaning out the stables and giving his thoroughbreds a good brush down and their feed. He wanted to go for a ride later, but he thought maybe he would wait until after school, when he could bring his sweetie, Celia Diaz, over for dinner and a nice ride. To his mind, that would be the perfect way to end the day.

He was headed to the house for a good washup and another cup of coffee when his cell sounded. He fished it out of his shirt pocket and answered with his usual gruff tone. "Garrett."

"Um, Big Jim? This is Ed Rollins."

"Howdy, Sheriff. What can I do for you today?"

"I got a call from Miz Dyer, the social worker, about you taking them little Mexican girls home to their mama and papa. I told her you and your family was the best people on earth and that she could trust you with the girls."

Big Jim made a sound between a growl and a snort. "Thanks for the reference, Sheriff. We'll be taking them down to Matamoros tomorrow."

"That's what I wanted to talk to you about."

Big Jim motioned for his sons to go on to the house, and he climbed up on the corral fence to get comfortable. It appeared the sheriff had a lot on his mind. "Go ahead, Sheriff. I'm listening."

"I got a call from the Amarillo office of Immigration and Customs Enforcement. Them are the guys who took charge of that little Valentina. I sent her tiny handbag over to them guys. They did something to her phone and checked all her messages and phone numbers. It seems she and her boyfriend, some creepy dude, were all about running a few girls from Mexico so they could be sold like slaves. They were part of some kind of network. Don't that beat all?"

"Yes, it does." Big Jim could feel his jaw tense up and consciously worked it. "But how did they end up in the Moore storage shed?"

The sheriff chuckled. "Here's where it gets interesting. Apparently, that was the handoff point. They would take young girls, who was scared half outta their wits, an' this Valentina girl would pretend to be helping them. She would hide with the girls up in the shed. Then they would be picked up to take them to wherever they was to be delivered. Ain't that the craziest deal you ever heard?"

"Crazy doesn't begin to cover it," Big Jim said. "So, how did this Valentina and her charges stay in the loft without someone finding out? I mean, the feed store is a business, and there were a lot of people going back there to get feed and stuff. How did they not get caught?"

There was a momentary silence. "Looky here, Big Jim. I don't want to burst your bubble, 'cause I know you and Vern Moore was good friends, but the big boys are saying there must have been collusion. Vern probably knew all about it and was gettin' a cut of the money."

"No!" Big Jim thundered. "Vern Moore was one of the most honest men I've ever known. He would never stand for something like that going on at his place of business. He would have gone straight to you if he even thought there was something illegal going on at his store."

"But I—" the sheriff began.

"No! Don't even go spreading that around, Sheriff, because you would be besmirching a good man's name."

"Um—sure, Big Jim. I won't say a word." The sheriff's voice was barely above a whisper.

"There has to be some other explanation," Big Jim said. "I will never believe that Vernon Moore was involved."

"Yes, sir. I believe you. I just wanted you to know what was being said." He paused. "But don't you worry. I'm sure there's some other reason the feed store was the handoff point for them white slavers."

"Vern would never deal with human traffickers." Big Jim disconnected and shoved the phone back into his pocket, thinking that Vern's integrity was probably what had gotten him killed.

Maybe this was not the day to go for a ride with Celia Diaz. Maybe he needed to check out the feed store again. Maybe he needed to pick up old Pete by the ears and give him a shake to find out what he knew about the illegal activities rolling out right under his nose. If anyone knew what was going on, it had to be Pete Miller.

Dixie and Ava were headed to the stables.

"But, Mommy, why do we have to clean up after the horsies every day?"

Yeah, why? Dixie ruffled her daughter's disorderly halo of light-orange tendrils. "Because those horsies are a messy lot. They expect us to make sure they have a clean house."

Ava's lower lip jutted out. "But it stinks in there."

"That's why we have to clean it." Resolutely, Dixie

opened the stable door. Indeed, the pungent aroma of horse manure assailed her senses. She opened the door wide to let the place air out a bit before subjecting her daughter to it.

She recalled performing this task with her father many times but didn't think the smell had been so pungent. "It's okay, honey. We're big girls. We can do this."

"But why?" Ava persisted.

Why, indeed? Dixie made an elaborate bowing motion to indicate to her recalcitrant daughter that she was to go inside. Lip still jutting, Ava stepped over the doorjamb.

Dixie followed Ava into the stable, leaving the door open for ventilation. "Because…we are strong women and we do not need to wait for some man to do it for us." She almost stumbled as her own words slapped her in the face. *Hmm…*

She began her task, mulling over her options. She replayed her conversation with Beau the night before. The conversation where he basically told her to step back and not get involved with looking into her father's murder. Several possibilities presented themselves. One thing she was sure of. She wanted to talk to Josh herself and not hear about it thirdhand from the moronic sheriff as filtered through her beloved and protective Beau.

Ava was propelling a push broom across the floor, while Dixie shoveled out the stalls. It was hard work, and it was dirty work. Was it man's work?

She huffed out an impatient snort. The entire male Garrett tribe did this and more on a daily basis. It was in their genetic code by now. Big Jim had raised his sons to work. But what if he'd had daughters?

Nah! Big Jim was one of those men who thought the "little woman" should take care of the house and do tasks like cooking and laundry. Her general irritation was fueling her actions with unexpected energy. In no time at all she had shoveled horse manure and befouled straw into the wheelbarrow.

Her mother's ringtone sounded, but Dixie didn't respond.

"Is that Gramma?" Ava sang out. "I wanna talk to my Gramma." She came to stand in the open doorway of the last stall Dixie was cleaning.

"Grandma can leave a message. I'm too busy to chat right now."

"But—"

"Enough!" She realized her voice was too harsh. "I'm sorry, honey. I just want to get this done and then get cleaned up." She turned to gaze into her daughter's big blue eyes...*Garrett eyes*.

Dixie straightened her shoulders. "C'mon and show me where this compost heap is." She picked up the handles to the wheelbarrow and rolled it in the direction Ava was heading. She knew full well where the compost heap was...the same place her father had designated so many years ago. It was located far enough away and downwind from the house. *Good plan, Dad.* Her next task was to scoop the contents out of the wheelbarrow and onto the pile. She was pretty sure the pile needed to be turned and that the material on the bottom had broken down into some pretty rich compost by now.

But not today.

Her lower back was aching, and her shoulders were

complaining as well. Maybe a hot shower and a couple
of Tylenol would fix her right up.

After Dixie had fed the horses and returned them to
their stalls, she was having delusions about that shower,
but as they retraced their steps to the house, her cell
sounded again. It was Roger's ringtone.

She hated to touch the phone with her filthy hands.
True, she had worn work gloves, but she could feel
germs multiplying on her skin. Gingerly, she fished the
phone out of her pocket with two fingers and accepted
the call. "Hey, Roger. How's it going?"

"It's going very well indeed. Poor dear Scott is
doing better. The doctor has had him in a medically
induced coma to help him heal, but they're bringing
him out of it slowly. He should be awake later tonight.
Isn't that fabulous?"

Dixie grinned. "That is fabulous. I'm so glad."

Roger went on for a while, his enthusiasm spilling
over. By the time he had hung up, he had gotten to speak
with a delighted Ava and secured a promise from Dixie
to visit the next day.

"I'll call first," she said. "Be sure and find out if the
doc is good with a visit." She rang off, heartened that
Scott was recovering. Happy that she would be able to see
him. Irritated when her mother's ringtone sounded again.

―⁓⁓―

Beau was back in his element. He and his brothers had
been working together just as they had for years…before
the return of his long-lost love and the discovery that he
was a father.

Not that he would trade Dixie and Ava for anything,

but for the moment, he was enjoying the camaraderie of working alongside his brothers, trading irreverent insults, and feeling amazingly productive.

As the three brothers made their way back to the house, Tyler slapped him on the shoulder. "Good to have you back, Little Bro."

Colton, the biggest big brother anyone could possibly have, looped his beefy arm around Beau's neck. "Yeah, bro. You've been missed."

"I've missed you two jackasses too, but I've got a lot going on right now."

Colton rolled his eyes dramatically. "Oh, we know. You're all about little Miss Dixie."

Beau removed Colt's arm and gave his brothers a long, steady gaze. "I love Dixie, just the way you love Misty and the way you love Leah." He took a step back, continuing to stare them down. "I have a daughter. I love her. When you have kids of your own, you'll understand." He turned and stomped toward the ranch house. At that moment, all he wanted to do was get the hell off the Garrett ranch.

He strode into the house, intent upon washing up and heading to the feed store to check on Pete and his undercover helper. But that was before he ran smack into his dad.

"Whoa!" Big Jim jumped back. "What's the hurry?"

Beau took a wide stance and hooked his thumbs in his belt loops. "Sorry, Dad. Colt and Ty have been giving me a hard time about Dixie. When will they realize that I'm a man and not their little brother? This is my life, and I want to spend it with Dixie and Ava. They're my family now." He stopped short, realizing his rant was aimed at the wrong Garrett.

Big Jim's face clouded. "What the hell? Of course they are, but they're my family too. My little Ava is the link. She's a Garrett. She and her mother will always have a place deep in my heart." His granite jaw worked. "I would lay down my life for your females …you know that."

Beau's chest filled with emotion. He spread his arms and walked into his father's embrace. "Thanks, Dad. I feel the same way."

"Get yourself cleaned up, and let's get out of here," Big Jim said. "I'm going to take you to lunch at the steak house, and then we can go to the feed store."

Beau complied, glad to have a little one-on-one time with Big Jim. He figured his dad needed some supplies from the feed store. Maybe he had called in an order. At least it would give Beau a chance to check on things without being obvious.

When he returned, Big Jim was talking to Leah and Tyler. Leah appeared to be excited. She wore a wide grin and spoke rapidly, her voice in a higher register than usual.

She grinned at Beau when she spotted him. "Hey, Beau. I'm going to Mexico." She covered her mouth to giggle. "I feel so silly. I've never been anywhere, let alone out of the country."

"I haven't been much of anywhere either," Beau said. "Don't feel bad."

Ty leaned close to her and gave her a kiss. "I'll be glad when we can get those girls back to their parents. The whole thing's got me worried."

Leah made a shooing gesture. "Oh, you're no fun at all."

Ty picked her up and swung her around in a circle. "I'm plenty of fun. We're having a baby, aren't we?"

Beau shook his head and walked toward the front door before he got steamed again. Why didn't Ty realize that Dixie was as precious to him as Leah was to Ty?

Beau paced back and forth between the array of pickup trucks parked in a row.

Finally, Big Jim emerged and strode to his own silver double-dually, extra-cab, four-wheel-drive truck, opening the doors with his remote. "C'mon, Son. Let's get on the road. I'm ready for that steak. How 'bout you?"

"Yeah, Dad. I could eat." Beau climbed into the front passenger seat, glad to be leaving his judgmental brothers behind.

Big Jim was silent until he turned onto the highway. "Don't be too hard on your brothers, Beau. They just remember how she broke your heart when she ran off without even a fare-thee-well."

"But Dixie's mother lied to her. Dixie's heart was broken too. She thought I had turned my back on her."

"I understand that, Son, but it's just gonna take a little time for your brothers to forgive her. They're your brothers, after all."

Beau tried to wrap his brain around that. On the one hand, he was glad to have brothers who cared about him, but he wanted them to realize how unfair it was to blame Dixie when she had suffered her pregnancy alone, thinking her father had disowned her and Beau had denied that the child was his.

His own pain had been visceral, becoming a part of every aspect of his life. He had finished the school year, his classmates constantly asking about Dixie. He had been relieved when Big Jim packed him off to college. Not that he had been an exceptional student, but at least he had been forced to turn his attention to his studies, graduating with a Bachelor of Science degree in land management and animal husbandry. Returning to the ranch, he was able to throw himself into work, and the pain of Dixie leaving him eventually lessened.

And now she's back…

"Are you all set to take care of little Miss Gracie tomorrow? You have to pick her up from school and keep her overnight, then take her to school the next morning."

"Yes, we're all set. Ava is really excited about having a sleepover with her friend. She thinks Gracie is a rock star."

Big Jim emitted a deep chuckle. "She's all that."

"Is there anything else you need done while you're gone?"

"Just help Colt. He's gonna have his hands full trying to get everything done all by himself."

"I'll be there," Beau said. "I might not be speaking to him, but I'll be there."

Big Jim gave Beau a rough pat on the shoulder. "Aw, get over that attitude. I'll tell Colt to keep his mouth shut about Dixie."

"That will help."

Big Jim drove to the steak house and made sure they were both stuffed to the gills before they left. His next stop was the feed store.

Beau had expected him to pull around to the back where something he had ordered could be loaded into the bed of the truck. But Big Jim parked in front of the store and was out of the cab before Beau could even comment. He followed behind his father, taking long strides to keep up.

Once inside, they found Pete in his usual place behind the cash register.

Pete looked less stressed than he had previously, a grin spreading across his face when he spotted the Garretts. "Well, howdy, Big Jim…and Beau. It's good to see both of you. What can I do for you today?"

Big Jim fixed him with an expression that was hard to read. One of his dark brows was raised. "I suppose you can tell me what's going on with your cousin Josh. That'll do for starters."

Pete's grin faded. He blinked several times in rapid succession. "Well, I'm not sure what you mean."

The formidable brows drew together. "C'mon, Pete. Beau told me your cousin has been in touch with you. What's going on with him? Why doesn't he come forward and tell Sheriff Rollins what happened out behind the shed?"

Beau realized that questioning Pete had been Big Jim's sole purpose for driving into town.

Fletch had come in and stood nearby, listening attentively, but Big Jim had not noticed.

Beads of sweat broke out on Pete's forehead. "I don't mean to be disrespectful, Mr. Garrett, but my cousin is scared for his life. If he could come in, I'm sure he would."

Big Jim planted his fists at his waist. "So you're saying Josh is a witness to the attempted murder of this Scott person, and he ran away like a sniveling coward?" His expression and tone of voice left no doubt as to his opinion of this particular kind of coward.

Pete swallowed hard, giving his bobbing Adam's apple a strenuous workout. "Well, sir, I suppose it's better for Josh to be a coward than to git hisself kilt."

Beau had to admire Pete's loyalty to his cousin. "I agree, Pete. Just tell Josh to stay under the radar until the sheriff arrests the shooter."

Big Jim turned a frosty glare on Beau. "It would be a helluva lot quicker if Josh would cooperate with the sheriff." He noticed Fletch leaning in the doorway to the room with small animals. "Who do we have here?"

Fletch came forward, extending his hand. "Hey, Mr. Garrett. My name is Fletcher Shelton."

"I suggested Pete hire someone to take Josh's place since we don't know when or if he will be back." Beau gestured toward Fletch.

"Good idea. You're Herb's oldest son, aren't you?"

"Yes, sir. I'm a local homegrown boy."

"Weren't you in the military? Seems I recall Herb telling me something about that." Big Jim stroked his chin thoughtfully.

"Yes, sir. Army…two tours in Afghanistan."

Beau could see his father's admiration growing. "Well, thank you for your service, young man. Glad you're home now."

Fletch grinned. "Me too, sir."

"Well, we won't take up any more of your time." Big Jim turned as if to leave.

"Hang on a sec, Dad. I need to get some more of that rabbit food for Ava's bunnies." He pushed past Fletch to enter the room that had chickens, ducks, and other small animals, and Fletch fell into step behind him.

"I'll help you," he said. "I just rearranged the small animal food."

When the two were hunkered down beside the shelves of rabbit pellets, Beau shook his head. "Sorry, man. I had no idea my dad was going to confront Pete about Josh."

Fletch spoke in a low voice. "No problem. We're monitoring Pete's home phone and the store phone. When Josh gets in touch with him, we'll be listening in." He winked. "And I'll be right on hand in case something pops here."

Beau paid for the rabbit food and climbed into his father's truck. Pete had tried to give him the bag of pellets, but Beau didn't want to establish any kind of precedent for nonpayment.

Big Jim climbed into the driver's seat and slammed the door. "Damn! Didn't learn a damned thing."

"I thought you were going to let the sheriff deal with things," Beau said.

Big Jim expelled a long breath. "Thought I was too." He smacked the steering wheel with the heel of his hand. "I'm worried that your little Dixie might be in big trouble. Vern Moore, her father, was killed at night, and they're trying to pass it off as a robbery, but then that other guy got shot behind the shed in broad daylight." He cranked the motor and revved the engine before putting it in gear and pulling out of the parking area. Once on the highway, he seemed to relax a little.

Beau looked out the window at the familiar countryside whizzing by. Fence posts, grasslands and various breeds of cattle passed in a blur. He thought about Fletch, undercover at the feed store, and about the phone taps in place. He had no idea what Josh had seen, but he hoped that the authorities would locate him soon and learn what he knew.

"And those little Mexican girls that were hiding in

the loft—what about them?" Big Jim appeared to come out of his reverie.

"What about them?" Beau echoed.

"They're the third strange thing happening at the feed store. Can you believe that Vern's store is a center for human trafficking?"

"Um, no, Dad. We're not sure what's going on. I think we're all going to have to be patient and leave it to law enforcement." He stopped abruptly. "But I agree with you. I told Dixie to stay away from the store, for Ava and for me."

Big Jim snorted. "How did that go over?"

A grin spread across Beau's face. "Yeah, just like that."

Chapter 17

DIXIE DROVE TO THE HOSPITAL IN AMARILLO WITH AVA strapped into her child safety seat in the back passenger side. She wasn't thrilled at the thought of taking her daughter into a hospital, which she considered a hotbed of germs and disease, so Roger had promised to meet her outside the entrance and take his favorite goddaughter for a lunch date at a small café across the street.

Dixie knew how much Roger and Scott adored Ava, treating her as a daughter instead of a goddaughter. They had been on hand all of Ava's life, and she thought of them as her uncles. Now she had two more uncles, a grandfather, and her loving and protective daddy. Quite an array of male role models. A girl could do worse.

An unwilling smile spread across her face. It was good to have more family, especially since Dixie had just lopped off communication with her mother, the doting grandmother. Her smile evaporated abruptly. She knew she would have to deal with her mother, but at the moment she was too mad. She needed to be able to control her inner rage and not lash out. She couldn't imagine any scenario in which her mother would have been justified in telling such hurtful lies.

She spotted Roger pacing back and forth in front of the hospital entrance. There was a covered drive-through area where discharged patients could easily be picked up. In this case, Dixie idled under the canopy to allow Roger time to remove Ava from her constraints. "I'll meet you two at the café after I visit Scott."

Roger gave a jaunty wave as Dixie pulled away to find a parking spot. Once she had hiked back to the hospital, she rode the elevator to the level where Scott had been transferred. She had no idea what a "step-down unit" was, but it did sound less daunting than intensive care unit.

When she stepped out of the elevator, she found the nurses' station with a cheery-looking woman working on charts. She asked for Scott's room and was given directions to a nearby cubicle with a window. Drawing in a sharp breath, she immediately noticed that Scott had lost his healthy tan and seemed to have also dropped quite a few pounds.

His eyes were closed when she entered the cubicle, but when she got closer, they slowly opened. A hesitant smile spread across his face as he recognized her.

"Hey, Dixie." His voice was just above a whisper.

She leaned down to place a kiss against his forehead. "Hey, big guy. You sure look out of place here."

"Tell me about it." His breath came in short gasps. "I want to go home."

"Don't blame you." She pulled a chair closer and sat down. "Any idea when they're going to release you?"

He sucked in a breath and expelled it. "Getting therapies…physical, occupational, and respiratory…guy got me in the lungs." Apparently exhausted, he let his head fall back onto the pillow and closed his eyes.

Dixie's own heart pulsed in her ears. "You saw the guy who shot you?"

His eyes snapped open. "Hard not to see him."

"What did he look like? Did you recognize him? Where did he come from?"

Scott raised one hand in supplication. "Slow down... the guy was just there...out back."

"What caused him to start shooting?"

His eyes closed again. "I was just looking...I went up some stairs...narrow metal stairs."

"Yes! I know what you're talking about. What did you find?"

"Nothing. I wanted to look...out the door up there, but...it was locked tight." His breath sounds were starting to sound labored and a little raspy.

She patted his hand. "Just rest and I'll tell you about the ranch. Ava is having such a good time getting to know Beau and the entire Garrett family."

Scott's expression morphed from exhaustion to annoyance.

"Did I tell you that Beau got her two of the cutest rabbits? Bertram and Anastasia. She just loves her bunnies."

"Don't make me gag."

"Aw, don't be grumpy, Scott. I'm truly happy, and so is Ava." She shrugged. "The fact is that my dear mother lied to me about my father and about Beau and the Garretts."

"Really?" His voice was heavy with sarcasm.

"Believe me. It took a lot to convince me, but I found my father's letters. I cried buckets." She pressed her lips together and drew in a breath. "I hurt him so deeply. I don't know how I could have believed that he disowned me."

Scott's expression softened. "Sorry, babe."

"And I caused Beau such pain. He had no idea why I

disappeared." She had to swallow hard to keep the tears at bay. "I have so many things to regret, but most of all I regret that Beau wasn't with me for Ava's birth. That he missed her first years."

Scott reached out to her, enfolding her hand in his. "I can't believe Mamie would do that to you...to all of us...but you seem to have it all figured out."

"I'm just glad that I'm on the right track now."

"Me too, but I'd rather you...live in Dallas."

"I'm getting back to my roots. But getting back to the feed store...when you were in the shed and went upstairs, what happened next?"

"Nothing. I tell you... There were some young girls... up there. They didn't speak any English." He sucked in another raspy breath. "I think they were playing some kind of game...like hide and seek..."

Dixie frowned. "Hide and seek?"

He nodded vigorously. "When they saw me...two of them scrambled...behind some big bales of hay."

"That makes sense. Then what happened?"

"I went back downstairs, and then this guy shot me." He sighed and closed his eyes.

"What guy?" She stood and leaned over him. "Just tell me what he looked like. Give me a hint."

Scott's eyes fluttered open. "I—I think my memory is...a little fuzzy. I was thinking...there was one guy... but now, I think there were two...or maybe more."

"Time's up!"

Dixie turned to see the nurse from the desk standing in the doorway.

"Short visits only. Doctor's orders." She gestured to the doorway.

"Oh, can I just say goodbye?" Dixie asked.

"Two minutes," the nurse said and left them alone.

Dixie leaned over to whisper. "Listen, Scott. You have to focus. Was there one man, or were there more? It's very important."

"I'm not sure... I really don't know." Scott's brows drew together. "I'm getting a headache."

"Oh, sorry. Please just rest and get well. Love you a bunch." She kissed him on the cheek and backed out of the room, bumping into the nurse on her way. "Sorry."

Dixie left the hospital and walked across to the café where Roger and Ava were entertaining each other. The sound of Ava's laughter carried from the other side of the eating place to where Dixie stood. She zigzagged between the tables to slide into the red-plastic seat of the booth beside Ava.

"Mommy! How is Uncle Scott?"

Dixie exchanged a glance with Roger. "He's good, baby."

Roger raised his brows. "Did you have a good visit?"

"Um—sure." She fiddled with the plastic-covered menu. "The poor man can barely breathe," she said under her breath.

"But he's so much better," Roger assured her. "He was on a respirator. The doctors tell me he's making amazing progress."

Dixie nodded her head, miserable that her friend had nearly lost his life. "I hate that he's struggling."

Roger shook his head. "You must not think of it as Scott struggling. He's a strong person, and he has a long rehabilitation ahead. I would take him back to Dallas, but he's making such great progress here, and he really likes his rehabilitation team. I don't want to do anything to impede his progress."

"No, of course not." She was touched by Roger's willingness to change his own life to be near the person he loved. "I'm sure Scott is so grateful for your support."

Roger's eyes misted up. "He's just so very dear to me." He pried a napkin out of the napkin holder and dabbed at his eyes.

"You're right. Scott is tough as nails. He's going to get through this." Dixie reached across to squeeze his hand. "We'll get through this."

───※───

Big Jim, Ty, and Leah dropped Gracie off at the elementary school in the morning and then headed to Amarillo to pick up the kidnapped girls.

Leah and Ty trooped into the social worker's office, while Big Jim idled out front. They walked down the hallway, hand in hand, locating the office in a niche near the drinking fountain. *Lorene Dyer, LSW*, was inscribed on the door. Leah reached out a tentative hand to knock and was rewarded with an invitation to enter.

Ty swung the door open, and Leah stepped through. "Mrs. Dyer?"

The woman turned, her lips turned down in a grimace. "It's Miss Dyer."

Leah stepped forward and extended her hand. "Miss Dyer. I'm Leah Garrett, and this is my husband, Tyler."

Miss Dyer shook hands with both of them, obviously appreciating the tall, handsome blue-eyed man towering over her. "Well, I—ah." A blush flamed her cheeks.

"These young ladies are going to be your charges until you turn them over to their parents. We usually don't operate this way, but Sheriff Rollins gave your father and your entire family such a good reference. He vouched for all of you."

Leah smiled. "That's good to hear." She gazed at the two young girls sitting close on a worn leather couch, their hands laced tightly together. They looked terrified, eyeing the newcomers with distrust.

Leah gave them a smile and waggled her fingers at them.

"The older one is named Sofia, and the younger is Ana," Miss Dyer supplied.

"Do they have a suitcase or something?" Ty asked.

Miss Dyer gave him a somewhat scornful look. "They were kidnapped. They didn't exactly have time to pack a bag."

Ty swallowed hard. "I see."

"Do I know you?" Miss Dyer stared up at him. "You look so familiar."

"My husband won *Country Idol* this last year," Leah said proudly. "Perhaps you saw him on television."

Miss Dyer's expression transformed from stiff and distant to smiling and warm. "I knew it! You were wonderful."

"He still is," Leah said. "Shall we get the girls into the truck? We've got a long drive ahead of us, at least ten and probably twelve hours."

"Yes...yes, of course." Miss Dyer handed Leah a paper to sign stating that they were taking charge of the sisters, and she gave her the number of the girls' parents' phone. Then she turned her attention to the two girls. "C'mon," she called, accompanied by appropriate hand gestures.

The girls stood, looking bewildered and afraid. The younger girl, Ana, had tears in her eyes.

Leah couldn't stand it any longer and crossed the room to embrace both of them. "Please don't be afraid. We'll take care of you."

"I'm afraid they don't understand a word you're saying to them," Miss Dyer supplied.

But Leah could tell the girls felt a little more confident. They met her eyes without flinching. She nodded and urged them toward the door that Ty was holding open for them.

When they had traversed the hall and were out on the street, Big Jim was standing beside the truck. He opened the back door and helped them up.

"I'll sit back here with them," Leah said. "I brought this book of Spanish phrases I got from the library. I'll see if I can say a few words to them."

"Atta girl," Big Jim said, closing the door behind them. He and Ty climbed into the truck, and they headed south.

Leah had brought some snacks in a small cooler and opened it. The girls seemed to be interested in the contents. "I have *leche con chocolate*." she said and passed them each a carton of chocolate milk. "And *empanadas*. Little meat pies. I got them at the bakery."

"Did you get some for us too?" Ty asked.

"Check the console. I got you things I know you like."

Big Jim's laughter boomed out. "Thank you, Tyler, for marrying such a wonderful woman."

"You're welcome, Dad. Let me know when you want

me to take over driving," Ty stretched his long legs out. "Mexico, here we come."

"*Nosotros vamos a México,*" Leah said, gratified when the girls appeared to be relieved.

———∽∽∽———

Beau got up extra early to finish tasks at Dixie's and then headed out to help Colton at the Garrett ranch.

By the time he finished, he was famished since he had not eaten breakfast. "What's for lunch, Colt?" he asked.

"Whatever we rustle up," Colt replied. "Misty's at work, and Leah went with Dad and Ty down to Mexico. We're on our own."

"Not a problem. Just lead the way to the fridge."

When they opened the refrigerator, they ended up taking everything edible out and lining it up on the granite countertop.

"We should be able to find a meal here." Colton gestured to the array.

"Yeah, but what are you going to eat?" Beau elbowed Colt out of the way and reached for a plate. "I am going to make sandwiches with everything on them. Maybe an entire cow." He reached for the bread, placing four slices on his plate, slathering them with mayonnaise, and stacking meats and cheeses on top. He mashed all the ingredients together to make two very fat sandwiches. He poured milk into two tall tumblers and nudged one toward his brother, who was rummaging through the food to fill his own plate. Colt settled for leftovers and heated them in the microwave. They took their food out onto the back patio and settled into two deck chairs side by side with a small table between.

Beau set his milk on the table and reached for one of the sandwiches. He made short work of it and was just ready to start on the next one when Colt brought him up short.

"You in a hurry, Little Bro?" Colt asked. "You're stuffing your food in like you've got someplace else to be. Does Miss Dixie have you on a short leash?"

Beau picked up his milk and drank it down. "That does it. I'm outta here."

"Wait. What's the deal?" Colt asked.

"I've had it with you bashing my relationship with Dixie. I love her, and if you can't respect that, then I have no reason to be here." He stood up, sandwich in hand, and strode through the house to the front room, where he retrieved his Stetson and barged out the door. Climbing into his truck, he looked back to see Colt in the doorway, looking puzzled.

Beau slammed his truck door and started it up, revving the motor. He managed to maneuver his vehicle off the Garrett property without dropping any of his sandwich.

He drove into town, knowing he had to pick Gracie up at school in a mere two hours, but he figured it was better to be early than late. Driving by the feed store, he noted that Pete was sweeping the front porch, industriously swinging the broom from side to side.

He turned the truck around and drove as slowly as possible, figuring he was going to park in front of the elementary school to wait for dismissal. But he saw Breckenridge T. Ryan pull into a parking place in front of his office. He tooted his horn, and Breck raised a hand in greeting and walked toward Beau's truck.

Beau pulled over and rolled down his window. "Hey, Breck. How's it going?"

Breck leaned in, smacking Beau on the arm. "Hey there, Beau. It's going fine. I sure do like having your sister-in-law Misty running my office. I feel like I can pretty much leave her alone if I need to, and she has the sense to keep things on an even keel."

"Yeah, Misty does have my oldest brother wrapped around her little finger."

"How about you? Is everything going well with Dixie Moore?"

Beau swallowed hard, not sure where to start. "Everything's great. I can't believe I have a beautiful little girl. My dad is crazy about her."

"I'll bet. Is Dixie getting things squared away at the feed store?" Breck looked at him intently.

"I might as well tell you, Breck...I've told her to stay away from the feed store. There are too many dangerous things going on related to the store. First her dad was murdered, and then her friend was shot. Now it looks like there is some connection to human trafficking." His mouth tightened. "I can't have Dixie spending time in a place with so much violence. I need her, Ava needs her."

Breck gave a slight shake of his head. "Tell her not to worry. I don't think her father would want her to be in harm's way. When this is all over, we'll see about her taking up the reins again. She's smart, and I'm sure she'll get it under control."

"Good deal," Beau said. "I'm trying to help out a little. Pete is completely overwhelmed...but Dixie is obsessed with her father's murder. I'm afraid she just can't leave it to the sheriff. Patience is not one of her virtues."

Breck let out a derisive snort. "Good luck with that. I know all about Dixie's lack of patience. I was surprised she came back to Langston after her little blowup during the reading of the will."

"Well, it took her by surprise, but she's here now, and so is Ava, so we're trying to make the best of it."

Breck touched the brim of his Stetson in a salute. "Good luck with that too, Beau." He stepped away from the truck and walked back across the street toward his office.

Beau shifted into gear, drove the few blocks to the elementary school, and parked. He knew that Gracie was expecting him to pick her up for a sleepover, but he was antsy, so he got out and leaned up against the hood of the truck. He figured he would be able to spot Gracie the moment she emerged from the building. There was a queue of yellow buses lined up on one side of the school. Other vehicles lined up behind his truck, he presumed driven by parents. In due time, a loud buzzer sounded, and students were released. The doors opened, and children seemed to all pour out at once. Adults exited too, apparently to monitor the exodus.

Beau pushed away from the hood, craning his neck to check out the students. He'd thought it would be easy to spot Gracie's mop of blonde curls, but there were a confusing riot of fair-haired youngsters mixed in among the brunettes and a few redheads.

"Uncle Beau?" And there she was, standing at his side, looking fresh-faced and eager. She had a backpack and a small duffel bag clutched in her hands.

He flashed a grin. "There you are. Ava is so glad you're coming for a sleepover. Are you ready?" He reached for her book bag. "This is heavy. How do you carry around all this stuff?" Beau opened the back passenger door of his truck.

Gracie shrugged then climbed up with Beau's help. "I got a couple of books from the school library today. I thought Ava might like me to read some to her."

It's going to be a great night at the Moore house.

Chapter 18

Dixie paced around her house. She had spent the morning putting masking tape on the woodwork in Ava's room. She really wanted to get the painting over with and start making the room into a little girl's delight. But she also knew that she couldn't begin rolling paint on the walls until Ty and Leah returned from their trip to Mexico. Not a good idea to begin a redecorating project with a young houseguest.

The color was to be purple, all right, but fortunately Beau had convinced Ava that the palest lilac would be the best choice. He'd told her that all true princesses had their bedrooms painted that exact color.

Dixie picked up her phone and replaced it on the dining table several times in succession. She was torn, knowing Beau would be furious with her if she made any move to try to find out who murdered her father and tried to murder Scott. Although Sheriff Rollins seemed to think the two events weren't related, she knew better. She picked up her phone again but placed it back on the table, clasping her hands together.

Making a loop of the house, she made sure she was prepared to entertain an eight-year-old houseguest. There was plenty of food on hand, Ava's room was all made up with fresh sheets, and several flavors of ice cream were stashed in the freezer.

The bunnies had been fed and their hutch cleaned. Nothing else to do…

Ava was wound up like a tightly coiled spring. She kept running to the front of the house to peer out the windows, eager for Gracie's arrival.

Resolutely, Dixie picked up the phone and punched in the numbers to the feed store. Of course, Pete answered.

"Hey, Pete. It's Dixie. I just wanted to talk to you about something."

"Why, of course, Miz Dixie. What can I do for you today?" He sounded less morose than usual.

"I want to talk to your cousin, Josh. I understand you can get in touch with him?"

When Beau pulled up close to the Moore house, he had one very excited little girl in the backseat.

Gracie was grinning and leaning forward to peer out the windows. "This is where Ava lives? This is a nice ranch. Does she have horses? We have horses and chickens too."

"Yes, we do." Beau grinned at her in the mirror. She seemed to have forgotten that he lived on the Garrett ranch too and had grown up there. "Let's go inside and get an after-school snack. I'm sure Dixie has something special for you." He climbed down and went around to open the truck door for her. She leaned out into his arms, and he swung her down then grabbed her backpack and duffel.

The front door of the house burst open, and Ava came racing out, a wide grin spread across her face. "You're here," she shouted.

Gracie ran toward her, and they clasped each other like long-lost friends.

"I've never gone on a sleepover before," Gracie said.

Ava squealed her delight. "Me neither!"

Beau cocked his head toward the front door Ava had left open. "Let's go inside, girls. This sleepover thing sounds like fun."

When he turned, he found Dixie leaning against the doorjamb with her arms folded across her chest. She was trying to suppress a grin.

"Really, Mr. Garrett? I seem to remember you as being quite good at sleepovers."

It seemed they had been driving forever. Big Jim was thankful that his daughter-in-law seemed to have some magic powers when it came to breaking through to kids. Indeed, she had enchanted the two girls in the backseat.

There had been a significant number of stops for gas and food and bathroom breaks, so everyone was quite comfortable.

Big Jim thought it interesting that, wherever they stopped, people accepted that they were a family. He took a deep breath and acknowledged that a beautiful family could be blended when the uniting factor was love. He considered Leah's daughter, Gracie, who had been officially adopted by his son Tyler and by all the members of the Garrett family. Gracie was as dear to Big Jim as if she were a Garrett by blood.

When Colton had married Misty, her orphaned twelve-year-old brother Mark had also become a part of the Garrett family. Big Jim thought of Mark as officially a Garrett.

And now there was Ava. He was thrilled to have the

little redheaded heartbreaker in his life. He knew his
youngest son, Beau, was over the moon. Big Jim needed
to adjust his thinking about Beau and stop character-
izing him as being the baby of the family. He was a
full-grown man and was taking on his new responsibili-
ties admirably. Fatherhood seemed to suit him. Perhaps,
if things went the way Big Jim hoped, there would be
more little redheaded grandchildren.

His only concern was Dixie.

This was the girl who had walked out on Big Jim's
friend, Vern, and broken his son's young heart. It was
hard for a father to forgive the person who had caused
so much misery.

Beau had been telling him some story about Mamie
Moore lying to her daughter, but surely the girl should
have checked it out for herself. How could she have
believed that Beau and the entire Garrett family would
deny responsibility? And even worse, how could she
have ripped the heart out of her own father's chest by
taking off and not looking back?

But she had been so young. He felt a muscle in his
jaw tighten. *That was then, and this is now*.

It was time to move on and support his son's decision to forgive past injuries and accept the good that had
resulted from their teenage coupling.

Ava…

Big Jim and Tyler had changed places several times,
but now Big Jim was rolling through Corpus Christi and
heading south.

Leah's chortles and frequent giggles emanated
from the backseat, giving evidence of the joy she was
creating while taking Spanish lessons from the two

sisters. For their part, the two young ladies had relaxed considerably.

Big Jim found himself smiling as he drove, and when he looked over at Ty, he had a big smile spread across his face too. As they headed south, the elder Garrett noticed how flat the terrain was, much like his beloved land in north Texas.

"They call this the Coastal Plains," he said. "King Ranch is coming up. One of the largest ranches in the world."

Ty nodded. "I read all about it when I was in college. There's a larger ranch in Hawaii. Parker Brothers Ranch, I think it was."

"Well. Ain't that nice. Good to know we're in such good company."

Ty gave his head a little shake. "Everybody's gotta eat, and we gotta feed 'em."

"Good attitude, Son." Big Jim reflected that he had thought his beloved middle son might abandon the ranch and not look back when he left to pursue his singing career. Big Jim had been rabid. In an effort to be fair to Colton and Beau, who were solidly bonded to family and to the land, Big Jim had gone to his lawyer, Breckenridge T. Ryan, and changed his will, cutting Tyler completely out of the inheritance.

Big Jim glanced at Tyler again, happy that he had asked Breck to tear up that document and that Ty had never known he had almost been cut out of the will.

The best thing was that Ty had been the first of his sons to choose a mate, and the woman he chose was the lovely Leah and her daughter Gracie. *Good deal*. He gave Leah full credit for taming his rebellious middle son and for her gracious ability to see the good in people. *One in a million.*

So the miles sped past. Big Jim was feeling pretty mellow, having mentally reviewed his family members one by one. Now he realized how truly blessed he was to be so rich in family. He felt a pang that his dear wife, Elizabeth, had not lived to enjoy it.

~~~

Dixie considered herself lucky.

Beau was grilling chicken legs and ground-beef patties. He also had some corn on the cob seasoned, wrapped in foil, and ready to throw on the grill. The man was a prince among men.

Anything that could get Dixie out of kitchen duties was a blessing indeed. She was quite realistic about her limitations in the kitchen. Huffing out a breath, she recalled that she had spent much more of her time being her father's little tomboy and had turned her back on learning the feminine arts from her mother. Of course, Mamie had always been on hand to cook for her and, later, for Ava.

Now Dixie was struggling to determine which side of the toast to butter. Fortunately, Ava was not complaining…nor was Beau.

For this meal, her task was to arrange potato chips on paper plates and pour drinks for the diners.

Right up my alley.

Since she was determined not to forgive her mother, she figured she would have to learn to cook at some point. Maybe Leah could teach her…or maybe she would just marry Beau, and he could keep on grilling.

In a short time, she and the girls were seated at the table, while Beau served up hamburgers and chicken legs. She thanked him and set about arranging lettuce, tomato, pickles, and thin slices of onion on her burger. The girls were happily following her lead.

"I'm making my own hamburger," Ava crowed.

Dixie saw that tomatoes were oozing out of the burger but didn't want to rain on her daughter's parade. "It looks delicious."

Beau was in his element. He acted as host, leading both girls in conversation. It seemed Gracie wanted to be a teacher when she grew up, but Ava wanted to be a fairy princess.

They finished the meal and tossed the disposables. Only a few dishes to wash.

"I hope you're okay if I go back to help Colton for a couple hours. With Dad and Ty on their way to Mexico, I need to step up."

She nodded. "Sure. I understand. That's what families do." She was actually a little disappointed but didn't want to voice any negativity when Beau and the girls were so happy.

She followed him outside to receive a toe-curling kiss culminating in a grab of one butt cheek.

He grinned. "Good stuff."

"Only the best for my cowboy."

When he had driven away, she went inside and locked the door. She had just settled the girls at the now-cleared dining table, Gracie with her homework and Ava with some coloring pages, when she heard a knocking at the front door.

She figured that Beau had forgotten something and

threw the door wide open, the grin freezing on her face. Swallowing hard, she drew in a breath.

"Mother! What are you doing here?"

Mamie Moore pushed past her. "Are you kidding? Why wouldn't I be here? This was my home too." She whirled around dramatically. "I have been going crazy. Why won't you answer my calls?"

Mindful of the girls happily working in the rear of the house, Dixie kept her voice down. "Are you kidding?" Her chest felt as though a tight band had suddenly been drawn around it. "You lied…and then you lied some more. You caused me to hate my father…and to hate the boy who loved me."

"I did no such thing," Mamie asserted. "You listen to me, young lady. I sacrificed everything to give you a chance at a decent life."

A mini-explosion went off in Dixie's chest. "You didn't sacrifice anything. What you did was take everything away…from me…from my dad…and from Beau. We were so much in love. Having a baby would have been the frosting on the cake."

Mamie's eyes narrowed to slits. "You have no idea what I sacrificed. I gave up my life, and it was for you."

Dixie made a scoffing sound in the back of her throat. "What did you sacrifice? You and your lies took everything away from me. I hate that you hurt people I love."

"Nonsense! I was just looking out for you. I wanted to save you from a life squandered in this wasteland."

"Mother! Are you crazy? I had the best childhood imaginable."

Mamie's mouth drew into a tiny bow. "You are an ungrateful child. You have no idea what I gave up just to give you life." She huffed out a sigh and fisted her hands on her hips. "You have no idea."

Dixie leaned back against the door. "Well, why don't you explain it to this ungrateful child? Just what did you give up for me?"

Mamie sniffed and raised her chin. Her expression was one of exquisite suffering. "I—I was a college freshman. It was my first time away from home." Her hand fluttered to her face. "I was so naive. Vern was the first boy who had ever paid any attention to me." She paused, pressing her lips together. "To make it short, I got pregnant. Vern impregnated me."

Dixie was rooted in place. This was the first she had ever heard about her mother's college experience and how she met her dad. The idea that her mother, not exactly a bundle of passion, had engaged in a love affair hit her hard.

"My—my parents were horrified. We had to get married, and I was hustled off to this godforsaken place to live my life in a cultural desert." She was wringing her hands together now. Mamie turned to Dixie, her eyes wide. "I gave up everything nice to live in this crude and rustic structure." She spread her arms and turned around in a circle, as though the sight of the living room made her stomach roil.

Dixie swallowed hard but remained silent. In their many mother–daughter conversations, Mamie had spilled no hint of how she really felt. Indeed, Dixie was shocked to hear the venom in her mother's voice.

"I gave up my tennis lessons and shopping at decent stores. I never got to go to the Dallas Museum of Art again or to Dallas Orchestra performances." Her eyes looked haunted, as though these memories were extremely painful. "Instead, Vern took us to rodeos and livestock shows. That was his idea of culture." Her voice took on a strident tone. "And the worst thing was the women around here. They wanted to bond over Bible studies." She threw her hands up, rolling her eyes. "We had nothing in common. In Dallas I had friends with brain cells who could converse about world affairs, about art and culture." She blew out a frustrated sigh. "Don't you understand? I gave my life to raising you. You, Dixie, were the only beautiful part of my life. I devoted myself to you. To preparing good, nutritious meals for you. To reading to you and making sure you had pretty clothes to wear, even if I had to order them from catalogs."

Shaken, Dixie tried to find words. "M—Mother! I had no idea you felt this way. I thought you were happy."

"I was happy that I had you. You were truly the ray of sunshine in this squalid wasteland. All I wanted was to get you raised and out of here. I knew that if I could raise you and get you to a decent university, you might have an opportunity for a better life. Travel, arts, culture…" Her voice trailed off as she seemed to fold in on herself. She sank down onto the rose-velvet chair she had favored during her tenure as lady of the house. "I just couldn't bear to sentence you to a life in this hellhole with some rustic farmer."

"Oh, Mom. I had no idea you felt this way." Dixie perched on the edge of her father's leather recliner. "I—I can't believe you had all this bottled up."

Mamie shook her head. "I was just trying to save you…and then our dear Ava." Her lips twitched into a faint smile. "She was so beautiful…so much like you.

When she was born, I realized I had a chance to make things right. If I could give Ava the life I had envisioned for you, everything would be all right." She reached to take Dixie's hand. "I've been working with Roger, that dear man. He pulled some strings and managed to reserve a space for our Ava to be enrolled in a lovely private school in the fall. I know it's just kindergarten, but it's a start. She can go to the best schools and be around the best people."

Dixie stared at her sadly, realizing that there was an ocean of difference between the future she envisioned for her daughter and her mother's version. "We'll have to talk, Mom." She stood and gestured for Mamie to follow. "Come on out to the kitchen. Ava has a house-guest. Her first sleepover."

Mamie rose unsteadily. "I can't wait to see my girl. I knew you'd understand when I explained things to you."

Dixie rounded on her. "No, Mom. I cannot forgive you for all the pain you've caused. But it's late, and it's too late for you to return to Dallas tonight, so you might as well spend some time with Ava." Her mouth tightened. "But let me warn you not to make any negative remarks about Beau or anything related to the Garretts."

Mamie's spine stiffened. "The Garretts! I can't stand—"

"Stop it! I am in love with Beau Garrett. He is the father of my child, and she loves him as much as I do. If you don't want to permanently end our relationship, you will keep any antagonism toward the Garrett family to yourself. They're all Ava's family…and they're my family too."

Mamie's color rose, and her jaw tightened. "Very well."

Dixie led the way to the kitchen where a very excited Ava greeted her grandmother. Dixie stood apart, watching the woman who had given birth to her and who thought she had sacrificed the world to stay with Dixie during her formative years. She had difficulty believing that anyone could hate living in this house with Vern as a loving husband. But she was giving her mother the benefit of the doubt. Now, if she could just keep her mother from infecting Ava with her skewed view of the world.

Chapter 19

"So this is Brownsville?" Leah was peering out both side windows as the truck rolled through the border city. "Everything looks so lush and green."

"We're quite a bit closer to the equator," Big Jim responded. "No harsh winters. While we're slogging through snow, these folks are sunning themselves."

Ty let out a snort. "They call this area of the coast the Texas Riviera."

"Well, it certainly is beautiful," Leah said. Indeed, there were flowering shrubs and trees lining both sides of the street along with a vast number of very tall palm trees.

Sofia and Ana had certainly perked up. They appeared to be almost giddy.

Leah fished out the phone number for the girls' parents and punched it in on her cell. "*Hola!*" she greeted them before handing the phone to Sofia.

A rapid conversation in Spanish followed, punctuated with squeals and a few tears. Ana got to contribute to the conversation as well.

"Ask them where we can meet them," Leah said.

A few more words in Spanish, and Sofia said, "Bridge. Mama say the bridge."

"The bridge?" Big Jim asked.

When Leah checked on her phone, she found there were three bridges, but Sofia pointed to the one where they were to meet her parents.

"*La Internacional*," she insisted.

"The International Gateway Bridge." Leah read aloud the address and programmed it into her phone.

Big Jim followed the directions, and soon they were in a long line creeping toward the bridge spanning the Rio Grande. When they got closer to the approach to the bridge, a uniformed officer placed his hand on the driver's-side door, and Big Jim lowered the window. "Good evening, Officer," he said pleasantly.

The officer leaned in to look at the passengers, his gaze falling on the two young girls in the rear seat. "Could you step out of the truck, sir?" The officer's expression was stern.

Big Jim's expression could best be described as grumpy. He climbed down, muttering under his breath.

"What's that, sir?" The officer motioned for one of his coworkers to join him.

Ty's brows drew together. "I wonder what that's all about."

The girls were wide-eyed, saying something that sounded like "lameegra."

"They're saying *la migra*—immigration. Are they ICE agents?" Leah asked.

"I'm going to find out." Ty opened the door and stepped out, only to be ordered back into the truck by the agent. "Wait a minute," he said. "That's my dad you're taking off there."

The first agent had escorted Big Jim inside the building, where they could see he was talking to two men in uniform.

Knowing her father-in-law's temper, Leah stepped out. "You stay here." She hoped her tone conveyed that she was not to be disobeyed, which would be a difficult concept for her very strong-willed husband.

"Ma'am." The first agent approached her, his hands raised in a "stay back" motion.

"I want to know what's going on."

"Ma'am, we noticed you were transporting two young girls who do not appear to be related to you. We were just trying to find out what's going on, but the gentleman is not cooperating."

Leah surprised him with a grin. "I'm sure he's not. Mr. Garrett is not used to being questioned. He's as good as his word." She extended a paper to the agent. "Actually we're transporting these two young ladies to meet their parents. They were kidnapped and were being transported north by a human trafficking ring."

The agent looked in at the girls again. "What are you doing with them?"

"They were rescued in Langston, Texas, and were in a juvenile detention facility. The parents could not afford their bus tickets, but we were worried that they were too young to go on a bus unaccompanied...so my wonderful father-in-law offered to drive them to meet their parents." She pointed to the paper she had given him. "That's the sheriff's number. He's the one who set it up for us to bring them here."

The agent gave her a stern look and told her to wait by the truck. He went inside to confer with the other agents.

Leah looked back at Ty and the girls, noting that all looked more than a little worried. She flashed a broad grin and gave a double thumbs-up. Sofia responded, returning the gesture.

Leah hoped she could defuse whatever situation Big Jim was adding fuel to.

The agent returned to the door of the enclosure and motioned for her to come closer.

Leah sucked in a breath and plastered a confident smile on her face. She thought about calling Breckenridge Ryan and telling him to stand by for trouble.

Beau was ready to take a couple of Tylenol and jump in a hot shower. His muscles and joints were screaming from his extreme exertion. He had worked so hard with Colton, and he knew he had overdone it just to prove that he could take the place of Big Jim and Tyler too. *Yeah, big tough guy.*

He turned onto the farm-to-market road leading to the Moore ranch. He pulled up in front, surprised when he realized that a very shiny Lincoln Navigator was parked next to Dixie's burgundy SUV.

The hair on the back of his neck was standing at attention. Whose car was this? He tried to control the churning in his gut as he opened his door and pocketed his keys.

He winced as he climbed out of his truck. Dixie would have to take it easy on him tonight. *Yeah, right.* If little Miss Dixie didn't have other plans. He wondered if this visitor was another of her "best friends" from Dallas.

He approached the entrance, not sure if he should knock or let himself in with the key Dixie had given him. When he twisted the doorknob, the door swung open with an eerie squeak. "Um, hello? Dixie?" But there was no response.

All his senses were on high alert as he stepped inside. Total silence greeted him, then a burst of shrill laughter.

A wave of relief washed over him. Ava was happy, and that was all that mattered. Now, all he had to do was find out where Dixie was and why the big Lincoln was parked outside. Had she traded up?

When he got to the kitchen, he felt as though he had been punched in the gut, hard.

His least favorite person on the planet was staring at him. Mamie Moore. Her face registered surprise and then loathing.

"Hi, girls," he said softly but kept his gaze fastened on the woman who hated him.

"Daddy!" Ava slid off her chair and ran to him.

Beau obliged by lifting her high and then settling her in his arms so he could return the hatred Mamie was sending his way. He turned to the other smiling face sitting at the table. "How are you doing, Gracie?"

"I'm good, Uncle Beau. Just finished my homework, and Mrs. Moore was telling us about the school Ava is going to in September. It sounds so nice."

Beau tried to control his anger. "I think Mrs. Moore is mistaken. Ava is going to be enrolled in Langston Elementary School for kindergarten."

He and Mamie exchanged hate glares.

"Where is Dixie?" His voice was terse. "Did Mommy go somewhere?" he asked Ava in a softer tone.

She shook her head, her arms laced around his neck. "Mommy has to go to the store."

"The store?" With all the food in the house, he couldn't believe Dixie would drive all the way back to town for a few items. Maybe she just wanted to escape the hateful person who was glaring at him.

Mamie cleared her throat. Her eyebrows were

raised almost to her hairline, and her lips were pinched together. "Dixie got a phone call from our—from her feed store. She said she has to go meet someone there and asked me to stay with the girls…which I am happy to do, by the way."

Beau put Ava down. "Dixie?" His voice was somewhere between a yell and a bellow.

Mamie shrugged. "Maybe it's an emergency. She's really upset."

Dixie came rushing out from the direction of the bedrooms, her eyes wide. "Oh, Beau. I'm so glad you're here. I need to go to the store. Josh is there."

Beau took a wide stance, his hands at his waist. "Josh? You mean the guy the sheriff is looking for? That Josh?"

She nodded furiously. "I asked Pete to get a message to him, so he called me." She stepped around Beau. "But he's not going to be there for very long, so I have to hurry."

He reached out to stop her, holding her by the shoulders and resisting the urge to shake some sense into her. "No, you don't. Let me call the sheriff, and he can pick Josh up."

"No!" she exploded.

"Dixie, that guy could be dangerous." He spoke just above a whisper, not wanting to alarm the girls.

She glanced at the three others and drew Beau into the living room before speaking. "Beau, I have to go. Josh said he would tell me who murdered my father if I just meet him and give him a little money. He sounded desperate."

Beau let out a derisive snort. "I'm sure he is, but I'm

not going to let you go running off to meet up with a wanted man—no matter how desperate he may be."

She gazed up at him, tears gathered in her eyes. "Oh, Beau. Don't you understand? I've got to do this."

Her lower lip trembled, and Beau's resolve crumbled. He heaved an exasperated sigh. "We'll do this together."

She threw her arms around his neck. "Thank you so much. I hope you understand."

He was afraid he did understand. She was feeling guilty for hurting her father, and this was a way to atone. "I do understand." He stroked her cheek. "Let's go tell the kids goodbye."

She was quivering with anxiety as they returned to the kitchen, hand in hand. "Mom, Beau's going to go with me." To Beau, she said, "Let me grab my purse." She ran back toward the bedrooms.

Beau raked his fingers through his hair. "Stay here… and lock the door." Striding to the front room, he reached for his cell and punched the number for Fletch Shelton. He needed backup.

"Hey, Beau. What's going on?"

"Dixie—she's going to meet with Josh."

"I know." Fletch sounded remarkably calm.

"You know?" Beau was definitely not calm.

"I know."

Before he could learn more, Dixie raced up to meet him. He tucked the cell back in his pocket and escorted Dixie to his truck. He was thankful that he had arrived in time to avert what he thought would have been a sure disaster.

～៳～

When Beau helped Dixie up into his truck, he was a little tight-jawed. She thanked him, but he remained silent. *Just as well*. She wasn't in the mood for a lecture.

She fastened her seat belt as he started up the powerful motor. It was probably a good thing that he was coming along, but she hoped he didn't frighten Josh away. She needed him to tell her the name of the person who shot Scott because that same person might have killed her father.

The truck bumped over the cattle guard, and Beau turned onto the highway leading to Langston.

Her stomach was churning. This day had been a roller-coaster ride for her emotions. Having her mother pop in had been bad enough, but now Dixie was considering that, in her own slanted way, Mamie really thought she had been acting in Dixie's best interests.

She had been rehashing Mamie's words and thinking of things she should have said and not concentrating on their destination.

When Josh had called, he'd sounded nervous. He'd said he would tell her who had shot Scott and who may have murdered her father...but he needed money. He insisted he was too scared to go to the sheriff with his information but said he would tell Dixie everything and then leave town.

She reasoned that the sheriff could just as easily hear the information from her if Josh was too big of a wimp to step up. Pressing her lips together, she hoped he really had solid information and wasn't just being a tool in an effort to get his hands on some cash.

Her cell chimed again. *Josh...* "*Where* are you? I thought you would be here by now."

"I'm on my way."

He disconnected.

Asshole...

Beau glanced at her, unable to restrain a slight shake of his head.

Dixie pressed her lips together. He just didn't understand. She had to know who killed Vernon Moore...she just had to. She swallowed a lump the size of a baseball. She owed it to her father. Perhaps she could atone for hurting him.

A short while later, Beau drove into Langston, Texas, and slowed the vehicle to the posted speed limit.

She sucked in a breath, trying to control her growing apprehension. She felt as though a feather pillow had burst inside her chest. Maybe she would actually know who shot Scott...and if that same person murdered her father.

They passed all the businesses that had closed down for the evening. Past the darkened office of Breckenridge T. Ryan, the attorney her father had used to tie up his estate. Tiny's Diner remained open, but very few cars were still parked outside. At the far edge of town, Moore's Feed and Seed was shrouded in darkness.

Beau braked and sat idling. "Well, where's your boy? Let's get this party started."

She moistened her dry lips. It was pitch dark now. "Um, would you pull around to the back? He's probably in the back, where his car is."

Beau sighed and followed her directions, the headlights slashing a path through the gloom.

She sat frozen in the truck with the lights on. Josh's old car still sat at the end of the platform in the rear of the shed, but there was no sign of Josh.

The waiting was working on her nerves. She was about to tell Beau they could leave when the back door of the shed opened and Josh stepped out onto the platform. He looked both ways and then motioned for her to come to him.

Beau started to get out of the truck, but she stopped him with a hand on his arm. "I don't think he can see you with the headlights shining in his eyes. Can you give me a few minutes? He may not be willing to talk in front of you."

He sighed, regarding her stonily. "Okay, but I will be right on your heels if he makes any kind of move on you."

"Oh, silly. It's not that kind of meeting. Josh is not at all interested in me personally."

Beau made a scoffing noise. "Now you're being silly. That guy's tongue was hanging out when he looked at you."

"I do believe you're jealous," she said.

"Not at all." He leaned over to kiss her. "If he lays a hand on you, I'll kill him."

A shiver coiled around her spine. She wasn't feeling good about meeting with Josh but wanted to get it over with. Taking the cash out of her purse, she tucked it in her pocket. Clenching her jaw, she reached for the Beretta she had taken from her dad's collection of weapons and shielded it from Beau's vision. She hoped it was small enough to go unnoticed. She slipped out of the truck and tucked the gun in the back waistband of her jeans. She pulled her shirttail out, hoping she didn't shoot her own ass off.

She took a few steps toward Josh before she spotted the dark stain where Scott had fallen, bleeding. A shiver the size of a tsunami slithered down her spine, followed by a wave of guilt. It was her fault that Scott had been shot. *All on me.*

She shook off these feelings and quick-stepped up the stairs to the platform.

"You got my cash?" Josh asked.

"Yes, but tell me first. I have to know."

"Let's get inside. It's too open out here."

Dixie snorted. "There is no one out here. Just the two of us. Don't be such a wuss."

Josh's eyes narrowed. "You think I'm a wuss?"

"Of course you are. A real man would have gone to the sheriff straight away." She lifted her chin, meeting his gaze. "But no...you ran away like a little girl."

Josh swallowed hard. He sucked in a breath and expelled it through his gritted teeth. "Little girl? Shows what you know." He spat over the side of the platform. "C'mon. I'll show you."

Dixie made no move to follow. "I don't need to be shown a damned thing. Just tell me who shot Scott."

Josh sneered. "Who's the wuss now?"

They stared at each other for some time. "What's inside that you're so all-fired determined to show me?"

A smile played around his mouth. "The man who shot your father."

Beau was not happy. All of his focus was on a certain stubborn redhead and her determination to get involved in something that could get her killed.

He'd watched her climb up onto the loading platform at the back of the shed. She was talking to Josh, and neither of them appeared to be happy. Grim would be a better description.

"Dammit, Dixie. Ava needs you. I need you." He made a sound like a feral animal in pain. "I love you, but I want to spank your gorgeous little butt."

Finding Mamie Moore at the Moore ranch house had been a shock for sure. She was the last person he would have thought Dixie would leave their daughter with.

When he was a teen, Mamie had been distant but not virulent. The many times he had gone to the Moore house to study with Dixie or just hang out, her mother had performed chores such as providing food and making sure they were on task, all the while giving no hint of her true feelings. Apparently, Beauregard Garrett would never be good enough for her daughter.

On the other hand, Vern Moore was always friendly and affable. He seemed to genuinely like Beau and made it a point to make him feel welcomed in their home. Of course, he and Big Jim Garrett were the best of friends.

Now the two families were intertwined...linked by blood. All Beau wanted to do was cement the relationship. Marry the mother of his child. Happily ever after, forever and ever.

"Now, what the hell is she doing?" His gut did a tumble and roll. He watched in horror as Dixie appeared to be entering the back of the shed with Josh. "Oh, hell no!"

―――

With great trepidation, Dixie peered into the blackness of the shed. Her stomach was roiling, and her heart pumped double time.

"After you, Your Highness." Josh gave a mocking bow with hand gestures to indicate she was to enter.

Dixie straightened her spine and stepped through the dark, gaping maw of the doorway. "Where's the light switch?"

Josh stepped in behind her. "What's the matter? Are you afraid of the dark?"

"I would like to be able to see this person who you claim killed my father."

He laughed. "Yes, Your Highness." He seemed to know the layout and walked around in the darkness with confidence. "Here's your light. I got it right here." He flipped a switch, and a dim light gave a little illumination.

It took a moment for her eyes to adjust, but her gaze immediately lit on a strange man sitting in a chair against the far wall.

Her throat tightened, cutting off her air supply. She swallowed convulsively, staring at the man with a combination of loathing and fear.

A barrage of questions filled her brain. Who was he, and why would he murder her father?

The man was large and beefy, and he was glowering at her as though she had gravely wronged him. He was way overweight, but his arms looked toned and powerful.

She took a few steps toward the man, but Josh put his hand on her shoulder. "Wait a minute. Before you go all crazy on him, where is my money?"

Dixie reached for the cash and practically flung it at him.

"Whooee!" Josh spread the bills into a fan and then folded them and stuffed the wad in his jeans.

"Who is this man?" Dixie asked. "And how do you know he killed my dad?"

The man struggled to his feet making grunting noises in the process, no doubt due to his girth.

She realized he was quite intimidating; his expression alone sent a chill scurrying down her spine. Josh was smiling. "Why, this guy is Troy Elmore. He drives a big rig. He and his girlfriend, some little Mexican chick, are the ones who kidnapped those girls and stashed them up in the loft."

Dixie's stomach churned. She glared at the man, spewing pure venom in his direction. "Why? Why would you murder a sweet, harmless man?"

Josh chortled. "Well, the old man found out about the girls. He was going to blow the lid off the whole operation."

She stared at the man, who was slowly advancing toward her. He was really huge, but he was also quite muscular.

"So, how about it, Your Highness? Don't you just wanna punch him in the face? Knock yourself out."

Dixie turned toward the man named Troy. When she got close enough, she noticed he was sweating profusely and his close-set eyes were bloodshot. His jaw was set, and he seemed to be angry.

"You little shit."

Dixie took a step back, fear roiling in her gut. The fear skyrocketed when she saw Troy take a large handgun from the back of his belt. Her own weapon seemed minuscule by comparison.

Josh spoke in a calming voice. "Now, Troy…I—"

"Shut up, you little weasel. You got my girl arrested." He waggled the handgun, and she realized the anger wasn't directed at her. Dixie whirled around to find

Josh shaking his head and holding his hands as though to ward off the huge man.

"Wh—what are you doing?" Josh asked, his voice an octave higher than it had been. "You know I did my part. I took care of your product. I got them food and water. You know I did."

Troy's rough laughter echoed off the metal walls of the shed. "Got your attention?"

"It wasn't my fault," Josh screamed. "It was her. Her boyfriend and his family got up in the loft. They're the ones who got Valentina arrested. Not me." He pointed at Dixie.

Troy's big head swiveled. His eyes seemed to bore into her.

She couldn't think…couldn't speak.

Troy huffed out something that might have been a laugh. "She ain't the problem. You're the problem." That was when Troy shot Josh. "Tell her the truth."

Josh shrieked and fell to the floor, clutching his thigh. "It was me. I shot him."

"It was you? You shot my dad?" She felt the room sway.

"I had to. Don't you see?"

"No! I don't see at all. Why would you kill him?"

"Tell her," Troy ground out, raising the gun again.

"Okay…okay!" Josh held up one hand in surrender. "Vern was nosing around the shed and asking questions. I couldn't let him mess up a good thing." He looked at Troy, his expression pleading. "C'mon, man. We're just a part of the system. The other guys are depending on us. We can't let 'em down."

"Shut it, you little weasel," Troy growled out. "I want Val back. How's that gonna happen?"

Josh made a motion that seemed to be directing Troy to calm down, but it wasn't working.

An anguished growl erupted out of Troy's cavernous chest. "Shut up." He raised the gun to point at Josh again.

Anger and fear were duking it out in Dixie's gut. She was terrified but furious to hear Josh so casually discussing her father's death. "Wait a minute. I don't care about your business dealings. I just care about my father." A wave of fear washed through her as Troy turned to glower at her.

Josh groaned in pain, grasping his leg with both hands. "It just happened. I had to do it."

"What about my friend Scott? Did you have to shoot him too?"

Josh was moaning in pain. He made a scoffing noise in the back of his throat. "That big dumbass went up into the loft even though I told him to stay down here."

Shock began to ebb while anger ratcheted up within her. "So you shot my dad and Scott to protect your human trafficking business?"

"And you got Valentina arrested and them girls picked up. I had plans for them two. They were gonna bring a big payday." He shook his head and aimed the gun at Josh again.

"Wait!" Josh pointed at Dixie again. "You can take her. Somebody oughta pay a pretty penny for her."

"No!" she shouted. She remembered the Beretta nestled at the back of her waist. "You can't do that!"

—∾∾—

Beau's gut was tied in a knot, and his jaw gritted together. "Oh, babe. What have you done?" As quietly as possible, he opened the driver's-side door and stepped down onto the pea gravel in the drive.

A shot rang out, causing Beau to freeze in his tracks. "Dixie!" He took off running across the parking area, leaped up the steps, and threw open the door to the back of the shed.

Dixie was wrestling with a huge guy. Josh was sitting on the floor, blood oozing from his thigh.

Beau threw himself at the man trying to contain Dixie. Beau pulled him off, but Dixie rolled up after him. She landed a solid punch straight to the man's face. It was solid enough to rock Beau backward onto the floor with the man falling back on top of him.

Beau was trapped under the behemoth of a man. He wrapped an arm around the man's neck, hoping to cut off his air supply, but the neck was wider than the man's face. "Back off, Dixie, and call the sheriff's office."

The man bucked violently, dislodging Beau and scrambling across the floor toward Dixie.

"Oh," she said, her eyes wide. She threw herself onto the floor, scrambling for whatever he was after.

Beau grabbed the man's booted feet and dragged him backward, away from Dixie. The man rolled to one side, twisted out of his boots, and leaped to his feet, fists raised. He launched himself at Beau, punching out wildly.

Beau sidestepped, avoiding the thrashing-windmill technique. He drew back his fist and landed one upper-cut punch to the man's nose, sending him flat to the floor flat on his ass. He shook his head but didn't immediately get up.

Beau turned to see that Dixie had snatched a large

handgun and was pointing it toward him with shaking hands.

"Dixie, put that away," he demanded. Being shot was not on his agenda for the evening.

At that moment a uniformed Fletch Shelton burst in through the back door, weapon raised. He was followed by another deputy in similar mode.

"You got here quick," Beau said.

"I—I didn't call them," Dixie said.

"I saw her drive up to meet with Josh," Fletch said, "so I called for backup." He jerked his head toward the doorway, now filled with other deputies.

"Josh has been shot." Dixie pointed to where Josh sat crumpled in a heap at the other end of the shed. "His partner in the human trafficking business shot him."

Fletch took the gun away from Dixie, and she removed the Beretta from her waistband, causing him to step back quickly. "Don't worry, if I were going to shoot anyone, it would be Josh. He admitted that he killed my dad and shot Scott. It was all him."

Fletch held his hand out tentatively, and Dixie handed over the gun, butt first. "Who's this guy?" He gestured to the man sitting on the floor, blood streaming from his nose.

"His name is Troy Elmore," she said. "He's Josh's partner."

The other deputy called for an ambulance, while Fletch handcuffed Josh and the big man.

"So, why were you wrestling with this Troy guy?" Beau asked.

Dixie's shoulders sagged. "He—he was going to sell me. He was ticked off at Josh and decided he could make up for losing those two little girls." She squirmed. "He put his hands on me."

"Come here, baby." Beau gestured for her to come into his embrace.

She rushed over to him, burying her face against his chest.

"Honestly, Dixie. Why the hell would you come inside here? I thought you were going to talk to Josh outside and find out what you wanted to know."

"Okay, I'm sorry. I couldn't help it."

"Really?" His voice dripped sarcasm.

She placed both hands on his chest. "No, I really couldn't. I had to know who killed my father, and the killer, for sure, wasn't going to admit it. But it was Josh. He was willing to do anything to keep his human slavery business going. He killed my father, and then when Scott was nosing around, he tried to kill him too." She gazed up into Beau's eyes, seemingly trying to convince him of the necessity of her actions.

"Slavery? You mean human traffickers?"

She nodded. "Yes, you understand. Apparently my father suspected something was going on, so Josh murdered him to protect his interests…and then he shot Scott when he poked around back here."

Beau huffed out a little snort. "Sounds like a bad man. Maybe that's why I told you to stay away from him."

"Um—well, yes. I can see that would have been a good thing to do, but you know how impatient I am, and I just couldn't wait any longer. Please don't be mad at me."

He lifted her chin. "What would you have done if I hadn't come in when I did? The big guy had you on the floor, and there was a gun."

Her lower lip jutted out a bit. "Well, I could have taken him."

"Excuse me for buttin' in, Beau," Fletch said. "But your girlfriend is crazier than a bedbug. This Josh guy shot two people, and then she saw him get shot by this other man here with her own two eyes…and she thinks she can take that guy in a wrestling match. He weighs three times what she does." Fletch shook his head. "I swear, Beau. You can do better. I have a cousin, Cheryl, who's just as pretty and has more sense than this'n." He walked away, shaking his head. "I'll give you her phone number."

The ambulance had pulled up, and two attendants were working on Josh. They had wrapped his thigh and were in the process of strapping him to a stretcher.

"That man is under arrest," Fletch said. He ordered the other deputy to escort the ambulance and to make sure Josh didn't escape.

Fletch took charge of the handcuffed and surly Troy and led him from the shed.

Beau stood in the cavernous space gazing at the totally crazy, headstrong woman he loved. He snapped his fingers. "Damn! I forgot to get Cheryl's phone number."

Dixie punched him on the arm.

Chapter 20

"This is really beautiful." Leah gazed out over the Intracoastal Waterway, enjoying the soothing sound of chop slapping at the bulkhead. Their waiter refilled her glass of iced tea and served her husband and father-in-law another beer. She was glad they had made the decision to stay overnight at South Padre Island as opposed to driving all night to get home.

"Sure is," Big Jim agreed. "I'm guessing there are a few fish out there just begging to be caught." He gestured toward the expanse of water that had been dredged by the Army Corps of Engineers and extended from Brownsville, Texas, around Florida and up the east coast. A series of sand bars, some natural and some man-made, protected the shipping channel.

Tyler just shook his head. "Knock yourself out, Dad. I'll take more of these incredible shrimp." He demonstrated by stripping off the shell and popping one into his mouth.

Leah recalled the fleet of shrimp boats they had observed when they had driven over the long Queen Isabella Bridge spanning the mainland and South Padre Island. "Maybe the shrimp was freshly caught." She stabbed a fork in one of the shrimp making up her shrimp scampi.

They were enjoying the evening with dinner at a restaurant before returning to their rooms at a hotel on South Padre Island.

"I'm just glad we're not all in jail," Leah said. "Those border crossing officers scared the daylights out of me."

Big Jim made a scoffing sound. "Not likely. You just stepped right up and spelled it out for them." He cocked his head to one side. "You, little lady, were the reason those guards helped us get together with those girls' parents."

Leah's chest felt tight when she recalled the moment that Sofia and Ana were reunited with their mother and father. There had been tears, of course, and a cacophony of voices all speaking Spanish at the same time. After hugs and farewells, the decision to stay over had been made. Leah was glad to be out of the truck and wasn't looking forward to sitting so long again.

"You were very clear when you explained to the border guards about the girls. Maybe we ought to send this little one to law school. What do you think, Ty?"

"Step away from my wife, Daddy dearest. We're going to have our hands full with Gracie and this new little one." Ty fixed his father with a grimace of mock ferocity.

Big Jim raised his hands in surrender. "I give."

Leah set her tea glass back on the table. "I think I'll be quite content to get settled into our new house before the baby comes. I can't wait to have a place for my grandmother too."

Big Jim beamed across the table at her. "Your grandma is one feisty little lady. I like her spirit."

"Let's eat up," Ty suggested. "I'd like to take my beautiful bride on a romantic moonlit walk on the beach." He reached across the table to take her hand.

The look he gave her sent a rush of heat to Leah's

lower regions. She smiled as Ty lifted her hand to his lips, glad the romance was alive and well in their marriage.

------ ∿ ------

There had been a bit of confusion as to who was sleeping where.

Dixie took a great deal of satisfaction in making her mother sleep in the same room she had shared with the man she betrayed.

"But—but I can sleep in the guest room," Mamie had insisted.

"No, Mom. Beau and I sleep there."

Okay, she had enjoyed getting that out there too. *Yes, I'm having wild sex again with the man who knocked me up in high school.* Smiling, she made sure there were fresh sheets in the master bedroom, and then she went to tuck the girls in bed.

She found Beau was already there. Pausing in the doorway, she heard his deep voice and realized he was reading to the girls. She felt as close to him as though in his embrace.

The girls noticed Dixie first, tearing their attention from Beau to smile at her.

Beau looked up, his face reflecting love. "There's my girl."

She stepped into the room, giving each girl a kiss and hug. "Enjoy your story. I have a few things to put away in the kitchen, and then..." She changed her focus to meet Beau's gaze. "Then I'll be getting ready for bed."

This elicited a wink from Beau.

"Mommy, are you and Daddy going to get married?" Ava asked.

"What?" Dixie looked at Beau, who also appeared to be surprised.

"Why do you ask, baby girl?" Beau asked.

Ava's dimples flashed. "My gramma asked if you and Mommy were going to get married. I told her I didn't know." She shrugged and held her hands up to indicate her lack of knowledge.

Dixie put a finger to her lips. "Shh… It is absolutely not any of your grandmother's business…and you can tell her if she wants to know, she should ask me directly." That her mother had been pumping her daughter for information was more than irritating.

The next morning, Dixie rose early and went to the kitchen, surprised to find her mother sitting at the table, sipping a cup of tea.

Girding her literal loins, she tightened the sash of her robe. "Good morning, Mother. I trust you slept well."

Mamie's mouth was turned down at the corners. "Not well at all," she whispered.

Dixie selected a cup from the cabinet. "Too bad. I would think you might feel right at home." She set the cup on the counter and rummaged for a tea bag. "Considering that you slept in that room for many years."

"I suppose you feel justified in beating me up emotionally, Dixie. I did leave your father." She gave a half-hearted shrug. "This was never my home. I didn't love it the way a woman should love her home."

Dixie's mouth felt dry. She moistened her lips before speaking. "How about your husband? Did you love him?"

Mamie sucked in a deep breath and expelled it slowly. She stirred her tea again, the tinkling of the spoon against the china cup working on Dixie's nerves.

"I did love Vern Moore…once. Then he brought me to this godforsaken place to rot for as long as we both shall live."

Her mother's bitter words stung like nettles, bringing an ache to Dixie's chest. "Wow! It's not such a bad place…and Dad loved it here. I'm sure he thought he was sharing a place he loved with the woman he loved."

Another deep sigh from Mamie. "I'm sure he didn't bring me here out of malice. I just never fit in here. I ached to return to Dallas—to a civilized life—but, of course, Vern couldn't even comprehend my pain. He thought I should be thrilled to be stranded here."

Dixie poured hot water over her tea bag and took the cup to the table. She took a seat across the table and, when the tea had steeped sufficiently, began to vigorously stir in a spoonful of honey.

Mamie gave out a brief little laugh. "Our own little tea ceremony. Another special mother–daughter moment."

Dixie sighed and set the spoon on the saucer. "Look, Mom. You were the best mother on the planet. I loved coming home from school to have the special time just for us. I can even sort of understand why you thought it was necessary to leave Langston."

Mamie nodded, her mouth tight but somewhat pleasant nonetheless.

"I'm only angry at you because of the way you did things. You could have left without taking me. You could have left me right here with Beau. We would have been married, and Ava would have had a father. She would have been a part of the Garrett family. A beloved child and grandchild."

"But not my family," Mamie spat out.

"It's normal for a child to be the binding between two families." Dixie gazed at her mother steadily.

Mamie Moore drove back to Dallas after breakfast.

Dixie and Ava waved goodbye from the front porch. Beau hung back, giving them their space. He sensed there had been a lessening of tensions between mother and daughter while granddaughter remained blissfully unaware of any discord.

When Dixie and Ava turned back to the house, Beau opened his arms, enfolding both in an embrace. "My girls," he breathed, ruffling Ava's curls in the process.

"Daddy, don't mess up my hair. Gramma fixed it for me." She patted her hair back down.

"Sorry, princess. Your hair looks fine." He watched her prance into the house. *Such a girlie girl.*

Dixie remained glued to his side, her arms locked around his torso. "Oh, Beau, I'm so glad things are back to normal. I don't ever want anyone to be able to drive a wedge between us."

He rubbed her shoulder. "Me neither." He pressed his lips to the crown of her flame-red hair. "Although I'm not exactly sure what normal is between us."

"I'm truly sorry that I upset you by contacting Josh, but you know, we might never have found out who murdered my dad—and I had to know."

"I'm just glad we both lived through it." He gave her a little squeeze. "I had my doubts there."

"But everything turned out okay. Josh Miller has been arrested for murdering my dad and for shooting

Scott. And that other man, the trucker, he is in jail for human trafficking…so it's all good."

He shook his head, knowing he would never be able to squelch her determination or convince her that she had taken a dangerous risk. Perhaps being impulsive and headstrong was a part of her genetic makeup. Perhaps that was a part of her charm. "This might be a good day to go get a marriage license."

She pushed away, gazing up at him. Her lower lip trembled, making her at once vulnerable and childlike. "Today?" Her voice sounded fragile.

Beau shrugged, looking around the sun-drenched landscape. "Looks like a good day to me."

"Well—I, uh…"

"You don't have to marry me until you feel like it, but we could get a license…and see—"

"Yes!" she said. "Yes. Let's go get the license today. I'm ready to make things official."

Beau was blown away. He called his brother Colt to let him know he was on his own for the day but didn't tell him why. Beau could tell from Colt's tone of voice that he was miffed, but he had to put Dixie first.

He dropped Gracie off at school and then drove to Amarillo with Dixie and Ava. Dixie seemed a bit anxious. He thought it was hilarious that she would face down a killer but was nervous about making a lifetime commitment when she had known him all her life. He reached over to squeeze her hand. "Everything is going to be great. You'll see."

Ava, for her part, was excited. She wasn't sure what she was excited about, but she was taking a trip with her mom and dad, so that's all she cared about.

Their first stop was the courthouse, where Beau and Dixie obtained the required license to marry. Beau was elated but noted that Dixie seemed a bit subdued. He hoped she wasn't having second thoughts.

She heaved an audible sigh when they climbed back in the truck. "That's done. I guess we can go home now." She buckled her seat belt and flashed a brief smile.

He started the motor, pausing before putting it in gear. "I have just one more stop to make. You don't mind, do you? We can grab dinner at a nice restaurant before we leave."

She glanced back at Ava. "Sure. That sounds great."

Beau drove to a large mall and parked as close as he could.

A wide grin spread across Dixie's face. "Well, a shopping center. Now you're talking. Ava and I know how to shop."

Beau was glad to see her good humor restored, but he wished she had more enthusiasm for the marriage license. He released Ava from her car seat and walked across the parking lot holding hands with each of his ladies.

Once inside, Dixie broke away. "I think Ava and I deserve some serious retail therapy. Where are you going to be, Beau?"

"Hey, I need you both with me. I have some serious shopping to do too."

Dixie gave him a surprised look. "Sure, we're with you. Where to?"

"Right over here." He steered them to a large jewelry store. "I thought you might like to help me pick out your engagement ring."

Dixie froze in her tracks. "What engagement?"

"You didn't think I was just going to drag you to my cave without all the proper rituals, customs, and folderol."

"Folderol?" Dixie's eyes opened wide.

"Sure. *Folderol* was one of my mother's favorite words." He kissed Dixie's hand and tucked it in the crook of his arm. "We need to go through all the folderol leading up to our proper and forever marriage."

Tears spangled her lashes, but she cleared her throat. "Oh, I'm all for folderol."

Tyler was driving, with Leah sitting up front beside him. Big Jim spread out in the backseat, enjoying the countryside.

When Ty drove over the cattle guard at the entrance to the Garrett ranch, Big Jim realized how he had missed his own domain, even after being gone for two days. Somehow the grass looked greener and skies looked bluer.

"It's good to be home, isn't it?" he asked.

Ty reached over to squeeze Leah's thigh. "I could have stayed at South Padre Island a few more days."

Leah patted his hand. "Yeah, it was really nice."

Big Jim realized that spending a little time alone would be a treat for these two. They really hadn't taken a honeymoon, not with Gracie needing her mom. Now she would feel comfortable staying at the Garrett ranch with her adopted grandpa, aunts, and uncles. He would have to see about sending Ty and Leah to a special place for a little romance…maybe a cruise. He had heard that was what lovers did for a little romantic getaway.

When Ty pulled the truck to a stop in front of the

Item ID: 31321006115102
Date charged: 02/24/2020
Date due: 03/16/2020

Item ID: 31321007748448
Date charged: 02/24/2020
Date due: 03/16/2020

Item ID: 31321007525309
Date charged: 02/24/2020
Date due: 03/16/2020

Item ID: 31321007440749
Date charged: 02/24/2020
Date due: 03/16/2020

Garrett ranch house, he tooted the horn twice before climbing out and rounding the vehicle to open the door for Leah, but Big Jim had already done that and helped her descend.

Big Jim chastised himself for automatically opening the door when the gesture would have meant more coming from Ty. He stepped back, spotting Colton emerging from the house. He looked ticked off.

"What's wrong, Colt?" Big Jim asked.

"Just glad to see someone in the family back here at the ranch."

Big Jim snorted. "Well, hell, Son. I didn't think you would miss your daddy that much, but come here and let me wipe your tears."

Colton rolled his eyes. "Just glad you're all home safe," he muttered and went back into the house.

Big Jim followed, wondering what was going on. It took a lot for something to get under Colton's skin. "Wait up, big fellah."

Colton turned, taking a wide stance and planting his fists on his hips. "Sorry, Dad. Little Brother came over and worked like a stallion yesterday, but he's goofing off today. I got a message that he was taking the day to be with Dixie and Ava." He huffed out a sigh. "I can understand him wanting to spend time with Dixie and his daughter, but...dammit! There's work to be done every day."

Big Jim frowned. "He's just trying to make sure Dixie and Ava stay right here because if they go back to Dallas, your brother is out of here."

Colton's dark brows drew together. He shook his head. "Yeah, I can understand that."

"Son, you gotta stop thinking of Beau as your little brother. He's a man with his own life. I hope everything settles down and they can work it out, but in the meantime, step back and give them a little space. Okay?"

"Sure, Dad. Sorry. I just knocked myself out today. I'll be okay." He raked his fingers through his hair.

Big Jim slapped him on the back. "You'll get over it, Son. Let's surprise Misty and Leah. We can throw some meat on the grill and take the load off the ladies tonight."

Colton nodded. "Sounds great. I'll go fire up the grill."

Big Jim took out his phone and punched the number for Beau. It went to voicemail. "Hey, Son. We're back from taking those little girls back to their parents at the border…and I'm celebrating by firing up the grill. Can you bring Dixie and Ava over for dinner? I sure do need to give my granddaughter a hug." He disconnected, hoping Beau would check his messages…wondering where the hell he'd been all day.

─᷈᷉᷈─

Dixie couldn't stop staring at the ring. It was gorgeous.

Beau had insisted on purchasing more stone than would have satisfied Dixie, but he had assured her that this was the only engagement ring she would ever have, so it might as well be spectacular.

And then he had selected a ring for Ava. It was a lacy butterfly design with a small diamond set in the middle.

He'd taken them to a late lunch at a nearby Italian restaurant while the rings were being sized.

Dixie wasn't particularly hungry. In fact her stomach was turning flip-flops. The day had produced so many surprises, the first of which had been when she arrived at a truce of sorts with her mother. At least she could understand, given Mamie's skewed point of view and events in her past, why she had been driven to estrange Dixie from everything Garrett. All in all, Dixie was glad her mother had chosen to show up unannounced. At least the burgeoning war between them had been dealt with. No clear winners, but the battleground was cleared.

She was still feeling guilty for dragging Beau into her quest to seek out her father's killer. He was right. She knew he was right but just couldn't admit it to him. She could have chosen to sit back like a nice little woman and let the boys handle everything, but such behavior was not in her nature.

The murder of Vernon Moore had been eating away at her insides since her return to Langston. Dixie knew that Beau and his brothers would react the same way she had if someone killed their father, but it was the traditional alpha-male mindset that said she, as a woman, should stand back and let the boys take care of things. She couldn't blame Beau. He had that "protect the little woman" thing going on—and she loved him for it, even as she rankled at the idea of being corralled by her man.

But today, after a very exciting night in which she had tracked down the man who murdered her father and confronted him—okay, she had watched him get shot and then, when threatened with becoming a pawn in their human trafficking enterprise, had resisted and wrestled with Josh's partner. For some reason now she felt disappointed—let down somehow. It was as though every conflict had been settled and all was right with the world, but why did she feel like an overwound cuckoo clock, ready to spew her innards in all directions?

Then to top things off, Beau had suggested getting a marriage license and then surprised her even more by taking her to choose a beautiful diamond engagement ring. It was all so normal, but she didn't feel normal... not yet.

On the drive back home, Beau got a phone message and glanced at it. "My dad is back home with Leah and Ty. We're all invited to dinner. Dad's grilling. Are you ladies up for it?"

Dixie had planned for a romantic evening with Beau after they put their daughter to bed. She wasn't really in the mood for the total Garrett experience, but Ava was delighted.

"Oh, Grampa! I like it when he cooks."

Beau glanced at her in the rearview mirror. "Well, I'm sure your grampa has something special for you."

Okay, I guess that's settled. Dinner at Grampa's.

Dixie turned in her seat, noting Ava's wide grin. "Sounds delicious. And the good news for you two is that I don't have to cook."

"Aw, honey. Your cooking is all right. Don't be so hard on yourself." Beau reached over to pat her hand. The hand with the spectacular ring on it.

Chapter 21

BEAU COULD SENSE THERE WAS SOMETHING GOING ON WITH Dixie, but she wasn't giving it up.

Big Jim greeted them profusely. "I was hoping you three were gonna make it." He squatted down with a wide grin on his face. "And I've been missing this little one something awful." He scooped Ava up in a fierce hug.

"I'm glad you're home, Grampa." Ava grinned in delight. "I missed you."

Beau caught Dixie's eye. She was laughing too. It was clear that little Miss Ava had her Grampa eating out of her hand. "Can we give you a hand, Dad?" he asked.

"Naw. We got it under control." Big Jim whirled around, dipping Ava like a tango dancer.

Ava shrieked with laughter.

Leah waved them inside. "Come on back, folks. Let me get you something to drink."

Beau shook his head. "I think you should take it easy, Leah. You had a hard trip down to Mexico and back. Don't you need to rest, little mama?"

Leah blushed. "I'm just pregnant. Not sick."

Ty joined her, sliding an arm around her shoulders. "I've been telling her to rest up, but she gets really antsy." He gave her a kiss on her temple.

She made a scoffing noise. "I don't like to be waited on. Honestly! These people. They won't let me do a thing."

"And yet we managed to put together a decent dinner with absolutely no input from the Kitchen Queen," Ty said.

"I helped," Gracie offered. "I made the salad."

"I can't wait to try it," Dixie said. "I love salad."

Beau loved her even more for recognizing Gracie's contribution. The entire party made their way to the back of the house to disperse around the kitchen and dining area.

"I can help," Dixie offered. "What do you want me to do?"

"We can set the table," Leah said. "That's about all they let me do now." She handed Dixie a stack of dinner plates. "Oh, let me see that." Her eyes were wide as she reached for Dixie's hand. "That's a beautiful engagement ring."

"What?" Big Jim spun around. "Engaged?"

Beau met his father's questioning gaze with a grin and a nod, setting off a series of whoops and hollers from all the Garretts.

Misty, Leah, and Gracie clustered around Dixie, making appreciative noises as they stared at the ring. Dixie appeared to be pleased but slightly embarrassed at the same time.

Tyler grabbed Beau around the waist and lifted him about a foot off the floor. "Let's hear it for our little bro. About time."

Big Jim glowered at Tyler. "That's enough of that 'little bro' talk. Show some respect for your brother. And congratulate him on his engagement to this lovely young lady."

"Sorry, Bro. Old habits die hard." Ty offered his hand. "Congratulations." The brothers shook hands, followed by a hearty shoulder pounding.

Beau turned when Colton approached with his hand

outstretched. "Congratulations. I hope you have a long
and happy marriage." He said the words, but his expression was on the grim side.

"Beau, come on outside and help me at the grill.
These folks want to eat." Big Jim cocked his head to
indicate Beau was to follow him.

Beau followed, glad to be free from his brothers and
their mixed messages. He stepped out onto the back
deck. "What can I do to help, Dad?"

"You can turn the meat on the grill. It's been smoking
slow." Big Jim took a seat in one of the wooden deck
chairs and leaned back, stretching his arms behind his
head.

Beau opened the lid, releasing a huge waft of savory
smoke. There were several chickens split in half, two
racks of ribs, and steaks. He carefully turned them,
using tongs to prevent releasing any of the juice. "Looks
good." He closed the lid and placed the tongs at the side
of the grill.

"Come sit here and tell me how you did it," Big Jim
said. "Grab us a couple of beers while you're at it."

Beau opened the cooler, and sure enough, an assort-
ment of longnecks were properly embedded in ice.
"Sure thing, Dad." He selected two and flipped the lids
off before slapping one into Big Jim's open palm and
settling into another deck chair. "How did I do it?" Beau
intoned softly. "Same way you gentle a wild horse."

Big Jim let out a roar of laughter. "Good analogy,
Son. Dixie is a wild little filly, for certain. Good one."
He took a long draw on his beer then made a satisfied
sound. "Getting a ring on her finger is a great thing, but
do you think you're going to make it to the church?"

Beau tilted his head back, letting the cold liquid roll down his throat. "I'm pretty sure. We got the license today."

Big Jim let out a whoop. "Hot damn! Can't wait to see the two of you up in front of the preacher."

"What's going on out here?" Colt stepped out onto the deck, one dark eyebrow raised.

"My son and I are discussing his upcoming nuptials. You got a problem with it?" Big Jim fixed him with a glare.

Colt crossed the deck and rummaged around in the cooler. He straightened and sauntered to a chair a few feet away from the other two. "Not a problem exactly. I just remember how broken up Beau was when Dixie left him the first time."

Beau rolled up out of the deck chair, leaning dangerously close to his older, bigger brother. "She's not going to leave again. That was all her mother's doing, and we've hashed that out, so leave it alone."

Colt gazed at him without rancor. He took a sip of beer and set it on a small table. "I'll try. It's just, when someone does something to hurt one of my family, it's hard to forgive."

"Easy, Beau," Big Jim warned. "Now, looky here, Colt. You need to step back and let the two of them work it out, and it seems they have. There's a ring on her finger, and they have the license." He leaned back in his chair, stretching his long legs out in front. "I'm ready to throw some rice."

Dixie hadn't planned on a big or elaborate wedding. She would have been just as happy to go to a justice of the peace...but no...

When they went to talk to the preacher, they found out Big Jim had already been in contact to make sure a date was available in the very near future. Okay, it was great that her future father-in-law was so eager to have her in the family—and her daughter. The man was totally sappy over Ava.

So a date was chosen just a little over a month away. Beau was ecstatic, and so was Ava.

Leah and Misty took a Saturday trip to Amarillo with Dixie and the younger females. They helped her choose a wedding gown. Although she had protested that white wasn't really appropriate, they argued her down. In the end she selected a gown in the palest cream to compliment her complexion and hair color. It had a scalloped neckline and cap sleeves to show off her slender, toned arms.

Leah and Misty would wear dresses in a soft apricot hue, while Ava and Gracie went for a pale green. All together the colors looked fresh and summery.

Big Jim had given Leah his Visa card with strict instructions not to let Dixie pay for a thing.

"Now we all need shoes," Leah announced with a grin. "We don't want to disappoint Big Jim."

"I think we need underwear too," Misty said, and everyone laughed.

Dixie was caught up in the whirlwind of activities.

The church ladies threw a kitchen shower for her, although she didn't tell them that the kitchen was not her favorite place to be. She smiled and graciously accepted each colander and ricer with a delighted gush of appreciation. She would figure out what to do with them later. The ladies had carefully printed out their favorite family recipes on index cards. Dixie's throat tightened as she read the little notes written in their handwriting.

Big Jim kept trying to find something to give the happy couple…something big and expensive. He reasoned that he had given both Colton and Tyler large sections of land and helped with the cost of building their houses. But Dixie had a house and land and wanted to live there…with some major remodeling. She thought it was close but not too close to the other Garretts. The entire Garrett clan was somewhat intimidating. She knew they meant well, but she was an only child, and all this crowding around all the time was a bit much. She figured that when Leah had her baby, Big Jim would have a new focus.

As the big day neared, Dixie found herself feeling more and more antsy. She knew Beau was concerned, but she tried to pretend there was nothing wrong.

One night, after they had tucked Ava in, Beau took her outside to sit and gaze up at the stars.

"Beautiful, isn't it?" Beau reached for her hand. "The sky is so big and full of stars…makes me feel small by comparison."

"We are small by comparison," she said.

"You sure do know how to kill a mood," he said. "Here I was being all romantic, and you have to pop my bubble."

"Oh, I'm sorry…I—uh…"

"I'm kidding." He sat up and looked at her. "But I know there's something bothering you. Come on, Dixie. Tell me what's on your mind. Whatever is wrong, we can work it out."

She took a deep breath and let it out slowly. "Beau,

nothing is wrong. It's just wedding jitters. I read all about it in one of the many bridal magazines Misty keeps buying for me." She gave a confident laugh. "I'll be fine."

He picked up her hand again, brushing his lips across her fingers. "Something's been on your mind. I wish you would just tell me. If I'm doing something wrong, let me know, and I'll change."

"Oh, Beau…it's not you."

He held up both hands. "Do not say it's not me, it's you."

"But it is me. I've just messed up my life something fierce. I know things will be okay between us and we're going to have a wonderful life together." She stopped for breath. "But I wish I had done it right the first time. I wish I had gone to you the second I knew I was pregnant and that we had gotten married and…" A tear rolled down the side of her nose. "And I wish you had been with me when Ava was born."

"Baby, we can't change what happened." He wiped at her tears. "We can just go forward from here."

A shiver racked her body. "But I feel sad about the past. I was so stupid not to question my mother. I hurt you. I hurt my father, and I'll never get to make it up to him."

He wrapped his arms around her. "I think the best way to honor your father is just to live a good life and be happy. That's what he would have wanted."

"I know you're right," she said, sniffling. "But can you forgive me for all the pain I've caused you?"

"It's already done. Dixie, when you agreed to marry me, you made me the happiest man on the planet. Yeah,

I'm sorry I didn't get to be a part of your and Ava's lives the past few years, but we have a chance to turn the page. Whatever happens from now on, that's our life."

Dixie stared at him, the moonlight clearly defining his features. "A blank page?" That made so much sense. She could envision herself turning a page with the past written on it—and now she had a brand-new page and a pen in hand.

"Yeah, brand-new. Just you, me, and Ava...and any other little ones who come along."

She leaned over and kissed him. "Thanks, Beau." He would never know how he had taken the guilt and maybe not erased it but at least given her a starting point. "From now on, everything will get better."

———⁓———

The wedding took place a week later. Beau was dressed in his best Wranglers, pressed with a little starch, and his dress boots were highly polished. The rest of his garb was dictated by his beloved sisters-in-law, who had appointed themselves in charge of...everything. This was why he was wearing a "morning coat" with his Wranglers. Leah had informed him that this was what the British princes had worn for their weddings, so she thought he should follow suit. Fortunately, she had compromised on the Wranglers and boots.

Big Jim cheered them on, gleeful that his youngest son was finally marrying the love of his life. To Beau, he appeared to be counting the minutes until the deed was done.

"Relax, Dad. It's happening right now." Beau tried to stand still while Big Jim adjusted his tie. "Leave it alone. Misty tied it and said that was the way it's supposed to be."

Big Jim took a step back. "All right, Son. You look mighty purty though."

His similarly attired brothers howled with laughter.

"You were always the prettiest one, Little—I mean Bro." Colton caught himself.

Big Jim slapped him on the shoulder. "Atta boy."

A knock on the door signaled that it was time.

"Here we go, Son. Let's marry that girl."

The four Garrett men headed down a hallway to the fully packed main church.

Beau had been playing it cool among his male relatives, but in truth, his gut was tied in knots.

The organist was playing something light and fluffy, which only added to his stress. The fancy tie Misty had arranged was choking off his airway. As the foursome clomped down the hallway, his anxiety rose. *What if she's not there? What if she takes off and leaves me again?*

One of the church elders was waiting for them, lining them up in readiness for the big event. When the preacher strolled out onto the dais, smiling at the entire assembly, the elder nodded for Beau to head for the altar using a side aisle.

His mouth felt dry, but he managed to smile and shake the clergyman's hand. He was aware that the entire town seemed to be crammed into the pews and a few men were standing against the wall. *Good turnout.*

The church organist was playing something classical, and everyone in the church seemed to be smiling. Maybe they had been waiting all this time for Beau to marry Dixie.

The double doors opened onto the central aisle, and there was Ava, looking adorable in a green dress with a circle of white flowers around her hair. The organist smiled but continued playing the same music.

Behind her, Gracie wore an identical outfit. They looked like angels to Beau. The girls seemed to be getting directions from Misty, who gently nudged Ava into action. Ava led the parade, followed by Gracie and then Misty and finally Leah. Everyone was staring at them and smiling.

The four walked down the aisle and took their places on the dais. Then the organist hit a dramatic chord, and the entire congregation drew in a collective breath as all heads turned to the open doorway.

Beau swallowed hard.

Dixie stood with her friend Roger at her side. She looked beautiful, smiling shyly as she gazed around the assemblage. She spied someone at the front of the church and seemed to relax. She took Roger's arm, and he patted her hand.

Beau saw that Dixie's mother sat in the front row with Scott, who was still in a wheelchair but, according to Dixie, was recovering quickly from his wounds. The two of them appeared to be happy, at least for the moment.

Everyone except Scott stood as the organist began pounding out the traditional wedding march.

Dixie met Beau's gaze and took the first step toward him, gliding gracefully.

He was saddened that Vern Moore did not get to give the bride away. Sorry that he was dead, but Beau figured that Dixie was happy that her friend Roger had stepped in. When they reached the altar, Roger handed her up the step, and then reached to shake Beau's hand before he took a seat in the first row on the bride's side with Scott and Mamie. When Dixie stood beside Beau, he felt the tightness in his throat release. "Hello, my bride," he whispered.

She smiled and handed her bouquet to Leah.

The preacher began the familiar words. It felt like a dream. He had wanted them to write their own vows, but Dixie had said she didn't want to share her feelings with the entire town, so they said their "I dos" and exchanged rings. He leaned down to place Ava's butterfly ring on her finger and was rewarded with a grin and a hug.

He caught his father's eye and noted the tears he was trying to hide. *Old softie*.

The minister pronounced them husband and wife and then said, "You may kiss the bride."

A radiant Dixie lifted her chin and placed her hands on Beau's shoulders. "I love you, Beau," she whispered.

He laid a kiss on her and lifted her off her feet, swinging her around in a circle. "I love you, Mrs. Garrett," he shouted.

"Whooee!" Big Jim's howl echoed off the stained-glass windows and brought the crowd to their feet, applauding and cheering wildly. It seemed everyone was glad these two had made it official.

Everyone except one sad-looking woman sitting in the front.

Beau met the gaze of his new mother-in-law. He hoped that time would change her attitude, but in the meantime, he was ready to celebrate.

Their reception was held in the back room of the

Eagles Hall. Leah and Misty had decorated the room
and hired a local restaurant to cater the event.

He sat grinning and accepting congratulations and
well wishes from the guests with Ava on his lap.

Dixie was given the task of opening wedding gifts.
Leah and Misty were making notes of who had given
which gifts for future thank-you notes.

Big Jim drew a chair up beside Beau. He appeared to
be supremely satisfied.

"Thanks for everything, Dad."

Big Jim held out his hands, and Ava crawled into his
lap. "It doesn't feel like I've done anything. Leah and
Misty have been working their little tails off though."

"Yeah, they've been troupers."

"I've had a little trouble figuring out what to give
you for a wedding present." Big Jim set Ava on her feet,
and she ran across the room to her grandmother, who
opened her arms, pulling her into a tight embrace. Big
Jim shook his head. "Don't know what you're going to
do about that."

"Not a problem, Dad. I think time will soften her up."

Big Jim gave a curt nod. "Hope you're right. I—uh,
I got something for you here someplace." He patted his
pockets and drew out a fat envelope, passing it to Beau.

Beau weighed the envelope, thinking it might contain
cash, but when he opened it, there were several sheets of
paper and a smaller envelope. "What's this?" he asked.

Big Jim leaned back in his chair and folded his arm
across his chest. "When we were delivering those two
little girls, I saw what a beautiful place South Padre
Island is and thought maybe you and Dixie might enjoy
taking a little honeymoon there. There are two tickets to

fly down there and a rental car you can pick up at the airport in Brownsville. You've got a week at a beautiful hotel right on the beach. It's mighty romantic there, so I thought you might think about giving me another grandchild." He let out a bellow of a laugh as though that was the funniest thing in the world.

"That's really nice, Dad. What about Ava? Where will she be while Dixie and I are enjoying all this romance?"

He made a scoffing noise. "Why, I will be treating that little princess to a week of being totally spoiled. What do you think?"

"Sounds great to me. Let me run it by Dixie."

"You should check out the other papers in that envelope. I deeded two sections of good pastureland over to you. This land butts right up to the Moore property, so it should be pretty easy for you to manage."

Beau half rose. "Damn! Dad, that's twelve hundred and eighty acres. This is the best gift ever."

Big Jim blew out a lungful of air. "I've given so much to the other two. Just tell Dixie this is your wedding present and a legacy for Ava."

Beau was stunned by his father's generous gifts. He was also surprised when Big Jim walked over to where Mamie Moore was sitting with Ava and struck up a conversation. It seemed his dad was going to make the first overture in healing old wounds. *Good man, my dad*.

Beau crossed the room to where his two sisters-in-law were clustered around Dixie.

She greeted him with a wide grin as he approached. "Well, here's my husband."

He returned her smile, holding out his hand to her.

"And here is my beautiful bride. Can I borrow her for a few minutes?"

Dixie rose, and he drew her out into middle of the room. "The band is tuning up, so I thought we should stake out a place here on the dance floor."

"How romantic," she said. "I'm so glad I called dibs on you when we were in grade school."

"Me too." He drew her closer into a dance position. "I wanted to tell you that my dad made arrangements for our honeymoon."

"Oh, I thought we were going to Dallas. Mom is counting on seeing us…and I think it would do her good to know that we will visit her with Ava."

"We can do that anytime you like, but Dad is sending us to South Padre Island for a week of sun and fun. How does that sound?"

Her eyes opened wide. "Are you kidding? That sounds great. What about Ava?"

"He said he will take care of her and spoil her something awful." He paused to gaze into her eyes. "And he gave us a couple of sections of land…the sections that butt right up against the Moore property, so we'll have lots of work to do."

"Whoa! That's quite a gift. I'm totally blown away."

He gave her a gentle kiss. "Me too. I think he is just glad to have you and Ava as part of the Garrett clan…I am too."

Dixie turned to him with a smile. "Oh, Beau. I'm so glad we did this. Everything is going to be great."

He brushed the backs of his fingers over her cheek. "We are great."